Yorkshire-born Domini Highsmith lives alone in the shadow of Beverley Minster, on the ancient site where this trilogy is set. (*Keeper at the Shrine* is the first book in the trilogy and the story of Simeon de Beverley is continued in her next novel, *Master of the Keys* which is available in hardback from Little, Brown.)

She has also written six thrillers as Domini Wiles, and, under her own name, two acclaimed semi-autobiographical novels about an abused child, *Frankie* and *Mammy's Boy*. She is also the author of the bestselling novel *Leonora* and its sequel *Lukan*.

ACKNOWLEDGEMENTS

The author acknowledges with thanks and affection all those whose help and encouragement went into the writing of this book:

The Reverend Peter Forster of Beverley Minster
David Thornton, Verger of Beverley Minster
Pamela Martin, Head of the Reference section,
Beverley Library
Librarian Jenny Stanley and staff at Beverley Library
Barry Roper of The Beverley Bookshop
Father X

and those special friends who helped keep the candle burning:

Alan and Beryl Parrot
Pauline Brown
Peter Harvatt Robinson
and
Roger Keith Driscoll

BEAVER-LAKE
Beverley 1180

North Bar

St Mary

Hengate

Archbishop's House

Town ditch

Cornmarket

Town ditch

Bar

Bar

Butcher Row

Fishmarket

Westwood

Lairgate

Hyegate

E

Minster

Minster Moorgate

St Martin

Town ditch

Keldgate

Keldgate Bar

Landing & Drawbridge

Lake

Copyright
Domini Highsmith, 1992

St Anne's Convent

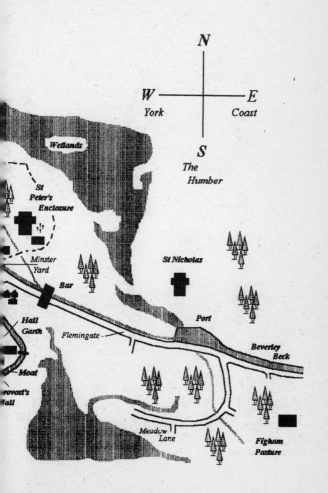

*Once again my book is dedicated to the Unknown Priest,
whose tomb now rests in the North Transept
of Beverley Minster.*

CHAPTER ONE

'Cedd? Where are you, husband?'

The moorland all about her was deserted. Two children and a man had been there when she last looked up. Now they were gone.

'Cedd?' She rose to her feet and used one hand to shield her eyes against the glare of a cloudless sky. 'Matilda? Arno?'

Nearby, her youngest child lay sleeping, the rough stuff of his carrying-cloth hooked up on a wooden stake to keep the bright sun off his face. Beyond the bundle three cows had been grazing. They too had vanished.

The woman was on the Swinemoor, gathering dung to shape and dry for fuel. She wore a robe of shabby wool, kilted at the waist by a twisted cord. From hip to ankle her legs were stained with dirt, and to each elbow her hands were gloved in cow dung. Beside her stood the family basket, packed now with stinking pats and furnished with a single band of leather. 'Husband?' Her voice rose to a shriek. *'Husband?'*

A man working some distance off looked up at the woman's cry, wiped his sleeve across his brow and threw his cutter down. For a moment he stood as if transfixed, then screamed a single word that chilled her soul: *'Run!'*

Instinctively she moved to scoop the infant from its cloth, and as she turned again the man and his dung basket were sucked into the ground. With appalling speed the dusty earth was transformed into glistening black liquid. The moor was cracking open and a silent, deadly pool of slime was oozing out.

The woman looked all about her in a panic, then wheeled to flee as the solid ground beneath her feet became a sticky pool that wrenched her down before she could cry out.

A clerk in holy orders, robed for the lengthy journey back to his chapter at York, paused at the edge of the Figham pasture to survey the town that lay in a haze of dust on lower ground. His horse had fallen lame and so the priest on whose account he travelled had generously supplied him with another, the better to reach St Peter's before the gates of York were barred at dusk. He threw back his hood to reveal a shaved crown that glistened with perspiration in the heat. He was a shrewd, ambitious man whose search for advancement drew him to any market-place where his particular merchandise might easily be bartered. This time the market-place was Beverley, the purchasers its priests.

He lifted his shoulders in a sigh and smiled as he signed the cross in humble gratitude for business well concluded. He had his new horse and his purse of silver, Father Cyrus de Figham had his information, and both had profited in the transaction. More than this, the clerk had played a sly but cautious double game, for he had learned that his archbishop, the little-loved, conniving Geoffrey Plantagenet, would willingly make handsome payment for other churchmen's secrets. That which he brought from York had fetched a decent price; that which he carried back might double his profit.

This clerk was sharp in his assessment of his fellows. Priest or pauper, beggar, monk or canon, all men might be corrupted for a price. He had heard it said that a scribe who sought to do secret business with the same Cyrus de Figham, canon of St Matthew's, had sold his information for his life. Some said an old servant in the priest's employ, covetous of the purse his master offered, had followed the visitor out to cut his throat, and the canon had had no part in what was done. Others believed de Figham gave the order for his visitor to be waylaid, then retrieved his purse and paid the servant well for his foul deed. The truth of it depended on the teller, and so this clerk was wise enough to take both rumours into his account. He carefully informed his host that he would travel by the regular route and join with other riders on the way. Then he made a complicated detour to the pasture and, mounted now on a fast and sturdy horse, intended to ride at speed for home as soon as he was rested.

He allowed himself to smile again. There was a certain satisfaction in foxing those in higher orders who might have common villainy on their minds. He would keep his well-earned purse along with his life, and if Cyrus de Figham sought to relieve him of either, the men sent out to do the deed would even now be riding hard upon a futile course.

Now the clerk dismounted and hooked a jar of watered ale from beneath the bundles tied to his saddle. As he drank he watched the mists roll off the wetlands that lay in hazardous patches all around the town. He snorted the brown dust from his nostrils and thought this a dirty, godforsaken place. But for the holy shrine of St John and the precious relics kept within his tomb, the pilgrims would not flock here in their thousands and the population would not breed like rats in their squalid hovels. Beverley survived while other places foundered, it prospered while many a worthier town did not, and some said the Devil had a hand in its endurance. Even its half-mended Minster church, halved in height by a hastily erected timber roof, stood with its fired-blackened tops encased in dust and had the look of some long-abandoned ruin.

'The canons of Beverley are welcome to it,' he said, so fiercely that his mount, unused to its new master, side-stepped in alarm. 'This town is either as wet as swampland or as dry as Hell's own ashes. God's teeth, no man is safe while this heat persists. One little spark, one candle wrongly placed, and Beverley will consume itself again.'

He was about to remount his borrowed horse and ride for

3

York when something held his gaze and caused the thin skin of his scalp to prickle and draw tight over his skull. He saw the marsh mist meet with the thicker dust beyond the scorched fields, and it seemed to him, a man of religious fears and superstitions, that two opposing forces met head-on. The result was a sudden upsurge of glistening fluid from certain points along the waterways, and there, before his disbelieving gaze, a score of swift and silent tragedies occurred. He saw a cluster of small ships moored at the port keel over like fainting women before a huge and muddy wave that moved upstream. Further north, a huddle of makeshift houses lying between the wetlands and the town ditch simply vanished. Buildings and farmyards, men and beasts alike, were sucked away as pools of slime appeared as if by magic. The clerk stared about him, saw a part of Cobbler Row wiped out in an instant, witnessed the sudden rise and fall of the Great Beck where its banks were at their lowest, and marked the empty, desolate places left behind.

'Dear God Almighty,' he muttered. 'What manner of events are these?' Dust stung his eyes but still he stared, unable to turn away his horrified gaze. 'By all that's holy, the rumours are true. This Beverley is cursed. May God have mercy on these stricken souls.'

He signed the cross and muttered his indecision in a prayer. It was too late for him to raise the alarm, and how would he warn an entire town against deadly mud-pools rising from the ground first in this place and then the other, with no sign where or when they would next rise up? He heard no sound, no cry of terror or concern, no peal of bell or blast of horn, yet men were dying right before his eyes. The sinister silence, more than the sight of death, caused his flesh to crawl. His conscience told him he was needed here, but instinct urged him to ride for York and put this cursed Beverley, its mud and its sly priests far behind him. He glanced at a creeping, glistening patch where once a barn had stood, then yanked at the bridle to steady the nervous prancing of his horse. Self-interest hoisted him into the saddle and jabbed his heels savagely into the horse's flesh, and as he dragged the beast's head round he saw the riders coming.

Three men were crossing the pasture at a gallop, and by their clothes he recognized Cyrus de Figham's creatures. While he had thought himself a cunning man and careful to a fault, that black-eyed priest, that silver-tongued de Figham, had outmanoeuvred him. Fear clawed at him with grasping hands, trapping the breath in his throat and threatening to pull him in a dead faint from the saddle. He saw the flash of blades and knew that he was doomed, ripped the purse from his belt and threw it down, hoping to trade the silver for his life. One man leaped from his horse to take the bait but the others came on without a pause. The clerk's mount suddenly reared up and, sensing its rider's fear, plunged into a fast and furious gallop toward the woodland. In a moment the clerk had regained his courage and was urging it on, determined to make the shelter of the trees before de Figham's men could run him down and murder him.

The Figham Ditch ran a crooked course across the pasture, coming from the north-east to the beck close by the port. Although reduced to a trickle of unsavoury water by the drought, its sides were deep and steeply cut and sometimes hazardous to grazing cattle. The clerk's horse took the jump with ease but on the far bank it stumbled. He heard the foreleg snap, felt the horse collapse beneath him and was catapulted forward from the saddle.

One of his pursuers laughed aloud and the clerk, now grovelling on his knees and babbling for his life, screamed at the heavens for God in His mercy to intervene on his behalf. As if in answer to his prayer the ground beside the ditch began to bubble and the nearest rider, grinning as he raised his sword above his head, was sucked into a great upsurge of slime. In an instant the clerk was on his feet and running, and in his blind panic to survive he cared not where he put his feet nor noted that the sun-baked earth grew softer where he trod. And then his feet and legs deserted him. He raised his head, uttered a half-gasp and was swallowed up.

The pasture then was as still as it had been, dusty and dry

as matchwood, its grasses scorched, its undulating contours undisturbed. No trace remained of mounts or swords or riders. Only the crooked ditch was changed as it glistened now with mud, and a pool of sludge, benign as a village pond, lay darkly in freshly cloven hollows on each bank.

There was no warning when the floods came. The weather was hot and dry and had been so for many weeks, yet in the space of a few short, horrifying minutes, the impossible had happened and many lives were lost. There was no time to sound the church bells in alarm, to carry possessions to safety or to drive animals to higher ground. The deluge surged upwards from the earth itself, flinging the river landward, forcing the beck and every lesser waterway to breach its banks. Within minutes the worst was over, leaving many streets awash with mud and countless homes destroyed. Whole settlements were buried, their occupants and livestock suffocated, while people living half a field away were spared. The deadly seepage came in sudden, isolated surges, and with such stealth that homes and farms were overwhelmed and the black slime settled before a man might turn his head to see the danger coming.

A cobbler raised his eyes from his work to see a row of houses devoured by a moving river of mud. A farmer saw his pasture turn to liquid which sucked his animals down so swiftly that they offered up no bleat or snort of dismay. A poor man fixing thatch to his roof, alerted by a sudden, eerie silence, glanced down to find his family gone and his modest patch of land turned into sludge. Men and women went about their daily tasks, unaware that, only streets away, whole families were being swallowed into the ground.

A priest stood screaming at the gateway to St Mary's, holding his altar cross aloft the creeping mass that had suddenly risen up from consecrated ground.

'Back! Back, you Devil's vomit,' he screeched. 'Back! Back, I say!'

'Father! Come away . . . the danger . . .'

A young boy rushed to save the priest, received a blow

from the swinging cross, clutched at his priest as he went down and both were sucked beneath the putrid mire.

The banks of the beck and the Great Ditch were breached in segments, driving the main flow landward so that the levels of water downstream were virtually unchanged. Thus honest townsfolk scoffed at reports of deadly swamping in other parts of the town. A well in Lairgate, serving a common enclosed square where children played and animals were tethered, suddenly belched out mud in such quantity that not a soul remained to tell of it. A house in Fishmonger's Row vanished with twenty people packed inside it, and when a large section of the fish market burst open, no one could estimate how many perished.

Some said that such a tragedy as this could never happen. It had been another hot September day with neither cloud nor wind to temper its oppressive heat. On the heels of an uncommonly dry summer, no rain had fallen for twenty-seven days, leaving the fields so scorched that the topsoil lifted in a haze of fine brown dust to hover in the air. Fire was the thing the people of Beverley feared. More than the wrath of God or the sting of famine, more even than the touch of pestilence, they feared the hot and deadly breath of flames running beyond any man's control. Fire-wardens patrolled the streets and lanes at night long after the *couvre feu*, the nightly cover fire, was called. At sundown every town gate was locked, every fire smothered, every naked flame extinguished, and any flame discovered burning after curfew might earn its careless owner a public flogging.

These precautions were observed with the best of reasons, for every man and woman in Beverley had seen at first hand what fire could do to them. On this day before the Feast of St Matthew only two years earlier, their town had burned from end to end and not one soul survived but that two more were taken in its place. If history were to repeat itself it surely would be now, while all was tinder-dry and the rains held off. To suffer flooding in this dusty drought was unimaginable.

CHAPTER TWO

By noon the number of persons known to have died in the spasmodic flooding at Beverley had reached two hundred, though fewer than a dozen bodies had been recovered. Looters and cut-purses were hard at work amongst the crowds that gathered at every mud-pool. Chickens and pigs were carried off while their owners searched for missing relatives. Possessions were stolen from unattended houses, produce and implements from unguarded plots. Even a pile of kindling-sticks, a kitchen broom or a decent fire-pot were spoils for thieves who traded one item for another in the streets. Soon every street and alleyway became a market-place, while goods were passed from house to house or changed hands through a convenient window opening.

'All thieves and looters will be clipped on sight.'

Such was the warning put about by many, but tragedy and opportunity go hand in hand, and so the robbers flourished and the good men of the town responded without benefit of clippers. One looter caught stripping the body of a drowned man was hoisted high by neighbours and tossed into the centre of the nearest mud-pool, where he sank like a stone, much to the crowd's amusement. Another had his ear cut off by an enraged pilgrim robbed of a pair of walking boots, and within the hour surrendered his remaining ear to the cooper whose tools he had snatched and traded on for a loaf of bread. In Walkergate, where the flooding was at its worst, a family of vagrants was discovered looting the house of a local man. Every member, including seven children, was hanged from the rafters as a deterrent to others of their kind.

Men using pole-hooks probed the mud-pools for the carcasses of animals to sell for profit or to fill the family cooking-pot. News reached the Minster church that certain shops in Butcher's Row were selling suspect flesh at less than half the price of regular beef and mutton. Two priests sent to investigate found the whole row besieged by a seething mass of would-be customers, all clamouring for their share of cheaper meat. The priests were promptly set upon and beaten to the ground by those who suspected them of trying to claim the better cuts ahead of people whose need was greater than their own. Fearing for their lives, the two took refuge in a yard behind the shops, and there were horrified to find a human hand and several severed feet amongst the baskets of offal. Their righteous protests fell upon deaf ears, for empty bellies cared nothing for the shape of the beast that provided them with meat.

Close to the Swinemoor pasture an acre of prime grazing land lay totally submerged. Scores of sheep and half as many cows were thought to have been sucked down by the mud and drowned, but the sons of Edward Blacksmith and their several friends knew well the truth of it. No sooner had the black pool risen up than they were out with staffs and sticks and barking dogs, driving the animals off. They did not rest nor slow their pace until they reached the market-place at Howden, where the beasts were sold from the open pens before that town had news of the Beverley floods.

On the Westwood pasture, too, men drove away their neighbours' animals even when they themselves had suffered no losses. It was, as in every tragedy known to man, a time of snatched advantage, rapid losses and swifter profits. At Grovall there was an embittered farm labourer who bore a grudge against his master for a past chastisement. When confronted by an invading river of mud that oozed from every ditch and well-hole on the farmer's land, he saw at a glance the means of his revenge. He struck down his employer with a single hammer-blow and hauled the body into the oncoming flow, then tossed the widow after it when she refused to lie with her husband's killer. Two children and a servant followed in like manner. Then the labourer delayed too long over the family's money-chest, and when he turned at last to make his escape, the mud had risen in a solid wave that ran him down.

How many debts were discharged in this way, how many grievances settled or grudges satisfied, no man could know with any certainty, but many fortunes were altered, lost or gained, diminished or improved, than owed any part to these natural disasters.

For Simeon de Beverley, master scribe, historian and canon elect of St Peter's, that sunny morning on the eve of St Matthew's Feast Day was to mark the end of two years of precious peace. With Osric the infirmarian and Antony the monk, he had ridden hard from York in the dead of night, a dangerous journey and an arduous one. Together they had swilled the dust and perspiration from their bodies and donned fresh robes in time to observe the morning offices. Afterwards they collapsed, exhausted, on pallets of straw in Simeon's scriptorium, only to be roused from their sleep a few hours later. They ran with ropes and staffs to first one place and then another to find whole settlements and families taken, and muddy lakes, some giving off foul steam, left in their places. Simeon spoke prayers to comfort the bereaved as best he could, but his heart ached for those who had died without Christian burial, unconfessed and lacking absolution and so, according to the Holy Catholic Law, doomed for all eternity. He would not have it so for those struck down in such a swift and terrible way and so, against the laws of Church and the teachings of Christian scripture, he gave each victim full and unconditional absolution:

'... *in nomine Patris, et Filii, et spiritus sanctus* ...'

'What? Full remission, Simeon? Without confession?'

Simeon turned from a mud-pool to meet the grim stare of

Antony the monk. 'Did these poor souls have time to make confession? Are they to die unshriven because no priest was on hand to given them even short shrift for their passing?'

'But the law requires—'

'The law of God,' Simeon cut in sharply, 'must be interpreted by men and priests according to what is written in their hearts. He is a God of goodness and compassion. He does not snatch life from innocents and then hold them accountable for the loss.'

Antony scowled. 'Tell that to your archbishop.'

'If I must.'

'You have absolved these people of sins that were neither identified nor repented,' Antony insisted. 'You do more than any priest should dare to do. God bless you for your courage, Simeon, but be sure the Church will not.'

'Full absolution,' Simeon answered shortly. 'The rest I leave to a much higher authority than any here on earth. Come, Antony, there is much to be done here.'

As he turned away the monk caught him by the arm. 'Have a care, my friend. Do as you must and as your heart dictates, but do it quietly, so that no word against you can be carried off to York for the benefit of your enemies.'

The big priest nodded and the monk was satisfied. Both knew the dangerous games played by the powerful men of the Church, and neither enjoyed the humble role of pawn.

Simeon de Beverley was a man of undeniable charisma. He was taller than most and broadly built, a handsome, impressive man with corn-coloured hair and eyes of an almost startling shade of blue. When surveying others his gaze was steady and he rarely blinked, so that the subject of his scrutiny often became discomforted, feeling himself too clearly seen, too closely understood. Indeed, this gentle priest could read another with his eyes and so detect a liar at a glance. He had the mild, inoffensive manner of a scholar with a genuine priestly calling, the delicate skills and infinite patience of an artist of some quality, the stamina and physique of a well-trained athlete. Simeon was a placid, compassionate man who rarely raised his voice or his hand in anger, yet few would care to put his quiet patience to the test, and fewer still would dare to stir the embers of his temper into flame. When justly aroused, the fury of this quiet man was legendary.

'Dear God, is there no stopping this?' he questioned.

Osric the infirmarian shook his head. He had seen much worse than this on the battlefield, and this sudden rising up of mud or water in marshy flatlands was by no means unfamiliar to him. 'In this oppressive heat the mud will quickly bake,' he said. 'Then winter will freeze it over and, come the spring, other homes and grasses will spring up in its place and these poor souls will be forgotten.'

'It is an obscenity,' Simeon whispered, and Osric smiled without a trace of humour.

'It is a *fact*, my friend.'

With a crushing sense of helplessness, Simeon watched the tough little monk from Flanders as he lay on his belly at the mud-pool's edge. The man's thick arms were shoulder-deep in the mire and his hands were groping blindly beneath the surface. At his sudden cry the two sprang forward to help him haul a blackened body on to solid ground. Then Simeon flung off his cloak, knotted a rope around his waist and handed its other end to a muscular youth in a leather skullcap. They used whatever came readily to hand: ropes and staffs, the branches of trees or even strips of clothing, anything to anchor each searcher to safe ground and keep him from slipping to his own death.

They pulled out seven bodies in all before the child was discovered. It was Simeon who found her. Wading thigh-deep just a short way from the edge, his face close to the surface of the mud as he stooped over, his groping hands met with another. To his amazement, small but desperate fingers grasped his own.

'By all that's holy!'

His voice was a bellow of disbelief that stopped the other searchers in their tracks. He stooped until his cheek was in the sludge, grabbed at an arm, a shoulder and a hood and, with a loud yell of triumph, hauled a living child up to the

12

surface. Half-suffocated, the girl had been cocooned in a leather hood in such a way as to keep out the slime while a pocket of breathable air was trapped inside. Unable to move against the sheer weight of mud which engulfed her, she had simply lain there, close to death, until the searching hand of the priest had closed around her own.

There was a deathly hush as Simeon waded to the pool's edge with the limp form in his arms. He raised her up and bent his head to blow his own breath into her empty lungs. When at last he stepped on solid ground she sucked in a gulp of air without assistance and let it out in a wail.

'God be praised,' the swarthy monk exclaimed, and he shook his dark head in amazement. 'She lives.'

'Aye, she lives,' Simeon nodded, holding the sobbing child against him. 'Her hood protected her, but a few minutes more was all she had. Thank God we reached her in time.'

'Simeon!'

He turned his head at the sound of his name and met the warning scowl of the infirmarian. Only then did he realise that the small crowd of would-be rescuers was silent, that none stepped forward to share his joy in snatching a living child from that terrible pit. Some men and women were already on their knees, others were signing the cross or clasping their hands together in prayer, and the whisper on everyone's lips was a single word: *miracle.*

A grovelling woman grasped his ankles in both hands and kissed his feet, oblivious to the filth with which they were stained. 'My little girl ... my Ava ... she was dead and you restored her ... bless you ... oh bless you, Father Simeon.'

'No, woman, I did *not* restore your daughter.' Simeon's voice was cold and harsh as the icy fingers of apprehension crawled across his scalp and down his spine. 'She was still alive when I found her in the mud.'

'No, Father, it was a miracle.'

'Not so,' he said. 'God's will and a stout hood saved her life. She did not die. Heed what I tell you, woman. Your daughter did not die.'

'This man is a saint!' the woman suddenly cried. 'Father

13

Simeon is a saint! You saw him do it. You saw him raise my Ava from the dead.'

'Woman, be warned,' Simeon cautioned through his teeth. 'What you say is a blasphemy. The church will not countenance—'

'But I saw the miracle for myself, Father Simeon. You kissed my Ava and she lived again.'

'Only a little air to help her breathe,' he protested.

'She was dead, I tell you, drowned like all the rest, but you made her live again. It is a miracle.'

Now the others gathered around the pool were joining in the cry: 'A miracle! We saw him do it. We saw a miracle.'

Appalled by this unwanted turn of events, Simeon handed the sobbing child into the woman's arms and stepped away. He found himself confronted on all sides by a press of people speaking of the so-called miracle he had performed before their eyes. An elderly pilgrim fresh from his journey to the blessed shrine of St John of Beverley compounded matters. But for him the story might have been safely contained but, seeking in honest faith to see a good man justly acknowledged, this pilgrim spoke his piece and did much harm.

'I know this man,' he said. 'Ten years ago a young man was killed by a savage blow to the head . . .'

'Have a care, brother,' Osric growled, stepping forward to grasp the pilgrim by the arm. 'It is an offence for a priest to claim a miracle to his credit. All claims so made on his behalf are taken to be his own.'

'But I know this man.'

'Then spare him with your silence,' Osric urged.

The pilgrim shook himself free and turned to address the people standing all about. 'I speak the truth. I was a witness to it. This priest brought a dead man back to life. I swear I saw him do it.'

'The man was stunned but still breathing,' Osric protested in a loud voice. 'And I myself have done as much while I was a soldier on the battlefield.'

'The man was bleeding,' the pilgrim declared. 'His skull was opened and his brains exposed.'

'Not so! Only his scalp was cut,' Osric contradicted. 'You all know that a man bleeds freely from a wounded scalp. He was stunned and nothing more. Father Simeon merely helped him breathe until his strength returned. Then, as now, there was *no miracle*.'

'I saw it ! I saw him raised from the dead!'

'Two miracles!' someone cried, and the now excited crowd took up the cry. 'Two miracles. Two souls raised from the dead. A saint twice over.'

Deeply disturbed, Osric and Antony drew Simeon away. Others were flocking to the scene beside the lake of mud, eager to know of the miracle and to see the once-dead child with their own eyes.

'Your limp, Simeon.' Osric growled the reminder out of one corner of his mouth. 'Do not forget that you were never healed of your affliction.'

The three men strode away, quickening their pace in order to put some streets and alleyways between themselves and the now clamorous crowd. They heard the whispers following after them.

'The priest is a saint.'

'He worked a miracle.'

'He brought a dead man back to life and now this child has also been restored.'

'Simeon is surely a saint. A twice-proven saint.'

As Simeon limped between his two companions, he knew that trouble once again was running at his heels. He could not find it in himself to regret the timely saving of the child, but in his heart he wished that someone other than himself had pulled her out. The hardships of ten years ago must not be allowed to repeat themselves, as they surely would if talk of miracles brought him into conflict with his Church for a second time.

He frowned now at the memory, still fresh after a decade, of the sudden storm of unholy proportions which had laid the better part of Beverley to waste. From its core a hooded figure came, bearing the naked, newborn babe who would change, enrich or destroy the lives of all who knew of him.

15

For reasons he would never comprehend, Simeon was singled out to be young Peter's guardian and protector. At the Minster's high altar, overshadowed by the shrine of Beverley's blessed St John, and with the raging tempest screaming in his ears, Simeon's crippled foot had been healed and his life of studious obscurity brought to an end. The repercussions of that terrible night had forced him to deny his healing and conceal the child, to live by lies and stealth so that his godson and those who served him might survive. Eight years were to pass before the mysterious figure appeared again, and with it a fire as merciless as any tempest. Simeon's life still hung precariously between the twin powers of Church and elements, each one as awesome and unpredictable as the other, and between the two he walked a narrow course of discipline and secrecy.

'It must not happen again,' he said now as he mimicked a cripple's gait. 'I will not be forced, by good intent or bad, to carry the burden of scapegoat yet again.'

'Then let us pray that *the other* has no hand in this,' Osric growled, and Antony muttered a hearty amen to that.

CHAPTER THREE

T he worst of that day was not over yet for Simeon. The
archbishop's house in the corn market was virtually
under siege, for mud had gushed from the beck and caused
much damage to the doors. Looters, some masquerading as
priests and rescuers, were forming groups and trying to get
inside, while priests and servants struggled to keep them out.
When the first door buckled under the pressing weight of the
mud, the warden and his family fled for their lives, leaving
the house and its contents vulnerable. Though little of value
remained in the archbishop's absence, its vaulted cellars
were rumoured to hold many caskets of fine wine and its
shuttered windows concealed such hangings as could raise
the means to feed a hungry family for many weeks. One
cellar chamber had been flooded to half its roof height.
Another had been guarded by two armed priests until the
mud gushed down the steps and pinned them like impaled
insects to the door.

'Father Richard of Weel is in there,' Simeon was told by a
would-be rescuer. 'He was fighting off robbers when the flow
increased. The thieves were drowned, but Richard and
another priest are trapped against a locked chamber door.
They can neither swim nor wade against this muck. I fear
we've lost them.'

'Father Richard? My own priest is down there?'

The rescuer nodded his confirmation. 'I'm sorry, Father. I know he was your friend.'

The big priest saw this same Richard in his mind's eye, a young man brave and loyal to a fault. He had risked his life many times in Simeon's service, had rescued many in tempest and in fire, and now he was trapped in an empty house belonging to an indifferent archbishop living thirty miles away in York. Brave men were not to be wasted in this way. Simeon would not have his friend die in such a petty cause as this.

Now he and his two companions joined the press of men who were trying to clear the mud from the narrow stairwell, though any eye could see the task was futile. They worked with their bare hands and with anything that would serve as a paddle to turn the flow aside, and it was as if they sought to shift an ocean from its course. There was a window in the wall above the level of the mud, but even when its metal grid was kicked away, neither a man nor a boy of any substance could pass through its narrow opening. The priests' cries for help could be heard from inside, their voices given a hollow quality in the vaulted darkness.

'It's hopeless,' Simeon declared at last as Antony, the smallest among them, struggled in vain to prise his shoulders through the window opening. 'The mud is still rising. We need axes and hammers to break these stones apart.'

'We'll never do it,' Osric gasped. 'These walls were built to withstand any assault, and even if we could breach the window stones, how could we hope to reach those two in time?'

'We must,' the big priest said. 'We have to get them out.'

'Let me help, Father.'

He turned to see a small figure standing at his side, and the sight came as a blow to him. The rags were unfamiliar and a leather skullcap hid his flaxen hair, but there was no mistaking those blue eyes.

'Peter! In God's name, boy, what are you doing here?'

'I am needed,' the boy said simply.

Simeon's protest died on his lips. There was no time to argue while men were being slowly crushed to death. He glanced at the window, then at the black sea making its slow, unstoppable way into the cellar.

'It is not possible.'

Peter nodded. 'I can do it. I can reach them with a rope and you can pull them out. Watch for me at that window there, the high one with the shutters.'

Simeon shook his head in doubt. 'Those shutters are made of solid oak. How will you lift the bars and free the chains?'

'I know a way. Listen ...' He cocked his head, his face turned up, and now only one voice called out from that dark place; the deep, familiar voice of Father Richard. 'I must go in. It is the only way.'

'Peter, I cannot allow it.'

'Then Father Richard will die,' the boy replied.

Osric and Antony had halted their useless labours and waited now for Simeon's response. This thing rested with him alone. He knew, as they did, that the boy was equal to the task. Someone must get through that narrow opening and scale the walls above the mud to save Richard's life, and if anyone could do it, Peter could.

'Are you sure of this, Peter?'

'Yes, Father.'

'So be it.'

Simeon called for a rope and, with a heavy wedge to weight its end, secured it around his godson's waist and lifted him shoulder-high.

'God keep you safe,' he whispered, and the boy replied, not doubting for a moment, 'Be sure He will.'

The skinny, ragged boy glanced back just once as he wriggled through the window. The blue eyes locked with Simeon's for an instant, the priest nodded his head and the boy was gone.

Simeon did not pray. His heart had risen to his throat and his mind was robbed of all but the image of Peter going into that dark hole. The mud was rising swifter now, filling up every space and hugging everything in its path in a sticky, suffocating embrace. The infirmarian stood with his fists clenched, staring at the shutters as if the fierceness of his glance might burst them open. The monk was balanced on the upper step where the mud had driven him. A pulse was throbbing in his cheek and his expression was as grim as any man had ever seen it. Long minutes ebbed away. The cries from the cellar ceased. Then, with a clatter, the shutters opened and the rope fell out.

'Dear God be praised.' The words were uttered as savagely as an oath as the tough infirmarian, a soldier for half his lifetime, was all but moved to tears by relief.

A dozen willing hands reached up to grasp the rope as it came down, and any man who could reach it gave his whole strength to the hauling. It came by inches, dragging a heavy load. Some braced their feet against the walls of the house to add more leverage, and as the rope descended other hands reached out to add what help they could. A cheer went up from below when the black and slimy figure of a man appeared at the window, and by his beard they knew that it was Richard.

The rest was easy. Richard clambered on to the window ledge and cautiously lowered himself down the rope. When his strength deserted him and his grip failed, he dropped the last distance into the arms of friends. The rope with its weighted end came after him. A pale face showed itself briefly at the window, the big priest nodded his thanks and the shutters closed.

Some minutes later Peter reappeared at the lower window, wriggled through and was helped to safety by several townsmen who had waded into the mud to see him safe. As they lifted him clear and set him on firm ground Simeon tossed the rope across the pool.

'Secure yourselves,' he called to those around him. 'Don't venture into the pool unless a man on firm ground has your lifeline safely held. This stuff has a suck as powerful as quicksand.' He turned then to Father Richard and caught him in a strong embrace. 'Bless your fine beard, my friend, it's good to have you back with us.'

'A lesser welcome would suffice,' Richard gasped. 'That Devil's brew has all but crushed my ribs. God's teeth, I ache in every joint and muscle.'

'There was a man with you ...'

Richard nodded. 'You knew him, Simeon. You heard his confession yesterday. He was Andrew, the exorcist, and he died well despite his pain. I heard the snapping of his bones. The pressure on him was all the greater because he was not a tall man and the sludge was very deep. In the end it reached his throat and choked him, but he died praising God and calling on the saints.'

'His faith was strong,' Simeon nodded. 'May God receive his soul in Heaven and judge him gently.'

'Amen,' Richard said, and winced upon the word. 'Simeon, I owe my life to that boy of yours. I couldn't move an inch to save myself down there. My chest was slowly being crushed and still the mud was rising. Who taught him to cling like a bat where there is no hand-hold, and to scale a wall as smooth and as flat as metal?'

'Not I,' Simeon smiled. 'Such skills are not of my teaching.' He turned his head, seeking the boy, but found no trace of him. 'Peter? Where is he?'

'The boy is safe,' Osric said, but his face was troubled. He had watched Peter turn and walk away, just another ragged child on Beverley's teeming streets, but as the boy reached the far side of the market-place, where a crooked lane would take him to the Westwood, Osric had glimpsed a figure by his side. It was the figure of a man dressed all in black, hooded and slightly stooped, familiar in shape and size. Osric had blinked his eyes and when he opened them again the hooded man was gone and Peter walked alone. He moved his thumb across his chest to sign the cross and told himself, firmly and repeatedly, that he had been mistaken.

'The boy is safe,' he said again, and knew it would be so. 'He took the lane to the Westwood. He's going home.'

Simeon called two men to assist Father Richard to the comfort of St Peter's infirmary, where Osric's people would see him well revived. He was frowning as he watched them skirt the mud-pool, supporting the injured man between them. 'How did he know of this?' he asked. 'How did Peter know that he was needed here?'

Osric dismissed the figure as nothing more than a shape glimpsed in a crowd, a brief error of eye and mind. He would speak no words to give that error substance, for he would not have that hooded figure here again in Beverley. His reply was gruff. 'How does that boy know anything?'

'And why would Elvira allow him to roam the streets alone, with no guards to protect him?'

'Why ask?' Osric met one question with another. 'No doubt he will be back with her before she even guesses he was gone. You know his ways, Simeon. You will not keep such a one as Peter under your full restraint, not while he knows every hole and tunnel in Beverley and slips unhindered in and out of either.'

Simeon nodded and looked about him to see what more could be done. The mud was creeping towards his feet, now moving at a slower rate because its bulk had filled up the cellars. The drama of Richard's rescue and the presence of the men of St Peter's had dissuaded the thieves who sought to make a profit from the breaching of the archbishop's doors. They had slipped away in search of other plunder, leaving the priests and rescuers to their work.

Simeon and his two friends left the market-place. Nearby, in Ladygate, they heard faint cries for help, and when they traced the source another tragedy was unfolding. The gate to a workman's house was barred against them, held fast by the weight of mud piled at its back. They scaled the outer walls and dropped to the roof of a lean-to hut which creaked and rocked beneath their combined weight. From there they could see a man chest-deep in the black morass, his face twisted in pain, his breathing broken and his nostrils leaking blood. The whole of his workshop yard was under flood. The well set at its centre had overflowed, pumping a river of stinking ooze into the yard, and the walls and fences, built close and solid to keep out thieves, now kept the sludge contained. Without movement the mass of it had begun to thicken and condense upon itself. Like Richard in the cellar, this man was firmly trapped and the mud was slowly squeezing him to death.

Antony secured a short length of rope to his waist, dropped lightly from the roof and waded in. His feet met with a grinding-stone submerged beneath the surface, and from it he stepped with caution to lower ground. He was thigh-deep before he recognised the danger. Mere inches from the grinding-stone his steps were halted, his legs gripped so tightly that he could no longer move in any direction or lift his feet clear of the clinging mass.

'It has me fast,' he cried, and there was real fear in his voice. 'It's thickening. It has found its level and settled on itself. It's turning to a solid mass. Help me. I cannot move.'

Osric and Simeon pulled him free between them and it was no easy task. The roof on which they stood was shifting sideways, its supporting structure so badly undermined that as they hauled they heard the timbers splinter. The little monk issued curses as he was freed, then touched his Tau cross and gave thanks for the strength and determination of his companions. His sandals were ripped from his feet and left behind and the skin on his calves, though weathered to the texture of well-tanned leather, had split in places where the mud had clung.

The man trapped in the mire was losing his battle for survival. They threw the rope a score of times and yelled at him to grab it and hold on, but the weight on his chest was such that he could barely breathe. Each time they thought they had him, one small tug upon the rope would pull it from his failing grasp.

'Help me,' they heard him gasp, but there was nothing they could do save make the passing prayer, relieve him of his worldly sins and stay to watch him die.

'I should have known,' Antony said. 'With no more space for it to move, this stuff builds up against itself and will not yield to any obstruction. I've seen it crack the hulk of a ship wide open. It is more deadly once it is contained. I should have known.'

23

'No more than I,' Osric replied. 'I have seen the speed with which it thickens once it comes to rest. Better to dig new courses in its path than to impede it. There was no way we could have saved him, not even if he had still possessed the strength to hold the rope.'

Simeon had not been aware of this but had supposed the mud would remain unchanged until the hot sun baked it hard and natural drainage did the rest. That a man could drown in mud was common knowledge, but that he could be broken of bone and sinew, snapped apart and crushed like a brittle twig was horrible. He stared at the man, trapped to his armpits with his head hung forward and his arms outstretched, and as he stared his cheeks drained of all colour.

'I taught them,' he said, a look of growing horror on his face. 'I showed those rescuers how to work in pairs with a rope between them.' He turned to his friends. Their faces told him, without need of words, that they too could see this tragedy repeated many times. 'I showed them. They are wading to their deaths on my instructions.'

The three men moved in unison. From the shifting roof they scaled the outer wall, dropped down into the street and sprinted off in different directions. At speed they ran from group to group, from pool to pool with shouted warnings. They grabbed at priests and townsfolk alike, yelling at them to spread the news that nobody must go near the mud unless it was still flowing. At every pool they yanked out the rescuers and sent them off with shouted warnings. Simeon roused the priests of St Mary's and, with hand-bells ringing and voices raised, these men rushed through the streets to clear the pools.

The friends met each other again at the North Bar, near St Mary's. By some authority the gates had been barred and teams of men and women were working where the ditch was breached.

From there they walked together, weary and smeared with filth, towards St Peter's. The Minster church stood in the distance, its stonework ghostly pale in the vivid sunlight. It shimmered where the dust blew up, black-tipped with charred timbers, still magnificent and still with the power to move men's souls.

'It's over,' Osric muttered grimly. 'The pressure below ground has been released and all the flows have halted.'

'God be praised,' Simeon replied, signing the cross.

They stopped close by the larger market cross. A woman was seated on the ground, the frayed end of a rope coiled in her lap, staring dull-eyed across the mire. The length of rope lay on the surface where the mud had hardened, its other end secured around a man's waist. He had been kneeling when the flow congealed, groping with both hands thrust beneath the surface, his face turned sideways and his mouth wide open. And there the pool had trapped him with too much of his body submerged for caring hands to pull him free. His eyes, still astonished, stared back to solid ground and she, the wife who held the rope, gazed back at him with equal disbelief.

They left the monk to offer words of comfort to the widow, and as they walked away Osric observed: 'I will never understand how life can be so precious and yet so cheap.'

CHAPTER FOUR

Figham House was set like a handsome jewel in the dusty, sun-scorched pasture. It had high walls around it and a fortified stone barn set at its back. A freshwater stream and two good wells lay enclosed within its walls, and there was neither knight nor bishop who did not covet the house and its excellent lands. A mile away the church of St Matthew lay in ruins, only its tiny chapel and bells restored, but here its canon lived in princely style and comfort.

Father Cyrus de Figham was seated in a carved oak chair, his legs outstretched and his long hands hanging loosely over the lion-head armrests. A gold ring with a huge black stone shone dully on the index finger of his right hand, echoing the murky depths of his dark eyes. He was glowering in frustration at the day's events, his brows furrowed over his elegant nose and his lips pressed tightly together.

'Damn it,' he muttered from time to time. 'Damn Beverley to Hell for crossing me again.'

De Figham was a man of striking appearance, an accomplished horseman and huntsman, as skilled with a bow as with a sword or dagger. His hair was very dark with a coppery sheen, an indication of his Norman ancestry. He wore it long, and not since the day he took holy orders had knife or razor touched his crown. Many priests argued that the tonsure, the earthly symbol of the heavenly crown, was a mark of obedience, an outward sign of a man's devout intent. Others maintained that all it proved about any man was that his crown was shaved. Even the popes who took their successive seats in Rome had failed to reach agreement, and decade after decade the dispute flared up and dimmed without resolve. Thus the priestly tonsure, although much favoured by the more devout, was still for some no more than a tiresome ritual of ordination.

'Damn it. Damn every stinking corner of it.'

Still brooding in his chair, de Figham drew in a deep breath until his nostrils dilated and, when he exhaled, the creases in his forehead deepened and his eyes became like polished slits. He was garbed in plum-coloured velvet edged with gold and silver thread, with a sleeveless coat of wolf-skin reaching to his booted ankles. He was every inch the arrogant son of a baron, and he guarded his powerful position within the Church as keenly as any baron's son might defend his noble standing in society. The Church was his profession, not his calling. He played the part and kept the rules where such was demanded of him, and he used the authority of his office to keep the rabble subservient to the Church. Neither man or priest nor pope would dare ask more of him than that.

Another man was present in the room, a sturdy individual with closely set eyes of no particular colour, set in a face of unremarkable feature. He was dressed in a modest priest's robe of brown wool, over which was hung a splendid crimson mantle with a hood. At his waist was a silver girdle set with jewels, and from the girdle hung a priest's knife of the finest quality. All these were gifts from a master who rewarded his servant for the use of his sly skills, and to prevent some rival buying off his talents. That the young priest had survived for four years in de Figham's personal service was to his credit. He was ambitious and had learned to use his wits for his advancement, and so he prospered.

This man was John Palmer, de Fighman's loyal steward and priest. He had been a palmer at the grammar school and, when his taste for corporal punishment outgrew the simple palm-beating required by his position, he was advanced to exorcist to keep him from temptation. De Figham recognised his skills, made him his steward and confessor, his puppet and his instrument.

John Palmer was well practised in the art of treading the quagmire of his canon's quicksilver moods. Like a well-trained hound obedient to an inconsistent handler, he had learned when to fawn and when to flatter and when to skulk away. Now John was waiting upon his master's pleasure while de Figham brooded in his chair. The crafty clerk from York was surely dead, but three men of worth were also lost, along with four valuable mounts and a purse of silver. He cleared his throat and chose his words with care, for this sullen canon was a man of dangerous undertows.

'My lord, perhaps they took the safer route along the main road after all?' He offered the suggestion lightly, knowing it was not so, for the signs were there for any man with half an eye to measure.

Father Cyrus raised one eyebrow in an arc, his gaze as sharp as flint and glinting black. 'They crossed the pasture.'

'That may well be so, my lord, but if the archbishop's clerk rode harder than our men expected of him?'

'Not on that short-winded mare I fobbed upon him,' de Figham growled and, in that moment, as he shook his head, an elusive ring of silver light played over the glossy surface of his hair. 'No, John, it is certain that they crossed the pasture, and when the ditch rose up they all were drowned. It cannot be otherwise.'

'An act of God,' John shrugged, and bit his tongue on the observation as he was fixed with a hard and mocking glare. To compensate for the slip he added quickly: 'A most unusual happenstance, my lord.'

'No, just one more reminder that this town is without solid foundations. It sits on water, mud and marsh, on land-faults and abandoned waterways. Another deluge like the one we saw ten years ago might well cause Beverley to slip its moorings and take to the open sea.' He raised a long forefinger in an elegant gesture, pointing it at John as his mouth curled upwards in a cruel smile. 'And that, my friend, would be an act of God for any man to savour.'

'You still hate Beverley, then, Father Cyrus?'

'With a passion,' de Figham spat.

'And yet you stay here when you could be elsewhere. In York, perhaps, or Lincoln, or even Durham?'

'Aye, John, I stay. I will not leave this hellhole to the likes of Wulfric de Morthlund and Simeon de Beverley. I will not walk away to serve their ends, not while the true wealth of Beverley still lies beyond my reach.'

'Ah,' John said, and the word came on a sigh of resignation. He was no stranger to this man's obsessions, nor did he underestimate the power wealth had to move the soul, to fire the blood to boiling-point and blinker the eyes to all but its existence.

Through many past centuries Beverley's ecclesiastical treasure had been the envy of more illustrious towns. It could be counted in gold and silver, bronze and pewter, in foreign ivory and jade, in precious jewels and illustrated manuscripts. It could be measured in chests of gold and silver coin, in caskets of amber and copper jewel-pieces, in saintly relics and priceless altar-cloths. Much of it had been laid by in secret by powerful men seeking to purchase a better place for themselves in Heaven, much by those intending only to enrich the Minster church, and much by those who meant to keep the treasure for themselves. Every decade provided its quota of royal tributes, papal gifts, archbishop's honours and noble bequests, and every year church profits and pilgrim's offerings swelled its coffers. Thus it had become a treasure worthy of any king, and no man knew, or could be made to tell, where it was hidden.

To this wealth were added the holy relics of St John of Beverley, founder of the town and its original monastery, the bones of John the Baptist, carried from Rome, and the jewelled dagger of King Athelston, gifted to St John for his protection. All these were concealed at the time of the fire and had not re-emerged in two long years, despite the efforts of expert searchers seeking a huge reward for their recovery. With the relics were hidden the church plate and the massive altar-cross of solid gold embellished with precious gems, its weight doubled by its tragic figure of the martyred Christ. Now unsuspecting pilgrims in their droves made offerings for the privilege of kneeling at an empty casket skilfully duplicated in polished brass with plaster gems. Trade flourished, poor men grew fat and priests grew rich, but still the whereabouts of Beverley's wealth remained a mystery. There were many men, de Figham not least among them, who would not know a moment's rest until they had that treasure in their possession.

John Palmer watched de Figham's brooding face, the gathered brow and gloomy stare, and he knew this canon to be consumed with such obsessions as would destroy a lesser man or separate him from his sanity. And those obsessions, while fashioned in unlike mould, were snagged upon a single spur that could be named with ease: *Simeon*. Each rage to which de Figham succumbed, and there were many, shifted its focus to hang upon his fixation.

There was a woman hidden in the town, a ditcher's wife whose gentle beauty had pierced de Figham's heart and left a raw wound there. Cyrus de Figham had seen her once, had held her in his arms and heard another speak her name, and for two years he had searched and plotted and lusted after her.

There was also that much-loved priest with his disputed imperfection, his crippled foot. In breeding, intellect and bearing they were so much of a kind that they were likened to the two sides of a single coin. Only at heart were they entirely dissimilar in the minting. Where one was covetous and lustful, the other was a true priest of the church. Cyrus de Figham was as dark as the underside of human nature, and in this, if in little else, Simeon de Beverley was his opposite.

'Ah,' said John again, another sigh of understanding, and his canon fixed him with a sidelong glance.

'You know my thoughts, John Palmer. That priest of St

Peter's is a deadly poison in my gullet. Try as I might, I cannot spit him out.'

'I know, my lord.' The clerk was inclined to add that such deep envy was its own contamination, that hatred for its own sake might eat a man away from inside to out and make an empty, useless shell of him. He was tempted, but he did not speak the words. Instead he pursued his lips and nodded, saying again, 'I know.'

'He has the woman hidden.'

'I understand so.' John spoke honestly, for that much he did believe of Simeon.

'And they have a son. That child of theirs is ten years old, and to think that once I had him ... I *had* him ...' His long fingers became hooked like the talons of an eagle gripping its prey as the memory jangled on his peace of mind. He could have choked the life from that scrawny neck or flung the boy to his death from the heights of the Minster church, had Simeon not robbed him of the pleasure.

'Their *foster* son, my lord,' John dared to say. 'It was given to him as an infant and the woman was employed to be its wet-nurse.'

De Figham glared. 'Damn you to Hell if you believe that fairy tale about a mysterious child, a celibate priest and an innocent ditcher's wife.' He raised his fist and brought it down with force upon the carved arm of his chair. 'She is Simeon's whore and the child their bastard son, and that priest's vow of celibacy is nothing but a sham.'

'You too have a woman,' John reminded him.

De Figham's laugh was harsh. 'A snivelling kitchen wench who does not please me.'

'And yet this very day you will challenge your fellow canons for the right to keep her under your roof.'

'On a point of principle from which I will not yield by the smallest shred,' de Figham said, measuring a minute space between a finger and a thumb and squinting at the gap through narrowed eyes. 'By not *one shred* to satisfy the sanctimonious bleatings of that priest of St Peter's and his company of fools. Let him be content with his own whore.

31

Let him breed a dozen bastard sons on her if he is half the man he thinks himself to be.'

'You too have a son, my lord,' John ventured, then stood back half a pace at his master's response.

'Damn you,' de Figham snarled again. 'Damn you for such an objectionable reminder. I will not name that peasant's brat, that dirty fish-cutter's whelp, as any son of mine.'

John sighed and spread his hands. How could this man be satisfied with anything he had while Simeon prospered? The hatred ran too deep for that, and when he had dangled helplessly from the Minster roof-space it was the strength of Simeon's hand that had held him back from certain death, and de Figham would never forgive the priest for that.

'Is that the prayer bell?'

'Yes, it is almost two. Will you keep the holy office?'

De Figham flexed his hands with sufficient force to make the knuckles crack. 'Damn the holy office,' he answered softly.

John sighed. The Figham house was the envy of most men, and as safe from flooding as it was opulent, its two wells meticulously maintained and its great barn stocked as amply as any castle keep. Even these advantages made Father Cyrus de Figham peevish, for he could see St Peter's enclosure from his boundary walls, and in that place, criss-crossed as it was with a web of little waterways and tightly packed with woodland, neither fire nor flood had claimed a single life these ten years past.

'They say he saved another life, this noble Simeon of Beverley,' de Figham complained.

'They speak of *many* saved,' John told him carefully. 'Have no fear, my lord, that any will criticise your own part in the day's events. I have dispatched servants all about the town with accounts of your own rescue work. They will speak of you toiling in this place and that as if they had seen your good deeds with their own eyes.'

'Your prudence does you credit, John Palmer, but he, that crippled scribe of St Peter's, was there to make his mark before genuine witnesses. I hear he rode all night from York to observe the morning offices, and before the noon bell toiled he was a hero.'

'And much the Church will make of it, my lord,' John Palmer answered. 'No matter if he met with him in York, as the clerk reported, our proud archbishop will tolerate no humble priest made glorious while he himself walks a narrow path between his supporters and his enemies.'

De Figham turned his head to survey his clerk with hooded eyes. Slowly, a smile transformed his sombre features and his eyes took on a bright silver lustre.

'Well spoken, John, and well observed,' he said. 'If history repeats itself, if claims to saintly talents dog him for a second time, I think the Church will not look kindly on the matter.'

'They say he gave full redemption to the dead and dying without confession or repentance to deserve it.'

'Did he, now?'

'And that he brought to life a child who had been drowned for an hour.'

'Indeed?' De Figham showed his fine white teeth in a smile. 'Then perhaps we should fan these small sparks into flame and quietly stand aside to observe the happy outcome. Who knows what the authorities in York, or even Rome itself, will make of his arrogant and blasphemous claims to saint-hood!'

'Indeed, my lord, who knows?'

'It seems to me that any witnesses willing to come forward should be handsomely rewarded for their reports, and that these matters should be clearly documented.'

'Yes, my lord.'

'You shall have the means to buy their tongues. Offer what you will, then use your skills to add the ring of truth to what you buy. These Beverley men would sell their kith and kin for a silver shilling or a loaf of bread to fill their empty bellies. They'll speak out all the more imaginatively if they believe they do Simeon de Beverley, and the Church, a loyal service.'

De Figham was animated now. He saw a way of striking at the priest who was the object of his envy and his hatred, and John was once again reminded that his own situation became all the more secure when he could drop some titbit into his master's venom.

'It will be done as you desire, my lord.'

'I owe you a debt of thanks, John Palmer. You can be sure your timely observations will not go unrewarded.'

'Thank you, my lord,' John said.

'So tell me, John, in your opinion, does Simeon know where the missing relics are to be found?'

John shrugged. 'He carried a package with him to York and came away with promises of the archbishop's patronage. The clerk was almost certain that he met with Aaron the Jew, son of that obstinate Josce, who was said to be the wealthiest man in the city until the mob cut him to pieces and the crown claimed all his wealth. These Jews are not known to trade with priests who come to them empty-handed. Both Geoffrey Plantagenet and Aaron, the archbishop and the Jew, are alike enough in this respect: they judge a man by the substance and the value of his bribe.'

'Indeed they do,' de Figham nodded. 'So what did our priest of St Peter's carry with him that would so impress the two wealthiest and most powerful men in York?'

'And the most dangerous,' John observed.

'All power is dangerous,' de Figham said coldly, and John the palmer, careful of his position, answered with measured respect, 'Indeed, my lord.'

'One thing he did without a doubt. He took a sample, some sop to whet their appetites. Whatever he got for himself in York was bartered with stolen goods. He knows where our treasure is hidden. He knows, and he would squander it, piece by priceless piece, to see that precious Minster of his restored.'

'I believe he would, my lord.'

De Figham's smile had faded now and his face was set with grim determination. 'Over my dead body,' he snarled.

'Or his, my lord?'

The dark priest bellowed with sudden laughter. 'Aye, his,' he said at last, savouring the thought. 'Over Simeon's dead body, John. And, as God is my judge, I'll have that woman and her skinny whelp, *and* the treasures of Beverley, in the process.'

John Palmer welcomed the change in his master's humour. There would be ways for him to advance his position while this pot of de Figham's ire was simmering. John knew the part he would be called upon to play, that of the visible, open target squarely placed between his master and his enemies. Already the pattern was set so that, should de Figham ever be brought to task for any crime, all blame would be neatly shifted to his palmer. He would not act unless it could be proved beyond doubt that John was the cause and inspiration of his deeds. Should his ill-dealing bring John into disfavour with the Church, he would confess his faults, exonerate his canon and be contrite. And de Figham would simply buy his pardon. It was a neat arrangement for their mutual benefit. If ever it proved otherwise, John Palmer would not hesitate to slip his blade between his canon's ribs and stop his heart.

CHAPTER FIVE

Another Beverley man was travelling from York on that hot afternoon, the eve of St Matthew's Feast Day. He came with a sprawling entourage of clerks and servants, priests and guards and carriers in attendance, all making a colourful spectacle along the open road. He came with a clatter of horse's hooves and a rattle of heavy wheels which dragged the dust in swirling clouds along the dry dirt road. Bright sunlight glinted on polished trappings and jewelled decorations, winking and flashing that here was a man of much importance journeying to Beverley. In quiet respect, farmworkers lowered their tools to stand and stare, while other travellers took hastily to the hedges as the group rode by.

A massive cart rumbled behind, decked out with fancy trappings and hung with curtains to keep the dirt from its lavishly furnished interior. In its dusty wake came lesser carts piled high with traded goods, food and cooking-pots, robes and carpets, all guarded by men on foot or riding donkeys.

Wulfric de Morthlund was mounted on a destrier of great strength and stamina, a horse bred for the plough and strong enough to bear the greater weight demanded of it. Its ornaments were trimmed with silver and laced with coloured thread, and here and there a flash of burnished copper shone with reflected sunlight. Over its muscular flanks a purple cloak was spread, the lower edge of which was heavily weighted with a band of embroidery set with silver discs. The rider was a man of huge proportions and magnificent apparel. Over his fancy canon's robes he wore a mantle of now scarce beaver-skin clasped at the shoulder with a ruby brooch. At his waist was a silver girdle of triple width set with precious gems, and on his hands he wore as many rings as he had fingers. That he displayed himself as grandly as any bishop was the measure of his conceit, for this canon of Beverley held himself above and beyond all laws save those he fashioned for himself. Wealth and status he had in plenty, fear and respect he could command from any. All else he took by any means, for all he lacked was any sense of self-denial or reserve. Wulfric de Morthlund acquired, by fair or vulgar means, everything his intemperate appetites desired, an easy task for a man unhampered by the yoke of conscience.

'Just listen to those cursed bells. Do the ringers of Beverley suffer an affliction that makes them pull on their ropes with such vexing enthusiasm?'

'Sounds travel far, my lord, when the air is still,' his companion said. 'Would you be more comfortable in the cart?'

De Morthlund shook his head and the rolls of flesh below his chin bounced one upon the other with the movement. 'No amount of swansdown pillows are enough to stop the jarring of my bones with every turn of the wheels, and with those curtains drawn it gets as hot as Hell in there.'

'Another hour and we'll be home, God willing.'

The fat man cast a mocking glance at the young priest riding by his side. 'God willing, Daniel? *God* willing? Make no mistake about it, we will be home in an hour because *I* will it.'

'Yes, my lord.'

They rode on in silence for some distance, and as they drew nearer the town they noticed flocks of crows wheeling and circling in the air, dipping and diving and settling in black patches on the ground.

'Carrion,' Wulfric said, clearing his throat and spitting, regardless of the proximity of other riders. 'This is a day of Christian fasting and yet those flying flesh-eaters are out in uncommon numbers, don't you think?'

Daniel, who had been observing the birds for some time with a superstitious eye, raised his head to watch a group soar over them and settle on the pasture.

'Some animal must have died,' he offered. 'A horse gored by a boar, perhaps, or a deer brought down by dogs, or even a grazing cow tripped by a rut and left for dead.'

'Fresh meat left out for crows? On a fast day and with half the town one bite away from starvation? I doubt it, lad. There are too many here for my peace of mind. God's teeth, with all this cawing of crows and jangling of bells, I have half a mind to turn back for York and eat wine-sopped bread for supper.'

The party of riders had reached the woodland marking Beverley's common pasture. They entered the cooler, shaded space beneath a varicoloured canopy of leaves, passing from dust and heat to autumn sweetness. Here, where the woods gave way to open pasture, they would stop to refresh themselves while footmen ran ahead to warn the town of their imminent arrival. Canon Wulfric had never been inclined to come and go without display. A man's status must be maintained by public recognition and acclaim, and he was not great who travelled about without it.

The first riders were almost through to the edge of the meadow when the cry went up. Some men were running for the woods, waving their cloaks and hoods in warning, and as they came on, the leading mounts took fright. Two stumbled sideways, pitching their riders off. Another went down heavily on its knees, throwing its rider into a tree with killing force. Two more were reined in sharply only to miss their footing on uneven ground and fall away into a deep hole, crushing the men they carried.

'God's teeth!'

The rider beside him reached out to grasp the bridle of de Morthlund's horse the instant the animal tossed its head and made as if to rear up in alarm.

'Have a care, my lord! You there! Look to your canon's safety!' The big destrier showed the whites of its eyes and side-stepped, and as its head went down de Morthlund pitched across its neck, all but unseated. His face turned purple and his breath was stopped as the sudden lurch caused his silver girdle to bite into the soft flesh of his belly. One foot slid from the stirrup-loop and paddled empty air, and the sudden imbalance of his weight brought the horse around so sharply that it collided with the rider closest to it, causing his horse in turn to whinny and prance. It took two men to right the obese canon in his saddle and two more to assist him out of it.

'My lord, are you injured?' His companion-priest dismounted with a flourish of his silk-lined cloak. Father Daniel was also called the Hawk, as much for his noble profile as for his hunting skills. His dark hair hung in waves about his shoulders but thinned towards his forehead. This loss was a source of much regret to him, since he was still young and pleasing in appearance. His threatened baldness was repulsive to his master, and since he depended for his living upon de Morthlund's pleasure, the thinning of his hair rendered his future uncertain. What passed between these two was love of sorts, but it bore an edge of malice that was razor-sharp.

'My thanks to you, Daniel Hawk,' the fat man said. 'Your swift thinking stayed my mount and prevented me from being thrown.' His face had lost its purple hue but the skin was beaded with perspiration and streaked with dust. His eyes were bright beads deeply embedded with his fleshy features, and when he smiled his lips glistened with saliva. This was not the first time Daniel had placed his master's safety before his own. Scars on his cheeks and hands, a knife wound on his chest and singed patches on his forearms were permanent reminders of his loyalty.

The runners from Beverley were standing at a distance, their hands cupped to their mouths as they relayed their news to others in the party. Their rough local accents offended de Morthlund's ears and bedevilled his understanding, so it was some time before the word from the town, sensibly translated, came to him. By then he was resting in his cart, supported by furs and cushions of swansdown, a goblet in his hand and a dampened cloth across his brow. Sprawled on his back, his girdle unbuckled so that his belly hung loose and unconfined, he gave no thought to the safety or the comfort of his entourage. He would have remained in York but for the date, which demanded the customary fast before St Matthew's Feast Day. He had no stomach for frugal ecclesiastical fare. Better to eat his fill in a dusty cart or at some village stopping place than to suffer the hardship of a day's starvation along with his pompous church superiors in York. He ate some mutton and a brace of honey-roasted starlings while lying on his back, then called for a roll of silk to cushion his head. He was dozing when Daniel slid the goblet from his fingers and dared to drink from it.

'My lord canon, we have lost four horses with their riders. some altar-robes and a donkey are also lost, and only two of our runners crossed the pasture with their lives intact to carry news of your return to Beverley.'

'What? Are we under attack from robbers?' de Morthlund asked. 'Out here on the open pasture, in broad daylight?'

'Not robbers, my lord. Floods.'

De Morthlund hoisted himself into a sitting position and shuffled forward so that his bulbous legs hung outside the doorway of the cart. He waved a huge arm towards the town where little could be seen save for clouds of hovering dust. 'Floods, Little Hawk? *Floods*? This place has suffered a season dry enough to scorch away the crops before they could grow to even finger-height. Look at it, lying there in dust as dry as old Adam's bones. It has seen no rain for a month or more, its wells are running low and yet you speak to me of *floods*?'

Daniel nodded, saw Father Wulfric's gaze flicker to his head, and self-consciously wiped his palm across his brow. 'Some parts of the town are flooded with mud and silt. The water must have seeped in from the river to undermine the ancient waterways and turn their banks to slime that would not hold to solid ground. Several wells have overflowed and many more are so polluted that there is a dire shortage of drinking water.'

Father Wulfric scowled. '*My* wells?'

'Safe, my lord. The greater houses, fed as they are by purer streams which are well maintained, have been little affected. Unfortunately, the archbishop's house in the market square has suffered—'

'Let the archbishop care for his own property,' de Morthlund cut in. 'Have my wells been placed under guard?'

'They have, my lord.'

'Good, good. I will not allow the common mob to help themselves and deposit their filth with me.'

'No, my lord, and repeats of last year's water riots are not anticipated. The monk from Flanders, brother Antony, has established water-points around St Peter's' walls, and the priests there are providing drinking and cooking water from their own streams.'

'Always the good man,' de Morthlund sneered. 'Always the selfless champion of the needy. And what of Beverley's darling, the handsome Simeon?'

'The people are saying that he saved a life already lost to all but God,' Daniel reported, 'that he gave full absolution to the dead and preserved the living with his blessing. His fame grows with every telling of every story.'

De Morthlund rubbed his several chins with thick, pink-tinted fingers. 'Ah, he raised the dead, did he?'

'So they are saying, my lord. A child was drowned in mud for over an hour, or two or three, depending on the teller. Simeon waded in to retrieve the body and knew by divine sign exactly where it lay. He blew air into it and the girl came instantly to life – or so they say.'

'Is that possible?'

'I believe so,' Daniel nodded. 'If the death is caused by a simple lack of breath and not by some mortal injury, and if the breath has not been stopped too long.'

'So, he raises the dead and gives full absolution in the absence of confession. The Church Fathers will not like this, Daniel.'

'No, my lord, they will not.'

'But they shall hear of it soon enough if I know Cyrus de Figham for the clever opportunist he is – and with some colourful embellishment, no doubt.' He chuckled and his great ungirdled bulk set up a trembling of its layers. 'At the canons' meeting this afternoon de Figham will be brought to account concerning the woman he keeps under his roof, and all because Simeon will not let the matter lie in peace. I'll wager Cyrus will not miss this chance to harass his enemy in return. There will be much amusement, Little Hawk, if Cyrus de Figham is once again to be rubbed across his tender grain by the fame of this unassuming Simeon of Beverley.'

Daniel's smile was polite but lacked his master's cruel anticipation of such diversion. He had little taste for the dangerous games these canons played in order to gain either pleasure or advancement at each others' expense. He loved his master, as well he must, since he could neither prosper nor survive unless de Morthlund loved him in return. He admired Cyrus de Figham, with his satanic good looks and aristocratic elegance, and who but a fool could pay scant regard to such a priest and such a man as Simeon de Beverley? Between them Little Hawk was often pulled in three directions, to please his master and to impress de Figham, to deflect or reduce any injury meant for Simeon. He knew himself to be a priest of no limited impairment, a sinner whose immortal soul was at risk of eternal damnation. With this in mind, and fearing for his master's place in Heaven, he trod a precarious line between his loyalty and his need of patronage, his admiration for Father Cyrus and his deep respect for Father Simeon.

'Sainthood,' he heard de Morthlund say with relish. 'Once more he aims for sainthood and the adoration of these muddle-headed fools in Beverley.'

'He repudiates the claims,' Daniel said.

'And so he might, for then these fools will praise him all the more for his modesty. This Simeon is very cunning in his ambition.'

'I do not find him so, my lord.'

'Oh?' The beady eyes glinted in amusement.

'I find him honest to a fault, a worthy priest, and ...'

De Morthlund caught hold of Daniel by the front folds of his cloak, pulled him roughly forward and placed a wet kiss squarely on his mouth. 'I think you find that pretty priest too pleasing, my Little Hawk.'

'He is ... he is admired by many ... a good man,' Daniel stammered, deliberately avoiding any reminder of the debt he owed to Simeon.

'And de Figham? Do you also judge him to be a "good man" worthy of our admiration?'

'Not ... perhaps not *good*, my lord ...'

'But praiseworthy nonetheless, in your estimation?'

'My lord, Father Cyrus is a powerful man and as such must be respected.'

'And you would be wise to heed your own words, dear heart. Seek not to divide your loyalties three ways. You are my creature, body and soul, and neither priest nor God Himself will claim any part of you that belong to *me*.'

Daniel bowed, wishing his head was covered. 'My loyalty is yours alone, my lord canon,' he declared, and there was nothing in his voice or manner which could be taken otherwise.

'So be it, Little Hawk. Now hand me my girdle and my purse and get these carts and horses moving. If the way is barred by flood we will go around it, and make sure the runners are well in advance of us. I will not have my entry into Beverley diminished by the fame of that crippled priest.'

Daniel Hawk bowed again and took his leave with some relief. Two years ago, when Beverley had been ablaze, he had offered his life to save his master from the swords of murderous thieves. Just one against many, he suffered much for his intervention. While de Morthlund fled to safety, Daniel managed to hold the thieves at bay until they overpowered him and beat him to the ground with fists and weapons. As the fire spread, he was left in its path, too badly injured to know his clothes were alight, and but for de Morthlund's return he would have perished. Near death and barely conscious of events, he was carried by his master to the priests of St Peter's, where Simeon and his friends had saved his life. De Morthlund had wept without shame, making no secret of his grief, and nurtured a hatred for those who had seen his weakness. Few men live easily with the knowledge that their frailties have been exposed for other eyes to see. The priests of St Peter's would earn no gratitude for saving Daniel's life; nor would his catamite benefit from his passionate declarations, for they had all seen de Morthlund despairing in the name of love. They knew his heart and would despise him for it, and he would never, as long as he drew breath, pardon them for it.

'Absolve me, Father, for I have sinned.' Those were the words Daniel had whispered to Simeon as the blond priest bent over his sickbed, taking his turn at the nursing and the dressing of his wounds. Simeon had heard his confession gentle-eyed and with no hint of recrimination.

'All love is precious in the eyes of God,' he had replied. 'If a man will willingly forfeit his life for it, dare others call that love a mortal sin?'

Now Daniel recalled that brief exchange with gratitude, for Simeon had helped to save his life with his skilled hands and his compassion, and he had offered some soul's ease with the mending.

At the edge of a pool of glistening mud where once a narrow ditch with a wooden bridge had made an easy crossing, Daniel Hawk considered the possible outcome of this sudden spate of flooding. Already there were reports of many deaths and widespread looting, and once again the town would be divided against itself. When hardship struck and men were tested, the good were often pushed aside while the less deserving prospered. Self-serving men such as de Morthlund and de Figham rarely came undone, yet those of undoubted quality and worth, like Father Simeon and Antony the monk, were often rewarded with malice and hostility. It seemed to him that humanity was flawed, that one Christ sacrificed would never be enough, so that any man's compassion might lead directly to his hanging.

Of late he had given much serious thought to matters that had not previously concerned him. He was a priest, the bed-mate of his canon, and he had been privy to a thousand ills and evils since the day he met Wulfric de Morthlund and became his willing catamite. The arguments that came and went through his mind these days were unfathomable. If the path of goodness led ultimately to a waiting cross, what purpose did it serve? If the worst of men might enter Heaven by virtue of confession or worldly wealth, while purer souls were damned by poverty or sudden death, God's kingdom must surely be populated by sinners and Hell itself by saints. What could it gain a saintly man to suffer his way into Paradise, only to find the likes of Wulfric de Morthlund and Cyrus de Figham waiting for him there?

'Ah, there you are, Daniel. Too much deep thinking mars a pretty brow with scowls, dear heart. These sudden moods of yours displease me.' A heavy arm fell across Daniel's shoulders. His nostrils caught the scent of spices blended with essence of roses as a jewelled brooch was pressed into his hand. The smile on de Morthlund's face was almost tender, if those hanging folds of flesh could be read with any accuracy. He pinched the young priest's cheek in podgy fingers, twisting the skin a little so that even that small gesture of affection had a measure of pain in it. 'What troubles you, boy? What do you ponder on?'

'Heaven and Hell, my lord.'

De Morthlund chuckled. 'Ah, the mysteries. Such things should not concern you.'

Daniel's smile was touched with bitterness. 'Such matters should not concern a priest in holy orders, my lord canon?'

'*Especially* not a priest,' de Morthlund grinned. 'Let the rabble with their empty bellies and ragged clothes concern themselves with the afterlife, and may they continue to pay us as well as they do for their gullibility. We priests are privileged to take our Paradise in the here and now, for when we turn to earth we are no more. Let the peasant hope for better things to come. Our lives are sweet, my Little Hawk, so clear that pretty brow of scowls and *savour* it.'

Daniel felt the big hand grasp his thigh, looked down at the jewelled gift in his palm and felt his dark thoughts shift and turn again. The image of the blond priest faded and his smile came easily, for life at that time was indeed as sweet as it might be for him. He leaned his thigh into the hand and whispered, 'Yes, my lord canon.'

CHAPTER SIX

The afternoon brought no further reports of flood or mudslides, and the town of Beverley, St John's own Beaver Lake, girded its ancient loins and took to the business it knew best: survival. New shelters were hastily erected from whatever materials came to hand. Streets were cleared and shops reopened, prayers were said at every church and altar for the living and the dead.

Townsfolk toiled in the dusty heat to clear blocked waterways, to redirect those mud-pools that threatened to overflow and cause fresh flooding, and to reinforce breached walls and broken dirt banks. Some worked like ditchers, naked from waist to ankle, while others stripped off all their apparel and worked with blackened bodies and faces as pale as masks. As the pools began to set like new stone in the heat, picks and axes were used to chop it free and carts brought in to carry it away. Those turbary workers used to cutting peat from the marshes now found themselves in great demand and well rewarded for their extra labours. It was a time for willing hands to earn a decent meal or a welcome coin for work well done, for women and children to work beside the men for fair reward, for righteous and sinner alike to offer their sweat to God for some small consideration in the afterlife.

Looters who sought to gain without due toil were violently discouraged by those who put their backs into the drudgery. So it was that little management from priests and landed men was needed to keep the workers at their various tasks. The townspeople were there to save their homes and livelihoods, their churches and food sources, and that they stood to keep for themselves what goods they managed to salvage kept them vigilant against the common looters.

Much time was lost while Father Wulfric's entourage passed conspicuously through the town. His runners came ahead of him to spread the word that alms would be distributed to the needy, gifts of bread and coin for those who met the party on its way to the canon's house in Minster Moorgate. Pilgrims and traders, workers and beggars, widows and ragged children gathered in flocks along the route, all hoping to reap a portion of the canon's generosity. Though kept at a distance by armed guards and priestly protectors, their numbers hampered the progress of the carts where streets were narrow.

Mounted between the rabble and his master, Daniel Hawk tossed coins from a leather purse and watched with some distaste the squabbles that ensued. Men snatched from women and women stole from children, all scrabbling in the dirt for coins and bread. He saw a pilgrim strike a woman down with his heavy staff to claim the bread she clutched to her breast, and Daniel wondered how that righteous man would tell St John of it when next he knelt before the holy shrine. He saw another take bread from the mouth of a blind man, and yet another leave a cripple half-choked for the sake of one small penny.

Another fistful of coins emptied the purse, and Daniel looked to his master for the next. De Morthlund gave it willingly, for he was buying his reputation while other canons chose to travel unnoticed. With bread and coin he served the twin demands of need and greed, and in return received a heartier welcome than any visiting bishop. This canon would pay a high price for his fame, yet counted every gift to his catamite as a debt outstanding. He took a twisted pleasure

48

now in handing over a purse of coin for Daniel to toss away to others while he possessed not one penny of his own.

'We feast tomorrow at de Figham's table,' Wulfric said. 'And tonight I sleep on my own feathered bed. God's teeth! This body of mine is sore with the discomforts of hard church pallets and leather saddles.'

'But the journey was well made,' Daniel observed. 'The archbishop was sympathetic to your cause. I believe you have convinced him that there is still a handsome profit to be had from Beverley, and that this town and its hidden wealth are virtually in your gift.'

Father Wulfric smiled and squared his huge shoulders. 'And so it will be. With the goodwill of our archbishop at my disposal, these Minster-servers will learn to dance to a tune of my composing, and when they do, much profit will find its way into my coffers.'

'To be shared with York?' Daniel's sideways glance was sceptical and his mouth curved in a smile.

De Morthlund reached across to pat the muscular young thigh. 'We'll see, dear heart, we'll see. And doubt not that I will use this feud between Cyrus de Figham and Simeon de Beverley to my best advantage. Those two will help me gain my ends. A wise man never allows the petty squabbles of his rivals to go unused.'

'Wise indeed,' Daniel observed, knowing his master's pleasure in setting two prize cocks, well matched and cleverly primed, to battle each other to the death while he wagered heavily on the outcome.

Both men turned in their saddles as a cry went up around the bread cart trundling at their backs. The store of loaves had dwindled while the press of beggars grew more impatient for a portion. They begged for charity, calling it a gift, but fought for it as if it were their right. A fat man in a cat-skin mantle mounted the cart and received the driver's club across his jaw, fell back and was trapped by one leg beneath the wheel. In a sudden tumult the cart was overturned and a man was killed. The mules were cut free and dragged into the crowd, and bodies surged to claim the rest like locusts on a carcass. Wulfric de Morthlund passed a third purse to his priest and signalled that the distribution of alms was to continue, while his heavy mount went forward, its steady pace uninterrupted.

While the vicars choral sang the psalms and led the holy office of Nones, their canons gathered in the provost's hall for an extraordinary meeting. Serious charges had been brought against one of their number and, because the dispute had been simmering for two years, both parties had agreed to have their grievances aired before their peers and to let the matter rest upon their verdict. Cyrus de Figham was the man accused, and Simeon de Beverley, supported by his canon, the accuser. Father Simeon had forced the issue by drawing the ageing Cuthbert into the debate, for he himself was merely canon elect and on this delicate point of ecclesiastical law, Father Cyrus had refused to make himself accountable. Now the canon himself had added his name to the charges, and Simeon de Beverley was determined to be heard in open court.

'He's a fool. Only a fool would test his enemy on so trivial a matter. Why can't he let it lie and enjoy this uneasy peace while it lasts?'

The speaker was Jacob de Wold, provost elect of Beverley. He had held the provost's seat for seven years without benefit of either official status or free privilege. He kept the peace between his canons and cast his vote where it would do least harm. He was little more than a figurehead, a leader of men by diplomacy and discretion. His main consideration was to steer a middle course through the calmest waters, so that Beverley in turn could remain on harmonious terms with York, its overlord. The role of provost was one of prestige and advantage and Geoffrey Plantagenet, York's archbishop elect, held it in his gift. He would not bequeath such a title to a Beverley man, and while this Minster lay half-ruined he would not offer so poor a living to anyone of stature. He kept the gift in tight reserve, and while they hung so lightly on his whim, the canons were merely stewards in his absence.

Jacob de Wold was over forty, tall and rigid in his bearing, slow and meticulous in voicing the swift adroitness of his mind. His head was bald so he wore no tonsure, though his whiskers were long and luxurious. A blast of fire two years ago had scarred his hands and face as it threw him backwards, damaging his back. His rescuer had done the rest. A young priest hoisted him bodily from the flames and carried him at a run down several flights of steps, across a blazing herb patch and over a high fence to safety. Jacob's life was saved by the brave and timely rescue, but the gruelling journey had crippled him. Had Osric not bound him so tightly to a wooden beam and kept him there for weeks despite his protests, his broken bones would have healed askew or perhaps not healed at all. Now Jacob could neither sit nor kneel nor bend his spine at any point, but he was alive and could bear the constant pain with the help of measured doses of tincture drawn from poppy seeds.

'He is a fool,' he said again, wincing as two of his dressers threw their combined weights against the buckles keeping his leather body-brace in place. The iron splints supporting his legs were buckled above his knees, and then the neck-piece, lined with sheepskin for his comfort, was more gently clamped in place. A third man wrestled his iron-strengthened boots over his feet and clamped them tightly at ankle, calf and knee. Thus bound and armoured as if for war, he received his tunic and his cloak and with these coverings none would guess that Jacob de Wold was unable to stand unaided.

Standing by a window in the provost's private chamber, Stephen Goldsmith, canon and craftsman, turned a golden seal-ring in his fingers, discreetly preoccupied while Jacob dressed.

'Simeon has a strong case against de Figham,' he said. 'If the facts are as he claims them to be, how can we allow such an unpalatable situation to continue?'

'He should weigh the improbable gains against the unavoidable losses,' Jacob replied. 'If he forces the canons to divide against each other he will place me in the delicate

51

position of casting my vote for one man or the other. If I cast against him, de Figham will never allow the case to rest. And should I find the charge unproven, Simeon will rightly appeal to a higher authority. Either way, I am firmly placed on the horns of a dilemma. We cannot afford to offend Geoffrey Plantagenet, or Rome, with such a scandal.'

Stephen Goldsmith nodded grimly. 'Our archbishop has trouble and scandal of his own at every turn. His moods are dangerously unpredictable. He is likely to eject us from our Church in favour of a handful of clerks from York, should any petition from Beverley catch him on a down-swing.'

'Indeed, and while it is his policy to issue excommunication as if dispensing alms to the poor, which one among us will put him to the test?'

'So what is to be done?' the Goldsmith asked. 'Where lies the middle course in this?'

'With the woman, Alice.'

The goldsmith peered at the provost under heavy brows which, like his hair and beard, were fired with tints of red and bronze.

'Can you allow a woman to be the deciding factor in a matter of such ecclesiastical importance?'

'I fear I must, if both parties can be persuaded to agree upon such a course. This Alice is the bone of contention here. Let her be brought from Figham House with de Figham's consent but without his prior knowledge, so that no claim of collusion can brought against him. If he denies the charge and Simeon persists in his accusations, the woman's testimony will settle matters.'

Stephen Goldsmith glanced at the men who had been helping Jacob into his body-harness. They wore the plain woollen robes of clerks, girdled with simple belts and hung with crosses. Two were folding garments into a wooden box while the third was on his knees, attending to his master's heel-straps. None appeared inquisitive of the conversation, yet Stephen frowned and shook his head sharply in warning. He knew the speed with which a careless word could reach the wrong ear, and he knew how swift men were to help it on its way for small reward. He lowered his voice to ask: 'Would she speak out honestly against her lord? Few men of courage would dare to cross de Figham, and half the case against him rests upon his ill-treatment of her. How, then, can this woman's word be relied upon as truth?'

'Because he will have no opportunity to manipulate her evidence,' Jacob whispered in reply. 'And because she will be made to swear on holy oath and so condemn her soul to hell if she speaks falsely. I do not doubt she stands in fear of Cyrus de Figham, but she was trained for holy offices and I believe she fears the Almighty as she should. It is the only way. If things go badly I will have her brought here.'

Jacob de Wold walked stiffly to the corner of the vestry where a wooden staircase led up to the canons' meeting hall. Once there he clenched his fists and locked his elbows and, with a man on either side, went up, every inch of his body rigid. Stephen Goldsmith followed in his wake, his red brows deeply furrowed. He did not see the third of Jacob's dressers lower the lid of the robe-box and slip from the building by a small side-door. Nor did he see this same man lift his skirts above his knees in order to run unhampered across the Figham moor.

Jacob de Wold was obliged to wait in an ante-room off the hall for two canons who had sent their clerks ahead of them with their apologies. Wulfric de Morthlund had come that day from York and begged the provost's indulgence while he removed his travelling clothes and swilled the journey's dust from his person. Cyrus de Figham had made good time in eagerness to defend his reputation, only to be summoned back to his house on a matter of the utmost urgency. Jacob sweated inside his iron and leather harness with its sheepskin padding, garbed from neck to toe in his heavy provost's robes. He silently cursed the heat and prayed that the meeting might reach conclusion before he toppled to the ground from sheer exhaustion.

The unpunctual canons arrived together, and some of less than charitable opinion might have declared their entrances neatly staged for best effect. First into the hall swept the mountainous Wulfric de Morthlund, dazzling and bejew-elled, his buckled boots marking a heavy tread upon the wooden floor. With a cloak of gold and royal purple billowing at his heels, he claimed his seat as he might a throne, with a wide, dramatic flourish. After him came Cyrus de Figham, splendid in white and blue beneath a scarlet cloak, his dark hood gathered around his neck and trim-mings of polished silver glinting on him. He claimed his seat with a casual elegance, his body posed and very still but his dark eyes wary.

Accompanying them were John the palmer in a yellow robe and Daniel Hawk in black with crimson panels. Both eyed each other cautiously, for there could be no trust between these two.

Eight canons were present in the hall, each with his clerks and other interested parties, making a total of fifty souls in all. The canons were dressed in their fanciest and finest, the clerks in brown or grey over white, with coloured hoods, polished brooches and brightly coloured tassels. All others in that room were well attired, for the fathers in Rome demanded that all men of the Church be recognised by their finery. Here was the real distinction between the two pre-destined levels of humanity. Those born to privilege garbed their pampered bodies in fine array; those born without it wrapped their bones in rags.

The provost looked from them to Father Simeon, who was standing near the door in a shaft of sunlight. The older man's stare was hard, for he disapproved of this unseemly quarrel over a woman when so much else in Beverley was at stake. As if aware of whose eyes were on him, Simeon turned his head to lock his steady gaze directly with Jacob's, a habit many found disconcerting.

'You are a fool,' Jacob de Wold spoke with his thoughts and left the words unsaid.

'I will not yield on this,' Simeon's unwavering stare replied.

The canon elect of St Peter's was dressed in a tunic of grey wool over a linen shirt. His breeches were cross-gartered from knee to ankle, his cloak rust-coloured with a dull red lining. His hood was a swirl of soft grey over his shoulders, his only adornment the plain metal brooch that held the hood in place. He was as modest in his dress as in his lifestyle. These other canons came like decorated peacocks, pranced and strutted in their conceit and still fell short of all this priest represented with his impressive simplicity.

'You must not find for him against de Figham.' The voice of Stephen Goldsmith was low and heavy with emphasis. 'Your admiration of Simeon will raise complaints if it is noted.'

Jacob looked at him sideways and in the next moment his face was closed, his thoughts too well concealed for any man to fathom. 'The facts alone will decide the issue.'

As Jacob made his stiff-legged way to his place at the head of the meeting, Cyrus de Figham leaned towards de Morthlund and observed: 'They say his outer body is shored up with iron and his innards pickled in extract of poppy-seed.'

'Indeed,' de Morthlund replied in a conspiratorial whisper. 'So little of him remains intact that we can only pray his common sense has not deserted him. I doubt if he will dare to find in Simeon de Beverley's favour.'

'Nor in my own. No, he will take the middle way, the impartial route that offends no one,' Father Cyrus chuckled. He looked at Wulfric then and closed one dark eye in a wink. 'And he will find no small impediment waiting for him there.'

The eldest of the canons, Father Cuthbert, sat dozing in his seat, a small, frail figure in grey and white dwarfed by the elaborately carved oak and high fringed canopy of his canon's chair. His chin was resting on his chest; perhaps because he slept, perhaps because old age and dedication to his devotions had set his neck in an attitude of prayer. This man was Simeon's mentor. He had taken a lame boy into his care and helped him realise his full potential as a priest and scribe. He claimed no credit for the transformation, for he had seen in Simeon many extraordinary qualities, and careful nurturing had done the rest. God's will had brought that lame boy to St Peter's. God's purpose, too, was in his nurturing. Thus it was that, when that other, stranger boy was brought to them through the tempest, Simeon the man was ready to receive him.

Despite the babble of voices in the hall, Father Cuthbert overheard the brief exchange between de Figham and de Morthlund. He was not unduly troubled by this hint of conspiracy. He had learned in his long years that while men squabble and debate like petty children, God's plan remains unaltered and the world unfolds exactly as it should.

The provost elect took his place among the canons, not seated in his ecclesiastic chair but standing at a high desk placed before it. As his senior clerk stepped forward to read out the matter under discussion, he looked about him at the blaze of finery gathered there and was reminded of the book of Genesis. It was written there that God made Adam naked. It might be argued that the original sin lay not with Eve, beguiled of the serpent, but with Adam, who, vain of his beauty, adorned his naked body with a fig leaf.

'... that the woman, Alice, was taken from the abbess under duress. That Father Cyrus did keep her against her will, in servitude and for his carnal pleasure ...'

The clerk read out the charges in a clear, strong voice and those in the great hall hung upon his every word.

'... and made her a prisoner to his base appetites ...'

Neither the accused nor his accuser let his thoughts be known. The clerk continued.

'... deprived of the comfort of family and friends, to share her master's bed under duress. That she be released at once and returned to the Sisters of Mercy from whence she came.'

Jacob de Wold gripped the edges of his desk and swayed a little on his feet. Small pools of perspiration had gathered in his armpits and his groin, in the small of his back and the centre of his chest. The sheepskin chafed his throat and had become so tight that he feared he would choke, for the neck-brace was buckled right cross his windpipe. In this low-ceilinged room, grafted on to the charred remains of the original provost's hall, stale air became trapped and fresh air could not circulate.

'My God, did I survive a fire and a shattered body only to die of suffocation?' These words were ringing in his mind even as he asked, in a steady voice, 'How do you plead, Cyrus de Figham?'

The reply was swift. 'I plead that this inquiry, however informal, is unacceptable. How can a priest be fairly judged by one who claims to be a living saint?'

There was a collective gasp at this remark and then a silence.

'Explain yourself,' the provost said.

De Figham shrugged and Father Wulfric, shifting mightily in his chair, was heard to snigger.

'This man,' de Figham declared, pointing an accusing finger at Simeon, '*this man* is putting it about that he has the power to raise the dead with a kiss. He gives full absolution to the unconfessed and even—'

'Enough! Be silent!' The voice of Father Cuthbert, rarely heard in indignation or impatience, rang out with such resonance that de Figham at once stopped speaking. 'These comments are based on wicked hearsay. The mindless talk of peasants is not in dispute here, and well this canon knows it.' The old man eyed de Figham and added coldly: 'This repeating of tittle-tattle is not worthy of him.'

Before the provost could interject, de Figham bowed his head and spread his hands in an apologetic gesture. 'Forgive my hasty outburst, Lord Provost. A fair hearing of my case is all I ask.' He bowed again. 'I retract my comments without reserve and beg the court's forgiveness.'

Such a babble was raised by this that Jacob had to rap his provost's ring against his desk before some semblance of order was restored. He saw the dismay on Simeon's face and knew what damage had been done, what doubts had been planted like poisonous seeds in the fertile soil men liked to call their intellect. No man present was ignorant of the whispers on the streets concerning Simeon. That these same whispers should be spoken aloud in the provost's hall was unforgivable. De Figham had done his worst and then retracted, knowing full well that his words, once they had struck at the very heart of ecclesiastical law, could not now be erased.

'How do you answer the charges?' he demanded.

De Figham got slowly to his feet and handed the clerk a roll of paper yellowed at its edges.

'This document proves that I took the woman from St Anne's with the full consent and approval of Constance, then lady abbess of that place. Alice came to me of her own free will and with the blessing of her abbess. I think, my Lord Provost, that you will find the charges against me spurious and vindictive.'

Neither Jacob nor his clerks could fault the document, with its indisputable signature and seal, and so it was accepted by the canons, duly entered into the records and the charge dismissed. Not even Simeon, with his keen scribe's eye and intimate knowledge of inks, could doubt the authenticity of the signature.

De Figham bowed and cast a mocking glance in Simeon's direction. He had been wise to force that wily old abbess to sign her consent to the abduction. She had been in his power then, when that terrible fire had left her injured and dispirited, robbed of her precious convent and all the authority it had provided. Despite her protests and her displays of righteous indignation, he had taken Alice with her full consent.

'As to the other charges,' de Figham said, and the elegant movements of his hand were more than just expressive, they were a prearranged signal to a clerk who waited at the door. 'I beg my Lord Provost's leave to call a witness in my defence, and I ask that the witness be questioned' he lifted one hand close to his chest and pointed a finger at Simeon, watching the priest through narrowed eyes ... 'by my accuser.'

CHAPTER SEVEN

A sudden hush descended on the provost's hall as a woman in a full grey robe and crisp white wimple was ushered in. Simeon and Osric exchanged glances. Neither doubted that Cyrus de Figham had primed his witness before allowing her to appear before the inquiry, but none could imagine how this served his ends. All testimony here was made under an oath of such solemnity that even a heathen would balk at speaking it lightly. A young woman trained for holy orders, raised in a convent and fearful of the judgement of the Almighty, would choose to die in grace before swearing a lie at the cost of her immortal soul.

'Enjoy the moment, Simeon de Beverley.'

Cyrus de Figham held Simeon's gaze, smiling a little as he reclaimed his seat. He spread his hands to convey that all was now in the priest's control, then sat back in comfort with one boot raised on the footstool near his chair. Wulfric de Morthlund leaned his bulk sideways and spoke from behind a hand adorned with many glittering rings.

'You have the cunning of old Lucifer, Cyrus de Figham.'

'I string my bow according to the game, Father Wulfric,' was the low reply.

Alice came slowly forward, flanked by two men from her master's house, her head demurely lowered. Some signed

59

the cross and many averted their gazes, but for all those who chose to guard their modesty as many more were ready to stare temptation in the face. If Simeon's charge was accurate, this woman had been snatched from the services of God to be Cyrus de Figham's whore, and every man who saw her felt that knowledge stir his blood.

She came with dragging steps and when she reached the dais two clerks took charge of her. The servants were escorted to a side-door, where another clerk led them down to ground level from where no word of the proceedings could be overheard. Men whispered now behind their hands, the righteous and the not-so-righteous all agreed that any fault, should such be proven, lay with the whore and not with the priest who kept her for his pleasure. When the curtain was replaced across the upper doorway, all conversation ceased and every eye was fixed on Alice. The judging and reckoning had been done before a word was uttered in her defence or her disfavour.

Simeon stepped forward to greet her and was surprised when she shrank from him, as if afraid. He was her only ally here, her last hope of escape, and yet her eyes did not meet his and she recoiled from his touch. She was deathly pale and thinner than when he had seen her last, with hollows in her cheeks and shadowed rings below her eyes. To any who had known her at the convent, serene and happy in anticipation of her holy vows, this once-bright Alice was a sorry sight. She took the sacred oath with much reluctance, touching the precious book as if it might sear the skin from her fingers. While she repeated the solemn and binding words of the declaration the clerks were obliged to support her by the arms. All present could see that she was terrified, but of God or of her master none could tell.

'Shall I proceed with the questioning, Lord Provost?'

'What?' Jacob de Wold was staring down the length of the hall to where several heavy curtains were draped across the doors and windows. There was a strange, perplexed expression on his face and his tight grip on the edge of his desk had turned his knuckles white.

'The questioning, my lord,' Simeon prompted gently, then noted the perspiration on Jacob's forehead and asked in a concerned whisper: 'Father Jacob? Are you ill?'

Osric stepped quickly forward to place a tiny horn-cup on the desk. The liquid it contained was thick and dark, its sweet strength guaranteed to separate a suffering man from his pain.

'There is a stranger here,' the provost said.

'None but the witness, my lord, and she is known to us.'

'Over there in the shadows, half-hidden by a curtain.'

'I see no one. Drain the cup, my lord,' Osric pressed.

'He is there, I tell you. A tall man in a hood.'

'No, my lord,' Osric spoke firmly, his words coming with a hiss. '*No, Jacob.*'

'I saw him over there. Who is he? Bring him forward.'

'There is no one, my lord,' the infirmarian repeated, and Stephen Goldsmith, helping to lift the horn-cup to the provost's lips, added his own whispered assurance. 'Pain fogs your vision, Jacob. There is no stranger among us.'

De Figham had grown impatient of this whispered exchange. He cleared his throat conspicuously and demanded: 'My Lord Provost, your canons would have this matter settled without delay. By your leave, sir, Simeon de Beverley, as my accuser, should hasten to begin his interrogation of this woman.'

'Continue', the provost elect replied at last, drawing his attention back to the matter in hand. He was troubled by what he might have seen at the far end of the hall, a hooded outsider, an eavesdropper lurking by the shadowed curtains. His head swam and his body ached from neck to ankle inside the metal harness. Then he felt the searching heat of the poppy extract begin to invade his body to ease the grievous pains in his chest and spine. With an effort he focused his eyes on Simeon's face and said, in a stronger voice, 'Proceed.'

Simeon inclined his head respectfully, then began his gentle questioning of the distressed woman.

'Do you remember me, Alice? Look at me. I am Father Simeon of St Peter's.'

She nodded her head but did not lift it up, and Simeon guessed it was because she knew his questioning would make public property of her private shame. De Figham's spite was clear in this, that both Alice and her advocate should be made to suffer by this inquisition.

'You have made the sacred oath,' Simeon reminded her. 'Your immortal soul is forfeit if your tongue speaks falsely now. Do you understand?' When she nodded her head he prompted her to make her answers audible to the court. 'Alice, you must speak out so that all may hear your words distinctly. Do you understand what is required of you?'

Several canons leaned forward in their seats, one with his hand cupped over his ear, the better to catch her whispered reply: 'Yes, Father Simeon.'

What duties do you perform at Figham House?'

'I am ... a servant.'

'And?'

'I ... I scrub and polish. I keep the rushes fresh.'

'And share your master's bed?'

She hesitated, then sighed as if defeated and replied: 'No, Father.'

'No?'

She shook her head, obviously intimidated by this company of canons and distressed by the close proximity of Cyrus de Figham. If only half the stories Simeon had heard were true, those two years under de Figham's roof had broken her in heart and spirit, and yet he did not believe that she would dare to utter a lie while under oath. She was aware that no priest could be censured for having a woman under his roof, and that carnal knowledge of a servant, even under duress, was no serious sin for a man in holy orders. De Figham's guilt would simply mean her freedom and after that he would never again be allowed to do her harm.

'Alice, are you being kept at the Figham house against your will?'

'No, Father.'

'Then you are free to leave if you should choose to do so?'

'Yes, Father.'

Simeon saw the misery in her face, in the hunch of her shoulders and the nervous, restless movements of her fingers. This was, for her, a humiliating inquisition.

'How old are you, Alice?'

'Twenty. Almost twenty.'

'And two years ago you planned to take holy orders. You were devout and dedicated to serving our Lord through the Little Sisters of Mercy. What caused your sudden change of heart?'

She cleared her throat and wiped away tears before speaking. 'Father Cyrus offered me a position in his house.'

'It took no more than that to sway you from your vocation?'

'Father Cyrus asked for me.'

'And you accepted of your own free will?'

Again that telling, painful hesitation. 'Yes, Father.'

He knew beyond doubt that she was lying now, for Elvira had seen her dragged away, screaming and sobbing and begging her abbess to save her from de Figham. The priest had snatched her in Elvira's place and he had sworn to make her pay two-fold for every day Elvira was kept from him. Now she was lying under solemn oath in defence of her tormentor. She was giving up her soul for his protection, and Simeon was baffled by this travesty. He glanced at Father Cuthbert, saw the veined head nod and asked another question.

'Were you wholly chaste in body when you left the convent?'

She hung her head and murmured. 'Yes, Father.'

'And are you still?'

A small convulsion shook her body and her legs began to buckle at the knees. The two clerks in attendance held her upright.

'Alice, remember your oath. Look to your soul and speak truthfully, before God and his servants. Are you still chaste?'

She nodded, sobbing loudly.

'We must have your answer,' Simeon said. 'On oath, with your soul in jeopardy, *are you still chaste?*'

'Yes,' she sobbed, then repeated the word in a strangled cry that echoed around the room: 'Yes! Yes! *Yes!*'

Simeon stood back and in the silence that followed her outburst, Jacob de Wold leaned stiffly over his desk and demanded: 'Look at me, woman.'

She raised her head and, though she shrank from Simeon, met the provost's gaze with the courage of a cornered deer meeting the huntsman face to face.

'This court has been convened on your behalf,' Jacob informed her coldly. 'While here you are under the strict protection of our church of St John of Beverley. Your testimony will determine whether you are given back to Father Cyrus or returned to the convent where the new abbess has been instructed to prepare a place for you. The answers you give must be the truth. Do you understand?'

She nodded. 'Yes, my lord.'

'Is it your wish that we return you to the convent?'

'No, my lord.'

'Is it your wish that we return you to Figham House?'

She hesitated, glanced swiftly at de Figham and replied in a soft, defeated voice, 'Yes, my lord.'

'Woman, are you content with this?'

'I am, my lord.'

Simeon was shocked to the core. He saw de Figham's crooked smile and de Morthlund's grin of satisfaction. Between the two canons' chairs Daniel Hawk stepped back so that his face, in shadow, became unreadable. Before the dais Alice sank to her knees and bowed her head into her hands, her sobbing broken and ugly. Jacob de Wold signalled the two men to raise her up and bring her to his desk.

'Woman, I ask again, are you content with this?'

She nodded.

He looked at her with pity in his eyes, then glared at Simeon for this gross miscalculation of de Figham's influence.

'So be it,' he said at last. 'Let the record show we find in favour of Father Cyrus de Figham. The witness is dismissed.

'And let the record show,' de Figham interjected in a voice

that carried clearly across the hall, 'that a respectable canon of this church has been the victim of a vicious campaign to besmirch his reputation. Let the record also show that Simeon de Beverley, priest of St Peter's, has sought to use this court to further his personal grudge against a fellow priest.'

'Your comments will be noted, Father Cyrus,' the provost responded sharply.

'And let the record show,' de Figham demanded, pointing an accusing finger at Simeon, 'that a certain ditcher's wife would not acquit her priest so well under holy oath as this woman has done today.' And in a lower voice he snarled at Simeon: 'You'll pay for this.'

De Figham was the first to leave. He bowed to his provost elect, shot Simeon a look of pure contempt and swept from the hall in regal fashion, his scarlet cloak billowing. John Palmer followed close behind with two clerks at his heels. Next the towering Father Wulfric made an impressive exit, pulling Daniel Hawk and his lesser clerks in his wake. Only then did the other canons leave their seats. They were divided as to where they would have cast their votes had they been called upon to judge the matter for themselves. Archbishop Geoffrey Plantagenet was their overlord and Jacob de Wold their surrogate head of chapter, but none doubted that de Morthlund and de Figham were the twin powers within the Church at Beverley. When a man is judged by his own integrity, he casts his vote where integrity dictates: when his worldly comforts are at stake he is prudent who learns to cast more cautiously.

Seated on the dais with his elbows on his knees, Simeon watched the canons and their clerks file out and knew that he had lost his two-year fight to free Alice from her miserable life with de Figham. More than that, he had left himself discredited on her account. That black-eyed priest would honour his threat to exact revenge from Simeon for this indignity. With the highest of motives, Simeon had challenged his enemy on her behalf. His failure lay not with his own inadequacies, or even with de Figham's sly manipulation of the truth. It rested solely with the very object of his concern, the woman Alice.

Ignored by the man whose ends she had served so well, she crouched now by the dais on her knees, a despondent woman who had known her soul was damned whichever way she chose to jump.

'Oh, Alice, what have you done?'

Her voice was barely audible. 'Forgive me, Father.'

'You vowed an oath, the most solemn of all the oaths, and you lied. I *know* you lied.'

'I am lost,' she sobbed.

Just then de Figham's men returned to claim her, and Alice allowed herself to be lifted up and led away.

'Not lost,' Simeon called after her. 'Never truly lost, Alice.'

He hung his head, staring at the floor. This time he had been sure he had de Figham trapped. This time the fox was cornered, and yet he neatly slipped the net and walked away unscathed, and a woman's immortal soul, thrown out as bait, had furnished his escape.

Alone on the dais, old Father Cuthbert remained in his chair with his hands clasped around the crucifix in his lap. Sunlight from the window made a sparse white halo of his hair and lit the blue veins on his skin where age had thinned it to a fine transparency. His body had slowed but his mind, when it could be harnessed, was still as sharp and as clear as any man's. Sometimes the edges of thought and reality blurred and lacked clear focus, but Father Cutherbert knew what God intended him to know. A storm was brewing, and once again his protégé, his beloved Simeon, was at the heart of it.

Stephen Goldsmith sat down beside Simeon on the high step of the dais. 'You were betrayed, my friend,' he said. 'Betrayed in innocence, if that be possible.' He nodded to where the provost elect, held stiffly by a man on either side, was being assisted to the stairs at the far end of the hall. 'He spoke unwisely of his intention to call the woman as witness rather than cast his personal vote for one man or the other. He has a dresser, a man named Otto, and this one I fear carried those careless words to Cyrus de Figham. You were betrayed.'

Simeon shrugged. 'So de Figham was warned and prepared his witness?'

'So I believe,' the goldsmith nodded.

'But what in Heaven's name might he have said or done to make her lie against the sacred oath? What threat of his could be greater than the certainty of eternal damnation?'

The goldsmith shook his head. 'I have no inkling.'

Simeon scowled then, his attention drawn to a small commotion at the farthest end of the hall, where Jacob de Wold was dragging heavy drapes aside and peering into alcoves as if in search of something that had been mislaid.

'What ails our provost?'

'Crushed ribs and a broken spine,' Stephen replied. 'Cracked bones and damaged joints that will not give him ease. And two years after he was left for dead, the remedy for his pain is eating away his intellect and distracting his mind with visions and visitations. He believes a spy was here.'

'A spy? What need is there of spies when de Figham and de Morthlund alone will spread the details of this meeting as far as they are able?'

'Poor Jacob sees through a haze of pain or a veil of poppy juice, and either way his vision is impaired.'

'He bears his suffering bravely,' Simeon said, and Stephen Goldsmith, rising to his feet, gripped the young priest by the shoulder and answered grimly: 'So must we all.'

Simeon shook his head again and felt the consequences of this day's events settle like a dark cloud over his head. 'Oh Alice, what have you done?' he muttered, rubbing his face with his palms. 'In God's name, woman, *what have you done?*'

CHAPTER EIGHT

The sky was copper when the sun went down. Over the woodland hung an eerie sheen, echoing the brighter colours of the sky, and even the clinging mist over the marshes had a brazen tint. Birds circled in black silhouette, drifting like specks of soot around a cauldron. It was a sky breathtaking to behold, so colourful that the dust itself was stained with it.

Dominating the town from the east side, not a full mile from the port, the Minster church of St John stood like a monument against the sky. Its blond stones, touched all over by the play of unusual light, took on a hot and shimmering glow, while the timbers, charred by the terrible fire of two years before, reached blackened fingers into the molten brightness of the sky.

Simeon had come from the provost's hall to St Peter's enclosure to pray at the tiny altar in his scriptorium. He needed guidance. He needed to believe that Alice had broken her oath in innocence, and that she could still be saved from the awful consequences of the deed. He could not accept that a loving God would place a lamb with a wolf and then condemn it for all time when it was savaged.

'There must be a way,' he said aloud. 'And if there is, dear God, show it to me.'

He left a candle burning at the altar for Alice, then joined the other workers at the water-point. After a while he became aware that the light was deepening. He set down his buckets and signed the cross over his broad chest, feeling his heart expand with this reminder that God's creation was both beautiful and strange. He had been carrying water from the little stream to the gate in the enclosure wall, and as the late-light fell upon the buckets, they were filled with pools of colour reflected from the sky.

Antony the monk was with him, aware of the wonder on his face and the blazing colour illuminating his eyes. Those eyes of Simeon's were as gentle as a babe's when his God was with him, yet that same gaze could shrink a man and strip a liar bare of his deceits with its intensity.

'Magnificent!' Simeon breathed. 'Magnificent!'

Antony nodded in agreement and did not say the words that sprang to his mind, that this blazing sky echoed too closely the memory of another St Matthew's Feast, when Beverley had burned. The floods were over and the town still lay like tinder awaiting a spark. That fiery canopy was indeed magnificent, but Antony of Flanders would have seen more beauty and more hope in a simple, less spectacular promise of rain.

Simeon's awe could be heard in his voice. 'Could any man look upon that sky and deny the existence of a loving God?'

Antony shrugged his shoulders. 'Life is hard, my friend,' he replied. 'Men lack the time to stand and stare and the spirit to ponder upon such things.'

'Then they deny their own needs,' Simeon said, still looking upward. 'Life is hard, all Christians know that to be their lot, but there are treasures lying all around us. An empty belly and an aching back are painful to endure, but a famished soul is a heavier weight to carry. Men need to feed on such as this for their spiritual nourishment. It is God's purpose, surely? Why would He paint such beauty but for us, to feed our souls?'

Antony smiled and raised his face. The sky had a warm glow to it that could be felt behind closed lids, sufficient to lift the spirits of the blind. His friend had touched upon a simple truth, that God's wonders are available to all.

The monk took up Simeon's discarded buckets and carried them to the gate, leaving the priest some respite from his labours while the need for prayer was upon him. As he left the enclosure he noticed that others were following Simeon's example and kneeling in prayer. He smiled and muttered his own thanks to the Creator. Since ancient times men had seen themselves as sheep in need of guidance. Sometimes God was wise enough, and kind enough, to send them a guide of Simeon's quality.

He met Osric at the gate. 'Leave him a while. This red sky has lifted his spirits. Sometimes this man is a child in his simple awe of God, his faith, his ... his ...'

'Innocence?' Osric offered.

Antony smiled at that. 'We two have seen him moved to an unholy rage, striking men down with his sword and caring nothing for whose blood is spilled.'

'In defence of the babe,' Osric reminded him. 'His cause was just. God guided his hand and his heart.'

'Still I doubt that "innocent" fits him comfortably.'

Osric nodded, watching Simeon, and slowly a smile transformed his grizzled features. 'My heathen priest,' he muttered.

'Stay close to him,' Antony said, touching the infirmarian's arm. 'This business with de Figham has unnerved him, and when he finds his equilibrium he will blame himself for pushing the woman beyond her allotted measure of human courage.'

'He tried to help her,' Osric protested.

'Aye, and only helped her cast her soul to hell.'

'Not him. It was de Figham's doing.'

Antony smiled and touched the weathered arm again. 'No, Osric. However noble the intent, the fault was Simeon's.'

A deeper dusk was extinguishing the colours of the sky when Antony stooped under the eaves of a hovel in Walkergate. In the squalor of an unlit room a woman lay in childbirth, sharing her last hours with hens and pigs, dogs and scavenging rodents. Her husband hovered close, for no midwife could be paid to sit out this vigil. In the gloom a clutch of filthy children watched dull-eyed as life and death wrestled over their prostrate mother. The birthing fever was on her. She had lost much blood and now had not the strength to even scream against the pains that tore her body. The unborn child lay fast across her pelvis and would not find its way into the world without the speedy intervention of a miracle. Antony saw at a glance that no physician's skills would save the mother, but a brief examination told him that her unborn child still struggled valiantly for life.

While the monk knelt by the pallet the husband brought a little pile of coins wrapped in a scrap of cloth.

'This is all I have,' he said, shamed by the insignificance of the offering. 'I have no more, but I can spare two hens and a corner-cloth of flour.'

Antony looked about him and shook his head. He counted six children huddled against the wall, all puny, half-grown things too young to be of much assistance to their parents.

'I require no payment,' he said.

'But it is the law. The priests insist . . .'

'No payment,' Antony repeated. 'Your wife is dying.'

The man looked stricken. 'Then take the fee and save her.'

'I cannot save her. She is near to death and no offering of yours will help her now. The child is trapped across the opening and cannot come to birth in that position. I can provide prayer and comfort, nothing more.'

'But the fee will buy her life . . .'

Antony lifted his face, his features stern. 'All the gold in Christendom will not save this woman,' he said. 'She will die and the child will perish in the womb. It is God's will.'

The man, a ragged, gaunt-faced individual of uncertain age, dropped into a squat on the dirt floor and covered his face with filthy hands. A wealthier husband would have insisted that his wife be cut, in Roman fashion, and the child

71

lifted from her belly lest it prove to be a valuable son. Such drastic measures usually proved fatal for the mother and a bitter disappointment if the child for whom the sacrifice was made should be a girl. These poorer men had different values. They bred babies on their wives until the women's bodies failed or the birthing fever claimed them, and at the end they mourned the help-meet and cursed the whelp that killed her.

Kneeling beside the filthy pallet, Antony clasped the woman's hands in his own, his Tau cross between them, and urged her to confess her sins and make her peace with God. He saw the terror in her eyes, the fear of the unknown now a pain more pressing than the ripping of her womb. In a corner a child began to wail and others followed suit, and by the bed the husband crouched in anguish. While he knelt there Antony thought of Simeon with his simple faith and uncomplicated reasoning.

'We Christians are blessed with the knowledge of an afterlife, a time when we will see an end to pain and share communion with our Lord. Because of this, no man need die despairing.'

Simeon's words came back to Antony now, but to the monk's ears they had a hollow ring. Despair was all around him. He saw it in the terror in a dying woman's eyes, in the tears of a man facing a bitter loss, in the futile lives of children who might never know anything higher in life than the gnawing of an empty belly.

'No man need die despairing,' he repeated softly. 'And yet they do. Dear God, they do.'

Father Cuthbert was stooped over the illuminated pages of a book, his failing eyesight assisted by a magnifying glass in an ivory frame, his thin forefinger tracing every line. A candle as thick as a man's wrist burned with a steady yellow flame close by the book, and the pages were stained with a tint of red from the high scriptorium windows. The peculiar lighting cast by this vivid sunset gave a healthy glow to his waxen fingers and softened the shadows in the room. Although the blazing sky was faded now and darkening, its burnished echoes lingered everywhere.

'Ah, an excellent work,' he muttered to himself. 'Splendid, quite splendid.'

The sin of pride was one Father Cuthbert found impossible to resist, and from time to time he begged forgiveness for it. This book was Simeon's own, his Chronicle of Beverley, a faithful and diligent history of St John's beloved Beaver Lake, and of this the ageing canon felt truly proud. His protégé was a scribe of exceptional talent and, more even than this, an honest historian. No word of it was censored. No line of it spoke what any one man would prefer to have posterity know of him. No portion of it was bought with either coin or threat or favour, and neither monarch, pope nor bishop had a hand in it.

'Splendid,' Father Cutherbert exclaimed. 'Every page, line and letter . . . splendid.'

Most historians copied down as many errors as facts from other scribes, adding, deleting or embellishing according to how best it might suit their vanities and their purses. Many who barely recognised the outside world filled up historical gaps with fabrication, or simply with the rumour of the day. One Alfred, known as Alured, translated the charters and annals of Beverley Minster into French. Determined to make his works more singularly consequential, he then ordered the original documents to be destroyed. By an act of love they were preserved and others burned in their place and, by a journey of half a century, came at last into Simeon's keeping. In this exquisite manuscript the true history of the town was recorded by a craftsman without equal, and posterity would have cause to thank Simeon de Beverley for a masterpiece.

Now Father Cutherbert turned another page and ran his dry, thin fingers over the exquisitely worked lettering. These skills of Simeon's had kept him here when that other archbishop, Roger de Pont L'Eveque, had been disposed to send him on a pilgrimage which would have kept him from England's shores, from Beverley and his godson, for seven years. It was a wise, compassionate God who blessed his servant with such artistry.

'Dominus vobiscum, Father Cuthbert.'

He heard the blessing. 'The Lord be with you,' and lifted up his eyes as best he could, for his neck was stiff with age and his shoulders stooped. A man was standing beyond the library chair, a tall man wearing a hood and with his hands clasped in his sleeves. The ageing canon half-recognised his visitor and, in his preoccupation with Simeon's manuscript, thought not to question how he had entered here.

'Et cum spiritu,' he responded. 'And with you.' The brilliant hues of the manuscript danced before his eyes and, set against the candle's yellow flame, impaired his vision as would a coloured veil. He saw the black robe and the hood but could not see the face. He felt a momentary chill, an involuntary reminder that he had already lived beyond his allotted three score years and ten. It occurred to him that here was the Grim Reaper, death's dark angel, come to claim him. 'Who are you?' he demanded. 'Have you come for me?'

The other shook his hooded head. *'I come only for your blessing, Father Cuthbert.'*

The voice was strange. It seemed to come from somewhere inside his own head, as if he imagined it, and yet he felt he knew this man, that he had met him before. He moved in his chair, the better to view the face behind the flame, but all he saw were shadows and reflected pools of light.

'Your blessing, Father Cuthbert.'

'Gloria Patri ...' he signed the cross in the air between them with a blue-veined hand. *'... In Nomine Domini.* In the name of our Lord, go in peace.'

'May our Lord keep and protect you, Father Cuthbert.'

'Are you a priest?' the canon asked.

'More than that, I am a friend.'

'I feel I know you. By what name are you called?'

'By many names.'

The flame of the candle flickered and lay sideways as if an undetected draught was dragging it towards the locked door of the scriptorium.

'I do. I know you,' Father Cuthbert said.

'*By many names,*' the other repeated. '*God bless you, Father Cuthbert.*'

The candle dipped again and then went out, leaving a stream of scented smoke trailing upwards to the rafters. Father Cuthbert was unaware that he had slept, but when he opened his eyes again the hour was late and Simeon was leaning over him.

'You were talking in your sleep,' the young priest said. 'Come, there is mutton in the pot and good wine in the jug. Will you eat with us?'

'Thank you, my boy. That one who was here, by what name do you know him?'

'No one was here,' Simeon said. 'You were dreaming, Cuthbert, and talking in your sleep about the Grim Reaper in his night-black robes. Do you fear to die, my friend?'

'Indeed I do, as we all should fear to die, but I will not be going just yet. My blessing was all he wanted, after all.'

'Your blessing?' Simeon asked, humouring his mentor. 'The Grim Reaper came all this way to demand a blessing of *you?*'

'And to warn me that a storm is brewing,' Father Cuthbert said, leaning heavily on Simeon's arm as they walked together to the door. 'That book of yours is a gift from God, my boy, a gift from God. The colours, the patterns ... beautiful, exquisite.'

'And did your Grim Reaper also sing the praises of my manuscript?' Simeon asked, his blue eyes twinkling.

'The Grim Reaper?' The old man stiffened in alarm. 'Was he here?'

'No, Cuthbert, you were dreaming,' Simeon smiled.

'Perhaps I was, but a storm is brewing, nonetheless.'

'Then we will give thanks for it. The land is parched and the water levels are dangerously low.'

'There will be rain, if our prayers are answered,' the old man told him gravely. 'But there will also be a storm, and very soon, with no rain to ease it.'

Simeon's hand was on the massive crossbeam of the door

when he paused to study his mentor's face with some concern. 'What is it, Cuthbert? What troubles you?'

The old man smiled and patted Simeon's arm. 'No more than a dream, my boy. No more than a dream. Have you had word from York?'

'I have their interest and their sympathy,' he said, hoisting up the bar to free the door. 'Now we can only have patience while they think on it. These things take time, especially when such a huge sum of money is involved.'

'Peter believes your petition will be successful.'

'I know. It was he who insisted I make drawings of my gifts rather than carry such precious things with me on the journey. He has a wise head on his shoulders, Cuthbert. A gift once seen but kept beyond his reach becomes the more alluring to a covetous man.'

'He asked a blessing, and blessed me in return.'

'Who? Peter?'

'The one who was here. Did you say you know his name?'

'No one was here, my friend. You were dreaming again.'

The old canon paused on the threshold to grip Simeon's arm with his bony fingers. He twisted his head at an awkward angle and Simeon stooped obligingly to meet his gaze. The faded blue eyes were moist and had a slightly unfocused appearance, as if their owner looked beyond his priest and saw much more. *Dominus vobiscum*, Simeon. The Lord be with you.'

CHAPTER NINE

The brilliant sunset had given way to the eerie half-light of dusk, that interlude of uncertainty when all familiar things take on an odd perspective and even a stout heart might become uneasy. Dusk drove the populace to seek the comfort of camp fire and shuttered shelter, and those lacking such remedies huddled as warily as animals in their secret lairs. The night crept in like a deep black mist, and with its coming the creatures of darkness emerged to scuttle and rummage amongst the shadows. Here were rats as cunning as men and human beings schooled in the rodent's skills. This was a time of dread and danger, yet in the passing of day through dusk to night most men believed, like Father Cuthbert, the world to be unfolding as it should.

Through the crooked alleyways of Beverley a black-robed figure moved at a rapid pace; a man of slender build and extraordinary height, head bent so that his face was hidden, all else concealed beneath a full black cloak. With every step he took, the cloak brushed the ground over boots that made no sound and left no mark behind them.

Three men held back in shadow to observe the stranger's passing. Each drew a weapon from his belt, blessing good fortune for this easy victim. These three were looters and robbers by trade, and they saw their fortunes changed by a single traveller. Only a fool or a priest would walk these lawless streets alone at dead of night. If a fool, then he deserved to surrender all upon his folly. If a priest, then he might eat the words he so smugly preached to those with no escape from poverty's grip, that those deprived of wealth in this world chalked up greater benefits in the next.

'Shall we have him?' one man asked, and the others nodded.

The robbers moved with accustomed stealth amongst the alleyways and cracks dividing one ramshackle dwelling from another. They stayed in the shadows, keeping the hooded figure in their sights, like hunters keenly stalking their prey. They crossed the foul-smelling ditch that oozed a sluggish course to meet the greater flow at Walkergate, ducked beneath the jutting eaves that made a long, dark tunnel of Cobbler's Row, and by this devious route prepared to meet their quarry at a certain corner. It was here, where rows of low-topped hovels huddled grotesquely against the ancient angles of the streets, that the trio of robbers hid themselves from view.

They watched him turn a distant corner where light from a vagrant's camp fire made his shadow leap. He came straight on, his cowled head lowered and his hands concealed. The robbers judged his height and width and knew that they, all armed and practised in their craft, would take this lone traveller and his goods with ease. A purse of coin would suit their needs, or a priest's girdle, his jewelled ring or his embroidered robe, and if this one were but a fool who carried nothing of value, his warm cloak and his death rattle would suffice.

Between the approaching figure and the lurkers, several poor houses leaned their roofs into the street, some with overhangs shored up in makeshift fashion, others trusting to fate for their support. In one of the dimly lit interiors a deal for silver coin was being struck. A young priest in a sable cloak had set the terms, while a hungry carter, robbed of his living when an unstable load slipped and shattered both his legs, knew he must take whatever price was offered. The man lay on a pallet in a corner by the empty hearth, the straw beneath his body alive with vermin. Someone had tried to set his bones with bits of wood and leather bindings, but a jagged edge of shin-bone had pierced his calf, and the flesh around it was swollen and discoloured.

'Must I go, father?'

'Your canon has asked for you,' the father said, too sick at heart and too much in pain to be anything but harsh toward the boy.

The priest looked on, his proud face set and his expression veiled. For Daniel Hawk this was the ultimate humiliation, that he should be set the task of procuring boys for his master's pleasure. That day a jewelled brooch and several small gestures of affection had come to him, but tonight he would sleep on the rushes outside de Morthlund's door while this lad, unwilling and terrified, would share the canon's bed. It was a familiar pattern now, for he was made to pay for any attention he received as catamite.

Now Daniel, hardening his heart against his task, was sharply reminded of the ways in which power and poverty fed upon each other, each with its own fair measure of dependency. Power rules best where poverty is greatest, and poverty flourishes under power's rule. As natural as night and day they were, each yielding to the other in its turn, and who but a priest or a poor man would question it?

'The poor are with you always,' the Christ had said, yet Daniel would not believe He meant it always to be so.

The boy chosen by Wulfric was young and fresh, a pretty child of nervous disposition, and while his father's legs lay in such ruin, this lad was the only means by which his family might survive.

'Here is the bundle of bread and meat we agreed upon,' the priest said softly, 'and sufficient silver for your needs until the boy returns.'

The sick man did not meet his gaze, nor did he watch his son exchange his dirty rags for the clean brown habit provided for his journey. The boy's face was deathly pale as his fingers fumbled over the cloth. He had heard much said of Wulfric de Morthlund, canon of St Matthew's, and what he knew of him filled his mind with terrible imaginings and turned his blood to ice.

'Come lad, the deal is settled and my canon will not take kindly to the long delay while you ...'

Daniel Hawk glanced up as a figure passed the window, a tall, thin figure in a full black cloak. For an instant he felt he knew the man, but when he stepped to the door the street was empty. Perplexed, he shrugged his shoulders and shook his head, attempting to dislodge a sudden feeling of unease that caused his scalp to prickle.

In another house two streets away, the monk from Flanders lifted the window flap and stuck his swarthy face into the street. The air outside, though heavy with the stink of human life, was fresher than that pervading the filthy hovel where he waited for a woman and her unborn child to die. He would remain until they breathed their last, for that was all he could offer this poor house. If his prayers and his faith could ease her transition from this world to the next, so be it, and if his comfort helped the living bear their loss, amen to that, too.

The street was dark, lit only by a single lantern hung on a corner beam where an industrious thatcher worked beyond the calling of the curfew. His gaze was on this patch of light when he saw a man pass by, a tall man in a great black cloak, hooded and slightly stooped.

'By all that's holy!'

It seemed to him that the figure hesitated for no longer than the space between one heartbeat and the next. A slight turn of the hooded head, a movement of the shoulders, just sufficient to indicate awareness of another's presence. Then it moved beyond the ring of light and vanished.

The startled monk withdrew his head and made for the door just as a thin scream issued from the farthest corner of the room. For a moment indecision held him in mid-stride, then he pushed all else aside and turned to where he was most needed.

Nearby, the three robbers waited in concealment. The shortest one among them took the lead. He was dressed in a filthy, knee-length tunic, his feet bare and his nose twice clipped to mark him as a thief. Those teeth still left to him were not sufficient in number to benefit his tongue, so that he lisped on every word he uttered as he sprang from his dark hole to halt the moving figure in his tracks.

'Hold up there, pilgrim.' The voice was rough and coarsened by the harsh East Yorkshire accent of his birth. 'We claim a traveller's fee for your safe passing through our streets.'

The hooded figure stood as still as stone. All three were out of hiding now. The second man was large and heavy-chested, and above his ragged clothes his head was tightly encased in a leather skullcap with its ties undone. The third was bow-bent at the knees and missing several fingers from one hand, his face sucked in at the cheeks, his body as thin as bone beneath a cat-skin wrap. They had two daggers, a short sword and a heavy club to lend weight to their cause, and all were grinning as they stood their ground.

'You'll part with a fee,' the lisping man repeated, 'or else this blade will part you from your entrails.'

There was an exchange of guffaws as the trio stepped forward to close the gap between them and their catch, but laughter and movement froze as the stranger raised his head to meet them face to face.

'Ye gods!'

The bigger man gaped, so shocked by what he saw, or thought he saw, that he let his short sword fall to the ground with a clatter. He lowered his body after it, his gaze fixed on the hood, his hands paddling the dirt around his feet in search of his fallen weapon.

'Holy . . . mother of . . . God.'

The thin man signed the cross over his chest. Then he turned on his heels and fled, his crooked legs bearing him away with ungainly haste. The lisping man bolted after him, pricked into action by his companion's flight, his dagger and club forgotten in his hands.

The bigger man, still crouched and groping blindly for his sword, made a whimpering sound at the back of his throat, half-turned as if to flee but lost his balance and sprawled upon the ground. He clawed at the dirt, making frantic, crab-like movements until he could regain his feet and make a dash for the nearest alleyway. Once there, cocooned in darker shadow, he found he had the strength to go no further. His heart had swelled until it seemed to overflow the cavity behind his ribs. All strength had drained from his limbs, leaving his body bereft of any support. He saw the hooded figure move away, head bent and cloak held close, continuing on its journey as if no circumstance had marred its progress. Then the big robber felt his legs begin to buckle and his body sink, and in that narrow, pitch-black alleyway he listened to his own heart pounding, felt it racing, heard it falter and marked the very instant when it halted.

At the door of St Thomas's chapel just outside the Keldgate Bar, a small boy in a short grey habit blinked his eyes at the darkness and cocked his head to one side, listening. Some sound had brought him from his bed, a small sound, like the cry of a night bird or the whispered calling of his own name from a far-off place. He held a tiny wax light in his hand, its spluttering flame barely enough to illuminate his clear blue eyes and fine, corn-coloured hair. He watched the darkness, shivering in the early morning chill, until he saw a shadow peal itself away from all the rest and move like drifting mist toward the chapel. Behind it stood the fortified North Bar with its row of lanterns and its sleeping watchman; ahead of it the Great Ditch, which embraced the town of Beverley as might some sleepy serpent.

'Peter? What is it?' Elvira's voice came from behind the boy, husky at first with sleep, then sharply anxious. 'The door! The door is unlatched!'

Watching the shadow-shape across the ditch, Peter raised his lamp so that his small, pale face was bathed in its yellow glow. His eyes were large and very blue, and neither fear, nor wonder, nor surprise was in them. He stared straight ahead at a face he could not see, into eyes that were concealed, and when he saw the hooded head dip slowly in a bow, the boy returned the greeting in like fashion. They stood thus for a long time, neither moving, their gazes locked in an uncanny stare which reached across the space dividing them. Once again the covered head dipped forward in a bow. The boy responded, lowering his own head while his gaze remained fixed hard upon the other.

'*Dominus vobiscum.*' He heard the words distinctly: the Lord be with you.

'*Et cum spiritu,*' he offered in reply. 'And with you also.'

Elvira appeared in the open doorway to hang a warmer robe about her foster son's slender shoulders. She wore a long white woollen shift and her feet were hastily pushed into linen boots. Her waist-length hair was hanging loose, a thick black veil that sparkled in the wax light. Wide-eyed, she stared beyond the door and the hand that rested on his shoulder trembled with concern.

'What is it, child?' her voice was low and edged with anxiety. 'What do you see out there?'

'It is nothing, Mother.'

'Did I hear a voice?'

'None but my own,' he told her, truthfully.

Elvira scanned the area beyond the chapel with an anxious gaze, marking the wide ditch and the locked bar beyond, the huddled dwellings dotted here and there, the crisp black sky and pale, cloud-shrouded moon. She saw nothing more than these familiar things, yet still Peter turned his head as if to catch a last glimpse of whatever had drawn him from the safety of the chapel.

'Peter, why did you open the door?'

His lips curved in a wistful scrap of a smile which had the power to warm or chill Elvira, to lift her heart or sink it, depending on the circumstances in which it was offered. She turned her head quickly to where he looked into the distance, and once again she could find no hint of what had caused the boy to lift the latch.

'Forgive me for disturbing you, Mother,' Peter said. 'As you see, there is nothing out there.'

She hugged him against her. 'We are not safe, child,' she reminded him. 'We can never be safe while our enemies lurk like hungry wolves in every corner. This quiet time of ours, this blessed two-year span of peace, could be undone by an act as simple and as innocent as the unlatching of a chapel door.'

'I know that, Mother,' Peter answered, seeing the tall, thin shadow turn and melt into the gloom. 'I know that.'

Elvira shuddered and felt a sudden stirring of unease. She thought of Simeon, reached for his strength and wished him comfort on this eve of St Matthew, when his memories would rob him of easy sleep. Then she drew Peter back inside and, casting a last worried glance outside, closed and firmly latched the door of the chapel against the night.

When the great bells tolled for the midnight offices the town of Beverley was silent and its streets as dark as pitch. The once-bright moon was wrapped in folds of cloud, the stars mere pinpricks in the blackened distance. A procession of priests wearing plain woollen cloaks over their fancy robes moved through the streets around the Minster, making their way with hooded heads from bed to altar. The sound of their murmured chanting and the flickering of their torches made a ghostly spectacle as figures slipped from open doors and gates to swell their ranks. At the Minster door a lantern burned, creating a welcoming glow of yellow light which drew the servants of the Church inside like eager moths to a flame. When all were safely in the door was closed and all was dark again outside.

Many unseen eyes watched the procession pass, for these devotees had privileges that were envied. The darkness hid those who would rob a priest of his ornaments and cloak, those who desired to share his comforts, those who compared his life to their own and begrudged his seat within God's inner circle. There were also some for whom the sight of the holy men forged a meagre link between the joys of Heaven and the cares of Earth. Knowing their lowly position in the greater scheme of things, they watched the priests and joined their prayers and hoped some residue of God's mercy would extend to them.

A youth wearing rags was standing in the churchyard, close to a window that allowed him to see the flickering candles and hear the choral voices raised within. He held a girl in his arms, a frail young thing too weak to stand unaided. In the light from the window her face, though gaunt and hollow-eyed with sickness, took on a look of rapture. The youth turned from the window as a priest passed by, a tall priest in a huge black robe whose hood concealed his face. Hungry and destitute, he forgot his empty belly as he shifted his burden in his arms and stepped away from the window.

'Your blessing, Father. I beg you to be merciful. My sister is dying. In God's name, will you heal her?'

He thought he heard the tall priest speak, but in his distress and with the soulful chanting of the midnight offices in his ears, the sound was strange. It seemed to him that the words were in his head: *'Is life so precious?'*

'It is,' he said. 'It is.'

The priest was standing very still, disturbingly tall and with no part of him visible amid the folds of his cloth. The youth's words tumbled out in a rush, for he knew in his heart that his sister would not survive another day of deprivation. 'I have brought her here from beyond the port, to die within sight and sound of our blessed Minster.' He lowered his head as if in shame, saw the small, sad smile on his sister's face and was fortified by it. 'I have nothing to offer as priest's fee but my own life.'

'Your life for hers, Edwin?'

His head came up. 'You know me, sir?' Puzzled, he peered into the hood but saw no features amongst the shadows there. 'Then you must know my twin sister here, a goodly, God-fearing girl who has a kindly heart and ...'

'Your life for hers?'

'Yes, sir,' the boy replied without hesitation. 'That would be a fair exchange.'

'Then take her to St Peter's. To Simeon.'

'Please, who are you, sir?'

The pealing of the Minster bells was in his ears when the strange voice came again. *'I am the Guardian at the Gate.'*

Young Edwin bowed his head, not sure that he had heard a voice at all, and when he raised it up again the priest had moved away. All around him there was darkness and deep shadow, and nowhere in that open place could he detect a human shape.

'Have courage, Edwinia,' he whispered. 'Have faith. All will be well now. I have paid the priest's fee.'

CHAPTER TEN

Two priests were standing in the open, watching for the
dawn, neither aware of the other's vigil, each with his
own thoughts and his own concerns. One was fair and
tonsured for his office, the other raven-dark, his crown
unshaven.

Simeon de Beverley stood alone on a small wooded hillock
within the walled enclosure of St Peter's. Against the cool
pre-dawn air he wore a cloak fully lined with squirrel pelts. A
heavy sword was at his girdle according to his priestly rights,
and a simple wooden cross was hung on a silken cord about
his waist. The thongs of his linen shirt were loosened to
reveal a bright golden ornament lying flat against his upper
chest. It was the brow-piece from the bridle of a horse, a solid
disc as broad as his own palm, richly engraved with symbols
and holy marks and bearing the name Christ gave to Simon,
His own chosen priest: Cephas. The Rock. Peter.

Simeon had worn that precious golden talisman for a
decade. It had been taken from the brow of the warhorse
which had ridden through a catastrophic tempest to bring a
child to Beverley; a horse which defied the elements and
burst its own stout heart to reach the town. Elvira had
witnessed both its coming and its death. She saw it race for
Beverley with that unholy storm close behind it, saw it rear up

87

to beat the broiling sky with its massive fore-hooves, then plunge to earth, its task accomplished and its brave heart ruptured. She saw the hooded rider, too, and knew the small, wrapped burden that he carried. Later she slipped that golden brow-piece into Simeon's hand, looked into him with her dark eyes and bound him, for a decade, by the heart.

'Elvira,' he whispered now, his thoughts reaching out beyond the high enclosure walls, beyond the town's strong barricades and treacherous ditch, to the tiny chapel of St Thomas, where his love and their mysterious godson lived in safety under lock and key. He was a priest, a celibate by calling. She was another man's wife and seemed to place her faith in everything but God. They loved across a chasm, worlds apart, yet love they did, and neither man nor God would alter that.

Great John, the ancient Minster bell named for its saint, rang clear and deep and sweet, and after it the voices of the choral priests rose up to sing their anthem to the dawn. Like a small echo the priests of St Peter's followed suit, and after them the more distant voices of St Mary, St Nicholas, St Catherine and St Martin. When he looked to the east, searching for the dawn, he saw that the blackness of the sky was fading. One by one, the stars were going out.

'Still doubting, Simeon?'

He turned his head to see the infirmarian approaching soundlessly across the grassy copse. The man moved like the soldier he once was, sure-footed and agile, as stealthy and as cunning as a wildcat and just as dangerous when cornered. Thin strands of silver shone in his dark beard, but Osric the infirmarian was a young man still, a fighter by training and by inclination. He too should live to see the boy to manhood.

'God's blessing, Osric,' Simeon said, then shrugged his heavy shoulders in a sigh. 'Yes, my friend, I confess my failing. There are still times when the night hangs over us with such a weight that I fear the dawn will never come again.'

'Heathen priest,' Osric chuckled. 'The storm that haunts you is safely passed ten years ago, the fire was quenched these two years past, yet still you stand in awe of both. You harbour superstition, my friend, like a simpleton.'

'That storm was the stuff of legend,' Simeon recalled, watching a cluster of stars being gently erased by daylight's probing fingers.

Osric nodded solemnly. 'And then the great fire came upon us, consuming everything in its path as if the very tongues of Hell were suddenly loosed among us. And now the mud-floods. This town of ours has seen its share of troubles.' He glanced about him in the uncertain light, noted the stone slab resting on the ground and with a firm hand drew his friend toward it. 'Come, heathen priest, I'll sit out the vigil with you.'

'Do you know the date?'

'Aye, Simeon, I do. Not one among us will ever again be allowed to pass this time of St Matthew's Feast with an untroubled mind. Come, let us watch the dawn and thank the Lord for it, knowing that for us the worst is over.'

They sat together on the stone slab, waiting in the new day, two friends who shared a thousand secrets and a single cause, and as the choral priests of Beverley lifted up their voices in the beautiful incantation for the dawn, both remained tight-lipped and grim, remembering.

On the Figham moor that other priest was standing. He wore a splendid cloak of wool dyed purple, its lining glossy black with rare and costly beaver fur. Father Cyrus de Figham, canon of St Martin's, held a gelding by its bridle, man and beast alike impatient for the morning's hunt. On one hip a brass-trimmed crossbow rested, on the other a quiver of feathered quarrels fashioned by a master weapon-maker. He stared through narrowed eyes at the paling horizon where hints of green and gold and copper were already visible.

His priest, still mounted, watched his master with wary interest, familiar with this pre-hunt agitation. De Figham was primed and eager for the kill, and when his blood was heated, thus, he was no less dangerous and unpredictable than the animals he hunted.

'Damn them to hell,' he spat in irritation. 'Where is my hunt?'

'They were preparing when we left,' John Palmer said.

'I told them to be here at dawn.'

'The sun is not yet up, my lord.'

'But *I* am up,' de Figham retorted. 'And I am not to be left clicking my heels while fools make ready according to the signs they read in the sky.'

A small shape scrambled from a hollow on the ground and showed itself to be a young boy with a weary face. Two hounds rose with him, wary beasts with clipped ears and distinctive brands burned deep into their shoulders: de Figham's hounds. No man would dare make off with them while they bore his mark so clearly on their hides.

The boy stepped forward gingerly. 'Shall I run back to the house and hurry them, my lord?'

De Figham waved his ringed hand in an impatient gesture and the boy took off, stumbling on the rough ground in his haste to do the dark priest's bidding. The hounds sprang after him, only to slink back, tails plastered to their bellies and shoulders hunched, at a growled 'to heel!' from their master.

From the hilltop Father Cyrus let his gaze range over Beverley. There stood the Minster church, ravaged by fire and looters alike, magnificent in its day but ugly now in its state of hasty and haphazard repair. Close by it stood the remains of his own St Martin's: ten years ago the parish church and rich in its endowments; today a storm- and- fire-damaged millstone hung about his neck. He had coveted that church for half his life, had struck down his ageing canon for want of it, but this St Martin's rendered inferior profit to him now, and in return he had no love for it.

His gaze took in the townscape with displeasure. Only two years ago this town had blazed from end to end like dry sticks put to the torch. Its homes were gutted and its churches razed, its markets and its mills burned to the ground, and the stench of burning flesh had clung to everything. It had been a fire of unsurpassed proportions, yet even this was not enough to put an end to Beverley, the tarnished jewel in the crown of York. This hell-hole had survived to prosper in its way. Local lords had squabbled over the spoils, priests fearing ruin had plundered their own altars, scholars of every nationality had abandoned their blazing schools and joined the gangs of looters rampaging through the town, and still Beverley refused to die. New hovels sprang up in place of old, fresh timber was patched to scorched, new masonry grafted on to old, and nothing really changed. The busy port was cleared and reopened within a few short weeks. Trade flourished, merchants and traders rebuilt and re-stored, and the Church regained its stranglehold on poor men's lives.

'And now the ground spews mud and slime, swallows up a few of these cringing beggars and settles back on itself as if such things were commonplace,' de Figham muttered.

'These water towns are prone to it, my lord,' John answered.

'Aye, and but for that bishop John and his monastery, this place would still be a breeding-ground for beavers. He should have stayed in York and left his precious Beaver Lake to the swamps that spawned it.'

'Many would agree with that, my lord,' John nodded cautiously, then heeled his horse so that it moved away to pace the ground until the hunt arrived.

On this morning of September 22nd, two years to the very day since Beverley's conflagration, Father Cyrus surveyed the uncomely Phoenix risen from its ashes. This town was indestructible, and by its obstinate survival it imprisoned him. He could not, would not, walk away and leave his enemy to flourish in his absence.

He shrugged his shoulders more comfortably into his cloak, cleared his throat and spat upon the ground. Down there, between the Minster and the wetlands, the high walls of St Peter's enclosure marked the only sizeable portion of Beverley which had managed to escape the fire. Some claimed it had been spared by divine intervention, but wiser men allowed that Simeon de Beverley was no fool. That blue-eyed priest had dragged every holy man from his futile prayers and set him to work with bucket and pan and ladle. A thousand hands had milked the waterways to douse the timbers of every building, every tree and woodpile, and so the sparks had been extinguished even as they flared upon the wind, and not a lick of flame could take a hold.

'I owe my life to you, Simeon de Beverley,' the dark priest growled. 'And I have made an oath upon my soul that one day I will discharge that debt by killing you.'

He saw the distant door of St Peter's church swing open and the pale, soft glow of candles light the space. The morning office was drawing to its close. Shadows were taking more definite shape and claiming back their colours from the night. Small camp fires were springing into life and already the scent of wood-smoke and cooking-pots was in the air. The Great Ditch stirred itself awake, turned muddy ochre in the gathering light, and all of Beverley's unsavoury little waterways came into view. Sunlight began to spread from the horizon, gilding the lower clouds, pushing the darkness back and lifting up the shrouds of mist that hugged the wetlands and the marshes all about.

'The Devil take this godforsaken hole,' de Figham spat, and then the flash of a small light caught his eye. Two men were at the edge of St Peter's copse where young trees crowded the spaces between old timbers. Two men, both cloaked against the dawn, and on the chest of one a glinting light, as if he held a candle to his breast.

Father Cyrus fingered a quarrel from his quiver and fitted it, using his boot for leverage, to the bow. He raised the weapon up, supporting its weight on one elbow, and closed one eye to sight the bolt more squarely. A living man made worthier prey than boar, and a priest a worthier target still, especially if that priest might by some chance be Simeon de Beverley. His fingers hooked across the firing lever, and that shimmering light, seen now not as a candle's flame but as the gleam of sunlight on a burnished surface, drew the eye and the quarrel point to itself. Then the sound of voices at his back brought Cyrus around, the crossbow lowered. His hunt was here.

Close by St Peter's church, Osric the infirmarian waited quietly for Simeon to have done with his devotions. The younger man was standing now, his face turned to the sunrise.

'Tie up your shirt, my friend,' Osric instructed gruffly when Simeon's prayers of thanks for the dawn were ended. 'That brow-piece you wear reflects the sun so brightly that it marks you out for robbers or bowmen, even at distance. Tie up your shirt and cover it, lest even good men fall to its temptation.'

For a moment Simeon turned the heavy golden disc in his fingers, seeing it catch the sunlight and cast it off in brilliant shards from its bright surface.

'Cephas,' he smiled, laying it flat against his chest and thonging his shirt across it. 'Peter.'

'Aye,' Osric nodded, returning Simeon's smile. 'Ten years we've had him here with us. Ten years, my friend, and ten times that number of enemies to outwit, and still the boy is safe.'

'He is well served,' Simeon said, gripping his old friend firmly by the shoulder. Osric's strong hand came up to grasp his wrist and, in that mute salute, they reinforced their secret bond.

Across the distance, high on the slopes of Figham moor, Cyrus de Figham heeled his mount and, knowing his shot would have fallen far short of its target, wondered what manner of man had filled his crossbow sights so briefly. Then he swept his heavy cloak about his horse's flanks, raised up his arm in a signal and led his hunting party toward the woodlands and the boar.

CHAPTER ELEVEN

When the hunt returned the morning was half-spent and he had a catch of five boars and two score rabbits to his credit. He would have them put to the spits without delay, for on this night his table would be attended by men well used to dining in the manner of princes. Nor would his guests be disappointed, for they would eat roast fowls in rich, hot sauces, pigeons in wine, plump hines of mutton, fresh-water fish, fresh eels and ewe's cheese with rare spices added. All this with succulent pork and beef, and as much of the finest wines as they could drink.

De Figham turned in the saddle to glower at the men following behind, strung out in their various groups of riders, carriers and walkers. He could hear a man screaming in the distance and the sound was an irritation to his ears.

'You paid too much for the sugar,' he complained, suspecting his personal priest no less than he would any other of cheating him. All were thieves when opportunity stared them in the face.

'Sevenpence a pound is exorbitant.'

'The king himself paid ten, my lord, and willingly. Our own archbishop was asked for eight with a cask of wine thrown in.'

'Was he, indeed? And you paid only seven?'

94

'I did, my lord.'

They had reached that area where the pool of mud had risen up and turned the earth black. Word had spread that a priest's party had been drowned here, and so the whole area had become infested with townsfolk picking and hammering at the ground for anything of value. The foreleg of a horse was clearly visible where the mud was being cleared, and the head of a sheep, raised high and open-mouthed, poked through the solid surface, its eyes glazed over. As de Figham turned his mount to skirt the pool, a wry smile played around his mouth and a chuckle gathered in his throat.

'Our Geoffrey Plantagenet will be displeased by the loss of a valued clerk,' he said. 'Perhaps he should order his fancy priests to ride from York and dig this mud-pool over. Their toil would be much appreciated here.'

'The archbishop would be displeased to learn that his clerk was ever here at all,' John said.

'Or that we are wise to his manipulations,' Cyrus added. 'He will not snatch this town's wealth from my grasp, not with the help of Simeon or Wulfric or a thousand men like them. While I am wise to the plots they try to hatch, no man will claim that treasure-trove but me.'

'Will you join forces with my lord Wulfric in the matter?'

De Figham eyed him sideways and smiled. 'It will appear so to that bloated peacock, but Cyrus de Figham shares his fortunes with no man. I will allow Wulfric de Morthlund to strut and preen and to fancy that he has the whole affair at his command, but I will cheat the peacock in the end, just as he would cheat me if he could. And I still say you paid too highly for the sugar.'

'Too high a price to sweeten tonight's grand feast, my lord?'

De Figham grinned and shook his head. It was a fact that some of the greatest men of both Church and state were the poorest martyrs to their worldly senses. Their benevolence rested in the lap of self-gratification, and their allegiance ebbed and flowed according to their more immediate needs.

These men were impressed first through the eyes and then the belly, and any host worth his salt knew well how to pleasure both without neglecting all those senses lying in between. None but a liar would dare to say that Cyrus de Figham skimped upon his table, or hint that his fortunes floundered for want of sufficient profit from his ruined church.

'You shall have a new cloak for services rendered, John,' he told his priest.

'Thank you, my lord.'

'And I have a mind to give you a purse of silver. Would that suit?'

'Indeed it would, my lord.'

Once again de Figham regarded his priest from the corners of his eyes. 'And any bribe Wulfric de Morthlund offers, I will double in price if you will tell me of it.'

John beamed and bowed his head. 'My lord, you are most generous.'

De Figham nodded. They were both aware that generosity was but a pretty word to hang upon an act of timely prudence. Loyalty was a thing of the market-place, a commodity to be bought and sold, and a prudent man must attach fair value to it. If he himself declined to buy, de Morthlund or some other surely would. The young priest was worthy of his keep and more, and de Figham meant to secure his continued loyalty at any cost, though he hoped to strike a tolerable bargain for it.

They slowed a little and turned as the sound of distant shrieking increased. Four foot-runners were struggling to cross the mudslides, unable to match their pace to the rest of the hunt. They carried a bundle between them and this writhing, bouncing burden produced the shrill sounds of a man in agony.

'We should have left the boar to finish its work,' de Figham said, and John agreed. 'We took a full man to the hunt and we bring but half of him back home. These sentimental fools surprised me by their willingness to carry such a burden all this distance. Good hearts they have, and strong limbs, too, but little sense. He will not live to thank them for their sacrifice.'

'Nor would he thank them for it if he did,' John said. 'Not with those wounds to bear and one eye plucked out.'

'Sentimental fools,' de Figham snorted, and urged his weary horse into a canter.

The gates of the house were drawn open as they approached, and he rode through as proudly as any knight. Inside he dismounted and handed his horse, crossbow and quiver to a servant. Then he waited, his cloak thrown back and his fists placed firmly on either hip, until the hunt was safely in with their catch. He was impatient to be inside the house. The ride had sharpened his appetite for good strong ale and mutton off the bone, and beneath his hunting tunic a heat burned strongly in his loins. This priest had no design on celibacy, that unnatural path trod by pious fools and clever churchmen searching after sainthood. Self-denial was a thing for ageing popes with shrivelled loins to ponder over, and for those who were less than men to take into their empty beds and unemployed embraces. Not for Cyrus de Figham such denial of the manly passions. He was as God had made him. His lust, along with eating and drinking, sleeping and defecating, was a simple human need to be placated.

The runners came at last, sweating and panting with their screaming bundle held between them. De Figham signalled for the gates to be barred and winced with distaste as the runners staggered forward, for blood was dipping in crimson drops across his well-kept courtyard.

One of his footmen, Ketel, a man much valued for his killing skills, had fallen foul of a cornered boar when the hunt was only minutes into the forest. The beast had flung him into a tangle of roots, then gored his legs and opened up his belly from breast to groin before the spearmen arrived on the scene to drive it off. De Figham had quickly declared the man beyond all help of human ease, and let the hunt continue. By some chance Ketel was still alive when they returned to the spot two hours later, though one of his eyes was gone and his lip was torn, as if some other beast had come across him and taken what it could before he drove it off. Four men, using a knotted cloak to bear his weight, carried him home between them at a pace, and Ketel had screamed and cursed God and de Figham all the way.

Now de Figham ordered the cloak set down on the ground and the man's wounds bared for inspection. He shook his head gravely, seeing that shattered shards of bone had pierced the once-strong legs in several places, and that only the man's own fingers kept his entrails from pouring out through the hole in his belly. There was no hope for Ketel, damn his error, and now the household was a good man short.

'At least we have the animal that gored him. See to it that his widow receives a shilling for her loss.'

Father Cyrus signed the cross and, eager to have the matter settled, withheld the lengthier passing prayer and offered instead a short shrift so that Ketel might die eased of his immediate sins and nothing more.

'Carry him to the infirmary at St Peter's,' he told the bearers. 'Let Osric, that arrogant healer of a thousand battle wounds, practise his skills where the boar has rummaged. We'll see then how much he knows of mending bodies.'

As he turned away he paused with one long index finger pressed against his pursed lips in a thoughtful manner, then turned back to John Palmer and asked: 'Where is the nephew of Sir Guy de Burton?'

'Still here in the town, my lord, assessing the damage. 'Neither his father nor his uncles will offer aid to Beverley unless it can be proved that aid is truly needed.'

'And unless any gesture on their part can speak so loudly that it reaches our archbishop's ears,' de Figham observed.

'I believe young Fergus has an interest here.'

'A woman?'

John Palmer nodded. 'His father is vicar of St Jude at Thorpe. He keeps her under lock and key since Fergus let his interest in her be known.'

'Surely he is not angling for marriage? What, marriage between a Burton and a country vicar's daughter?' De

Figham laughed and shook his head. 'She will die a virgin while he hopes in vain.'

'Unless young Fergus finds a way to tumble her while the vicar is at his altar. He seems determined that it will be so.'

'Does he, indeed?' De Figham tapped his finger to his lips again. 'This information serves me well,' he said at last. 'Bring Fergus de Burton here to me at once. Tell him I have important work for him. Have him prepare to ride to York this very afternoon, and after that, if all goes to my plan, he will tumble the maid to his heart's content and the vicar of St Jude's will make no protest.'

'I will go at once, my lord,' John said with a respectful bow of his head.

'And for God's sake clear that mess out of my courtyard.'

The shrieks of the dying man grew more piercing as he was half-dragged on the bloodied cloak across the cobbles to the courtyard gates. His bearers, already wearied by the long run home and aware that they performed a thankless task, would be less gentle on the journey to St Peter's.

A smile on Father Cyrus's face marked the twists and turns of his thoughts as he strode for the main door of the house, his eyes bright from the kill. Simeon de Beverley would rue the day he thought to bring this better priest to heel.

The young woman, Alice, met her master at the door of the house, her gaze downcast in obedience and her gown undone. Once she had been defiant in her hatred of de Figham, but now she attended to his every whim without complaint. It had been easy, in the end, to break her. Pious she was and proud in her suffering, until he set that brand upon her breast and bade her wear her gown undone so that all who saw it would know her as his property.

On a table in his private room the woman had set blood pudding and mutton on a deep bread trencher, a cup of ale with a fresh egg added, fruit in a bowl and sliced fruits laced with heated honey. He watched her as he ate. Alice was small and dark, with high, firm breasts and well-rounded hips. Even now she bore a small resemblance to Elvira, the ditcher's wife and now the lame priest's whore, the woman Simeon raised from filth and poverty to a life of idle pleasure at the Church's expense. For all his vows of chastity, Simeon de Beverley was flesh and blood like any other man and not yet thirty years of age. His loins were no doubt as potent and as urgent as his neighbour's. Elvira was beautiful beyond the God-given rights of any woman to be so. She was a temptress, pale and cool yet as hot as fire beneath her saintly exterior, with undercurrents designed to inflame all men who saw her close.

Elvira's face came to him now and, with the memory, hunger. Just once he had held her in his arms, by chance in the market-place, and after that, no other woman did more than bring a temporary ease to his desires. Nothing would ever convince him that Simeon de Beverley kept his vows in the face of such temptation, or that the woman spurned her handsome protector. His jealousy burned each time he thought of them, burned like a hot knife through his very soul.

De Figham shoved his cup aside and the woman refilled it with a trembling hand. His brand stood out in vivid scars above her breast, and he despised her for its ugliness. This was his property, this cringing substitute for the true object of his desire, this spiritless cur who bore his brand. Neither Simeon nor his canons had managed to lodge lawful cause for her removal, and with the regular and savage venting of his lust on her, de Figham nurtured his dangerous obsession.

'Damn,' he hissed, his eyes two slate-grey slits below furrowed brows. 'Damn that priest and his dark-eyed whore.'

He glared at Alice. The hunt and the ale had livened his loins and thoughts of Elvira had stirred the ever-present embers of his lust. That ditcher's wife was a plague upon his senses, but in her absence Alice would suffice.

'Come here,' he growled.

She stood meekly before him while he ripped her gown from chest to hip to bare her breasts. She scarcely flinched at the roughness of his hands on her bruised flesh, so he applied more pressure until he saw the tears of pain spring to her eyes. Her resignation did not please him beyond the fact that he was master of her.

100

His lust was heightened by the memory of her solemn oath before the holy canons. It was a heady power that had allowed him to force this pious wretch to damn her soul to hell by her own words. Ultimate power: no man could ask for more. He was free to use her now in any way that suited his requirements. The woman was damned. Her soul was forfeit. In the eyes of God and man alike she was now no better than the dirt beneath his boots.

He snapped his fingers and jerked his head toward the dirt floor, and Alice obediently raised her skirts and bent to assume the posture of a dog. As he prepared himself, he vowed afresh that one day Elvira would kneel before him thus, and her degradation would be the last thing Simeon saw in this world before de Figham's sword dispatched him neatly into the next.

CHAPTER TWELVE

While Ketel screamed and Cyrus de Figham took his lustful revenge on Alice, two men, known as robbers and looters, were at the water-point outside St Peter's wall, telling those gathered there of strange events. They were given bread and pig's head soup, and this simple midday fare encouraged them to embellish their tale as the food went round. Today was St Matthew's Feast Day, and soon the festivities would begin, the Saint's procession and the merry-making. Already the market stalls were filled and carts were rumbling through crowded streets, bringing in their mer-chandise. At all the five bars streams of oxcarts, handcarts, loaded mules and burdened men and women joined the rush of pilgrims pouring into the town. Sailors left their vessels at the port, farmers their fields and villagers their homes to join the feast. Life did not slow or halt its forward flow when tragedy struck. The floods were stopped, the dead indifferent, the living eager for distraction.

Outside St Peter's wall the group drew closer as the two men told their story once again.

'It was an apparition,' one looter declared in solemn tones, and although his nose was twice clipped with the thief's brand, none took his words for anything but truth. 'It was twice the height of any ordinary man. It was as slender as a willow's branch and made no sound, not so much as a footfall on the ground or a rustle of its cloak.'

'Death,' his companion nodded, crossing his body with a hand which lacked three fingers and half a thumb. 'The angel of death was abroad last night. We two passed right across its path and lived to tell of it.'

'What did it look like?' someone asked, eager for detail.

'Did it have flesh like living men?' another demanded. 'Arms and legs? Did it have a face?'

'Thin, you say? All bones then, was it?'

'Did it have the stench of the grave on it?'

The questions came from each listener in turn, accompanied by a chunk of bread well soaked in soup from the simmering pot. A woman speared an onion with a stick, pulled it from the camp fire and held it out, charred and smoking, just beyond the storytellers' reach. When the clipped man reached for it she pulled it back. 'What did it say?' she demanded. 'What did it do?'

The man sighed heavily and picked at a rotten tooth, wincing as he did so. ' "Say?" Nay, woman, it uttered not a word. "Do?" It murdered our friend, that's what it done.'

A murmur went around the ragged bunch of men and women at the camp fire. The steaming onion was released and the looters divided it with their bare hands and gulped it down with bits of bread. They shared a cup of watered ale and let the silence lengthen, the better to make their story worth the price. The gaunt-faced one with hollowed cheeks took up the telling of it.

'You all know Judd, the sanctuary man who was driven from Lincoln on false charges. You know him well. He wore a leather helmet slashed at the nape, and he carried a sword well notched to mark his courage. He was a big man, as strong as any of his size, with a wide back and a stout heart in his chest.'

'I know him,' someone said, and one by one they all agreed that Judd was known to them.

'Well, this same Judd, God rest his soul, was brave enough to challenge the apparition with his sword. As God and my

103

good friend here were witness to it, that apparition struck poor Judd to the ground without a blow. It felled him like a rotten oak put to the axe and left him dead. Is there a drop more ale? This business has given me a hearty thirst.'

While he drank, his lisping companion offered his portion of the tale. 'At poor Judd's boldness it rose up even taller than before, threw back its hood and pierced him with its eyes. The force of its stare threw him backwards at a stagger. We fled in fear of our lives, and when we dared return to search for him we found him slumped in a nearby alleyway, and he was dead.'

'Dead? How dead? What wounds? Was much blood spilled? What limbs were ripped from him? Was his skull caved in?'

'Not a mark,' the looter said, holding out his empty cup to the holder of the ale jug. 'No mark was on him, no bone was broken, no drop of blood was spilled. His body still lies in the alley where it fell, close to the Cobbler's Row, where anyone who has the stomach to view it can see for themselves how Judd was stricken down.'

Around the camp fire men and women whispered fearfully amongst themselves and, while they speculated, the two looters crept away to tell their tale and taste the fare elsewhere.

In an isolated corner of St Peter's enclosure, four men had bound a tangle of thorns aside to dig a pit in the dry ground underneath. Here the oldest and stoutest sections of the ancient walls met at an angle, reinforced by nature's handiwork and dividing the enclosure from the treacherous wetlands. St Peter's marked the end of the settled area to the east of Beverley, and these bastions were virtually impossible to approach from the lands beyond. Intruders faltered on the rocky, weed-infested mud outside the walls, where deadly pools and cavities of mud could suck a man to oblivion before his last cry was even uttered. Any who survived this far would need a rope and irons to scale the walls, then meet with the impassable growth of thorn protecting their inner sides.

The diggers stood back, wiping sweat from their faces as Simeon and Osric and six priests approached through heavy woodland. All but Osric were dressed according to their offices, carrying candles, prayer-books and incense pots. This burial, though held in secret and unsanctioned by the archbishop, was to be conducted in the proper manner.

'It is a good spot,' Simeon said, well satisfied.

'Aye, he will be safe here,' Osric nodded, handing a purse of coin to be divided amongst the diggers. These four were also priests and fiercely loyal to the Church. They would have toiled willingly for love, but Osric had been a soldier too long to disregard the hearts of even the most devoted of men. They labour best and serve most loyally who are adequately rewarded for their work. These priests of St Peter's rejected the common practice of selling their prayers and services to the poor, but priests must eat and drink like other men. They must be allowed to prosper in their offices, lest they become too destitute to be of any value. So here at St Peter's a priest might expect fair payment for his labours, then serve and succour according to his conscience.

There had been two other burials that morning; a woman dead in childbirth while her crippled babe survived, and the huntsman, Ketel, one of de Figham's men. This man had borne horrific injuries for five long hours after being savagely gored by a boar at dawn. Half-crazed with pain, he screamed vile curses upon all manner of God's creation, and in the end his rage turned on itself. The hands that had held in his innards through the gaping hole of his stomach began to pluck them out, and with his own fingers he disembowelled himself.

The box containing the remains of Father Bernard, gentle canon of St Martin's, a man of true and honest faith, lay on the ground close by the pit which had been sunk to receive it. The coffin was lined with lead, and within it the body was wrapped in its finest regalia, its rings and jewelled girdle, its precious priest's knife and a cross of gold. For a while the cask had lain in the garden behind the provost's house, beneath a splendid oak reputed to have stood in that same

105

spot for five hundred years. Father Bernard had spent long hours there in his lifetime, sifting his thoughts while the old tree kept the summer sun from his head and the winter chills at bay. A windborne mass of blazing thatch had burned the oak tree down, and after the fire the men of St Peter's had rescued the coffin from looters and stakers and carried it to their little church where it could be protected. Only now, two years after the Great Fire, when hopes of finding a more suitable place had faded, was Father Bernard to be properly reinterred.

'*Kyrie eleison,*' Simeon said in his richly-timbred voice. Lord have mercy.

The response from the gathered priests was sweet and melodic: '*Christi eleison.*' Christ have mercy.

Osric stood back a pace or two to listen, letting the Latin words wash over him. He knew the Latin but had no need of it, for the calculated shape and weight, the ebb and flow of word and phrase, was in itself enough to reach the soul of even the most ignorant of men. There were times when he found the ritual and repetition demanded by his faith unfathomable, but the simple truth of Christianity had not left him since first he heard it so clearly expressed by Simeon. All men were pagans, this he did believe, yet this faith offered hope to the pagan soul. However he lived, in anguish, want, depravity, in affliction or in ignorance, no man need die despairing.

Now clouds of incense wafted sweet scents from swinging ropes while soft singing filled the woods within St Peter's. To move a body after burial is to tear a soul from Paradise. God's grace would nurse poor Bernard through this cleaving, and draw him back to Heaven from a safer resting-place.

Simeon's voice was deep and full of hope. 'We commend to Thee O Lord, the soul of Bernard, Thy faithful servant.'

The coffin was lowered into the pit, the soil smoothed over and the thorns cut loose. The growth of centuries, freed from its unnatural fetters, fell and settled back into its rightful place so that the earth was quickly reclaimed and no eye could detect what had been done.

'*Spiritus sanctus Deus,*' Simeon intoned.

'*Misere nobis,*' came the soft response.

As those selected for the task drew near to begin the long, hypnotic Litany of the Saints, Simeon and Osric stood aside in the dappled sunlight filtering through the trees. Their faces had grown sombre and their thoughts ran parallel.

'A good man murdered,' Simeon said. 'And an innocent hanged for the deed.'

'Aye, it was a sorry time, my friend, that saw a good man murdered by his priest.'

Without turning his lowered head, Simeon regarded the infirmarian from the outer edges of his eyes. 'You do truly believe de Figham struck him down?'

'Do you doubt it?' Osric challenged.

Simeon shook his head. 'And now the killer wears his victim's vestments, carries his titles and puts claim on his church.'

Osric laughed harshly at that. 'And what paltry benefits St Martin's has allowed him for his pains.'

'What paltry benefits St Martin's offers *anyone*,' Simeon sighed, 'with its altar fallen and its roof still breached.'

'It will not prosper while de Figham has it,' Osric told him.

Now Father Richard, moving with care for his recent injuries, detached himself from the chanting priests and joined his companions in the shelter of the trees. His eyes were bright with unshed tears, for he had loved the ageing canon dearly, and his death had held a particular sting for him. It was Richard who first stumbled upon the body lying in a dark stairwell in the Minster, and who helped Father Simeon prove the deed as murder.

Now Simeon gripped him by the shoulder and stared into his bearded face. 'You are in pain?'

Richard shook his head. 'I thank the good Lord for my life if not for my physician. My ribs are smeared with knitbone and bound so tightly that I can scarcely breathe. This Osric has had me all but pickled in a brew most Christians would be ashamed to feed their swine. I will heal. The injury is bearable.'

'That wall of mud did you less hurt than this,' Simeon said, indicating the burial with a movement of his head while keeping his gaze firmly locked with Richard's. His eyes said that he knew the other well and shared his loss.

'If I had gone earlier to that stairwell ...'

'Richard, my friend, you punish yourself unjustly,' Simeon said. 'Our brother Bernard rests in peace and safety now. However sharp the pain of it, we must at least give thanks for that.'

'And for a life well spent,' Osric added. 'God will not find him lacking.'

'But He will find him unavenged,' Richard complained, still bitter in his heart. 'A good man lies mouldering while a bad one prospers, and for all my prayers I cannot be at peace with such injustice.'

Simeon grimaced. 'Then shoulder it wisely and bear it, as you must, until the Almighty brings the wrongdoer to account.'

'Thou shalt not murder,' Richard quoted hotly.

'Indeed so, Richard,' Simeon said, gripping the shoulder more tightly and searching the tear-bright eyes with his own far-seeing gaze, 'and you'd be well advised to remember that above all else. Neither for gain nor for revenge, thou shalt not murder!'

Chastised, Richard lowered his head and asked forgiveness for the wrath still burning in him. Simeon touched his thumb to his lips and signed the cross on the young man's forehead. He knew the true weight of his pain, the guilt and sorrow that he bore in equal measure with his anger.

'Go in peace,' he said, and watched the young priest limp away.

'Peace?' Osric repeated bitterly. 'There'll be no peace for him while de Figham lives.'

'Nor, I think, for any of us, my friend,' Simeon answered gravely.

Just then a movement caught his eye, a shadow amongst the deeper shadows of the trees. He threw back his cloak and drew his sword, holding it in a two-handed grip, point lowered. On the instant Osric, too, was fully armed.

'What is it, Simeon?'

'A man. I saw a man there in the trees. A tall man, fleet-footed and wearing a long dark cloak.' As Simeon spoke his narrowed eyes searched every tree and every gap between.

'Could it be Richard, doubling back?' Osric wondered, stepping towards the trees. His own eyes were shrunk to slits and his knees were bent and firmly braced, a fighter's stance, prepared for any attack.

'Too far to the south for Richard. And too tall.' He suddenly leaped to the right and his sword came up. 'There! Over there where the sun slants in! Do you see it?'

'I see only trees and shadows,' Osric confessed, and under his breath he prayed, 'Dear God, let it not be *him*.'

'It was a man. Damn your eyes, Osric, I tell you, it was a man.'

Even as he spoke the words, two women in the light grey habits of the order of the Little Sisters of Mercy came into view. They stepped lightly from that same direction with their headclothes sparkling in shafts of sunlight. They stopped abruptly when they saw the swords.

'Did a man pass by you?' Simeon demanded. 'A tall man in a black cloak and a hood?'

The sisters exchanged glances. 'No, Father, we saw no one,' one of them offered, 'except for Father Richard, at a distance.'

'Father Richard's cloak is green with a yellow hood. A man in black. Come, woman, you must have passed right by him.'

The woman shook her head and her companion echoed the denial. 'We passed by no one, Father.'

'But that's impossible,' Simeon said, and slowly his face began to drain of colour. As he lowered his sword tip to the ground his eyes grew wide. 'God forbid it,' he whispered hoarsely, and again: 'Dear God forbid it.'

'A shadow, Simeon, just a shadow,' Osric tried to insist, but in his face, too, there was a certain look of apprehension.

They allowed the nuns to pass by on their way to Father Bernard's grave. Then, with their swords still out, the two men made a rapid but thorough search of St Peter's wood.

109

When they reached the farthest side they searched the copse, the vegetable gardens, the little orchard and the herbery, and after that the buildings, one by one. No eye had seen what Simeon had seen, and none believed there was a stranger loose in the enclosure.

'A trick of the light,' Osric insisted. 'The play of sun on shadow, nothing more. Our talk of Cyrus de Figham has unnerved you.'

'I wish I could believe that,' Simeon said, white-faced. He turned to Osric and his eyes were troubled. 'They must be brought here, now, within the hour.'

Osric nodded, his thin face pinched and grave. 'It will be done. God's teeth, I hope you are at fault in this, my friend.'

Simeon stared about him, searching still, then turned and strode toward his scriptorium. 'See to it, Osric,' he growled over his shoulder. 'Within the hour, and under heavy guard. I want them *here*.'

Osric nodded at Simeon's departing back. A hooded figure, tall and wearing a long black cloak, glimpsed in the shadows of their own enclosure. Disaster dogged them, unless the priest had been mistaken. He shuddered despite his soldier's courage, re-sheathed his sword and signed his chest with the cross. One sighting might be a fancy or an error, but two independent sightings came uncomfortably close to certainty. How many others might have caught a glimpse of that same dark shape, only to keep the knowledge to themselves, as he had done? He felt his forearms prickle with apprehension. Was their hard-won peace to be so short?

'What will he bring upon us this time?' Osric asked the untroubled sky above him.

A moment later he had gathered his wits together and was striding toward the infirmary, pulling men from this task or that as he went. At Simeon's bidding and on his own keen instincts, he would have the woman and the boy inside the walls of St Peter's without delay.

CHAPTER THIRTEEN

Elvira came by boat from St Thomas's chapel, anonymous in her long grey habit and with her hair concealed beneath a large white wimple. Only her eyes and the long, deep scar along her left forearm revealed her true identity, and these she kept well hidden, her eyes beneath demurely lowered lids, the scar inside the wide sleeves of her robe. She placed herself in the centre of the group, one sister amongst the many, so quietly inconspicuous that none would guess how well this one was guarded.

Simeon was waiting with two other priests near the ruin of St Martin's, watching the crowded landing-place where Elvira's boat would stop. Osric was there to meet the boat, and with him Thorald, the fierce, bull-tempered priest of St Nicholas's at the port. Each carried a short sword and dagger hidden beneath his cloak, and each was wary of every man and woman at his elbow. Two monks were in Elvira's party, and with them a young priest from the chapel itself. Others had come on Osric's instructions from St Catherine's, St John's, St Andrew's and St Peter's. All were armed and had their trusted clerks beside them. Nineteen in all, a near score of willing escorts for her journey, yet still Simeon feared that she might come to harm. Two years of peace they had enjoyed since the great fire and its troubled aftermath and yet, knowing that peace of any sort might only be maintained by strictest caution, Simeon was ever vigilant on Elvira's and the boy's behalf. This new alarm fretted his mind, this glimpse of a hooded figure in the woodland, and every time he thought of it he prayed to God that he had been mistaken.

'Two men over there by the ruin,' Osric whispered to his companion, one hand gripping the sword hilt at his belt.

'I have them in my sights,' Thorald replied. 'One is Sir Guy de Burton's man, the other a merchant from Durham. They are here to meet de Figham's agent.' He turned his head to scan a group, picked out a shape he recognised and nodded in that direction. 'The stout man in the green hood over there. More food arriving for his master's feast, I'll wager.'

'De Figham!' Osric almost spat the name. 'That blackhearted priest would gladly trade his shipment for ours if word has reached his ears of what we are expecting.'

Thorald smiled grimly and squared his massive shoulders. 'His men would be here in force if that were so. Our goods are well protected, Osric, and our keen eyes and our swords will keep them so.'

The flat, low-sided boat approached the landing. Too heavily laden with merchandise and people to move with any speed, it sat low in the murky water as the boatman and his lackeys poled it along. Simeon saw Elvira amongst the tightly pressed crowd of passengers. There was nothing to distinguish her from her fellow travellers, yet even from that distance he picked her out. It was his heart that recognised her first, and it quickened in his breast at the sight of her.

He glanced about him, then at the seething mass of humanity surging forward to the landing-place, at the press of people at his back and the crowds on either side. One hand slipped beneath his cloak, his fingers gripping the hilt of his sword in readiness for any sign of trouble. His handsome face was set in concentration, his blue eyes keen, his senses alert to every danger in that bustling place. He saw the boat being tied up and the group of passengers disembarking, the first men roughly elbowing others aside to make a way for those behind. Elvira raised her head just once and turned her face in his direction and after that she kept her eyes cast down.

'God keep you, lady,' he whispered as, flanked by his priests, he followed the group at an unobtrusive distance through the crush of people around the great Minster church. His nostrils caught the odour of scorched timbers. Here at the Minster, as in so many other places, new had been patched to old and fresh wood pinned to burned, so that the clean new roofing and beams were impregnated with the scent of fire. As ever, it saddened him. The Minster stood on valuable land owned by the archbishop of York, its canons divided as to its future, and while the pilgrims flocked there as before with offerings and gifts, the interests of St John were poorly served.

The church top was left untouched for want of money to meet the restoration costs, and while old men and profiteers clucked their tongues and wagged their heads over the problem, St John's remained, in part, a ghostly and smoke-blackened ruin. The clerestory windows all were blinded now, the parapets and stone ledges fallen away in several places. For a moment Simeon found himself distracted by a painful memory. He had been up there, trapped in the roof-space when the fire took hold, and but for the grace of God and a small boy's courage, he would have perished in the flames with all the rest. It was no mystery to him now, for he believed he had been spared because his life had purpose.

They passed the Minster church and entered Eastgate, where new hovels had sprung up like ragged mushrooms almost overnight, hugging the banks of the stinking ditch which ran a parallel course by St Peter's wall on its way to the beck. A group of priests still tended the water-point, sharing St Peter's' fresh supply with those who were in want, and giving comfort to those who flocked to its walls.

Simeon did not relax his vigilance until the group of women and priests was safely over the little bridge, through the enclosure gates and making its way to the modest church beyond. There the guards dispersed and went about their midday duties, for it was near the time of Nones and soon a meal would be on the refectory tables.

When Osric spoke, his voice betrayed relief. 'It is done as you directed, Simeon. We have her safely under our protection.'

'And the boy?'

The infirmarian laughed and shrugged his cowled shoulders. 'Your own rule is that they must never travel conspicuously together. Young Peter will arrive here in his own time and by his own route.' He shook his head and his smile was askew, showing a broken tooth. 'They say he vanished from a room that would have sealed up a rat. That boy of yours has learned to come and go as if by magic.'

'St Peter himself was given the special powers of binding and loosing,' Simeon reminded him. 'Perhaps the good saint's namesake has inherited his gifts.'

'Or else purloined them,' Osric said, feigning disapproval. Then he gave his friend a searching, sidelong glance and asked, 'Are you less troubled now, Simeon?'

He nodded. 'I did not see the figure clearly, nor can I even swear I saw it there at all. Even so, with Peter and Elvira close at hand we are prepared, and if we are in danger . . .'

'If we are?'

'If we are then he will come again and show himself. Until he does, we can but wait and maintain a careful watch against our enemies.'

'Your trust in that apparition astounds me, Simeon. I trust it only for the calamity that follows in its footsteps.'

Now Simeon smiled again. It was the smile of a priest, a man whose faith was just as enduring and as uncertain as the flickering light from a single candle. A thousand wicks could be lit from it and still its own flame would not be diminished. Sometimes it faltered, for it was vulnerable, but in its simplicity it had the power to ignite a forest or else to hold the darkest night at bay with its modest glow.

'He will not fail us,' the blond priest said with quiet conviction. 'Calamity is every man's lot in life, my friend. However we may try to hedge and parry it, misfortune will always trip us in the end. But be assured of this, he will return if we have need of him. He will, for he too must protect the boy.'

Great John began to toll the noontime offices, reminding them of other obligations. Simeon observed the ritual in a quiet corner of his scriptorium where a small stone altar had been set. His clerks and copyists knelt beside him, their voices low and mellow in their devotions. Candlelight sent golden reflections dancing across the silver cross with its tragic figure of the crucified Christ, and agitated the shadows that hung like trembling cobwebs over the altar. They had reached the Angelus, the prayer to commemorate the incarnation, made each day at sunrise, noon and sunset, when the kneeling priest became aware of another's presence in the room. His concentration wavered and his eyes came open, and after that his prayers were scantly uttered.

It was a journey of two crooked miles from the chapel of St Thomas beyond the Keldgate Bar to Simeon's scriptorium. Peter had come alone, with nothing but a wooden cross and his courage to protect him. He had come by a secret and perilous route, following the caverns and streams beneath the town, negotiating the long two miles in the near total darkness of the underground. Now the boy waited discreetly for the office to reach its close, keeping himself concealed from view but knowing that his godfather was aware of his arrival.

The scriptorium of St Peter's was a spacious building made of solid, enduring Yorkshire stone. Its heavy roof timbers were reinforced by an intricate network of long stakes cut from oak and thorn and yew, the whole covered over with plaster and lead to keep bad weather out. Two rows of windows, set very high and securely latched against intruders, let in the maximum amount of daylight required by Simeon and his lesser scribes. There were two elaborate library seats at one end of the room, scribes' desks and tables set before the walls, some sleeping benches and a great stone hearth. Half the room had hanging timbers over it, creating a place of privacy within the roof-space. A single door of metal-strengthened wood gave access, and this was barred from the inside by a heavy wedge of oak housed in iron fittings driven deep into the stone.

There was an old dry well in the very centre of the scriptorium, its mouth half-covered by slabs and cloths to provide extra seating on that section closest to the hearth. Over it was fitted an ancient iron grid whose joints and fastenings had long since rusted into disuse. The sound of running water could still be heard in the chimney of the well but, like so many of Beverley's older streams and brooks, this one had dwindled from gush to trickle over the centuries. It now ran at a distance of two poles from the rim of the well, matching the heights of sixteen men, each standing on another's shoulders', too deep for a simple bucket and rope to reach. That no upsurge of mud had reached this far was the source of much thanksgiving. Had it done so, had it breached the well in that much-fortified building, many precious books and manuscripts would have been destroyed and those inside would surely have been lost.

The office at last concluded, Simeon dispatched his clerks and copyists to the refectory for their midday meal. He dropped the oak log into its metal slots across the door, then strode to the well and spoke into its hollow.

'Come out, boy. Show yourself.'

At once a small hand poked itself between the bars of the metal grid to slip a heavy bolt aside and release a rusting section from its casing. This section, wide enough to receive a man, swung upward with a creak of protesting hinges. Simeon caught it in one hand and reached for the boy with the other, lifted him clear, then dropped the well-guard back into its place.

'God's blessing, Peter,' he said in formal greeting.

'God's blessing, Father,' Peter responded gravely. Then Simeon spread his arms and the boy leaped into them and, scooped up into that strong, familiar embrace, he entwined his skinny arms around Simeon's neck and his legs around his waist.

For long moments the big priest held him there, feeling a

116

quiet joy surge through him as the small body pressed itself to his. Each like embrace filled his heart with a sense of triumph. This was his precious godson, as dear to him as any child of his own loins could ever be. For Peter he had bloodied his sword more times than he cared to number, had stood fearlessly against those who came like Herod's men of old to murder an innocent. He had disobeyed the ruling of his church and openly defied his own archbishop to protect the boy, and he would do as much again, if it were asked of him. He may never understand why he should be singled out for such a task as this, and in his heart he did not need to know: love was enough.

He put Peter away from him now and seated himself on a low stool to regard him with a father's scrutiny. The boy was thin and slight for his ten years, but was blessed with perfect health and a wily agility more valuable to him than mere width and muscle. His face was slender and very pale, the features those of a fledgling aristocrat and the eyes a clear, strong blue beneath his cap of fine blond hair. Elvira called him beautiful, an inappropriate, feminine description for a boy, yet there were times when Simeon looked into that fine-boned face and found no other word with which to name it. Peter *was* beautiful. He was also wise beyond his years and had about him a serenity that belied his tender age, a stillness that might be interpreted as saintly or sinister, according to the colour of the observer's conscience.

'It was a brave thing you did yesterday,' Simeon told him. 'Father Richard is a loyal friend to all of us. You saved his life. God bless you for it, boy.' He looked more closely into the boy's blue eyes and asked, 'How did you know?'

The ghost of a frown played over Peter's brow. 'I came where I was needed,' he said at last.

Simeon nodded. The boy was both intuitive and intelligent. News of the flooding had pricked him into action. To him it was a simple matter.

He hugged him again, then ruffled the soft blond hair. 'Come, boy, you are to eat your meal in the refectory with Osric and Antony the monk. Father Thorald is with them, no doubt with a hundred tales to tell, all fresh from the mouths of sailors and merchants passing through the port.'

Outside the scriptorium he took Peter's hand and called two priests to stand guard at the door, then walked with the boy beside him down the long slope to the refectory building near the southern wall.

Looking to his right, he saw the half-ruined Minster set against the sky above the ancient Eastgate wall. 'One day,' he said in a whisper that was fierce with determination. 'One day our holy church will stand once more like a monument to God's glory.'

'Indeed it will be so,' the boy replied.

'And the shrine of St John will be restored to its rightful place. No man or woman will ever kneel again to bare a needy soul at an altar where no saint is resting.'

'It will be so,' the boy repeated softly, and Simeon felt a now familiar prickling of his scalp in response to the quiet conviction in the words.

They looked at each other closely, the priest and his mysterious godson, and in their exchange was a burden of truth and trust that neither could refuse to carry. For an instant Simeon saw himself as he had been ten years ago, holding a naked newborn in his arms while an unholy tempest ripped the Minster church apart and shattered its great east window into a thousand deadly, flying shards of glass and twisted leads. A simple scribe he had been then, lonely and lame, a priest with but half a faith and few ambitions. Everything had changed for him when Peter came to Beverley.

It will be so, the boy had said, and Simeon knew it would, in God's good time.

CHAPTER FOURTEEN

The bells were ringing to herald the start of prayers for the saint's feast-day procession when Simeon gave the boy into Osric's care. As he turned from the refectory door, he saw Elvira coming from the church. Discretion held him back from greeting her, and instead he walked behind her as she made her way to the scriptorium. The priests on guard stood back to allow her through, and Simeon, silent, followed her. She was standing by the well when he stooped through the doorway, her back turned to him as she unfastened the hated wimple from her hair. Seeing her slender shape and feeling her gentle feminine presence in the place that was his home, he felt his heart shift with its own acceptance. She was his love, his earthly joy and a constant source of comfort. Using both hands, he dropped the heavy bar across the door so that it clattered in its iron brackets. She turned at the sound, her raven hair brushing her elbows with its length and shimmering darkly in the sunlight from the windows. He saw her gaze soften the way it had when first she looked at him a decade past, and her heart was in her eyes. She came to him without a word and he held her close against his chest, gathering her soft, warm body to his own.

'Elvira ...' Her name was drawn from him on a gasp and now, as ever when he held her thus, he experienced the resignation of a drowning man reaching for death and glad of its embrace. The time had long since passed when he would try to stand off from all he felt for her. 'Elvira ...'

'My love ...'

Her voice was husky with emotion. She clung to him, slowly moving her head to leave a trail of kisses across his lowered cheek, her mouth with stealthy passion seeking his. He turned his own head, eager for her taste, and for a moment they were held motionless, their mouths no more than a breath apart. He heard her say his name just once, felt the whisper of it pass between his parted lips, and in that moment Simeon was lost, to God and to himself, as all his soul reached out from him to her.

A rapping at the door divided them, a brief tattoo produced by the striking of a dagger's hilt upon the wood, Osric's signal. Simeon set Elvira from him, keeping her faced cupped in his palms, reluctant to disengage his gaze from hers. His sigh was deep and filled with pain. He was a priest and bound by a solemn vow of chastity that his Church had neither demanded nor required of him. It was a vow of his own making, a bargain struck between himself and God. Elvira was another man's wife, and Simeon had kept her by him all these years to be his comfort and his godson's mother. This love of theirs cut right across the grain of his vocation, and yet he knew no power on earth would ever part them now. They sinned and yet they did not sin in truth, they erred but did not err in fact. Even in its innocence, their love offended every law but God's.

He was slow to release her, and even as he moved towards the door, their outstretched hands still clung one to the other, their fingers straining to maintain the contact.

Osric stepped into the scriptorium bearing a large wooden platter piled high with food and drink. He saw the bleak, unhappy expression on Simeon's face and knew that his arrival was untimely. The woman's cheeks were flushed, her eyes as bright as polished jet, and there was a tell-tale trembling in her hands. Her beauty still had the power to surprise him. It seemed to him that time held fast for her, for she grew more lovely while other women faded. More than this, she bore her chaste, ill-fated love the way a flower bears its bloom, untouched by bitterness or ill-will.

'We thank you, friend, for this,' Simeon said, lending a hand to set the platter down, and Osric knew he was also being thanked for his intrusion. The priest's unspent, unnaturally harnessed passion was in his voice, and a look of sadness mingled with resignation was in his eyes.

Osric glanced from Simeon to Elvira and was offended in his own manhood by the waste. The priest tormented his senses with this woman. He tried his solemn vows to their fragile and uncertain limits and still he denied himself, and her, those pleasures their love demanded for its expression. He kept his vows and by doing so condemned the woman with him to a celibate existence. Osric believed his friend to be a fool; sincere, devout, courageous, but a fool. God in His vast compassion would never hold a good man to the letter of such a well-intentioned vow. And if this priest would only heed a loyal friend's advice, he would gladly tell him: 'Have her and be damned.'

They ate their food with unaccustomed awkwardness, their conversation strained, until a small group of men arrived to join them. Young Peter slipped between their legs to hand Simeon the book he had been given, a lengthy chronicle of St John the Evangelist's life and teachings, set down in Latin by a foreign scholar of high repute.

'From Father Thorald,' the boy said proudly. 'It came on the ship from Athens, carried in a lead-lined box with silver clasps.'

'A fine gift,' Simeon told him. 'Guard it well. The words of scribes and scholars have a value far beyond that of gold to a hungry soul. One volume such as this may lift a poor man from the gutter and make him rich beyond measure.'

'But sir, is it not a sin of pride for a man to reach above the place God gave him at his birth?'

'So the Good Book tells us, and a sin of ingratitude to fall below it,' Simeon said, 'but a man's mind is the life-blood of his soul. He who wastes it starves his soul and is surely guilty of the greater sin.'

'Yes, Father.' Peter's face was grave, his eyes wide and unblinking as he looked up at the man who was his guardian and his mentor. Such men should walk in sunlight all their lives with neither cloud nor shadow to invade their peace of mind. It should be so, but Peter had seen *the other* in the darkness by the North Bar, and he knew the shadow that soon would fall on Simeon.

'Peter? Why such a solemn expression? What troubles you?'

Peter's hand slipped into that of his godfather, small and cool within the larger one. Father Cuthbert believed that all things had their allotted time, all words their proper moment to be spoken. Believing this to be so, Peter said, 'I saw the twins, the brother and sister who came in the night seeking your protection, Father.'

'Simeon nodded. 'The girl is very ill. It is Osric she needs, not I.'

'But it was you they asked for.' The small brow puckered in a thoughtful frown. 'They are the same, except that the brother is taller. But for his height, how would we know one from the other?'

Simeon grinned and squeezed his godson's hand. 'Peter, my boy, we would know them as we know a ewe from a ram. Now, go join your foster mother while I greet my friends.'

As Peter moved away Antony of Flanders nodded a silent greeting to Simeon.

'God bless and keep you, Simeon.'

'And you, my friend. How are the boots?'

'Too large by far, but a gift for which I am grateful, at least until my begging earns me a decent pair of sandals.'

'We thank God those battered old sandals of yours were all we lost of you.'

Antony grinned and rubbed his sun-browned face. It was lean and deeply lined, with a long, straight nose and a narrow beard at the chin. His eyes were of a clear, unremarkable blue and, though often restless and suspicious, they shone with the light of true compassion for his fellow man. This monk was a clever linguist much admired by the many pilgrims who flocked to Beverley. When far from home and wearied by the miles, a foreigner was blessed indeed to find a man who spoke his mother tongue.

Antony's true origins were known to none. Even that he was born in Flanders was speculation given credence by its long currency. Some said he was a one-time criminal struggling now to atone for many evils, some that he was a saint destined for martyrdom, a dangerous heathen frocked as a monk, a wandering pilgrim, a vagrant or a beggar. One story made him a sailor, shipwrecked in some foreign tempest and brought ashore at Beverley after three long years spent floundering through the ocean's wilderness, and when he stepped ashore he was converted. The myths and fabrications surrounding Antony's origins were legion, and Simeon neither believed nor disbelieved a word of them. Better to ask if a man may now be trusted, to honour or dishonour him as he deserves, rather than judge him good or ill according to the bare facts of his pedigree.

'Any sign?' Antony asked, and Simeon hushed him with a warning glance toward Elvira, then shook his head and saw the monk's relief.

'I'm glad. Last night I thought . . .'

'What did you think?'

'I thought perhaps . . .' Antony shook his head as if to shake an unwanted image from his mind. A tall, thin man wearing a hood had passed the end of a street, no more than that. A glimpse was all the monk had seen, and that too uncertain to warrant any alarm. Precautions had been taken to protect the boy and his foster mother, and if no other eyes had seen the figure, and seen it clearly, then it could be argued that it was never there at all.

'Last night you thought?' Simeon prompted.

Antony shook his head again. 'That the floods would increase,' was all he dared to say.

He was momentarily unsettled by the steadiness of Simeon's stare. It was as if the priest had read the lie and now sought out the truth. His discomfort was cast aside as Thorald, who had been hovering at the door watching Elvira, strode forward now to greet his fellow priest. Here was a giant of a man in stature as in fame. He had a full hand's edge on Simeon's own considerable height, and carried such bulk in solid muscle as might be generously divided between two men of average size. His chest was as round and as hard as a cooper's cask, his shoulders huge, and the size of his feet dismayed all but his regular shoemaker. Thorald's was the force behind the swift reopening of the port after the fire. His vigour kept the trade and relief boats passing freely through the town, and his voice and presence drew sailors, merchants, traders and pilgrims to St Nicholas's, the Holme church where he served. Thorald de Holme was as vital to the survival of Beverley as was his thriving port. And to this end he had been blessed with the build, the strength, the bellow and the temperament of the bull.

Now Thorald's laughter boomed like thunder as he flung Simeon against his great chest in a rib-crushing hug of greeting. They had not spoken for several weeks until today's tense meeting at the landing-site, and both had given thanks for this reunion.

'God's blessing, lad,' he said with true affection, then held the young priest from him and grinned into his face. 'God's teeth, you're still as handsome as a saint.' He lowered his voice to a rumble of sound and added: 'And that woman of yours could tempt all the saints from heaven with her beauty. How fares "the vow"?'

'Intact,' Simeon told him sadly. 'Or perhaps it would be more honest to say unbroken.'

The bigger man glowered, his grey eyes sharp as steel in his weathered face. ' "Better to marry than to burn," so said our own St Paul on the subject.'

'Better to burn than to fail God,' Simeon countered.

'God did not ask such a sacrifice of you.'

'No Thorald, I gave it freely. He knows my heart.'

'Aye, and He knows your loins,' Thorald insisted. 'He knows. He made you manly and robust, and if you prove to be no more and no less than He Himself intended, you will still have served Him well enough.'

Simeon smiled. 'My friend, such reasoning is not new to me. I've stood between these twin fires for a decade, not knowing in which I am to be consumed.'

'And so you suffer both in equal measure? Damn it, lad, your logic defeats me.'

'I made a solemn vow,' Simeon answered firmly. He extended his arm and Elvira came forward to place her hand in his. 'Come closer, lady, and greet our dear friend Thorald, come from the Holme church.' And with Elvira set between them, the subject of his chastity was closed.

'What news of the floods?' Antony asked of Thorald. 'Was much damage done?'

The huge priest nodded and brought his eyebrows down in a ferocious frown. 'Reports of twenty lost when the ground split open close to the port, at least a score of homes destroyed and many men and women still unaccounted for. The crypt of my church was damaged when the stones were split apart with the sheer force of the mud flow rushing upward. Part of the burial ground is lost but, God be praised, the church was little affected. As for the port . . .' He spread his massive hands and smiled. 'Our blessed St Nicholas takes good care of sailors and merchants, so there were few losses amongst his devotees.'

'God is merciful, then,' Simeon declared, signing the cross.

Elvira shook her head but held her peace. However much she searched her heart, she could not thank God for those He spared unless she also blamed Him for those He did not spare.

The conversation around the refectory fire grew low and easy in its ebb and flow as those who shared a common cause renewed the ties that bound them so securely in their friendship. Young Peter sat in a corner by the fire, his pale head lowered over the pages of his Latin text. He appeared to be preoccupied, yet all the while he sat apart and kept his eyes fixed firmly on his book, he missed no word of what the men were saying. The boy had a practised ear for fireside talk and whispered conversations, and those to whom he looked for his protection had learned to respect his skills.

Richard of Weel sat beside Elvira on the low wall set around the guarded well. He stroked his beard and watched her as she stared down into the darkness where soft echoes ran through the subterranean tunnels and drifted up the well-shaft like whispering voices.

'God's blessing, Elvira,' he said, and watched the softness of her smile as it played around the corners of her mouth.

'It is good to see you again, friend Richard,' she replied. 'Last week I glimpsed you running with Simeon and you were falling far behind. For shame, you are the younger man.'

'But I lack his stamina,' John admitted. 'All those years ago he swore not to waste the miracle of God's healing even though he is forced to hide it from public view. So many nights of tracing the entire boundary of the town at a steady gallop have made an athlete of him. Our lame scribe of St Peter's is no ordinary man.'

Elvira smiled at this and turned to where the big priest was seated on a stool, his handsome face in profile as he spoke with his friends. As if conscious of her attention he paused to turn his head and look at her, and in the meeting of their gazes much was conveyed that Richard could not interpret. Her dark eyes shone as she turned back to him and softly repeated: 'No Richard, Simeon is no ordinary man.'

Elvira lived a lonely and unsettled life, staying first in one safe house and then another, with every home a temporary place and each new friendship open to suspicion. Her daily life followed the same rigid pattern as that of her companions, except that she could never be one of them. She wore their clothes and ate their food and kept their holy offices. She observed the silences and obediences and yet, a decade on, she found herself no closer to Simeon's all-seeing, all-knowing God than ever the common ditcher's wife had been. She did not pray, for prayer to her was nothing more than a repetition of words. Nor did she place her trust in anything divine, for she was too much in the natural world

126

for that. The things in which Elvira believed were simple. She knew of mindless hatred and petty spite, of the good and evil in men's souls, of unwavering trust, cruel indifference and true uncomplicated love. Human things she knew about, and feared or cherished them according to her human capabilities, but all the rest was mystery to her.

'Are you content, Elvira?' Richard inquired, feeling her loneliness as a tangible thing.

She glanced again at Simeon and the darkness of her eyes took on a softer glow. 'I am content,' she said, nodding her head. 'Here, beneath this roof, I am content.'

As Simeon watched the fire in the grate he felt Elvira's hand rest on his shoulder and reached up to cover it gently with his own. For a while he was at peace, sharing this quiet time with those he loved and trusted. There was comfort in the simple fare they shared, safety in the bar across the door, close companionship in their conversation. Fear had no place at this friendly hearth. No other had spoken out about what he might or might not have seen, so that Simeon now convinced himself that a play of light and shadow, of sunlight on trees, was all he had detected in the woodland.

CHAPTER FIFTEEN

St Matthew's Feast Day brought the town alive with celebrations. The market-places swelled to overflowing, while every corner, street and alleyway became a site where men could buy and sell and haggle over all manner of merchandise. Here were stalls crammed high with pies and puddings, cakes and spicy offal sausages. Every inch of space held a table laden with tools and clothes and shoes, or frames bedecked with animal skins and leathers, or poles hung with poultry and wild birds or bending under the weight of dogs and cats and rabbits to be skinned and eaten. Where better stalls could not be had, many traders spread sheets of cloth upon the ground on which to display their wares, while others carried their goods about their person in sacks and slings. Salts and spices, eggs, honey and lard were set out beside linens and kitchen utensils. Pigs were traded alongside corn and oatmeal, blood puddings with wool, fruit and vegetables with herbal cures.

Men carried pigs and sheep across their shoulders, women bore baskets of vegetables and bread, and even small children offered bundles of faggots, herbs and wild flowers for sale. The bells of every church were ringing out in honour of the saint, and everywhere the clamour grew to such a height that those who would converse with one another were forced to do so at the fullest exertion of their lungs.

In the corn market, the mud that had swamped the archbishop's house and crushed a priest to death was now a saleable commodity. Chopped up in pieces small enough to carry, it went for tokens or for building matter, and those who bought it hoped to find some treasure trapped inside.

One man in a monk's robe carried a sack of carved and coloured animal bones, some slung around his neck on leather thongs and all declared to be relics from the body or the birthplace of a saint. He plied the crowds with great enthusiasm, grabbing at likely passers-by and thrusting his dubious bones and teeth upon them.

'See, here's a phial of ash from the ruin of Sodom, a piece of bone from the thigh of John the Baptist, a sliver of wood from the holy cross, a tooth hacked from St Luke's own jaw, a lock of hair from the head of our Lord Jesus Christ.' The peasants were gullible and trade was good, and any scrap of chicken or cow bone became, for the day, as sacred as the saint it represented.

The noon procession brought even greater numbers of people flocking into the streets, yesterday's tragedies forgotten in the rush to see, and perhaps to touch, the effigy or the hangings of the saint. Musicians and jugglers, harpers and jesters pranced among the priests, while cut-purses and beggars sought to profit where the press of bodies was thickest. The effigy was carried from the Minster church to each of the five town gates in turn, beginning at the South Bar, between St Peter's enclosure and the port. While it made its slow, laborious journey, the town made merry and the floodings were forgotten.

A man declaring himself to be the agent of Sir Guy de Burton waited inside the gates of St Peter's enclosure while a priest was dispatched to the infirmary on his behalf. He had four riders with him. His manners were impeccable, though he refused to leave the premises until he had spoken to Father Simeon in person. He was impressed when he saw the big

129

priest coming forward with the messenger trotting dutifully at his heels. This Simeon was more than worthy of his reputation, and were it not for that lame left foot dragging awkwardly behind the other in a cripple's gait, he might have had half the maids in Beverley sighing after him.

Simeon surveyed his visitor and saw a fair, presentable young man who sat his mount with the arrogance of youth and the confidence of good breeding in equal measure. He had light blue eyes under lashes that were as straight as the bristles of a brush and palest blond in colour, though his hair was tightly curled and neither brown nor blond but a shade between the two. That thick, strong hair betrayed his Celtic blood, as did the stocky build and freckled skin. His cloak was splendid and his boots were laced with silver buckles, and his smile was quick and warm as he leaned down with his hand extended in a friendly gesture.

'Fergus de Burton,' he said, and his eyes were a-twinkle as he spoke. 'I know you well by reputation, sir. It is an honour to meet with you at last.'

'You are welcome here,' Simeon answered cautiously. He saw a vivid smile that revealed good teeth as it set engaging dimples playing in its owner's cheeks. With it came fine temple-lines to accentuate the laughing eyes, and a gaze that seemed both open and sincere. The young man's manner could not be faulted, though Simeon's instincts told him otherwise. Such a wealth of charm could disarm a man in seconds, and a man so disarmed by a stranger was vulnerable to treachery.

'I come in search of the archbishop's clerk so that I and my guards may escort him safely back to his master in York. By your leave sir, I would speak with him.'

'I know of no clerk of York's,' Simeon replied. 'As you were informed by our keepers when you first arrived, such a man has not been here in many months.'

'Cyrus de Figham's witnesses claim otherwise.'

The smile remained untouched, the manner easy, and for these facts alone the priest was suddenly distrustful of his visitor.

'Then his witnesses are in error – or they lie. No clerk from York was here.'

'Certain men insist they saw him come inside. Perhaps some other here can shed some light on this mystery? If you would be good enough to inquire on my behalf, so that when the archbishop asks my opinion ...'

Simeon bowed his agreement. He did not miss the implication here, that it was in his own interests to appease this man. He would grant de Burton's request but he would keep this smiling stranger in his sight. He called to a group of priests and their assistants and ordered them to inquire for the clerk in every building within St Peter's enclosure. Then he called for wine and bade his uninvited guest take ease on the stone bench set by the infirmary door. They spoke together in friendly tones, but cautiously, before the young man observed: 'You people of Beverley leave your looters hanging to rot as a deterrent to others who might follow their example.'

'It is the way of things,' Simeon said.

'And so the whole town is plagued by hungry crows.'

'That, too, is the way of things.'

'And now the gulls are flying in from the coast for easier fishing here in Beverley.'

'Where there is death the scavengers will feed.'

'Ah yes, the way of things.' The young man grinned and rested his head against the wall on which he leaned, turning his face into the sun's hot glare. 'Some men are so blinded by it that too much of life becomes acceptable to them. Better to be a soldier who keeps a good edge on his blade and knows the shape and number of his enemies, or a lord with a fat purse and a loyal guard upon his wall. Would you not agree with that, Father Simeon?'

The priest looked fully into his visitor's face and saw that the eyes were open like slits against the brightness of the sky. 'We are shaved of our hair, sir, not of our faculties.'

'Well countered, Father,' Fergus de Burton laughed. 'They warned me you were an expert in debate.'

'They?'

'Your reputation runs ahead of you, Father Simeon. I have long desired to engage you in conversation, or even have you join my hunt to test my skills against your own. They say you are also an expert with the sword,' here he glanced conspicuously at Simeon's feet before adding, 'despite your lameness.'

'They say much,' Simeon shrugged.

'They do indeed.'

The two were still sitting together on the stone bench when the priests returned with shaking heads and nothing to report on the matter of the missing clerk.

Fergus de Burton drained his cup and bowed respectfully to his host before climbing back into his decorated saddle and taking up the reins.

'I thank you, Father Simeon, for your forbearance,' he said, his cheeks still dimpled and his eyes creased in a smile. 'Please forgive this intrusion and remember that others will swear the clerk was here.'

'Are you assured that he was not?'

'I am indeed,' de Burton nodded, eyes sparkling. 'However many might say otherwise. God's blessing, Father Simeon. I will ride for York and hope to find him there.'

'God speed your journey,' Simeon said.

The gates swung open and the men rode out with the laughing Fergus at their head, leaving Simeon staring after them through narrowed eyes. This meeting had served no purpose but to warn him that de Figham had some plan of sorts against him. He was suspicious of the young man's motives, and what concerned him most was de Burton's remarkably engaging manner. No man should need to cultivate such a veneer of innocence unless what lay behind it was at fault.

'A fine young man,' the priest beside him said.

'And persistent,' Simeon answered.

'Perhaps, due to the nature of his business, yet he lacked the sharp teeth by which his family is known. I took to him on sight. What a pity we were unable to oblige him.'

Simeon scowled at this effortless disarming of a man. 'I

132

believe we obliged him well enough,' was his grim reply, as he walked away, perplexed.

The festivities in Beverley lasted well into the evening, and only when the sun was going down did the revelry begin to reach its peak. By then half the town was in its cups, and of all those who had been employed to act as fire-wardens for the day, not one remained at his post when the cover fire was called. It was left to priests and those citizens who feared for the safety of their properties to go about ensuring that fireplates were set in place or shovels of dirt thrown over cooking fires.

It was the custom for teachers of renown to settle, with episcopal licence and under the protection of the church, in towns to which decent numbers of students might be attracted. Beverley, with its long-established grammar school and illustrious collegiate church, was no exception. On feast days the streets were filled with groups of students who, with no adequate supervision and no family ties to hold them in restraint, roamed from place to place in search of amusement. They plagued the local girls with their licentious advances, stole from the market stalls, cut swine from their tethers and drove them squealing into crowds to be taken by any hands swift enough to grab them. These young men roamed in packs and drank their ale without temperance and, where they met with bands of local youths, much rowdiness and drawing of blood occurred.

In York the festivities were on a much grander scale. The noon procession took almost three hours to wind its way through the crooked, congested streets with its burden of saintly effigies and banners. There were twenty-two carts in all, some hung with colourful canopies or altar curtains, others bedecked with autumn greenery, many carrying seated dignitaries of the church. The cart that bore the relics of St Matthew and travelled ahead of all the rest also bore His Grace the archbishop, Geoffrey Plantagenet. Garbed in his finest robes and bishop's cap, bearing his crook in one hand

and his gold orb in the other and flanked by no fewer than twenty men-at-arms, a less obliging champion of St Matthew's Feast could not have been found in all of Christendom. He was here under sufferance, on the advice of his counsellors, making a public demonstration of his good intent. Geoffrey was the bastard son of King Henry Plantagenet, a man of secular tastes holding an office for which he had no inclination. His refusal to be ordained into the priesthood was a matter of much contention in the Church. This show was designed to win over the people, and every laborious turn of the wheels was a grave assault upon his temper.

'My God, is there no end to this banality?' he complained.

'Another half-mile, perhaps less,' his deacon said.

Just then the men-at-arms were halted by a solid mass of traders, pilgrims and merrymakers with their sundry hand-carts and barrows. The mounted men drew back in a tight mesh about the archbishop's cart, as much from confusion as for the protection of their lord. The trundling cart ground to a halt as the horses drawing it forward began to rear and whinny, agitated by the noisy gaggle of people and animals barring their way.

'Protect the holy relics!' Geoffrey Plantagenet yelled to the priests and guards around him. 'Look to your archbishop and your saint! Lower the drapes!' His bishop's orb and crook fell to the floor of the cart as he flung off his jewelled cloak and reached for the short sword hanging at his girdle. 'Move, damn you, *move*! You'll burn in hell for all eternity if your archbishop comes to harm.'

Men rushed to do his bidding as the cart was surrounded. Voices screamed above the din for blessings. Hands reached out to touch the cart and the sheer weight of numbers drove the horses of the men-at-arms back against the wooden structure so that it rocked precariously on its iron-clad wheels. With the heavy tapestries lowered and the leather curtains tightly strung together, the archbishop set himself behind his priestly protectors with the great chair at his back and his sword held in a double-handed grip across his body. He feared a trap. His cart was halted in a crowded, narrow street with the rabble up ahead and the lumbering procession strung out in its entirety behind. High buildings enclosed him on either side, and from any window a bowman or a spearman might even now have him squarely in his sights. This archbishop of York was not to be cut down like Thomas à Becket of Canterbury, butchered by jealous enemies and a king with a careless tongue. He, too, had his enemies, not least his brother the king, and he had learned that yesterday's friends and allies were today's obstructions and tomorrow's foes.

A large stone hit the upper framework of the cart, bounced on to the canopy and caused the fabric to sag beneath its weight. Other missiles followed after it, littering the canopy with sticks and stones, vegetables and bits of broken crockery.

Geoffrey bellowed at the top of his lungs for his drivers to whip the horses and strike at the peasants with swords, if they must, in order to get the cart's wheels back in motion. His voice had reached a shrieking pitch and his face had coloured up. 'Get me home to my palace at once! Am I to die like a cur in this stinking market-place? Move! Move! I am archbishop here. My kith and kin are kings of England. I will not be held in uncertainty by this rabble!'

At the rear of the cart, divided from the archbishop's throne by religious hangings and the painted plaster images of saints, a man spoke softly to his travelling companion.

'He will bleed like any other when his time comes.'

'He will, despite his doubtful pedigree. As God is my judge, I would be happier sharing kinship with wolves than with these perfidious Plantagenets.'

'Henry his father was a worthy monarch,' the first one said, defensive of the old king.

'Worthy enough to have a bishop slain at his own altar,' his companion countered, for he, like so many, revered the murdered Becket.

'Had he not done so, Heaven would now be one saint short. The crafty Becket overreached himself and died for his error, but he owes his sainthood to his murderers.'

These two who spoke in hushed tones were a pair of

canons sharing their archbishop's cart. They were here to serve him and to do his bidding, and they hated him as only a pious man can hate an ungodly overlord.

The cart lurched forward, canopy swaying, accompanied by the sound of blade against wood, stick against bone and flesh against flesh as the horses forced a pathway through a crush of human bodies. The sudden movement caused the archbishop's orb to be dislodged from the place where it had been cast down. It rolled across the floor of the cart, shaping a winding course until it reached the spot where Geoffrey stood braced against the cart's supports. One crossbar of its jewelled cross held it balanced there with the golden orb turning in circles over the wood. When Geoffrey kicked it angrily aside it was retrieved by the deacon, who gathered it into the folds of his robes and muttered a prayer over it.

'Keep moving!' Geoffrey bellowed like the soldier he was at heart. 'To the palace! Make haste! Make haste!'

The crowds were scattered and stalls were overturned as the cart took speed with twenty furious men-at-arms swinging their swords like scythes to clear the way. Those townsfolk who were left outraged or injured in its wake vented their spleen upon the unguarded carts behind, and on that holy Feast Day of St Matthew the streets of York became a battlefield.

CHAPTER SIXTEEN

Geoffrey's mood was little short of murderous. He paced the palace hall from end to end and back again, one moment ranting and raving, the next morose. In a corner of the room his clerks were gathered together in a nervous huddle, not knowing which of them would be singled out to take the brunt of their archbishop's disfavour. He blamed his deacon and his church advisers. He blamed his carters, priests and his men-at-arms. He blamed his canons and his counsellors, for he knew his enemies would make much of this disastrous episode.

Now that the grand parade had limped its battered way into the palace courtyard, some assessment of the damage could be made. Several men had died, two priests among them, and many more had been injured in the fray. A number of carts had been overturned and stripped of everything they carried. Many animals had been so badly wounded with picks and knives that it was considered merciful to destroy them. Four excellent horses from the palace stables had been cut from their traces and ridden off by thieves, and although Geoffrey sent his armed guards back to the streets once he was safely inside his palace, not a single cart in the procession reached its destination intact. Two canons who tried to protect the holy banners were dragged into the crowd and robbed of every stitch of clothing they were wearing. One reached the palace an hour later, beaten, dazed and naked. The other had not been seen since he was taken.

'Someone will pay for this,' Geoffrey insisted. He halted in his pacing from time to time, slapped one fist into his palm and bellowed: 'God's teeth, someone *will* be made to pay for this.'

It was suggested that troublemakers had been employed to incite the crowds to riot, or that Jews had plotted against him in the way that Jews must always, by their very nature, conspire against their Christian neighbours, or that certain men of high renown had used the church parade to bring their lord archbishop into disrepute.

'Surely a conspiracy, Your Grace,' one man presumed. This suggestion bedevilled his peace of mind, for he was not yet fully consecrated in his archbishopric, and until he was, his fortunes could be altered. Hubert Walter had wanted York for himself and made complaints to the pope when King Richard elected Geoffrey in his stead. Hugh du Puiset of Durham, a powerful figure in England's northern lands, had wanted it for his nephew, the simpering Bourchard. He, too, had appealed to Rome on the grounds of Geoffrey's illegitimacy and his refusal to be ordained, and both believed their exclusion from the election rendered Geoffrey's archbishopric invalid. While King Richard looked to his crusades and harboured an unmanly regard for the wishes of his mother, Queen Eleanor, and while Prince John was so desirous of England's crown, their bastard brother grabbed what power he could at any cost and knew himself to be vulnerable. Powerful men would hope to make a pawn of him, but Geoffrey Plantagenet, son of a much-loved king, half-brother to the present monarch and burning with ambitions of his own, would play the hapless pawn in no man's game.

'A conspiracy,' he said aloud as he flung his cloak aside and called for wine. 'My enemies will say I went out to meet my flock and it turned on me with sticks and stones and curses. They will say the people hate me. They will argue that

I cannot lead my flock and so am not deserving of consecration as York's rightful archbishop. They will declare me unfit. *Unfit*!' He stopped his pacing to glare at a face he did not recognise. 'Who is this man?'

Before his deacon could reply, the man in question bowed with a courtly flourish, then stepped forward and dropped to one knee to touch the ring of his archbishop against his lips. This pleased the Plantagenet. Surrounded as he was by fawning churchmen who idolised the holy apparel while despising the man who wore it, he welcomed a show of genuine courtesy. He looked hard and long at the fine young man of quality who knelt before him.

'Rise up and state your business,' he commanded.

'I am Fergus de Burton, Your Grace. I come direct from Beverley.'

The archbishop's eyes grew narrow with suspicion. 'From Beverley?'

'My father Hugh and his brothers, Guy and Stephen, own much property in the area. They are most diligent on your behalf, sire, and have set me up as agent in the keeping of peace there.'

Here Geoffrey smiled. 'Young man, I know your family well by reputation and it occurs to me that if any man of the de Burton clan works diligently at any task, it is on his own behalf, not his archbishop's'.

The young man grinned and bowed his head. 'Your Grace is no less wise than I had hoped.' He leaned forward a little, lowered his voice and added: 'I did not ask my family's leave to come here, sire, and if I am in error by so doing I will accept any rebuke for my actions Your Grace may feel inclined to offer.'

The words were so neatly and humbly spoken that Geoffrey was impressed. 'What matter brings you here on a feast day, when the roads are more perilous than usual, and without your father's leave?'

'A personal matter, Your Grace.' De Burton glanced about him and seemed reluctant to speak while others were within hearing. 'I was to meet Harold, your clerk, in Beverley and provide him with safe escort back to York.'

Geoffrey Plantagenet raised his hand for silence. 'My clerk was in Beverley?'

'Yes, sire. He went there yesterday at first light.'

'For what purpose?'

The young man spread his hands. 'I know only what others say, that he met with certain canons there, de Morthlund, de Figham and de Beverley.'

Geoffrey was alarmed now. He called his deacon to his side and, with their heads together, they shared a brief exchange of whispered words. Then Geoffrey bade Fergus follow him to a window recess across the hall where cushions were set for those who wished to linger over the view of the gardens below.

'My clerk left York not two hours after Father Simeon and Father Wulfric were in the town. He has not been seen since then. What business did they have together that could not be settled here in York, so saving the clerk a journey of thirty miles twice over?'

'Your Grace, I understood that as your personal clerk he travelled to Beverley at your own behest.'

'At no behest of mine,' Geoffrey retorted.

'Then I am in error, Your Grace, and beg your pardon.'

'What others did he meet there? Who else has employed the services of my personal clerk, and for what purpose, while my back was turned?'

Fergus de Burton chose his words with care. 'I believe Wulfric de Morthlund had need of him.'

'That mountain of pig's fat has his own clerks by the score.'

'I have no proof of this, sire. Who knows what servants will invent in the hope of pleasing the one who holds the purse? I was seeking only to place myself at the clerk's disposal for his journey home. If I had guessed that he was ... that all was not as I was led to believe ...'

Fergus sighed and spread his hands again and knew he had the Plantagenet convinced. This man suspected a plot in every corner, and Cyrus de Figham had done well to play upon the weakness. Whatever business Wulfric and Simeon may have had in York was made ambiguous by their connection with that missing clerk.

'I like it not,' Geoffrey muttered, stroking his chin where once a beard had grown. 'Such double-dealing smacks of treachery. I like it not.'

'Your Grace, I will take no credit for drawing this matter to your attention, since my intentions were more self-serving than noble.'

'Oh?'

'Forgive my honesty, sire. I will not deny that I feared your anger if the clerk made complaint to you against me. I offered my services as his protector and failed to meet his needs. It was remiss of me, though I swear I have searched for him in every place he spoke of visiting. I even insisted that Simeon search his compound.'

'And did he oblige you?'

'Indeed he did, sire. He sent his priests and clerks to inquire in every building, since I was informed your clerk had entered there.'

'Informed by whom?'

Fergus held the archbishop's gaze and chose to speak the truth. 'By Cyrus de Figham.'

'I see. Plot, counter-plot and sub-plot. How well do you know this Simeon?'

'Not well, sire, though I am familiar with his reputation and I was keen to see for myself if he was truly lame.'

Here Geoffrey laughed wryly. 'Such unseemly hysteria followed Beverley's tempest that the only miracle lay in the fact that its after-shock was not felt in Rome itself. Roger du Pont L'Eveque, who left me a troublesome legacy with his rash promises and unwise gifts of high positions within the Church, soon proved to his satisfaction that the so-called healing was a sham.'

Fergus cleared his throat delicately. 'If you will once again forgive my bluntness, sire, your predecessor's hasty inquisition proved only that a man may limp convincingly when he finds it politic to do as much.'

Geoffrey Plantagenet looked sternly at his young visitor for a moment before his rugged features softened in a grin. 'Your wit is as swift and ready as your smile, my friend. I like you well enough, Fergus de Burton, and I believe your presence here is to my own advantage. What say you? Was this clerk plotting against his own archbishop?'

'Sire, I would have struck him down where he stood, had I suspected it was so.'

'Why else would he sneak away to Beverley without my consent, bent on visiting men who had been under his very roof not hours earlier? And where is he now, this loyal clerk of mine?'

'Sire, I cannot say. Perhaps he was attacked along the way. Perhaps some ill befell him at the hands of those he served against your interests.'

'And perhaps he took a purse or two from those scheming canons of Beverley and rode off in a new direction?'

'I cannot say. I took him for a loyal man.'

'Then why was he in Beverley at all?'

Once again Fergus turned his head as if afraid of being overheard. 'My lord archbishop, if one clerk was at fault, perhaps these others ... I do freely confess I fear for my own safety. Cyrus de Figham and Wulfric de Morthlund are canons of no little power in Beverley, and Simeon's temperament I cannot judge. If any one of them should suspect my part in bringing this plot to your attention—'

'Plot?' Geoffrey started visibly. 'Then you believe they *do* make plots against me?'

'Your Grace, I know only what words have passed between us here, and it seems your clerk was not an honest man. There is a boiling cauldron of high ambition in Beverley, with secrecy and collusion behind every door. If you and I could speak together privately...'

'Of course. It shall be done at once,' Geoffrey declared, and Fergus knew then that he had the archbishop eating out of his hand. 'Come lad, you will sup with me in my private chamber and tell me all you know of this conspiracy.'

The clerks left hovering outside the door of Geoffrey's

142

chamber pressed close to overhear the talk inside. De Burton spoke of floods of mud and many dead, of bribery and spies within the palace, and of a priest, a canon elect who seemed bent on claiming sainthood for himself.

An hour passed before Geoffrey reappeared. He roared instructions to his deacon, a soldier again beneath his ecclesiastical robes. 'Bring me the money-lender, Aaron.'

The deacon was astounded. 'Your Grace, a *Jew*? Brought here to the archbishop's palace? On a *saint's day*?'

'To the gatehouse, then. Have him brought at once to the gatehouse,' Geoffrey conceded.

'But this is Saturday, Your Grace. It is their holy sabbath, when no business may be transacted and no agreements entered into.'

'How strange that you did not remember such an important detail when you tried to convince me that Jews were responsible for that fiasco in the streets,' commented Geoffrey with a caustic edge to his voice.

'Your Grace?'

'No Jew would allow himself to pass within a mile of that holy procession on his sabbath day, let alone incite a crowd to do it violence.'

'He might have bribed others, Your Grace,' the deacon persisted.

'And any man here might well have done the same. Have him brought to my gatehouse.'

'Your Grace, I beg you to reconsider. This Aaron is a *Jew*! The chapter will be outraged.'

'Fetch him!'

'I doubt he will agree to come.'

Wearied by this exchange, Geoffrey thrust his face so close to that of his deacon that he fancied he could taste the fear upon the other's breath. 'Send for the Jew,' he snarled. 'I will meet him in half an hour. And if this Aaron declines to appear when His Grace the archbishop of York, son of Henry Plantagenet and brother to England's king, demands it, *you* will stand accountable in his stead.'

The deacon scuttled out, calling two clerks to follow him,

and as he went he struggled as much with his conscience as with his anger. He could not condescend to present himself in person at the house of any Jew, for that would strike too hard at the core of his Christian beliefs, yet if he sent his clerks instead, and if this Aaron refused to receive them, it would incur the wrath of his archbishop. He chose the middle way. His clerks would go ahead while he remained at a discreet distance, ready to confirm the summons if he must. This was a scandalous and humiliating errand on which to send a servant of the Church. The bishop of Durham would hear of it, and Hubert Walter, too, and if they felt, as this deacon did, that Geoffrey Plantagenet abused his holy office, then word of this outrage would fly to Rome and to his brother, King Richard.

The Jew came like a prince into the cobbled yard which led to the rear door of the palace gatehouse. Garbed all in black, he strode so proudly through the gates that those with their faces pressed to the windows around the courtyard crossed themselves and spoke out prayers against him. A group of priests, hands clasped around their hanging crucifixes, joined forces in reciting the cursing psalm: 'When he shall be judged let him be condemned, and let his every prayer become sin ...'

Aaron the Jew was tall and angular and conspicuous in appearance. He carried his head so high and proud that his hooded black eyes seemed to view the world and its inhabitants with disdain. His nose was over-long, his cheekbones high, and the colour of his skin alone was enough to mark him out as a foreigner. He wore a long robe loosely girdled with a silken cord, and over this a cloak of strange design. A six-pointed star, the ancient symbol of King David and feared by many as a sign of magic, hung on his chest from a metal chain pinned to the shoulders of his undergarment. He came bareheaded, his hair a tangle of tight black coils on his shoulders. Men watched him with their middle fingers hooked to repel all evil, appalled to have this heretic within their walls, and that he despised them in return they had no doubt. Good Christian men had killed his father and many more were now in Aaron's debt.

Between the archbishop and the Jew few words were wasted and few niceties observed.

'As archbishop I demand to know what business you had with Simeon de Beverley, a canon elect under the holy patronage of York.'

'I am a money-lender,' the Jew replied. 'He came to beg a loan for the rebuilding of his Minster.'

'How big a loan?'

'The full cost of the restoration will be in excess of three thousand pounds. His canons are unable, or unwilling, to raise so princely a sum unaided.'

'*Three thousand pounds!*' Geoffrey exclaimed. 'With half that figure added on for your interest. What hope does this canon have of ever honouring such a debt?'

'With the help of benefactors,' the Jew replied. His voice was rich and deep, his intonation slow and very precise. His hands seemed oddly elongated and moved expressively as he spoke. They were the colour of earth and yet as pale as sand on their undersides, flat-palmed and deeply etched with lines and creases. 'He hopes that, if a bargain can be struck, many prominent men, yourself included, will be willing to join forces to repay the debt and restore the Minster to its former glory. For a fraction of the cost, their names will be remembered in the Minster's annals and prayers for their generosity offered up for centuries to come. And if his architectural dreams come to fruition, men everywhere will praise the benefactors for their foresight.'

'And Beverley will prosper,' Geoffrey said thoughtfully.

'Indeed, we estimate that its revenues to York will more than double as its fame is spread. A worthy plan, it seems to me, by a man who seeks no personal distinction in the matter.'

'Except, perhaps, a sainthood.'

Aaron's hands moved together, then apart, the fingers following each other as if to mimic the delicate flutterings of a peacock's tail feathers. 'I saw no ulterior motive in Simeon.

I saw only that it was a worthy plan.'

'A worthy plan indeed, if it be so.' Geoffrey stroked his beardless chin and recalled his meeting with the blue-eyed priest. He had taken to Simeon from the start. That mixture of pride and humility was an attractive combination. He had seemed honest in his petition and now the Jew's words confirmed that honesty, but Fergus de Burton, harbouring no ill-intent, had cast a shadow over those first impressions.

'What inducement did he offer?'

'A metal chalice,' Aaron replied without hesitation.

Geoffrey sat forward in his chair. Perhaps that priest was not so honest after all, if he could offer altar cups as bribes to money-lenders. 'A chalice you say? A holy vessel?'

'Not holy to any man of the Christian faith.'

'What then?'

'A chalice from my country, from Ethiopia. It is a portion of the legendary treasure of our one-time king, Tirkahah. It was stolen many centuries ago from the holy vessel-house, and it has been sighted in many lands since then.'

'So how came this Simeon by such a relic?'

'It was found in Egypt and brought here by the Flanders monk, Antony. It is of neither interest nor value to any but my own kind.'

'Does it have jewels?'

'Once, yes, but it has suffered much since it was stolen. However, its archaic prayers and invocations are intact.'

'Prayers and invocations?' Geoffrey growled.

'In my own tongue, sire, harmless things that hold no threat to Christians.' That the chalice was of solid gold and bore the fabulous Ethiopian Topaz and a host of priceless opals, the Jew declined to mention.

'He offered me a set of illuminated manuscripts edged with gold,' Geoffrey said at last. 'My hands are tied until I am consecrated in my office, but I am sorely tempted. I would give much to acquire them for my own church.'

'And at a mere fraction of their value,' Aaron said, and this time dared to smile. 'By offering each what pleases most, this Simeon de Beverley does not mean to waste the gifts he has.'

146

'Will you lend the money?'

'Perhaps. Will you help repay it, if I do?'

'Perhaps,' Geoffrey Plantagenet replied.

Outside a man was waiting in the hall, a man with a handsome face and a swift, almost angelic smile. He nodded to the Jew, too fascinated by this dark stranger to turn his face away. He had never seen a Jew close to before and was intrigued as much by the contours of his face and the liquid blackness of his eyes as by the nut-brown colour of his skin.

'Good day to you, sir,' Aaron said, judging this man to be in some way involved in this affair. That he had been listening at the door Aaron had no doubt, and his response to the greeting confirmed the fact.

'Good day, Master Aaron. I have heard much of your father, that other Aaron who fell in the riots. He was a famous man of no little standing here in York.'

'My father was a much-loved man, for a Jew,' Aaron replied.

'Are you a priest?'

'I am a Jew, called rabbi or teacher.'

'My compliments on your excellent use of our language.'

'You flatter me, sir. My English is not half so good as my Latin or my Greek,' the Jew replied. 'Nor as flawless as my Hebrew or my Arabic.'

Fergus roared with laughter, then bowed with an elegant flourish. 'Master Aaron, both your talents and your modesty leave me humbled.'

They bowed to each other, both amused and seemingly at their ease.

'You are from Beverley, I believe?'

'Indirectly. I am Fergus de Burton. My family seat is at Burton, close to Beverley.'

'Then perhaps you will be so kind as to carry my greetings to a canon there, one Simeon de Beverley of St Peter's?'

'It will be my pleasure to do so,' Fergus said with another bow and a twinkle in his eye. 'Good day to you, Master Aaron. I hope we meet again.'

'I am sure we will. Good day, sir.'

147

As he left the building Aaron felt many eyes upon him. He was well satisfied that Geoffrey Plantagenet was appeased, and that the vanity of Fergus de Burton would encourage him to convey the message to Simeon on his return to Beverley. When he received it, Simeon would know that trouble was afoot, and would recognise the face of the man who spoke against him to his lord archbishop.

That interview between the money-lender and the arch-bishop, conducted on consecrated ground and following as it did in the wake of a riot, triggered a spate of ill-feeling against the Jews. Aaron left the palace by the narrow Judas door set into one of the gates, and as he turned to walk away a bucket of kitchen slops was tipped from an upper window. The mess struck him on one shoulder, staining his cloak from neck to hem and soaking his hair with oily, stinking liquid. On reaching his house he discovered that the homes of several prominent Jews in the city had been robbed and set alight. Many others had their windows broken or their shutters daubed with paint. He did not think for one moment that Geoffrey Plantagenet would be in any way disturbed by these events. On the contrary, it would salve his wounded self-esteem to have it put about that York's arch-bishop had fallen victim to the Jews, rendering these swift 'reprisals' justified.

Within his palace, Geoffrey Plantagenet instructed a servant to pour more wine into the cup of Fergus de Burton. The young man had accepted his archbishop's offer to feast with him that evening and to join his falconer's party at first light. This man was tired of whimpering priests, fawning servants and the mind-killing routine of ecclesiastical life. He was a man of action, a professional soldier trapped in an archbishop's gown. For a while, at least, he would enjoy the company of a more suitable companion, and damn the priests and canons who would try to persuade him other-wise.

'I have a mind to take this Simeon to task,' he confided to his visitor. 'My enemies need a scapegoat on which to focus their indignation if I am ever to know a moment's peace

148

from their endless bickering and complaints of me.'

'It is your right, indeed your duty, Your Grace, to examine any man who sets himself up as a living saint. Rome will not take kindly to his claims, nor to any reluctance on your part to put a stop to his blasphemous assertions.'

'Hearsay,' Geoffrey declared. 'I cannot be seen to act against a canon on nothing more than hearsay. No charges have been brought against him, and without complaint I can do nothing.'

'He has a bitter enemy amongst Beverley's canons,' Fergus said. 'A man with powerful friends. A man who will bend many others to his will in any case that could be brought against Simeon de Beverley.'

'Cyrus de Figham.'

'The same. He bears a long-standing grudge against Simeon de Beverley. They say that even now his clerks are taking written statements from those who worked with Simeon while the floods were at their height. This man would prove a rigorous ally, Your Grace. His bitterness goes deep.'

'And you?' the archbishop demanded. 'How deeply does your own grudge reach?'

Fergus laughed in genuine amusement. 'I have no grudge, sire. Indeed, I even like the man, if first impressions are to be trusted any more than reputations.'

'Why should I trust what you say?'

'Because you need me, sire. I have no axe to grind, no friend to defend, no enemy to blind me to good reason, no rancour to play upon my better judgement. I am merely, as you can see, a useful servant waiting to be used.'

Geoffrey leaned forward in his seat to grasp the young man by the shoulder in a bruising grip. His eyes were keen and small in a face made florid by too much wine. 'Speak the truth to your archbishop, Fergus de Burton,' he said in a threatening tone. 'What do you hope to gain by striking up a friendship with me?'

'The truth, Your Grace?'

'I insist upon it.'

149

The young man hesitated and dropped his gaze, then looked the Plantagenet bravely in the face and said: 'I fear you will not like it, sire.'

'I will like a lie the less, you can rely on that.'

'The truth, then,' Fergus conceded with a sigh. 'Your Grace, I am a younger son with no inheritance to call my own. The time has come for me to consider more than the pursuit of pleasure and the raising of maidens' skirts. My brothers and cousins have little love for me, so I must find a way to make my own fortune, if such is ever to be made. I could play the squire to the canons of Beverley and hope to win their favours, but fate has brought me here to York and I am not blind to where advantage lies.'

'A self-serving man with courage enough to admit to his interest,' Geoffrey said with obvious admiration. 'Ye gods, lad, most men in your place would lie and fawn and swear it was love of me that fired their hearts.'

'I fear I have no subtlety for that, Your Grace,' Fergus replied with a smile. 'My face is too easily read and my memory too short. To be a liar requires a host of skills, most of which I lack unless my life depends upon employing them.'

'But I'll wager you can charm many favours with that smile of yours.'

'It has helped me lift some skirts and a few fat purses,' Fergus admitted with a show of modesty.

'And impressed these various canons of Beverley?'

'I do believe it has,' the young man grinned.

'Would you work for me, if there was profit in it?'

'Your Grace, I am as yet untried. Perhaps I would be persuaded to work for *any* man if there was profit in it.'

Geoffrey Plantagenet roared with laughter and signalled his servant to replenish their goblets with wine.

'Fergus, my friend, you are as a breath of fresh, clean air in a room grown stale with other men's whimperings. Stay close to me and you shall have your fortune.' He paused and once again his look was harsh as he gripped the younger man by the shoulder. 'But if you cross me, if you prove false, so

150

help me God, I'll have that smile of yours impaled on a stake above the palace gates so every passer-by will know your treachery.'

Fergus grinned. 'Your Grace, I accept the warning even though I do not fear it. May I speak freely?'

'I insist upon it.'

'Well, sire, I had but small ambition before your clerk went missing. To serve the canons of Beverley was my ultimate aim, since I was blessed with the talents for little else. Now you have opened up a wiser and a worthier path. To serve an archbishop, the son of one king and the brother of another, is now my single purpose … so long as I am not required to take either holy orders or a vow of celibacy.'

Here Geoffrey laughed heartily once again, and in the merriment Fergus knew that he had made a conquest of this power-seeking man.

'You will prosper in my service, Fergus de Burton.'

'You can be sure of that, Your Grace.'

'We ride to the hunt at first light. My stewards will provide you with all you need.'

Fergus dared to tap his finger against the archbishop's breast in a friendly gesture. 'And be sure you will be admirably tested in the hunt, for I have not learned the subtleties of fawning. I will not concede if the kill is rightfully mine.'

'Your challenge is accepted, sir,' Geoffrey laughed. 'We'll see who is the better man when the deer is in our sights.'

'We will indeed, Your Grace, we will indeed.'

It was a matter of consternation to the men who hovered at the door, for this hunt was planned for the sabbath and their archbishop's drunken laughter could be heard ringing like thunder around the palace.

CHAPTER SEVENTEEN

At dusk Simeon sat with Elvira on a small bench in the clearing where Father Bernard, the murdered canon, lay newly buried. Nearby a smaller grave was overwhelmed by a decade's growth of weed and bramble. Unmarked by even the simplest cross, it rested close to the wall dividing the enclosure from the marshland at its back. The sun was lowering, leaving a bright star hanging in its wake and streaks of pink and green across the western sky. All about them the day's rich colours were slowly being drained from every living thing. Dusk sucked them dry and left a dozen shades of black behind, and where the enclosure had been bright with life just hours ago, it was silent now and shrouded in preparation for the night. Above the walls the Minster's blackened shell loomed high and sinister against the sky, an injured sentinel watching over all.

Sounds drifted from the streets, where music still played, and voices reached the enclosure from beyond the fish market, some happy in their carousing, others raised in anger or alarm. Another hour would see the streets deserted, for now the fire-wardens and their agents were out in force, and where fires still burned many people were arrested.

Elvira leaned her head against Simeon's shoulder. She was staring at the weeds where an infant, wearied by the struggle of life just three short days after he was born, now walked in Paradise or fell to dust, according to what was written in the hearts of those who cared.

'If he had lived,' Elvira said softly, 'how changed our lives would be.'

Simeon touched her cheek and sighed, remembering. 'If your son had survived you would not have come to St Peter's to sell your milk. You and I would not have met and Peter would have died that night the soldiers came to kill him.'

'I lost a son and was given another in his place,' she whispered, and there was both pain and gratitude in her sigh.

'The Lord giveth and the Lord taketh away. I fear His purpose has cost you dearly, my Elvira.'

'But it cost him more,' Elvira said, still staring at the grave. 'It cost the babe his life.'

Simeon closed his eyes, wounded by her simple reasoning. He did not consider Elvira's child a sacrifice, only a tiny piece in a complex game, and yet, had he survived, their precious Peter might even now be lying in his place. She had seen a newborn child brought to St Peter's that night and, distraught and wretched in her poverty, had sought to sell her milk to pay the priest's fee for her own child's burial. Her tender nursing of Peter had saved his life just as her gentle nature had touched the hearts of all who met her. She had blossomed like a flower grown in savage soil. She had stripped away her old life with her rags, and when the grime was scrubbed away Elvira, the ditcher's wife, was found to be a gift from God Himself.

Simeon touched the golden headpiece hanging inside his shirt. This, too, she had offered for her dead son's soul, and somewhere in the bargaining she had captured the heart of a priest and they had both discovered a love beyond themselves.

'God's designs are often more than we can fathom,' he told her now. 'We can only accept, and trust that He is kind to us.'

'Was he kind to the mite who lived but could not suckle?'

'He was kind,' Simeon said with feeling. 'Your child is safe in Paradise, Elvira. You must believe that all life has its purpose. However short, be it wretched or exalted, no life is ever wasted. Never doubt it for a moment. Your son was a part of God's design and now he is in Paradise.'

Elvira held fast to Simeon and was comforted. She did not feel the presence of this God in whom he trusted, yet any words of his could ease her fears and still the doubts in her mind and in her heart. What Elvira did accept could not be found in books and religious teachings. Her faith began and ended here, with Simeon.

In the silence as he held her close against him, Simeon saw a rectangle of light appear at the infirmary door and several men come out, Osric and Thorald, Antony and Richard among them. While one man paced and another shook his fist or slapped his brow, they appeared to be in heated conversation. Beyond his hearing, their talk was filled with anger and concern, and none were sure how they would tell him of its cause.

'You saw it too?' Thorald demanded. 'You saw it and said nothing?'

'Aye, as *you* did,' Osric growled. 'It was a glimpse, a quick, uncertain glance in a crowded place. I held my tongue because I hoped I was mistaken.'

'I saw it by lamplight,' Antony cut in. 'No more than a glimpse, as you had, but I saw him, I know that now.'

Here Richard used his fingers to count the sightings. 'Jacob de Wold was convinced he saw a hooded man lurking in shadow during the inquiry yesterday. Father Cuthbert describes the same man standing beyond the candlelight in Simeon's scriptorium.'

'I saw him from my church,' Thorald told them grimly. 'He was standing in the yard where several graves had been recovered after the flooding. His face was hidden, but I know he looked me in the eye. I felt his gaze. He nodded. No words were spoken and yet I swear I felt him ask if I was well prepared.'

'For what?' Osric demanded. 'Prepared for what?'

154

'I do not know. I simply told him, yes, I am prepared.'

Here Richard cut in. 'And what of Peter? What has the boy seen that he chooses not to speak of? What made him unlatch the chapel door in the dead of night? How did he know that I was trapped in that cellar by the mud, and that only he, with his slightness and his climbing skills, could save me?'

'He came when he was needed, and he will admit to nothing more than that.'

'One thing is ceratin, the lad knew of it,' Thorald nodded. 'And now we have this Edwin, who will neither eat nor drink nor close his eyes because he believes that same hooded figure sent him here to die.'

'We should have spoken out at once.' Osric ground the words through his closed teeth. 'If that figure has come to warn us, as it did before, we must take heed and be prepared for trouble.'

'Peter seems unconcerned.'

Osric glanced at Antony sharply. 'Have you ever known him to be otherwise?'

'Not I,' the monk shrugged. 'He faced death at the hands of Cyrus de Figham without so much as a whimper, and then he calmly led us from the worst of the fire to a place of safety. When the child exhibits so much courage, would we dare own to less?'

'God's teeth, but *I* would,' the great Thorald confessed at once. 'Men of flesh and blood I can deal with, even two or three at a time if I be pressed, but this apparition, this hood without a face . . .' He spread his hands and shook his head as if the very contemplation of it defeated him. 'What can we do but close our ranks against whatever ill it brings to us?'

'Do we tell him, then? Do we speak to Simeon?'

It was Osric who made the decision for them all. 'We tell him *now*,' he said, and walked away.

Simeon recognised Osric striding for the scriptorium, where the priest on guard spoke briefly to him and placed a restraining hand upon his arm. Osric shook it off and strode toward the bench at the edge of the copse, slowing his steps and clearing his throat conspicuously as he approached.

'God's blessing, Osric.'

'Forgive the intrusion, my friend, the matter is of some urgency.'

'The girl?'

Osric shook his head. 'She will survive. Her weakness owes more to deprivation than disease, though I doubt she will ever be robust. The boy is starving, too, though he will neither eat nor drink to help himself. He believes that he must die if his sister is to live.'

'The superstition of a twin?'

'No, Simeon, because a priest asked it and he, having no fee to buy the blessing, readily agreed. His life for hers.'

'What nonsense is this?' Simeon raised Elvira up and put her gently from him, though her hand remained in his. 'What priest would demand such a price?'

'The one who bade him carry her here to you. The one who spoke your name and promised she would live. His life for hers, that was the bargain struck.'

'What priest was this? Can the boy describe him?'

Osric shook his head and his eyes glinted brightly in the half-light. 'He called himself the Guardian at the Gate. He wore a long black cloak and a hood that hid his face from view.'

Simeon felt a shudder pass through Elvira's body as she gripped his hand more tightly than before. His voice was barely audible when he asked: 'Was it *the other*?'

'It was he,' Osric nodded.

'Very well, I will come at once.'

They saw Elvira safely inside the scriptorium with several trusted clerks and a guard at the door for her protection. She parted from him reluctantly.

'Take care,' was all she said, but her fingers fluttered across his cheek and then his chest, brushed lightly down his arms and over his hands, as if by their action she might hold him close and safe while he was absent.

By the time they reached those waiting outside the infirmary, Simeon knew from Osric what they all had seen.

He made no criticism of their silence. They were but honest men and fallible, with hopes and fears that played upon their peace of mind and doubts that fogged their judgement.

'Every sighting must be recorded from now on,' he told them. 'However vague, however improbable, every glimpse of that hooded figure must be discussed among us. Where is the boy, Edwin?'

Inside the infirmary, several beds were set against the walls and the atmosphere was heavy with the scents of herbs and potions. A wide arched alcove held the pots and jars, mortars and pestles, weights, spoons and measures for the various remedies, while above them hung bunches of herbs and wild flowers drying out for future use. When he reached the bed where the girl lay sleeping, Simeon paused to shape the sign of the cross over her. He touched her forehead briefly and was pleased to find it cool, though her rapid, shallow breathing was an indication of her body's weakness. Her eyes fluttered open as he looked at her; soft brown eyes that seemed untroubled despite the glistening of tears on her dark lashes.

'Father Simeon?'

'Yes, child, I am Father Simeon.'

She smiled and closed her eyes. 'Then all is well,' she sighed, and slept again.

The boy who was her twin was crouched in a corner on the dirt floor with his arms tightly folded across his body, his fingers spayed against his back, thin bones against thin bones. When he raised his head Simeon was astonished by the likeness to his sister. His face was similarly shaped, pale and with dark shadows beneath the wide brown eyes. Like hers, his light brown hair had grown long and dull through lack of care. The soft mouth and the cleft chin were the same. Even the tears on his lashes might have been borrowed from his sister.

'The likeness is uncanny,' Simeon smiled.

'Father Simeon?'

'Yes, boy, I am he.'

'Sir, forgive me ... I ...' Edwin jumped to his feet,

staggered blindly and would have fallen but for Simeon's timely grip on his upper arms. The priest signalled for food to be brought, then eased the boy to a bench and sat beside him, and only with his strong arm around the lesser shoulders was he made aware of the other's lack of physical substance. He wondered how long these two had survived on no more than was sufficient to keep body and soul together, and was reminded of the words of the Christ: 'The poor are with you always.'

'I know your story, Edwin,' he said. 'I know it and I feel you are in error.'

Young Edwin shook his head. 'I know I must die. I gave my word to the priest, the Guardian at the Gate, my life for hers. I gave my word, but I fear death, Father Simeon. I fear to die and yet I know I must, for Edwinia's sake.'

'Your sister will not die,' Simeon told him firmly. 'You are in error, boy, I am sure of it. The priest you saw would never demand such a sacrifice of you. Tell me the words, Edwin, the *exact* words that were spoken. Omit nothing. If I am to help you, I must know them.'

The boy was exhausted. When the mutton broth and bread were brought to him he waved them aside, but his eyes were bright and he salivated at the sight and scent of nourishment. Beneath his thin shirt his belly was hollow and his ribs stuck out, yet with a strength of spirit few men could match, he turned his gaze away and would not eat. While the food was left tantalisingly close on a low stool near his legs, he repeated word for word his brief exchange with the hooded priest.

Simeon nodded as he listened, and when the boy was done he said, convinced that he was right: 'There is no need for you to die. There are other ways to give your life for your sister. Look at me, Edwin. I gave my life to God a lifetime ago and yet I live. Men give their lives to a woman, a cause, a dream, and yet they live. Our lives can be given over in many ways without wasting the God-given gift of life itself.'

The boy watched him, wide-eyed and clearly struggling with his conscience. 'A priest? Am I meant to become a priest, like you?'

'Perhaps. That would certainly be one way to honour the debt, and one you may or may not decide upon in the fullness of time. But there is another way that I can see quite clearly now. I know the one who spoke to you. He sent you here to me, Edwin, because he knows I am to be in need of loyal allies.'

The boy stared back, unblinking, as he repeated what he recalled of the figure's words. *'If you would give your life for your sister, take her to St Peter's, to Simeon.'*

'To me, Edwin. Not to the grave. To *me*.'

Edwin was gaping now, and there was something more than hunger in the brightness of his eyes. The look of new hope was shining there. 'Can it be so? Can it really be so?'

'Think on it for yourself,' Simeon smiled. He reached for the bowl of soup and passed it to the boy. 'But first you must eat your fill. No man can reason rationally on an empty belly. Here you have food and ale for your body's needs, a bed on which to sleep and a safe roof over your head. Take them and thank the Lord for all His blessings. In the morning come to me at my scriptorium and we'll talk again, and I will ask that same question of you: can it be so?'

He stayed to watch the boy devour his soup and half a loaf of bread, then led him to the low, straw-covered pallet which had been set up for him in a corner. Edwin was fast asleep before the rug was over him.

Simeon signed him with the cross and touched his brow. When he passed the girl's bed he paused again and shook his head.

'An uncanny likeness,' he said. 'Quite uncanny.'

'I must see him,' the woman said. 'Please, I must speak to him now, before it is too late.'

'Father Simeon is at his prayers and must not be disturbed. Come back in an hour.'

The woman was cloaked in a rough brown blanket that hid her hair and most of her face. Her feet were bare and soiled and she used one hand to cover her mouth as she spoke. 'Please, in God's name, tell him I am here.'

159

'He is at prayer,' the gatekeeper repeated.

'I am Alice, Elvira's friend. Have pity, sir, I must speak to Father Simeon at once.'

'Alice, you say?'

She nodded. 'Elvira's friend.'

'You are the woman who spoke at the provost's inquiry?'

She hung her head. 'Yes, I am she.'

The gatekeeper crossed his arms over his chest and looked at her as if he saw a leper at the gate. Had he been free to act as he saw fit, he would have broken his staff across this wretch's back and left her for the rats to feed upon. Instead he cleared his throat and spat contemptuously at her feet. 'Wait here, woman, while I fetch a priest, but it won't be Father Simeon who comes. I doubt he'll want to waste his breath on the likes of you.'

Alice sank to her knees outside the gate. She did not weep, for she was far beyond the relief of tears. Nor did she pray, for she was too burdened with shame to open her heart in prayer or even to lift her gaze to Heaven. She huddled in the dirt outside the gate, rocking to and fro the way a child left alone might rock itself in search of some small comfort for its loss.

It was Elvira who came when the gates were opened. With no more than a whispered, 'Alice, my dear,' she brought the wretched woman inside and led her to the tiny stone chapel attached to the infirmary.

'Here is a seat, Alice. Word has been sent to Simeon that you have come to us. He will be here directly.'

'But his prayers . . . the holy office?'

'He will be here,' Elvira smiled and kissed her friend's forehead. She was troubled by the way Alice shrank from her, by the gauntness of her face and the fact that she kept her eyes downcast even while clasping Elvira's hand so tightly that her fingernails bit into the skin. 'Oh, Alice, what have we done to you? How poorly you have fared on our behalf.'

'I chose my own way,' Alice answered tightly. 'Remember that, if you are still my friend. I chose my own way.'

'*If* I am still your friend? Dear Alice, I will *always* be your friend. Now that you have come to us at last I will take care of you. I will repay every hurt, every indignity you endured for love of us.'

'Too late . . . it is too late.'

The door of the chapel opened and a tall, broad figure was framed in the light from a torch hung on the lintel. For an instant Alice gaped as if in terror, then recognised the priest and flung herself upon the ground, prostrate before him.

'Father Simeon, forgive me. Forgive me.'

'Poor Alice, you are condemned out of your own mouth. Only His Grace the archbishop, or His Holiness the pope, can absolve you now,' Simeon replied.

'You don't understand,' she cried, and began to beat the ground with her fists. 'You don't know. You don't understand.'

'Alice, if you repent, truly and unconditionally, then God in his mercy—'

'*No!*' She almost screamed the word, then shuffled forward to grasp at Simeon's ankles. 'I do not ask for God's forgiveness while the greater offence is yet to be committed. I ask for your forgiveness, Father Simeon. *Yours!*'

'I give it, Alice. I give it gladly,' Simeon said, stooping to raise her up. On her knees she turned a tear-stained face to him and he was deeply moved by the agony he saw there.

'I betrayed you with my lies.'

'Poor child, you did yourself the greater harm.'

'Will you hear my confession?'

'Alice, for any wrong you have done to me I readily forgive you, but I cannot absolve you of the rest and if, as you say, the greater sin is yet to be committed—'

'It is, and I am lost.'

Elvira made as if to go to Alice, caught Simeon's warning glance and turned away. As she left the chapel she placed her hand on Simeon's arm and looked into his eyes. She saw compassion there, and that fierce sorrowing of one who knew that, by his kind intent, the very soul he sought to save was forfeit.

'Never lost,' she whispered, reading the anguish in his eyes and knowing that this man, in his faith in an all-forgiving God, had dared to give full and unconditional absolution to the dead without confession. 'There is nothing de Figham can do that God can not undo.'

'God bless you for your wisdom, Elvira.'

'Though he will not bless me for my lack of faith?'

'Your soul is open. That is faith enough.'

Elvira glanced at the prostrate figure on the chapel floor. 'She suffered in my place and now she comes to you to be healed of all her hurt. Is *that* faith enough for the God you serve so well, Simeon de Beverley?'

'It is enough,' he told her, and she saw that he believed it to be so.

CHAPTER EIGHTEEN

I n the canon's house on Minster Moorgate, Wulfric de
Morthlund's face was dark as he shrugged his massive
shoulders more comfortably into his cloak, while Daniel
Hawk, sullen and silent, fixed the folds with a silver brooch
against one shoulder. The cloak was of a brilliant, vibrant
scarlet, its colour produced from cockles and known not to
fade in sunlight or to deteriorate in rain. The lining was of
violet silk, the whole set off to much effect by a wide panel of
embroidery worked with silver and copper thread. He wore
his favourite silver girdle of triple width over a grey silk tunic,
high boots elaborately decorated and a jewelled sash across
his chest. De Morthlund was hungry, and with his belly empty
he was peevish. He peered into Daniel's handsome, aquiline
face and saw there something that unsettled him.

'These dark and silent moods do not become you, Daniel
Hawk. Are you unwell?'

'I am quite well, my lord.'

Wulfric nodded. He could not read his face, nor did he
welcome the growing sense that he no longer held total
control over his catamite. There had been a time when
Daniel was so pliable and obedient that Wulfric had no
reason to consider him as separate from himself. Something
had changed. A slow, insidious process of alteration had

begun with the Beverley fire, when Daniel had almost lost his life and uncovered a dangerous weakness in de Morthlund's character. As master and servant they could live according to the natural order of things. As lovers the power between them was divided, and so the master surrendered his control and, by degrees, became the lesser man. Now he suspected Daniel of playing upon the flaw, of giving and withdrawing himself at will and so assuming a measure of equality to which he was not entitled.

'Your moods have become too feminine for my liking, dear heart,' he said acidly. 'And too frequent for my comfort. Why are you wearing black?'

Daniel shrugged, discomforted as much by the question as by the suspicion he sensed behind it. Although his loyalty had been sorely tested, his attachment to de Morthlund had not faltered from its course in sixteen years. No man could read the colour of his thoughts, yet it amazed him still that this man, who had owned him body and soul since he was barely into his teens, could look at him and fail to read his heart.

'I am wearing black because it pleases you,' he said. 'The robes are new. You had them made for me in York.'

The huge priest scowled. 'Cyrus de Figham favours black. Perhaps you hope to charm him with your apparel while you dine so prettily at his table?'

'The idea had not occurred to me,' Daniel said, then swore softly as he pricked his finger on the sharp stem of the brooch.

'Your hands are clumsy,' de Morthlund remarked. 'Do my words strike so close to home they make you nervous?' He grabbed the finger and squeezed it hard until a drop of blood glistened on the surface of the skin, then thrust it into his mouth and sucked on it so violently that Daniel winced in pain. When he had done he flung the hand away and looked contemptuously at Daniel's crown. 'You should cover your head, dear heart. No amount of pretty robes will compensate for such a dearth of hair. Your baldness ages you before your time. It displeases me.'

'I regret the loss, my lord.'

'And so you should. It does not become you.' He strutted across the room, swinging his cloak about him so that the lining flashed brightly against the rustling crimson. At the reading table he halted to examine a book whose pages were marked with narrow strips of silk. 'You think too much. I do not keep you in my house, at my own expense, so that you may waste your energies in *thinking*.'

Daniel shrugged and smiled. 'All men must think, if they have minds, my lord. Would you have your personal priest less healthy in mind than are the priests of other canons?'

'I would have my priest *obedient*,' de Morthlund snapped.

'And so I am, obedient and loyal.'

'You read too much for my comfort. Reading creases your brow and sours your humour. It is a futile, feminine occupation.'

'But surely it is my duty as a priest to read the scriptures regularly,' Daniel answered mildly. 'I do no more than I am duty-bound to do.'

'Your duty is to me, not to the words of a handful of pious old men who have been dead and buried for countless centuries. These pitiable scratchings are for fools and children to ponder over.'

'But my lord, the scriptures . . .'

'. . . are empty words to be quoted and recited *only* according to your duties as a priest. They are not for intelligent men to take seriously. Give up the habit, Daniel. I find it irksome.'

'As you wish, my lord. I will remove the book.'

As Daniel approached the table, Father Wulfric took up the book and held it from him. 'Go fetch your cloak and have the horses brought to the door for our journey to de Figham's house. I am drooling at the mouth for want of food to fill my belly.' He held the book close to his chest so that the rings he wore sparkled and gleamed against the leather cover. 'Be quick about it. I will dispose of this.'

They rode to the house at Figham with an escort of seven men, for in his finery de Morthlund was a target for

165

common thieves, and Beverley, with its pilgrims and its laws of sanctuary, harboured more than its fair quota of evil-doers. They took the shortest route across the meadow, sending three riders on ahead to ensure the ground was safe to ride upon. At the door of the house they were greeted by their host, Cyrus de Figham, who noted de Morthlund's peevish glances and his priest's glum features, and thought to grasp the moment while he could.

'My compliments on your princely attire, Father Wulfric,' he said with a smile. 'And on your priest's appearance. Such a handsome companion does you much credit.'

He noted the narrowing of the fat man's eyes and the sudden stiffening of his back. He had touched a raw nerve and the result was to his liking. Jealousy was a weapon men gave into the hands of their enemies. It was a barbed string by which they could be manipulated, and de Figham could not resist the plucking of it.

'Handsome?' de Morthlund repeated. 'Yes, I grant that he was handsome enough when he had more hair upon his head.'

'But the loss is hardly drastic,' de Figham persisted. 'In fact, it is little more than a receding of the hair above the forehead. It gives him an air of distinction, don't you think, since the highness of the brow so well becomes his noble features?'

'Handsome? Distinguished? Noble? God's teeth, sir, your pretty words offend my stomach. You'll have him preening like a woman on your flattery.'

Daniel caught de Figham's glance, the conspicuous wink and the glitter of triumph there. De Morthlund saw it, too, and was incensed.

'Don't bother to dismount,' he roared at Daniel with fury in his eyes. 'Get back to the house and return that spiritless whelp to the hovel in which you found him. You served me ill in that respect. He does not please me.'

De Figham feigned disappointment. 'You are too harsh, my friend. A place is set for Daniel at my table. The feast is ready to be enjoyed and this errand will make him late.'

'Late?' de Morthlund scowled, struggling down from his horse with the assistance of a duo of hefty servants. 'Tonight he will not dine at all. I fear my priest prefers reading dusty books to filling his belly with the best of fare. Let him take his fill of the scriptures and sup on ale and cheese like the common man he is.' He turned to Daniel with a hot flush on his cheeks. 'And in the name of decency *cover your head*. It sickens me to see your crown exhibited.'

'As you wish, my lord.' With a bow Daniel lifted his hood, then turned his horse aside and rode away.

De Figham examined the black stone in the ring he wore on his tapered index finger. 'Does your ... er ... priest no longer please you, Father Wulfric?'

'I find him sullen,' de Morthlund admitted, hoisting up his girdle with both hands. 'He thinks too much on matters that depress his spirits and set a wedge between us.'

'Ah, yes, I fear the fire has left its scars upon us all.'

'What do you mean by that remark?' De Morthlund looked sharply at his host. He did not think the priest would dare make open reference to those humiliating scenes at Daniel's bedside. De Figham caught the flare and knew that he had touched the raw nerve for a second time. He spread his hands in a gesture of innocence and probed the wound.

'I only observe that, after spending so much time with the priests of St Peter's, your Daniel Hawk seems to have undergone certain changes. Perhaps Father Simeon is responsible?'

'Meaning what? Speak out, de Figham.'

'Only that Simeon may have planted the seed of doubt in Daniel's mind. He has a persuasive tongue, and if he has designs on drawing your priest away...' Again he raised his hands, then turned to watch the dark-clad figure riding across the meadow. 'Can he be trusted?'

'I'll kill him with my bare hands if he can't.'

'And Simeon de Beverley, if he is the cause?'

'Then be sure I'll kill him too,' de Morthlund growled, then added, for de Figham's benefit, 'as I would kill any man who tried to pilfer what belongs to me.'

De Figham laughed and slapped his guest's broad shoulder. 'My friend, I do believe you would at that. We can only hope that your priest keeps a decent distance between himself and Simeon. Come, let us eat and drink together. The others are already inside. Tonight we dine in royal style, with or without your pretty Daniel Hawk.'

As he steered de Morthlund inside he turned to give a silent signal to the man who kept his dogs. He wanted Daniel followed and his movements reported back to him in detail. Let Daniel Hawk spend just one hour in seclusion, with no witness to his movements, and de Figham would have a probe to lay this fat man's raw nerves open to the bone.

Daniel Hawk was seated in his master's chair, staring into the grate where a fire still burned. The flames had died to glowing, crimson embers, and all around them ash had settled. The object on which the flames had fed was still identifiable, its pages blackened and its leather covers burned away. Wulfric de Morthlund had been as good as his word when he said he would dispose of Daniel's book. He had burned it. The act itself, although a sacrilege, was of little genuine consequence, since copies were available through the church. The message behind it, though, was incontestable. What Wulfric provided, he could take away, and whatsoever displeased him he would destroy.

Daniel stared at the embers in the grate. He had been deprived of his place at the feast and sent home like a punished child to run errands and take his supper in the kitchen. He did not need this charred reminder of Wulfric's power over him, nor his own dark thoughts to prompt his inner disquiet to the surface. He could not touch the source of his discontent, for it lacked shape and substance, but he was troubled. His future was at stake and yet he felt himself to be powerless against a vague and baffling shifting of the ground beneath his feet. His love for de Morthlund had not diminished despite the many cruelties he received, but it was changed. Now he feared for their immortal souls. Now he looked out through the eyes of a man instead of those of a child, with reasoning rather than blind obedience, and what he saw disturbed his peace of mind.

'Sir?' It was a small voice, nervous and uncertain. 'Forgive me, sir.'

'What is it, boy?' He did not turn his head.

'You said I was to be taken home.'

'What?'

'Home,' the boy repeated. 'To my father's house, sir. I do not know the way.'

Daniel pulled his gaze from the charred remains in the grate. The boy was standing just inside the door, an untidy bundle clutched in his hands and too much of the world in his young eyes. This, too, was new to Daniel Hawk, this peculiar thing akin to pain that he sometimes felt for those outside his comfortable sphere, those who ate and drank and survived another day only upon the whim of other, stronger men. The weak were meant to be enslaved by the strong, the poor by the rich, the small and insignificant by the mighty. He knew this to be so. It had been so since Adam left the Garden, and would be so until the close of time. It was the law, the natural way of things. Why, then, had Daniel Hawk, who owed his own survival to his master and held his own future in a fragile grip, begun to question this, the very first of Nature's principles?

'What is your name, boy?'

'James, sir.'

'You were named for a saint. Were you aware of that?'

The youngster merely shrugged his narrow shoulders.

'Well, James, are you ready to go?'

'Yes, sir.'

Daniel rose to his feet and took the youngster by the hand. The fingers in his palm were very small and unexpectedly firm, and the glance he received from their owner would have touched his heart, had he believed he owned one. It occurred to him that he might choose to lead this child to the river and throw him in, or sell him for a pittance in the market-place, or beat him to death in an alley simply because it amused his fancy to do so. He might lead him from Wulfric de Morthlund's bed to that of other men who would use him just as ill, but he had agreed to take him home and so James had taken him at his word. Trust was the thing he saw in those sad eyes, and that this boy should dare to trust him, with so little cause, was inexplicable.

They walked together through the darkening streets and when James saw an area he recognised he slipped his hand from Daniel's and ran ahead. He limped a little and his steps were unsure, but in his haste to rejoin his family, any pain he had suffered was forgotten. In the narrow street he paused several times to retrieve a scattering of discarded cabbage leaves, then vanished through the door of his father's hovel. Daniel should have left him then, his errand completed, but something drew him after the boy until he found himself ducking through the narrow doorway and into the single room of the family's hovel.

The room was dark. No fire burned in the grate, and the stink that met his nostrils caused his stomach to heave. As his eyes became accustomed to the gloom he was able to make out the shape of a figure on the bed with the smaller, more familiar shape of James kneeling before it. Two younger children huddled in a corner, clinging to each other like filthy, frightened monkeys. The movements of a wooden cradle caught his eye, and as he stared he realised that a company of rats was feeding there. More rats were on the bed, feasting boldly on the dead man who still held Wulfric de Morthlund's meagre purse of silver in his hands.

'Come away, boy,' Daniel said sharply, then grasped the youngster by the shoulder and pulled him roughly to his feet. 'Your father is beyond help. Come away.'

To his consternation the boy suddenly clung to him and buried his face in the folds of his cloak. Sobs shook his body and made strange animal sounds in his throat, and with his first instincts Daniel was tempted to thrust him aside and hurry from that place. Then his own hands moved to the youngster's head in a gesture of comfort, and after a moment he gathered him in a close embrace and held him while he wept.

170

'Is this what He wants?' Daniel muttered to himself, and the question seemed to cut right to the core of him. 'Is this what God wants for His own? Can He, whom men call good, be this indifferent?'

He stood for a moment beside the deathbed, struggling to harness words into a coherent prayer but finding each short, familiar sentence fragmented in his mind. He prised the strings of de Morthlund's purse from the dead man's fingers, closed the staring eyes and signed the cross, and when he left he took the children with him.

In the little chapel inside the St Peter's enclosure, Simeon de Beverley raised his eyes to heaven and prayed for guidance. The woman had wept and bared her soul to him, and now he knew how she had been persuaded by Cyrus de Figham to risk eternal damnation by lying upon the sacred oath. That priest had threatened to give her in marriage to the one-eyed hunchback, Knut, whose body was infested with running sores and so hideous that children ran from him in terror and grown men avoided passing close by him in the street. If Alice failed to do de Figham's bidding she would be bedded with Knut. If she agreed, she would receive absolution for her sins. All this the priest had promised her and afterwards had laughed in her face and set the marriage date. Alice would have her hell beyond the grave and suffer a hell on earth before she died.

When Simeon's prayers were ended he looked down at Alice with a heavy heart. She was kneeling on the ground with her face pressed into his lap, exhausted by her own misery.

'Stay here with us,' he said at last. 'Let Cyrus de Figham rant and rave and do his very worst, and we will keep you from him, by force, if necessary.'

'I am his property,' she reminded him. 'By my own oath I am his willing and obedient chattel. How can you hope to do the things you say? How can the Church allow a priest to confiscate the property of a canon?'

'I'll find a way,' Simeon promised. 'And if I fail in that, you will be taken far from here to begin your life anew.'

171

Alice's laugh was harsh as she got to her feet and moved toward the tiny altar where a candle burned before an icon of the blessed Virgin Mary. 'There can be no new life for me,' she said, touching the candle's flame with her bare fingers. 'No life but the one Cyrus de Figham dictates. He despises me the more because I am useless to him now. He will bring another woman to take my place and I will be given over to that hateful hunchback.'

'You are wrong, Alice. You must not despair. A new life *is* possible, far from this place where you are known, with a good and decent husband, even children.'

She turned on him then and threw aside her cloak to reveal the hard round bulge of her belly. 'With this?' she cried. 'And with this?' She tore open her gown so that the livid brand of de Figham stood out like a hideous wound upon her breast.

'Dear God in Heaven!'

'His devil's mark is on me,' she groaned, then began to clutch fitfully at her clothes as if she might tear the growing child away. 'And his devil's spawn is inside me, growing fat on my flesh and on my soul. It is an evil thing and I am cursed. *Cursed!*'

'Alice, Alice.' Simeon went to her and took her in his arms but, even as he tried to comfort her and she to cling to him, he felt her belly quicken with the movements of de Figham's unborn child. 'Is this the greater sin you spoke of? The sin yet to be committed? The birthing of de Figham's babe?'

'It must not live,' she sobbed against his chest, and all her despair was in the cry. 'This monstrous thing must not draw God's air into its devilish lungs.'

'Hush, child. We'll find a way.' He quoted Elvira's words to strengthen them both. ' "There is nothing de Figham can do that God can not undo." '

Alice pulled a simple cross made from twigs and wire from beneath her cloak, pushed it into Simeon's hands and closed his fingers around it. 'Father Simeon, will you take this to Elvira? It is all I have to give to mark our friendship. Will you ask her to come to me here?'

'I'll go at once,' Simeon smiled, moved by the sudden strength he felt in her. 'She will take care of you, Alice. You will be safe with us.'

He had reached the chapel door when she called his name. 'Father Simeon?'

'Yes, child?'

'Do you forgive me? In your heart of hearts, do you truly forgive me?'

'I do, with all my heart,' he said, and left her standing beside the little altar.

When he returned with Elvira a few minutes later the chapel was empty. The candle on the altar had been extinguished, leaving a scent of smoky tallow drifting from the wick. A finger of anxiety stroked his spine.

'We have lost her.'

'Simeon, I will not ask what she told you in confession, since I know you can repeat no word of it, but let me say what troubles me. When I tried to hold her in my arms she shrank from me. At first I assumed her misery to be the cause, but now . . .'

'What is it, Elvira? I have come to trust this extra sense of yours.'

'There was something she wanted to keep from me, something terrible. I am a woman, no stranger to these things. I believe she is with child, and if that is so . . .'

Trusting her sound intuition, Simeon prompted, 'If so?'

Elvira turned her earth-dark eyes to him. 'She said in my hearing that the greater sin is yet to be committed. She needed your forgiveness for her peace of mind, but she believes your God will not forgive what she must now do.'

'She will attempt to destroy the child,' Simeon said flatly. 'That wretched woman means to kill her unborn babe.'

'And more,' Elvira told him sadly. 'Poor Alice means to take her own life, too.'

173

CHAPTER NINETEEN

The hunchback came at speed across the meadow with a wooden cradle strapped across his back. He lurched from one ungainly foot to the other in a lopsided, crab-like shuffle with which he could out-distance many healthy men. He was an outcast and a thief, a beggar and an object of ridicule, for the world did not take kindly to twisted bodies and drooling mouths. He lived on his limited wits, by thieving and begging and on the occasional mercy of Beverley's priests. Such a one must be quick and agile if he is to catch his coin before his benefactor drives him off.

Knut the hunchback had never mastered the art of common speech, though he understood simple English well enough, some French and a little Latin. Yet he could read a man's face and limbs with an accuracy vital to his survival. He could recognise the signals of a coming blow before a hand was even raised against him, and he knew a gift when it was handed to him. Cyrus de Figham had given him the woman, and Knut was wise enough to realise that his miserable life was altered from now on. Alice was whole and strong and beautiful. She would work for him and share his bed as any true wife was obliged to share the bed of her lawful husband. She would give him a normal, healthy child before St Thomas à Becket's Feast Day in the last week of December.

Men from the town would come to his door and pay him money just to lie with her. They would envy him because his life was changed, and he would feel as whole as other men. Now he toiled with his thickened tongue to shape the name of his salvation through a mouth half-filled with rotting teeth: 'Alice.'

Knut threw back his hood as he came in sight of the ramshackle wooden hut set in a hollow on the Figham pasture. His home was safe from thieves because he was the poorest of men, and because in his misshapen ugliness he was suspected of being in league with hobgoblins and other hideous terrors of the underworld. He wiped a hand across his dribbling chin, hoisted the cradle more firmly over his hump and hurried on. Even though his back was twisted and his legs curved in twin arches, he was forced to crawl on the ground to enter the hut by its low door. Once inside he drew himself up and groped for a candle, and by its light he saw his dreams and all his hopes undone.

She was hanging by the neck from a rope attached to the single crossbeam of the hut, her tongue and eyes protruding. Beneath her gently swinging feet, lying like a glistening carcass in the filth, was the thing that was to have been his child before the year was out.

'Alice.' Knut shaped a wet, pathetic semblance of the name he had been practising for so long. 'Alice.' He shuffled around the body of the woman, viewing it from all angles in his quest for comprehension. He poked it with his finger so that it turned in lazy circles on the rope. He nudged the carcass of the child with the toe of his boot, then tugged at the hanging skirts as if by doing so he might revive their owner. He began to make whimpering noises in his throat, stamped his feet and waved his fists in the air. Then he flung himself from the hut and scuttled back across the Figham meadow, sobbing and screaming all the way.

Simeon found Daniel Hawk in the gatehouse where the keeper, concerned by the appearance of Wulfric de Morthlund's man at St Peter's gate, had bade him wait. The young

175

man was dressed in black with silver trims. His luxurious dark hair fell in waves to his cowled shoulders, and his bent profile, with its long nose and high, strong forehead, had a certain Latin look to it. He held a sleeping child against one shoulder, and with his free hand he traced the words of a book left open on a reading table. The back of the hand was scarred and the nail from the middle finger had been burned away, but it was neither ugly nor clumsy as it moved across the page. Absorbed as he was, he did not hear Simeon enter the room and was unaware of his presence for some time. He turned the pages of the book, and when he finally closed it he allowed his fingers to trace its cover with a kind of reverence.

'The psalter,' Simeon said at last. 'The Book of Psalms, translated from the Latin.'

'It is a work of great beauty and great skill.' He looked up then and nodded a greeting. 'God bless you, Father Simeon.'

'God bless you, Daniel. No title is required. My gateman tells me you have brought three orphaned children into our care?'

'Will you take them?'

Simeon nodded. 'The purse you offer belongs to Father Wulfric. You must return it to him.'

'I cannot do that,' Daniel said. 'It was given to the children's father before he died, as payment for his eldest boy, James.'

Simeon sighed and shook his head, weighing the meagre collection of coins in his palm. 'So small a purse for his innocence. Life is cheap.'

'And harsh. They lived amongst rats and other vermin.' For a moment Daniel closed his eyes and a look of pain passed over his handsome features. 'Simeon, I could not speak the passing prayer for their father. I tried, but the words would not be brought to heel. The blessing I left with him was scant.'

'You brought his children to a place of safety. Is that not a worthy blessing, Daniel Hawk?'

'Is it enough?'

'It is enough. No one will harm them here.'

'The boy . . . young James . . . Wulfric de Morthlund . . .'

'I know,' Simeon told him. 'Such a thing will not be repeated here. James will be safe with us.'

'Thank you.'

'And is there nothing we can do to help *you*, Daniel?'

The young man shook his head and Simeon remembered how, so many years ago, this same Daniel Hawk had pressed a scribbled note into his hand in a crowded place, a note with three words written on it: 'You are betrayed'. Those words had helped save Peter's life and Daniel had risked his own to pass the message.

'I owe you much,' he reminded Daniel. 'Let me offer a little something in return.' Simeon took up the psalter and handed it to Daniel. 'It is small enough to slip beneath your cloak and inconspicuous enough to avoid your canon's interest. Please take it with my thanks, and with my blessing.'

The look that passed between them was long and steady. Daniel knew that these calm blue eyes could see things others did not see, could reach inside a man and share his secrets. His own gaze did not waver. He was not afraid of Simeon's scrutiny. It seemed to him there was no judgement in it, and there was little of Daniel left concealed after Simeon had nursed him back to health in those weeks following the fire. These two were men of the Church who were ordained to serve the same God. They should have been allies, they might even have been friends, were they not set on opposite sides, with Wulfric de Morthlund standing in all his earthly majesty between them.

'I must leave now,' he said at last.

Simeon nodded and indicated the sleeping shape curled over Daniel's shoulder. 'Someone is waiting outside to take the child.'

'I do not know her name.'

'No matter, but you may have saved her life by bringing her here. No mean achievement, Daniel Hawk, three lives preserved in a single act of kindness.'

177

'It will not go well with me if Father Wulfric discovers I was here.'

'Then do not attempt to lie to him,' Simeon warned. 'He has more informants than Beverley has rats, and you are too easily recognised to slip unnoticed through St Peter's gates. Confess at once that you brought the children here.'

At the gatehouse Daniel handed the sleeping child to a woman in a grey robe and a wimple. He touched the small head with its crusted, dirty hair, and wondered briefly how the child would have fared outside these walls. As he turned away he noticed a skinny youth struggling to right a crooked slab of stone upon a plinth outside the infirmary. The bricks below had crumbled at their edges and the dead weight of the slab had caused it to tilt, so adding to the damage. The boy had long brown hair, a pale, thin face and soft brown eyes. He worked the stone this way and that in jerky movements, easing it slowly back into position.

'Another orphan,' Simeon explained. 'He is Edwin. He came to us half-starved, with a sickly sister. His body is exhausted, yet he sleeps for only an hour or so before he leaps up, wide awake and eager for work, and later he falls quite suddenly into sleep again.'

'Is he ill?'

'It is too early for us to say. Only time will tell us if he is afflicted or just temporarily beyond his strength.'

Daniel frowned. 'He is too slight of build for such a task. If that stone should slip . . .'

Even as he spoke the words, a brick from the plinth crumbled away and the heavy slab slid sideways against the boy's narrow chest. With a yell of warning Daniel rushed forward with Simeon close behind. Together they took the weight while Edwin, quick to recognise what must be done, wedged a fresh brick in place and tapped it home with a lump of stone. When the slab was settled back upon its plinth, Daniel took the boy by the shoulders and looked fiercely into his eyes. He was no more than sixteen years of age, yet he was almost as tall as Daniel himself and already there were hints of a handsome ruggedness developing in his face.

'You might have maimed yourself for no good cause, lad. You must learn to know your limitations. You are far too skinny for such a heavy task.'

'I'm sorry, Father Daniel.' The small face with its dark eyes was crestfallen. 'I thought I could shift the stone by small degrees.'

'And so you might have done, had the plinth below it been solid enough to take its weight. A little extra thought, some common sense, would have shown as much.'

'Yes, Father Daniel.'

'Do I know you, boy?'

'No sir, but I know of you.' The soft eyes brightened. 'You live at the canon's house in Minster Moorgate and your hands are scarred because you risked your life to save your master in the great fire. You ride a beautiful black horse with a blaze on its forehead and white hairs in its tail. You own a falcon, too, and you can make it obey you from a hundred miles away . . .'

'A hundred miles?'

'Yes, sir, and you can fire a crossbow further and faster than any. You are Daniel Little Hawk, a famous man.'

'Famous, am I?' Daniel laughed, and Simeon, looking on, had the distinct impression that this troubled young priest had not laughed so easily in a long, long time.

'And what is your own claim to fame, young Edwin? Tell me about yourself.'

'Father Simeon says I am to be taught how to read and write,' Edwin said with a happy grin. 'I might become a gardener, or a herbalist, or a priest.'

Daniel looked at the bright brown eyes, so full of hope and expectation, and he was moved to shake him very gently by the shoulders. 'Then be sure you survive to take advantage of his generosity. Let there be no more shifting of heavy stones without help and supervision. Work well within your limits from now on, young Edwin. I expect to see some flesh and solid muscle on those bones of yours when next I meet you.'

'Yes, sir, and I will learn my letters, too. I intend to be a model student for Father Simeon.'

179

'Be sure you are, for I may test you on your lessons.'

The boy's face lit with pleasure. 'Does that mean you will come to see me, sir?'

Daniel glanced at Simeon, saw his smile and nodded to the boy. 'Yes, Edwin, I will come.'

'And will you teach me riding and hawking, how to use a sword and a crossbow and recite the holy offices and …'

'Slowly, now, Edwin, slowly.' Daniel was laughing again, an easy, good-natured laugh that made his eyes sparkle and his face crease. 'Like all of us, you must begin at the beginning. Learn well and be obedient to your teacher, and I will come again to check your progress when my duties give me leave. Will that suffice?'

'Oh, yes, sir,' Edwin beamed. 'And you will meet my sister when she is well again.'

'I look forward to it,' Daniel said. His smile faded as the soft brown eyes glazed over and the lids begin to droop. He felt the shoulders sag beneath his grasp and a moment later caught Edwin as he collapsed.

'Bring him inside,' Simeon said. 'Here's Osric. He will carry him to his bed.'

Daniel scooped Edwin into his arms as Osric strode toward them. 'What manner of affliction is this? By Heaven, the lad is as limp as a rag. What ails him?'

'Hand him to me,' the infirmarian said. 'I will take him to his bed and this time keep him there, even if I have to tie him down with ropes.'

As the boy was taken away Daniel turned to Simeon in concern. 'What is it, Simeon? Could it be the mortal sleeping sickness?'

Simeon shook his head as he drew Daniel away. 'We hope it proves to be nothing more serious than exhaustion. There is no seizure involved, no spasm of the brain, though he seems quite unaware of the coming of these sudden collapses. Come, he is in good hands. It seems you are something of a hero in his eyes. He is quite taken with you, Daniel.'

'And I with him. He reminds me of myself when I was

180

young, eager to please, untried and ...'

'Vulnerable?' Simeon offered.

Daniel nodded. 'There are so many just like Edwin.'

'The poor are with you always.'

'And so we must provide for them.' He looked sideways at the bigger man. 'You do not suspect my motives, Simeon?'

'Motives, Daniel?'

'In befriending the boy.'

'I see compassion in it, and perhaps a mutual need for friendship.'

'And nothing else? Nothing more sinister?'

Simeon looked into Daniel's eyes and saw in them what this young priest himself did not yet know, that God was taking a hand in his existence. How he received that help was up to him, but Simeon knew he would not harm another in the process.

'I see only hunger and a reaching out,' he said. 'Seek and you shall find, Daniel Little Hawk. Read the psalter. It will comfort you.' He offered his hand and Daniel shook it warmly. 'Be sure you will always find a welcome here, and remember your promise to Edwin.'

'Thank you. I am grateful.'

'Go with God, Daniel.'

Daniel nodded, and his expression was grim as he walked towards the gate. When he looked back, Simeon was watching him, a big, impressive man whose strength and honesty were almost tangible. He wanted to say what was in his heart, that he could never betray Wulfric de Morthlund, but as he briefly held Simeon's gaze he knew the priest had read as much in his eyes.

By the time Simeon reached Cyrus de Figham's house the feast was over and the evening's merrymaking was at its height. He brought four priests with him as witnesses, Osric and Antony for his own protection, and Father Cuthbert to lend authority. He also carried a written summons signed by Jacob de Wold and bearing the chapter seal. It was a demand that the woman, Alice, be taken into custody at once. The

181

Church would know why she professed to be intact while heavy with child, and why she swore willing obedience to de Figham when his brand was burned into her flesh. This was a serious charge against de Figham, that he had kept a woman against her will, manipulated the Church inquiry and forced a witness to lie under holy oath.

Despite his wish that it be otherwise, Simeon and his party were ushered into the main hall where the feast had taken place. The tables were littered with animal, fowl and fish bones, some with sufficient meat left on them to feed many hungry mouths. Grease-smeared bowls and half-eaten bread platters were scattered on every surface, and much of the food had gone to feeding the two dogs lying sprawled and satiated before the fireplace. The head of a boar, its tusks intact, lay on a tray amid onions and apples, prunes and figs, all baked in a wine and honey sauce to complement the pork. There were minstrels present and several young women from the town, all with their faces flushed and their gowns undone. An empty cask of wine stood on a table, and beside it a second cask already broken.

There were canons here as well as priests, men stuffed to bursting with de Figham's food and wine, men purchased with a feast of over-indulgence and barely aware that they had passed through the market-place. In a corner on a stool sat an elderly man in shabby clothes. He was ill at ease and his wine remained untouched, and only when he raised a hand in greeting did Simeon recognise him as the vicar of St Jude, the church at Thorpe. The man shrugged and looked miserable, as if he did not understand why he was here and would have given much to be elsewhere.

'I must return to my church, to my house,' he muttered, wringing his hands with agitation. He had been summoned unexpectedly to the presence of his canon and, in high hopes that the matter concerned a gift of money for his crumbling church, had come at once, on foot because he owned neither horse nor donkey. For two long hours he had waited, and all the time he feared for the safety of his wife and daughter, and he dreaded the journey home to his village of Thorpe.

Simeon saw that de Figham had relinquished his place at the head of the table in favour of Wulfric de Morthlund, a fact that spoke volumes for his true intentions. The fat man's clothes were stained with grease and wet with dribbled wine. He was slumped in the big carved chair like a beached whale hung with sparkling jewels, his eyes unfocused and his features slack. Beside him de Figham was a picture of sober elegance, for this host knew how to accommodate the appetites of his guests without losing his clarity of mind.

'You interrupt the pleasures of my guests, Simeon de Beverley.'

'We could have met privately, in another room.'

'Would I wish to deprive you of your audience?' de Figham smiled. 'These men have already seen how you perform in public. The provost's inquiry has provided us with an amusing topic of conversation during our meal. Say what you have to say. State your business and be gone, sir, if you please.'

'We have come for the woman, Alice.'

'She chose to stay.'

'She lied. We know that now.'

De Figham smiled and raised his hands, palms upward, in a gesture of innocence. His priest, John Palmer, handed him the summons bearing the chapter seal. He broke it open and read the words, then nodded. 'I believe you have also entertained an important guest this evening, Simeon de Beverley.'

'You are misinformed, sir. I have had no guest.'

'Oh? Do you deny, then, that Daniel Hawk spent the evening at St Peter's?'

Wulfric de Morthlund jerked himself from his stupor and leaned forward in his seat until his great belly overhung the table. His eyes were suddenly clear and sharply focused as he fixed Simeon with a look of purest hatred. 'What's that he says? My priest was at St Peter's?' His fist came down with force upon the table, scattering food and dishes everywhere. 'My God, I'll break his bones for this, I'll—'

'Father Wulfric!' Simeon's voice, though low, had a cutting

edge that reached across the room. 'You sent your priest on an errand that made him responsible for three newly orphaned children. He did what the Church expects any priest to do in such circumstances. He brought the orphans to a place of safety.'

'And stayed an hour,' de Figham commented.

'He stayed only long enough to fulfil his duties as a priest.'

'He could have left them at the gates,' de Figham insisted.

'Damn him to hell!' de Morthlund exploded. 'He should have left them to the Devil! I gave him no leave. He has no right to go sneaking around St Peter's in my absence. So help me God, I will break every bone in his body for this disobedience.'

Father Cuthbert stepped forward and raised a hand for silence. 'Brother Wulfric, you are in error. Look closer to home if you would vent your anger.' He glanced at Cyrus with a warning scowl. 'Look to the one who would stir that anger to his own advantage. We have come here for the woman, Alice.'

'Then take her and be gone,' de Morthlund spat. He jabbed one sausage-like finger in Simeon's direction and hatred was written in his purpled face when he added: 'And be sure I have not yet done with *you*, Simeon de Beverley.'

Cyrus de Figham rose to his feet and bowed politely to his guests. 'Gentlemen, if you would be kind enough to accompany us to the other room, I would have you all bear witness to the claiming of the woman. Since you were all present when she returned to the house two hours ago, I wish you to observe her safe removal from my house.'

They followed de Figham through a curtained doorway into a shaded room with candles set in sconces all around. A table in the centre of the room was covered by a sheet of yellow cloth, and under it a body lay. As they filed through the doorway a figure scuttled from a dark corner and flung itself over the corpse. Some crossed themselves in haste, others drew back, for Knut the hunchback was grotesque, and in the half-light he was like an animal.

'This man found Alice in his hut on the pasture,' de

Figham said. 'She was his woman. She was to have his child, but while he was fetching wood she hanged herself.'

'Lies, all lies,' Simeon exclaimed, then strode to the table and snatched back the cloth, only to gasp out loud at what he saw. The rope had been hacked some distance from the knot, leaving the fibres biting into her flesh. It was Osric who cut it free and Antony who closed the bulging eyes.

'She lied under oath,' de Figham said, addressing the entire room in superior tones. 'You were there. You all heard her. She swore before God that she was chaste while all the time she was the hunchback's whore. See for yourselves the dead child between her legs. She was Knut's whore, a liar before God and a fornicator with the most base, the most disgusting form of human life. See how he fawns and drools upon her body. Question him for yourselves. He understands words and can nod or shake his head like any man.'

'This is your doing, de Figham,' Simeon said, and his voice was cold.

'*My* doing? Have a care for your accusations, Simeon de Beverley. It is already known that you are conducting some kind of personal vendetta against me. Before this company of trusted men, how will you substantiate claims that this is *my* doing?'

Simeon hesitated. He was a priest and Alice had come to him in private confession. Her words must not be repeated here, and so he could not accuse de Figham openly. There was only one thing he could do for Alice now, he could expose the last vestige of her shame for all these curious eyes to gaze upon. 'Your brand is on her.'

'What? What is this latest slur you make upon me with your whispers? Speak out. Let these men know what new crime you add to my account.'

'Your brand is on her,' Simeon said, and there was a gasp of horror in the room. 'You marked her as you mark your beasts. She stayed because of your barbaric mutilation, and you shall answer to the Church for it.'

Cyrus de Figham drew back in mock amazement, then turned an open-handed appeal to all those present. 'My

185

brand?' he questioned, as though the suggestion appalled him. 'My *brand*? Would I dare commit such an outrage on any human being? Brand-marks are for curs and cattle, not for people. I am a canon, a servant of the Church. I would not stoop to such a heinous crime. Father Cuthbert, Father Wulfric, Father James … I appeal to everyone gathered here. Will you allow such open defamation to continue? I am accused unjustly, most unjustly.'

'Then how do you explain this, Cyrus de Figham?' With a muttered 'Forgive me,' Simeon drew the cover down. There was much blood on Alice's clothes. When he opened them a gaping wound was there, a wound as large as a man's hand and deep enough to expose the bone beneath. De Figham's brand was gone. It had been hacked from Alice's body with a knife.

CHAPTER TWENTY

There was uproar in the room which would not be subdued for many minutes. Simeon's rage overwhelmed him and ran from his control. His left hand closed around the folds of de Figham's tunic. His right came up, the hand balled into a fist, and would have smashed into the other's face, had Osric not hung the weight of his arm upon it. De Figham, held fast with his face only inches from Simeon's, stood with his hands in the air as if to declare his innocence in the matter. His near-black eyes bored into Simeon's, narrow and glinting, as he challenged his enemy to reveal the full force of his rage.

'Do it!' he goaded softly. 'Do it and damn the rest.'

'You killed that woman,' Simeon growled into his face.

'Prove it.'

'You cut out the brand.'

'Did I?' de Figham smiled.

At his back, de Morthlund lumbered forward with his arms outstretched. He felt a weight against his chest and looked down to find the little monk from Flanders in his path. Barely reaching as high as the fat man's shoulder, he gripped his pilgrim's staff in both hands so that its bulbous end made a hollow in the stained tunic and the flesh beneath it.

'Step aside, you cockroach,' de Morthlund grunted.

'By your leave, sir. Stand off,' the monk replied. 'This matter is personal. Let them settle it between them.'

'What? You impudent cur!' With a belch the fat man swayed on his feet, groped for the arm of a chair and dropped heavily into it, too blown with food and wine to make more than a grumbling protest.

The two priests stood like stags with antlers locked, glaring at each other, their faces set. Osric still gripped the raised fist that would break de Figham's face, and those looking on were struck by the resemblance these antagonists shared. The priest of St Peter's had the same noble profile and lordly bearing as the canon of St Martin's and, were it not that one was Norman dark and the other Saxon fair, they might have shared the same aristocratic family line.

'Strike me if you dare,' de Figham hissed. 'Shake off your ugly nursemaid and strike me.'

'Have you no conscience?' Simeon demanded. 'You killed her as surely as if you had tied that rope around her neck with your own hands, and then you cut your brand away to hide your guilt.'

'No other man will dare say that of me.'

'I know it for the truth, and you will pay, de Figham.'

'Not I.' The black eyes flashed as the mouth curved in a cruel smile. 'The woman harmed herself in a fit of shame, then took her own life in the hunchback's hut. Or perhaps the hunchback did it. Ask him. He will admit to anything.'

'It was you. *You* ordered the brand hacked from her flesh.'

'Your word against mine, priest. I charge you again to prove my guilt.'

Simeon struggled to free his arm from Osric's determined grip. 'I'll see you in hell for this, de Figham.'

Osric gripped him more tightly, reached over with his free hand until his arm and shoulder were wedged between them, then began to prise Simeon's fingers from de Figham's robes. 'Unhand him, Simeon. Your anger works against you.'

'I'll not stand by and . . .' Simeon snarled, and there was an unfamiliar hardness in his eyes.

'Let go, Simeon!'

'Aye, unhand me, priest.' With these words de Figham managed to dislodge the loosening grip and draw back a pace. He turned to those around him and began to protest with a show of righteous indignation. 'By all that's holy! This priest has lost his senses. You heard, you saw ...'

'Devil's cohort! I will silence you!' Simeon strained against Osric's grip to take hold of de Figham again. The canon stepped away, just far enough to incite the other's anger with his close proximity.

As the others gathered closer, de Figham crossed himself and held his hanging crucifix aloft. 'See how he strains as a mad dog fights the leash? I call upon you gathered here to remove this person from my house. Where is my priest? Where is my guard? Come close, to me. See how your canon is in need of your protection. Am I not safe from attack in my own house?'

When all was calm again de Figham stood with his hands clasped in priestly fashion, reciting a prayer for the soul of the man who now struggled between two others for the freedom to strike him down. It was a fine performance and Simeon, robbed of all reasoning by his impotent anger, played well the part in which de Figham had trapped him. Even Father Cuthbert, flanked by two clerks for his personal protection, doubted the evidence of his own eyes and ears.

De Figham's party filed back into the hall where the debris of their feast still littered every table. They allowed their goblets to be refilled with wine and in their turn they offered their host sympathy and promises of support. Not one among them offered a word in Simeon's defence, for those few who saw the whole scene as manufactured were loath to risk offence by saying so.

Cyrus de Figham watched the party from St Peter's carry the body away. They had come for Alice and he had dutifully obliged them. He had been surrounded by company when the hunchback came a-blubbering and took two men from the yard to cut down the body and carry it to the house. No hint of guilt could rest upon him. He was as innocent of this death as the other priests who had been sharing his table when the news was brought. Now he stood in the courtyard with his priest and his guard close by him, and all the dinner guests in their finery gathered at his back. The other party, led by Simeon, bore the bodies of Alice and her unborn child on a wide piece of oak, covered by the yellow cloth and a woollen blanket, as if the extra covering might keep the chill of death away. De Figham smiled as he watched them go with their torches blazing to light the way, their hoods turned up and their steps matched one to the other.

'You are my witnesses,' he told his guests, so loudly that no man in the departing company would miss his words. 'This Simeon de Beverley has once again sought to destroy my reputation with his lies. That canon elect of St Peter's is deranged. He claims to have the qualities and the powers of a saint, but any sane man can see how the Devil moves in him and drives him to this, this unholy obsession.'

Osric turned his head to throw a threatening glance at the grinning, black-clad Cyrus.

'Leave it be,' Simeon told him, so calm now that his voice was icy cold. 'God's face was turned when this foul deed was done. The Devil has had his hour this night. I swear it, Osric, the Devil has had his hour.'

A shabby man came creeping from de Figham's house, skirted the watchers and dared to approach his host.

'Father Cyrus, you sent for me some hours ago and . . .'

'What?' the vicar of St Jude's was seen to flinch as de Figham's black gaze was turned directly on him. 'What is it? What do you want of me?'

'I come from Thorpe, my lord canon. You sent for me. I hoped . . . I wondered . . . perhaps a small endowment for my church? St Jude's is sorely in need of repair and all my petitions so far have been in vain.'

'St Jude's?' De Figham passed a hand over his brow, then tipped a few small coins from his purse and said: 'Here, take this for your trouble. My priest will see that you are taken safely back to your village. That ranting canon elect has vexed my mind until I cannot recall why you were summoned here. No matter, you may go now.'

'But sir, I had dared hope . . .'

'Go at once. Return to your family, and if this night has inconvenienced you in any way, be sure to place the blame where it belongs, with the man who brought us all to a state of distraction. Blame Simeon de Beverley. The repercussions of this night – and I fear there may be many – will owe their shape and substance to that mad priest. Pray for his soul. God knows, he needs our prayers.'

The vicar was led off, clutching his coins as tightly as he held his disappointment, to a saddled donkey waiting at the gate. De Figham watched the torches moving across the distant meadow, then drew his priest, John Palmer, to his side.

'Get news to York of this,' he told him in a whisper. 'Tell Fergus of the details, embellished as you think fit, and have him make sure the archbishop hears of it before I make my official complaint to him. And tell young Fergus his woman will be at the house we agreed upon by noon tomorrow.'

'All has gone splendidly, my lord,' John said. 'This night's events are much to your credit.'

'The night is not over yet,' de Figham told him. 'Simeon's star is falling and nothing can be over until it strikes the earth and blows itself apart.'

'What more is to be done, my lord?'

'What more?' De Figham counted on his elongated fingers. 'We must question the hunchback in the presence of a witness to set the fact that Alice was his woman and the child she bore was his. We must take a written statement from every guest.'

'But the hour is late. They are ready for their beds.'

'They are ready to serve their injured canon,' de Figham corrected. 'And the more weary they become, the more readily they will serve in order to rush home to sleep. I will have those statements while these events are fresh in their minds. My complaint to Geoffrey Plantagenet will be carried to York tomorrow.' He turned his face to the sky and smiled, then placed an arm around his priest and added: 'I have a mind to send messengers to Rome. His star is falling, John.'

191

That night, when the vicar of St Jude's returned to his home with only six coins for his efforts, he found his wife beside an empty hearth, weeping and tearing at her hair in grief. Some men had arrived during his lengthy absence and carried off their daughter. One man among them paid the mother eighteen shillings to relieve her loss and vowed the girl would be returned when his master, whom he declined to name, had tired of her. In that poor house in the shadow of a crumbling village church, the vicar and his wife counted out their coins and wept and prayed together.

In York the Jew, Aaron, sent his pupils to their homes long before their lesson-candles had burned down. He was unsettled by the atmosphere in the town. The archbishop and his friends were at the hunt, a thing unheard of on the Christian sabbath. There was unrest at the palace and noisy gatherings in the streets around the Minster, and there were rumours that the Jews were at fault. A Jew had been allowed within the palace walls, seeking an audience with the lord archbishop, and he had gone there openly and boldly on the Jewish holy day. Now the archbishop himself was flaunting holy Christian law by riding out to hunt on their own sabbath. Some whispered that the Jews had turned the St Matthew's Day procession into a riot and so Geoffrey Plantaganet had sought to bring their rabbi to account. If this were so the archbishop was at fault. Others said that Aaron had presented himself at the palace unannounced, to protest against the harassment of his people. While some blamed the one and some the other, that element bent on toppling Geoffrey from his throne put word about that the rabbi and the archbishop were plotting together to plunder the coffers of their own blessed church of St Peter, York's wealthy Minster. The people were suspicious, so they blamed the Jews.

When the last student had left his house, Aaron closed all the shutters and slipped the bolts in place. His house was close to Coppergate, within sight of the ruin of his father's house in Coney Street. Every Jewish house was conspicuously built of stone, with neither brick nor thatch to match it to its neighbours, for they were more vulnerable to attack than any other. Most Jews of any substance practised usury, a thing outlawed to Christians by their pope. It brought them heavy interest and it placed men in their debt, and every promissory note they held was some man's personal curse. It was believed that Geoffrey's predecessor, Roger du Pont L'Eveque, had borrowed heavily in order to rebuild, on a lavish scale, his Minster's choir, so that he would be remembered after his death. That debt had grown while the see of York was in the greedy hands of the crown, with no archbishop at its helm, and now it was said to stand at more than £4,000. All Christians knew all Jews to be their enemies and hated them the more while paying interest.

It was close to midnight when he heard the rapping at his door.

'Who is there?' he called in Hebrew and again in English.

The answer came in muffled tones through the door. 'Hozah, the wood-carver. Give me refuge, Rabbi. I am pursued.'

Aaron unlatched the door, identified the man and bade him step inside. 'What is it?'

Hozah was nervous and so breathless he could barely deliver his message. 'They saw me. They saw my face. I was recognised.'

'Calm yourself,' Aaron said. 'Tell me what happened.'

'The priest, the one who was dragged from his cart in the Christian procession yesterday. He has been found, stripped and beaten in an alley close to Fossgate. The hunt was late returning to the palace, and many of the young men from the archbishop's party refused to seek their beds. They went about in groups, carousing through the town in search of women and entertainment.' He paused to gasp a few ragged breaths. He was not young and the dash from Fossgate, in fear of his life, had left him exhausted. Aaron led him to a chair, poured wine for him and watched him drink.

'Can you continue?'

Hozah drained his cup and nodded.

'Then tell me first why you were on the streets at this late hour.'

'I was returning from the deathbed of an infant scalded by a cooking-pot. My cousin was with me and we came by the alleyway to avoid the carousers. There we found the priest and tried to help him.'

'He was still alive?'

'Barely. He had been savagely beaten. My cousin covered him with his cloak and offered comfort while I ran for help, but before I had reached one end of the alley, the arch-bishop's men were upon us from the other. The cry went up that a priest had been killed by a Jew. I hid myself. I was afraid. There were so many of them and they were incensed. I was too afraid, too cowardly to help my cousin.'

Aaron poured more wine, pulled up a stool and sat beside the older man. 'No man will call you coward for concealing yourself from a mob of angry Christians. Where is your cousin now? Did they take him away?'

Hozah looked up and his eyes were bleak. 'They stoned him.'

'May God have mercy . . .'

'They stoned him and then they fell on him with sticks and swords. He made no sound, but the priest cried out before he too was killed.'

'They killed their own priest?'

'In a frenzy,' Hozah nodded. 'He received some blows meant for my cousin. I must have uttered a cry, for suddenly I was seen and the mob came after me. Had I not been familiar with those alleyways and yards . . .'

'You must remain here tonight,' Aaron told him gently. 'I will seek a meeting with the archbishop tomorrow and speak for you. I will tell your story as it truly happened and we must pray that we can douse this dangerous flame before it runs beyond control.'

'I do not trust him,' Hozah said. 'Whatever promises he makes are valid only for the duration of his mood. King Henry is dead and with him our guarantee of security. Your own father was amongst the first Jews to die in the riots

194

marking Richard's coronation. Henry looked to the future and served us well. These sons of his would profit from our misfortune and toss us to the mob without a qualm.'

Aaron's reply was stopped by the sounds of running feet and raised voices in the street beyond the door. A mob was outside, hurling stones and yelling obscenities, but their presence was mercifully brief. Their cries diminished as they ran into other streets, and with their passing the rabbi muttered a prayer of gratitude that his house was spared.

'Go upstairs to my bed and rest yourself,' he said to the trembling Hozah.

'Rabbi, if I stay here these Christians will accuse you of harbouring a murderer in your house.'

'So be it,' Aaron sighed.

'I had nowhere else to go. I fear I have endangered you to save myself.'

'Go up and sleep, my friend.'

'What will you tell the archbishop?'

'The truth. Now go up.'

He watched the older man climb the wooden stairs, then listened until only the steady breathing of his guest could be heard from the upper room. He pulled on a long-sleeved shirt that reached his knees, leaving the neck unthonged so that his muscular chest with its tight black hairs contrasted sharply with the crisp white line. The six-pointed star that was the symbol of his faith glittered on the chain around his neck. Above it his face was grim, the hooded eyes troubled. These flash-fire spats between Christian and Jew unsettled him. It was a problem never to be solved. No Jewish physician dared refuse to treat a sick Christian, yet if his patient died they called him murderer. No money-lender dared refuse a loan to a Christian, yet if the borrower defaulted, the Jew was blamed for his high interest rates. Even the so-called protection of a monarch served but half its purpose, for when a Jew died his wealth and property passed by law to the crown, and his promissory notes became crown property. Many a gentleman had owed a Jew whose death left him indebted to a king, and many a king demanded settlement with a heavier hand than would the money-lender.

'*Aaron of Ethiopia.*'

He looked up with a start, believing he might have dozed on his stool and failed to hear Hozah climb down the wooden steps. 'What is it?'

There was a figure standing in the shadows beyond the hearth, a tall, thin figure swathed in black and wearing a hood that completely concealed his face. Aaron glanced at the door and saw that the latch was still in place, at the shutters and found them closed, at his sword-belt hanging above the fire grate.

'Who are you? What do you want with me?'

'*Aaron of Ethiopia.*'

'Yes, I am he.' There was an oddness in the voice. He pushed his stool aside and rose to his feet, aware that he had locked gazes with this stranger even though he saw no features in the hood. His mind was clear and yet his thoughts surprised him, for in spite of the circumstances he was calm and unafraid. 'How can I help you, friend?' He was puzzled by his own words, yet into the silence he asked again: 'How can I help you?'

The figure raised a hand and signed the Christian cross as if in holy blessing for the Jew. Then it stepped back into the shadows by the wall and faded from his sight, but before it vanished it spoke a single word, a word that seemed to come from Aaron's own head: '*Simeon.*'

CHAPTER TWENTY-ONE

Fergus de Burton had undergone a change of heart which caused him to view his life and his ambitions in a new light. The hunt had gone extremely well. Geoffrey Plantagenet had proved to be as good as his reputation, a superb horseman with a brilliant mind. He tuned his thoughts and his instincts to those of the beast he hunted and, by a combination of skill and cunning, turned the animal's flight to his advantage. Fergus liked him. He liked the dangerous undercurrents of his personality and the rapid changes of mood that carried him from mirth to rage in an instant. This clever, irreverent archbishop, with his lust for power at any cost, his zest for life and his constant fear of plots against his person, had shown young Fergus a better way ahead.

'You impress me, boy,' Geoffrey Plantagenet bellowed as he slapped his new friend on the shoulder and grinned into his face. They were eating breakfast in the palace hall, and last night's high spirits still coloured Geoffrey's humour. 'You have more courage of your own than all my minions could gather up between them. I like that courage, lad, I like it.'

'Some call me a headstrong fool, my lord, and blame my youth for it.'

'I call it courage when a man dare hunt beside me and not bend by a single inch to give me favour.'

'I play the game to win, my lord.' Fergus looked sideways at his host and offered up the gift he knew could melt any heart, his winning smile. 'Even against the best of men.'

'Well answered, lad, and win you shall, for I have a mind to make something of you. Stay here in York and be my chancellor.'

'Your chancellor?' Fergus laughed aloud at that. 'I have no skills to be anything of the sort. My lord, I am a younger son without land or expectations. I have spent my life in the pursuit of pleasure. I lack the discipline to be a clerk, let alone a chancellor, and if you think for one moment that I am fit for the taking of holy orders . . .'

'Ye gods, I would not wish such a curse on my enemy,' Geoffrey roared. 'Can you read and write?'

'Of course.'

'Latin?'

Fergus nodded. 'I served my time in the classroom.'

'And French?'

'I was two years at court.'

'Well then, you have your talents and your wits, charm in abundance and a blade-sharp mind. These things could make you chancellor within a single month.'

Fergus allowed his smile to fade and now his face became by contrast serious, his blue eyes grave behind their veil of straight, fair lashes. He looked at the archbishop steadily, knowing that here was a crossroads in his life, a chance to leave his old path for the new. It was as if he had a fine stag squarely in his sights. To win it, all he had to do was shoot his arrow straight and true so that it hit the target.

'My lord, I would be much more than your chancellor.'

'More? You ask for more?'

'I do, my lord.'

Geoffrey Plantagenet sat back in his seat and scrutinised the man seated beside him. He saw a handsome, elegant youth only lately into his twenties, a laughing charmer with an open face, and as stimulating a companion as could be found in the whole of Christendom. He had taken to him wholeheartedly. He was of a mind to endow the lad, but was not disposed to barter for the quality of his gift. By demanding more than the generosity offered, this Fergus de Burton might leave the archbishop's palace empty-handed.

'You disappoint me,' he said coldly.

'I think not, my lord, if you will hear me out.'

'I have heard enough to judge. You would be *more* than chancellor.'

Fergus de Burton pushed a bowl of meat aside and leaned his forearms on the table. His face had a look of concentrated gravity and his tone was intimate when he said: 'I seek to be your personal man-at-arms, your adviser and your friend. Men take to me with ease and I have the talent to make them trust me. They talk openly in my presence. Do you think they would be so open with your chancellor?'

'Go on,' the scowling Geoffrey said.

'I can be your eyes and ears in both York and Beverley. Give me a dozen trained men from among your soldiers who click their heels in idleness for want of occupation, a new suit of clothes and a purse to pay my way, and I will guarantee that no conspiracy or slur will flourish against you.'

'And no treasure will be disposed of by those canons of Beverley?'

'Not so much as an altar candlestick, my lord.'

Geoffrey looked about him with narrowed eyes. 'I trust no one amongst these fawning self-seekers with their silver tongues.'

'And wisely so, my lord.' Fergus leaned a little more intimately over the table. 'There is not a man close to you who has not already tried to get the measure of my loyalty, and I doubt they do it solely for your benefit. Your treasurer, for instance . . .'

'My treasurer? He plots against me?' Geoffrey demanded, his whole body stiffening at the merest suggestion of treachery.

'As yet I cannot say, though he is most eager to know with whom I am camped and if I might be turned against your lordship.'

'What? The snake! I'll have him thrown into the street.

Let's see how well he fares without my patronage.'

'Have ease, my lord, have ease.' Fergus's open hands and his ready smile diffused Geoffrey's rising temper on the instant. 'Why place a snake where you can no longer watch its movements, and perhaps install another in its place?' He saw the other man nod and check his fury and he was satisfied. That small hint was sufficient to clear the way for Fergus to the treasury, for any objection raised on his account would cast a greater doubt in Geoffrey's mind.

'My personal man-at-arms, you say?'

'The clothes will suit me better than a chancellor's pretty gown,' Fergus grinned.

'And my spy in Beverley?'

'Your eyes and ears.'

'And you will guard my back while I am surrounded by scheming priests and grasping clerks?'

'Your back and mine,' Fergus replied. 'Be certain of that, my lord archbishop. I will guard you so closely that any spite intended for you will have to pass through me to reach its target.'

'A comforting thought indeed.' He scratched the skin from which his fine beard had been shaved. 'De Burton. Would any man dare trust the name de Burton?'

'My lord, can any trust the name Plantagenet?'

The archbishop roared with laughter, slapped his thighs and thumped the table in amusement. Then he put up his hand, one elbow balanced on the table. 'Let us palm the deal, you impertinent whelp.'

Fergus slapped his palm into the other, the fingers locked, the elbows close together. Fastened thus they wrestled, laughing and straining one against the other, until the archbishop proved himself the stronger of the two.

Fergus was standing at Geoffrey's side when the Jew was shown once again into the gatehouse. By then the young man was wearing a tunic of grey and green from Geoffrey's private robe-chest, a girdle of gold heavily encrusted with gems, and borrowed boots that fit so well they might have

200

been his own. His presence, so grandly dressed and in such obvious good favour, caused a murmur of discontent among the priests and clerks already gathered there.

The rabbi told his story without embellishment. His voice was beautiful, low and deep, with a certain resonance that brought the big priest, Simeon, into Fergus's thoughts. He liked this tall, good-looking Jew and he believed his story to be true.

From time to time the archbishop, fully dressed in his ecclesiastical robes, leaned toward his young companion in the next chair, inviting comment or advice. He was not unaware of an air of sullen resentment in the room caused by the swift elevation of this charming stranger. Not one owned courage sufficient to complain and risk affront, so their discontent was centred upon the Jew. Two priests spoke out against him in their turn, intent on making his the hand that raised his people against innocent Christians.

'I have a mind to make an example of him,' Geoffrey whispered. 'The downfall of one of these rabbis will subdue the rest and pacify my priests. Besides, he is reputed to be amongst the wealthiest of our city's Jews. All he owns, including his promissory notes, will be forfeit if he is disgraced.'

'Aye, but to the crown,' Fergus reminded him. 'You will gain nothing from it. Your brother the king will claim it all to further his campaigns among the heathens.'

'True,' Geoffrey frowned. 'What course do you suggest I take?'

'My lord, you must not be seen to have a dubious part in this affair. It would not be fitting for your hands to be stained with this man's blood, or your reputation to hang upon his disgrace, simply to appease a gaggle of squabbling priests.'

Geoffrey chuckled at the description. 'What, then, do you advise?'

'Let it be known that you accept his story as the truth, then allow events to prosper or fail as they will. If things go well for the Jew you will be praised. If things go badly, ensure he has a fair and public hearing, then reinstate him as an honest man. Thus you will preserve his wealth intact, earn his devotion and prove yourself beyond the influence of those who conspire to use this innocent man against you.'

'Conspire? You see conspiracy in this?'

'Alas, I fear it must be so, my lord.'

Geoffrey's fist came down with a crash on the arm of his chair. 'Damn it all! I will not be manipulated.'

'Have ease, my lord,' Fergus said in a whisper. 'Do not lose your advantage by showing your mettle too soon.'

Geoffrey slumped back in his chair and glowered at the Jew. 'You say this Hozah is now with you? You harbour a fugitive, a possible murderer, in your own home?'

The Jew spread his two-toned hands, their pale palms uppermost. 'I simply gave an old man refuge from an angry mob.'

'His cousin was caught in the very act of murder,' a priest exclaimed, stepping forward with his two fists in the air. This was the keeper of Geoffrey's treasury and today he found no favour with his lord.

'Hozah and his cousin are innocent,' Aaron repeated evenly. 'Does it offend so deeply that a dying priest was comforted by a Jew, even though the Jew was stoned to death for his pains?' He turned his head and looked closely at the archbishop, his dark eyes hooded. 'Your priest, sir, might have lived, had he been given Christian help and not forced to wait until some passing Jew had mercy enough to attend him.'

A cry went up, a roar of outrage at the rabbi's suggestion that only a Jew could be relied upon to assist a dying priest. Their indignation was the greater because they knew the words as fact, and they knew no Christian would have done as much for any Jew.

Fergus leaned sideways in his chair. 'Take control, my lord. Bring them to heel and show them who rules here. Release the Jew and demand that no reprisals are brought against him, and see which of these priests dares flaunt your orders.'

'A hare to the hounds?'

'And more, my lord. We cannot know the number of our

202

sinners until we dare to tempt the virtuous.'

Much later Geoffrey said again: 'You impress me, Fergus de Burton,' and Fergus answered, much to his lord's amusement, 'You impress me too, my lord archbishop.'

When the rabbi had left the gatehouse under guard for his protection, and while Geoffrey Plantagenet attended to other matters, Fergus stood off in an ante-room, alone. His new cloak was about his shoulders, a vivid, luxurious thing of crimson and purple with a sable hood and fox-fur trims. As he surveyed his reflection in a mirror, he saw the man he desperately wanted to be. Here was a Fergus raised up before his time, no longer a younger son without a fortune but a man of no little power and quality. He wore a girdle of gold set with no fewer than forty precious stones, though his whole life of twenty pleasure-seeking years had never equalled a single one in value. Just hours ago his sights were set no higher than the bedding of a country vicar's daughter. Now he was ally to one of the most powerful men on England's shores, a man who would be king, so it was rumoured.

He grinned at his reflection in the mirror. His life was changed, his future was assured. For him the time for childish games was at an end. He knew he must act and think, conduct and advertise himself as a gentleman from now on, and before another year was out the name of Geoffrey Plantagenet, archbishop of York, would not appear on any man's lips unless that of Fergus de Burton shared the same breath.

The girl and a local woman hired as servant were in the house alone when Fergus de Burton and his men of York arrived to claim de Figham's gift for services rendered. She was no beauty but pretty enough despite her family's poverty, and she was not unwilling to be claimed by this fine young man. A husband would be found for her easily enough when her abductor tired of her, and if her life was hard from that day forward, she would have fond memories of being carried off and bedded by a gentleman.

'Is she unharmed?'

'She is,' the servant replied.

Fergus nodded. The girl was smiling and glancing coyly in his direction. His loins moved with a young man's needs, for he had desired this girl, without success, for many weeks. He could have taken her without fear of punishment. The daughter of a humble country vicar would not count herself disadvantaged by such an encounter, so long as her parents were fairly paid for the temporary loss of her company. The temptation was strong in him but his itch for power was far the greater. He saw himself as he had been reflected in Geoffrey's mirror, and he knew that image deserved much more than a rough-voiced country lass upon its arm. For his reputation's sake he could not have her, and for that same reason he would use her and her family well.

The girl was given a cloak and a purse of gold, then set upon a cart packed high with flour, wine and salt, with woollen blankets, candles and a heavy, fur-lined cloak of quality enough to see the impoverished vicar through the next several winters.

The vicar of St Jude's was an old man long before his time. His clothes were shabby and his eyes were dull, as if the light of hope had died, or perhaps had never shone there. Beside his gate were seven graves where his first wife and their six small sons were buried. His well was dry, the roof of his house was badly in need of thatch, his nearby church was falling down around his ears and all his stores were empty. No benefactor had been found in twenty years to keep this modest Norman church in good repair, and were it not for the mice and the birds that scurried around its altar, his sermons would often be heard by none but God.

'All this? All this for me?' While the girl greeted her weeping mother and went indoors to nurse her disappointment, her father stood outside with his mouth agape, staring at the cart. By his manner he was sorely unacquainted with good fortune.

'All this and the horses too, for your inconvenience. My men believed they were acting in my interests. I hope to convince you that I had no part in this abduction, and I beg you to accept my goodwill along with your daughter's safety.'

'Sir, I am overwhelmed ... quite overwhelmed.'

'By the look of your church, it too is overwhelmed,' Fergus replied drily, eyeing the broken roof where several ravens gathered like death's own watchers. The windows were covered over with leather, the stones crumbling in places, the threshold cracked and split by tufts of grass. The whole of it was in a sorry state.

The vicar sighed and shook his head. 'I fear St Jude is sadly neglected by the town and its canons. My own villagers trek a mile to worship at the altar of St Anne's, where they may kneel in prayer without fear that the roof will come crashing down on their heads.'

'St Jude? I do not know of him.'

'His Feast Day is October 28th, though few observe it. He is the patron saint of all lost or hopeless causes.'

Fergus cleared his throat and asked: 'The patron saint of *what*?'

'Of hopeless causes.'

Now the young man blinked his eyes slowly and deliberately. His mouth twitched at its corners, but otherwise he held his face in check. He nodded once, curtly, and walked away, his lips pressed hard together and his fists clenched. When he reached the group of horsemen gathered by the gate, he slipped between their mounts to conceal himself from view, released his pent-up breath and roared with laughter.

At last he managed to gasp: 'Would you believe that this miserable, god-forgotten village is served by the patron saint of hopeless causes?'

Chad, the sharp-featured man to whom he spoke, looked all about him with a critical expression on his face. He had come from York to this and he was displeased by the exchange. 'I would.'

Fergus shook his head, still laughing. 'St Jude, the hapless overlord of all things failed. Did you ever see such a desolate place as Thorpe? Every tragedy that ever saw the light of day must be drawn here as bees are drawn to a honey-pot.'

'Perhaps this saint works a contrary ministry,' the soldier mused. 'Perhaps we are intended to bring him a worthy cause so that he may reduce it to a state of hopelessness.'

Fergus laughed again. 'You could be right, my friend. Even the vicar's daughter, as comely and as willing as she is, has failed to get herself tumbled when all the signs were promising that she would. St Jude the hopeless, saint of all things undone!' He peered over the neck of a horse, coughed the laughter from his throat and brought his smile, though not the merry dancing of his eyes, under control. 'I fear our mockery will offend the vicar who serves this unfortunate saint.'

Chad looked down the length of his nose at the shabby little man who was helping to unload the cart and offering profuse and grovelling thanks for every item carried into his house. 'That miserable face is enough to discourage grass from growing,' he observed.

'A village fit for starving mice and famished ravens,' Fergus chuckled. 'Lost causes, indeed! This place is choking on them.'

As his amusement diminished, Fergus strode to a hillock from where he could view the location as a whole. It had a broken church and a vicar's house, and beyond them a huddle of homes which made up the village. It owned two streams, some fields and a few narrow ditches, and to the north was Bygot Wood, with good timber and, no doubt, some decent game. What really interested Fergus was the many things this neglected village did *not* possess. It had no canons fretting over it, no lord to steal its resources, no wealth for greedy men to haggle over. Nobody would be offended if he took it as his own good cause and kept its sorry church from total ruin. He could endow it with a modest altar to St Fergus, with a good supply of candles to be lit at evensong, so that every day his name would be remembered.

'It needs a worthier saint than this unhappy St Jude,' he muttered. 'It can be done. This place can be raised up and I can do it.'

In his heart he knew this was no idle boast. A man was much admired for the work he did and the money he gave to benefit the Church. Good deeds would earn him gifts from other churches, gifts of money, altar-cloths and furniture, robes and hangings, stones for rebuilding and leadings for broken roofs. And so the deed attracted other deeds and was greatly increased at small initial cost. The benefactor's name was spoken on many lips and remembered in others' prayers. His fame was passed from church to church, his reputation coloured and multiplied. Here was a cause young Fergus could believe in, for it would return high profit on his investment. Beverley lay just two miles to the south, with all its trade and pilgrimage to offer. Not far away the River Hull ran wide and deep for the port, the Humber estuary and the sea. If Geoffrey Plantagenet owned this land, and Fergus was sure he did, then Fergus would have it from him as a gift. He would build his house here, make himself the patron of St Jude's, and he would feather his new-found nest with Geoffrey Plantagenet's favours.

He watched the ravens circling and cawing, their rest disturbed by stones thrown up by Chad. 'Thorpe of the hungry ravens,' he mused, half to himself. 'Or Ravensthorpe, that has a prettier ring to it.'

In York, as in any other town of ecclesiastical importance, those young men and boys who were the sons of the nobility were employed to assist the canons with the many complexities of their robing and disrobing. These dressers passed from one man to another, learning to dress correctly every rank and office, to bear the required accoutrements, to perform according to the holy hour of the day and its strict religious demands. They were no more than servants to fancy masters, but they had ears to hear and lips to tell, and few were ever content in their employment. For three days Fergus had observed the way of things inside the archbishop's palace. What he found there was a cauldron of hostility and simmering discontent, and all it lacked was a clever man to stir it to the boil.

One of the youths who dressed the archbishop saw a silver shilling on a rug beside the couch where Geoffrey often took his rest. When it became clear that he alone had seen it lying there, he covered it with his foot and kept his silence. A fallen glove was all the deception needed. He stooped to retrieve the glove and, when he moved away, the coin was gone.

'I have him,' Fergus said, and winked an eye.

'Tempting the virtuous, Fergus?'

He grinned and winked again. 'One loose tongue can be more valuable, and less cumbersome, than an army.'

'And less expensive,' Geoffrey noted.

It cost another shilling to discover the plot against the Jew, a petty plot that might be left alone and come to nothing. The intended victim was the old man, Hozah, but Aaron was to know of it in advance and when he went to defend him, as he surely would, he too would be attacked. Six men from the achbishop's palace were involved, though a single gardener would lead the rabble on their crafty errand. This was as simple, and as hazardous, as setting the hungry fox amongst the fowl, for no one could predict where the jaws would bite. If the rabbi chose to intervene on his innocent friend's behalf, and if some faceless Christian struck him down, the archbishop's disapproval would be meaningless.

Fergus took down the names of three canons and their clerks for future use, outlined his counter-plan to Geoffrey and, with his archbishop's blessing, rode at once to the rabbi's shuttered house near Coppergate. When he met the Jew at the door he knew why he had been so anxious to act on this. He liked the man. He saw in him those qualities most obvious and most admirable in Simeon de Beverley. Here, too, was a brilliant scholar who suffered and yet preserved a deep compassion for his fellow man. Here, too, was a man of faith who could throw off the shackles, the pomp and show of religion and look his god full in the face and still believe. Like Simeon, this Aaron was a man among men, and such a thing was never to be wasted.

'Be gone within the hour,' he said. 'These men of Geoffrey's will guard your house from looters and arsonists, but you must be gone from here before the townspeople can make a scapegoat of you.'

'So, the archbishop will protect my property but not my person?' Aaron remarked, and there was resignation in his smile.

'He can do no more than his Church allows and his enemies will tolerate,' Fergus told him. 'Protect yourself. Meet the archbishop halfway in this. Do you have a horse?'

'What need has a Jew of a horse?'

'Then you must use mine. Here, take it and be gone from here before the streets are filled and the gates are barred.'

The Jew's smile was slow and cynical. 'What, should I take your mount and be apprehended as a horse-thief, on your orders, before I have ridden half a mile from here?'

'You do not trust me,' Fergus said, and his surprise was genuine.

'Why should I trust you, Christian?'

'Because I like you, Jew.'

The two men surveyed each other at close quarters, the hooded brown eyes intense, the blue defiant. Then Aaron took the reins and said: 'I am prepared to leave at once.'

'How so? Were you warned of these events?'

'I was, but not by any living man. God bless and keep you, Fergus de Burton. When a man dances between so many sharpened blades, he may not know which one it is that draws his blood.'

'Go safely, rabbi.'

As Aaron rode away the sharp-featured soldier known as Chad leaned down and offered his muscular arm to Fergus. The young man grabbed it and swung himself lightly into the saddle behind him.

'St Jude of hopeless causes will welcome him,' Chad commented grimly. 'He has some powerful enemies. His days, I think, are numbered.'

'Aaron will find sanctuary.'

'Not under the sanctuary laws of Beverley,' Chad reminded him. 'No Jew, however deeply in need, would be accepted there. The law is for Christians, not for Jews.'

'He will find sanctuary,' Fergus repeated.

'Ah,' Chad said. 'Another clandestine move. You choose your friends unwisely, my young friend. The subtleties you toy with can be costly.'

'Aye, but they're exciting,' Fergus laughed, heeling the horse.

'Your life will be a short one, lad.'

'But I will live it to the hilt,' Fergus vowed. 'And I will make my mark. Are you with me, Chad, or would you rather be drinking in some ale-house?'

The older man twisted in his saddle to look his grinning passenger in the eye. 'Would a sane man forfeit his ale for the sake of a rabbi and St Jude?'

'No, but he'd do it gladly for a fortune and St Fergus.'

They were laughing as they rode the protesting horse toward the archbishop's palace. Already noisy groups of men were gathering in the streets. Jews were closing their shops, locking their doors and fastening down the shutters on their windows. Soon the baiting would begin, and Fergus was satisfied that one particular Jew would soon be safely outside the gates of York.

CHAPTER TWENTY-TWO

There was concern amongst those living within St Peter's enclosure. The man to whom they looked for leadership and guidance had become troubled in his mind and in his soul. There were times when Simeon de Beverley, that gentle scribe, wore a mood of such ferocity that his friends dared not approach him. When he fenced with Osric or Antony in the sheltered clearing by the eastern wall, the clash of steel on steel and the meeting of heavy wooden staffs proclaimed the anger bottled up inside him. At night he made his circuit of the city as before, only now he made a detour across the marshes, pitting his fleetness of foot and his stamina against the treacherous pools and hidden currents there. He took his turn amongst the labourers, felling trees, chopping logs and carrying bricks for the lining of the new well. He even spent long hours in the blacksmith's yard, swinging a heavy, long-handled hammer until the iron on the anvil rang as loudly as a tolled bell.

He was fighting with Antony and using staffs of metal instead of wood when he underestimated the little monk's considerable skills and took a blow from the iron across his forearm. The bone was not broken, but the blackened bruising so concerned Osric that he forbade any further use of iron staffs and admonished Simeon for his lack of wisdom.

211

'You drive yourself like a madman,' he complained. 'You boil inside and your anger goes nowhere. Would you have the others, young Edwin or young Peter, follow your example and open each other's skulls because they do not own your skills?'

'Forgive me, Osric. I am much distracted.'

'Aye, distracted.' Osric deliberately knuckled the bruise on Simeon's arm until he winced. 'Careless men make dangerous teachers and are likely to get themselves hurt. Find ease for it, Simeon, before that anger of your eats up your soul.'

'I will seek God's guidance.'

'A wiser man would seek his woman's bed.'

'Perhaps.'

'You need Elvira, Simeon.'

The blue eyes softened and the feelings of his heart were in them when he said: 'I know.'

That night he wrenched his shoulder in a fall from one of the boundary walls. He had been running for an hour in total darkness, and when he came to leap the wall his body was too weary to clear its height. He came home limping, his right arm hanging, and made no more than a grunt of protest when two men using leather straps threw all their weight against it until the joint clicked back in place.

'My love, how can I help you?' Elvira asked, and in her dark eyes he saw himself reflected in miniature, as if her love had captured him and trapped him there, in duplicate.

'I am tormented,' he confessed.

'I know that.'

'My prayers avail me nothing. I seem to flounder in a mire without direction, blind to all but my own impotence.'

'Bury Alice,' she said. 'Do what must be done in its allotted time. All else will come when He is good and ready.'

'So I do believe, Elvira,' he nodded. 'And yet I cannot rest or still the turmoil in my head. When God at last is ready I fear I will be too exhausted to do His work.'

'I do not speak of God,' she said. 'It is that hooded figure we all wait upon, the one who shapes our lives and bids us be prepared without a hint of why or when or how.'

Simeon took her in his arms and stooped to press his lips to her soft cheek. Her breasts were firm against the muscular hardness of his chest. Holding her like this, so warm and yielding in his arms, was one more torment added to his store.

'He will not take the boy,' he promised her.

'Can you be sure?'

He nodded, holding her more tightly. Then his hand came up to stroke her hair, and all his love welled up in him for her. 'Oh yes, I can be sure. The boy is ours. He will not be taken from us.'

'I wish I had your faith.'

'And I your strength, Elvira.'

Alice was buried beside Father Bernard, close to the enclosure wall where her grave would be covered by the same wild growth which hid the murdered canon's final resting-place. It was a simple service in which Simeon, with his friends' approval, offered full absolution of her sins. He stayed beside the grave long after all the others had left, squatting in the dirt with an aching heart. Her life had been so full of hope and promise until Cyrus de Figham crossed her path and marked her out for tragedy. Elvira had known that she would choose to die rather than bring a hated child into the world. In that hunchback's filthy hut, with nothing left in this world or the next to offer solace, she had died alone with none to pray for her.

'I'll pray for you, Alice,' he promised. You shall have a candle every sabbath on St Mary's altar, and you will be remembered for your suffering and your courage.' He rubbed his eyes where tears were stinging, cleared his throat and added: 'And you will be avenged. Somehow, some day, I swear I will bring your murderer to account.'

He returned to his scriptorium and sent away the priest who was guarding the entrance. A hole had been drilled in the massive oak of the door, and through it hung a length of stout chain, the other end of which was fixed to the heavy bar that held the door fast from the inside. Elvira was not strong enough to lift the bar unaided, and there were times when she must be left alone in the scriptorium. This simple iron pulley had been devised to allow him access or to lower the bar when he was forced by circumstances to leave her unaccompanied.

He frowned now at the chain. It had been pushed through the access hole although no signal, no prearranged rap on the door with the hilt of a knife, had been given. It was unlike Elvira to be so lax about her own security. He felt his scalp grow tight and knew that this sudden apprehension for her safety was but a small part of the price he paid for loving her. He grabbed the chain and heaved on it until the bar was lifted and, when the door swung open, stepped inside.

'Elvira?' A glance told him that she was gone. He rushed to the ladder that leaned against the crossbeam. The upper platform where she slept was empty. 'Oh, God. Elvira.'

On the rushes by the fireplace he found young Edwin curled asleep with his knees drawn up and one thumb held loosely between his teeth. His face was slightly flushed, the eyes unfocused, their lids only partly closed. One of his sudden sleeping fits was on him.

'Edwin! Edwin, wake up!' Simeon shook him roughly, then hoisted him up and, gripping him by the chin, shook him again and repeated: 'Wake up, Edwin!'

Despite the rough handling, many long minutes passed before the boy began to stir. The instant his eyes snapped open Simeon shook him by the chin again, demanding, 'Where is she, Edwin? Where is Elvira?'

He regained his senses rapidly. 'A small boy came to fetch her, Father Simeon.'

'Peter? Was it Peter?'

Edwin nodded. 'It was the little boy with the yellow hair and strange blue eyes. He came up from the well and when she had gathered a bundle of things together the lady followed him back inside.' He paused to issue a long and noisy yawn. 'She said I was to tell you that a man had been injured by robbers and his horse and baggage stolen. The lady took food and water and medicines.'

'Who is he? Did the boy say who he is, or where?'

'No, sir, only that his head and his ribs were injured. He does not wake but mutters in his sleep in some foreign tongue.'

Just then Simeon saw that his translation of Beverley's history had been left open on a library table, the intricate coloured frontispiece clearly visible. Among the swirls and sweeping lines Elvira had left a mark, and by this he knew exactly where the injured man had been taken. No map that could be identified had ever been made of the maze of tunnels running beneath the town but, with the help of Peter's expert knowledge, a secret map existed. Incorporated into Simeon's pattern of knots and spirals and curving lines was every twist and turn of every underground cavern and passageway. Elvira's mark showed the vaulted area close to the chapel of St Thomas. Dire circumstances must have persuaded the boy to take a stranger there, even though he might wander for days and find no exit from that subterranean maze. Those tunnels were jealously guarded by all who knew of their existence, for at their heart lay the relics of St John of Beverley, and near to them the entire of Beverley's ecclesiastical treasure.

Simeon would have followed directly after Elvira, had not a messenger arrived at the scriptorium to announce that Daniel Little Hawk was at the gate. Young Edwin jumped for joy and smoothed the crumpled leather fronts of his new tunic.

'He kept his promise,' he beamed. 'Father Daniel has come to see me, as he promised.'

Behind him the messenger indicated that Simeon should come at once. 'Father Daniel has been injured in an accident,' he said. 'Osric is at the Minster church with Father Cuthbert, and our visitor will speak to none but you.'

Simeon hesitated with a glance toward the well, then brushed away the mark Elvira had left for him and closed the embossed cover of the book. 'I will come,' he agreed, and followed the messenger out.

Daniel Hawk was waiting in the chapel with his back turned to the door. He was leaning heavily on a stick and his unlined hood was raised. He turned as Simeon and Edwin entered, watched the happy smile fade from the boy's face and made a brave attempt to replace it with one of his own. It was a sorry effort, for his face was badly marked, his mouth swollen and one eye, surrounded by livid bruising, was tightly closed.

'A fall from a horse,' he said, speaking awkwardly from the less damaged side of his mouth. 'How are you, Edwin?'

'I am well, sir. You suffered a fall? But how can that be? You are the best of horsemen.'

'So I am told,' Daniel replied lightly. 'But even the best of us sometimes make mistakes and horses have a habit of stumbling on uncertain ground.'

Edwin moved closer, his brown eyes wide with concern and his fingers fluttering as if he sought to touch the wounds but did not dare. 'I think it must have trampled you, Father Daniel.'

'Aye, lad, I think perhaps it did.'

'Let me inspect that jaw,' Simeon said. 'By the look of it, I'd say that it is broken.'

Beneath the bruising and swelling, the jaw appeared to be intact, though Daniel's splendid teeth had pierced the inner side of his mouth in several places. A deep cut ran along the side of one eye and under his brow. But for an inch or less, he would have been blinded. When his hood was lowered a long wound was revealed from his crown to his ear. Another was on his neck and yet another could be seen across his shoulders.

'That horse of yours did a fine job on your face,' Simeon observed. 'With Osric's help it might heal cleanly. You were lucky not to lose an eye and half your teeth. Why do you need the stick?'

'My leg is bruised.'

'How badly?'

'Enough for me to need the stick,' Daniel answered wryly.

Edwin filled a cup with wine and handed it to Daniel. That it was communion wine already blessed for the evening service did not occur to him, and had it done so he would not have faltered in his offer.

216

'Show me the leg,' Simeon ordered, and when Daniel's robe was raised he saw that every inch from knee to ankle had suffered serious bruising. When he touched his thigh, albeit gently, the young priest swayed on his feet and his face drained of colour. Simeon led him to a stool and helped him sit with the injured leg outstretched. 'Edwin, go swiftly to the Minster and fetch Father Osric. Tell him to come at once but do not mention the cause by name in the hearing of others. We must keep Father Daniel's presence here a secret.'

'Yes, sir. Is he badly hurt?'

'I fear he is, but he will mend in time.'

'Will you stay with him?'

'Of course I will.'

Reluctantly, the boy slipped out and sped off for the Minster and the infirmarian. When he was gone Simeon locked the door and helped Daniel off with his cassock. He wore a long shirt beneath, and when this was unfastened and raised the full extent of his injuries finally came to light. His left leg was black and blue right to the hip. He had much body hair, but through the thatch of it could be seen an area of heavy bruising right across his chest. His back was laced with marks that had split the skin and bled through his linen shirt in a criss-cross pattern.

'No fall produced these wounds,' he said gravely. 'And no horse kicks so precisely as to damage a man's entire leg in such a way. Your attacker was an animal of a different breed, I think.'

'Cyrus de Figham had me followed when I came here two nights ago. I stayed too long. My master was displeased.'

'Wulfric de Morthlund did all this?'

Daniel nodded. 'Father Cyrus told the truth about the woman. She was not murdered. She hanged herself.'

'I know that.'

'His man, the brute who keeps his dogs, cut out the brand before it could be seen and his master chastised for it.'

'I know that, too.'

Daniel Hawk closed his shirt over his chest, hiding the bruising and the thick dark hair. 'They will destroy you,

Simeon, if they can. Cyrus de Figham's clerks are preparing statements for the archbishop concerning your claims to sainthood through the raising of the dead.'

'I have made no such claims,' Simeon protested.

'A source of either well-paid or well-meaning witnesses will swear you have. He records your giving of full absolution without confession, and the miraculous healing of your crippled foot. He cites that old charge against you of fornication, of siring a son and keeping another man's wife for your pleasure while claiming the saintly virtue of chastity.'

Simeon chose his words with care. 'He has always been too much preoccupied with those old charges against me. They were disproved two years ago. Archbishop Roger was content with the verdict then, and if any doubt persists, it is of de Figham's stirring.'

'There is doubt, and he will play upon it, Simeon. Letters of serious complaint against you, witnessed and endorsed by several priests and canons, have been dispatched to York and Rome. He flings a net about you, Simeon, and this time he is determined you shall not escape it. I heard about the unfortunate incident at his house. There were many witnesses who will speak against you. It seems that temper of yours was used to good effect, and much to your detriment.'

'A man's rage can be a terrible thing,' Simeon agreed, fingering the wound on Daniel's head. 'Sometimes it flares and feeds upon itself like a woodland fire, running beyond control regardless of consequences. This wound will have to be reopened and cleaned. Some hair and dirt are trapped inside where the healing has begun.'

'I saw the woman, Simeon. Two years ago, when I was mending after the great fire.'

'Two years? You have known of her for two whole years and yet said nothing?'

Daniel's smile was twisted in his swollen face. 'I owe you my life ... and more.'

'No man is in debt to me. To God, perhaps; to himself, but not to me.'

218

Daniel closed his eyes, remembering. 'I watched her tending the sick and giving succour to the dying. She was beautiful. No, she was more than beautiful, she was exquisite. You must love her deeply.'

'As deeply as any man can love a woman, yes.'

'Is she your wife?'

'No, Daniel, not my wife in any sense. I have made a solemn vow of chastity.'

'Then perhaps your love, though you profess it to be deep, falls somewhat short in measure?'

Simeon smiled and shook his head. 'Not so. I know it to be the greatest love. Only my love for God Himself is greater.'

'Can that be so?' Daniel asked, and in his eyes was the hope that it could be so. 'Can spiritual love transcend the very stuff of which man is made?'

'It can transcend all things,' Simeon replied, softly and with true conviction.

'Human love is brutal,' Daniel said bitterly. 'It embodies every vice hell ever produced.'

'Indeed, some find it so. But human love is also magnificent, Daniel, and when it is, it embodies every virtue known to God.'

When Osric came at last he made a brief inspection of Daniel's wounds and immediately demanded: 'What manner of man did this to you, Father Daniel?'

When he saw that Edwin hovered by the door, the young priest repeated his story of a fall from a stumbling horse. Osric did not believe it for a moment, though he had caught the glance and respected Daniel's discretion.

'No beast that is capable of inflicting such injuries is fit to breathe the same air as decent men,' he declared. 'This wound on your head will have to be reopened.'

'So I have been informed,' Daniel groaned.

The knife was out and the wet cloths laid in place when Edwin's eyes glazed over and his lids began to droop.

'The boy! Look to him, Simeon!' Daniel shouted the timely warning so that Simeon caught the boy as his body sagged. Then he cried out again, this time in pain, as the infirmarian's blade sliced into the deep gash on his scalp.

219

The man Elvira tended was tall and muscular in build. His legs and arms were long and thick, his shoulders powerful and his fingers longer and more tapered than any she had seen. Peter had found him near the old convent lake, wandering dazed through a patch of marshy ground in search of shelter and drinking water. He had been badly beaten, stripped of his clothes and robbed of all he possessed, and a blow to the head had left him all but senseless. Had Peter not found him when he did, the man would surely have died. Had he not brought him here, to this safe place, he might have become the victim of common stakers. His golden star had been ripped from around his neck, but she knew this man for what he was: a Jew, and no Jew was ever welcome in Beverley.

'He is so black in colouring,' she said, 'and yet the palms of his hands are almost as pale as yours and mine. See how the lines are deeply etched, as if some scribe had traced them with his pen.'

'And the soles of his feet, also,' Peter told her. 'And look at his face, mother. Did you ever see such features on any man?'

'Never,' Elvira said, as she lifted the cover over his woolly chest. It seemed to her that Jesus Christ, also a Jew, should be the very link that forged goodwill between this man and his Christian enemies.

The man on the bed began to turn his head this way and that in fitful sleep, muttering words they could not understand. His voice was striking in its depth and, against the dark skin of his cheeks and lips, his teeth, with their wide centre gap, were milky white.

Peter pushed a roll of cloth beneath his head to make a pillow. Where sweat stood out on his skin his hair was clinging in shiny black coils. Elvira watched his face in fascination. It was a face that might have been carved from darkest, smoothest mahogany. His nose was long and thin, with flaring nostrils, his lips full and wide, his forehead broad and strong. His eyes flickered open, so dark that the black pupils were indiscernible. The whites were tinted blue, the lids hooded as if weighed down by the thickness of his lashes. She saw his gaze focus upon her face, the strange eyes widen with a kind of wonder, and for a moment his fitful movements stilled.

'*Shalom,*' he said, and his voice gave the word such charm, such resonance, that she was captivated.

'*Shalom,*' she repeated, the alien word falling lightly off her tongue.

He smiled and moved one two-toned hand as if to touch her face, whispered the greeting again, and then slept.

CHAPTER TWENTY-THREE

When Fergus de Burton returned to Beverley six days
after the annual Feast of St Matthew, he was convinced
his fortunes were assured. He had Geoffrey Plantagenet, a
man whose arrogance, vanity and mistrust ran equally deep,
eating out of the palm of his hand as readily as would a docile
raven. The archbishop had sent him here on trust, to see and
hear, and then to judge the climate in the town. If Cyrus de
Figham stood to achieve his ends he would have York's
support. If not, he would be left to stand alone.

At Burton, in the house where his family had lived for several
centuries, Sir Hugh de Burton accepted this good fortune tongue in cheek. His son had been for too many years an amiable
wastrel to convince this iron-handed man that he would ever
improve himself by either skill or wit. At twenty young Fergus
was still a fool, for all his endearing qualities. He chose his
friends unwisely and tupped his women without a thought for
anything beyond his lust and their availability. That he now
had the favour of York's archbishop was much to his credit;
that he had the judgement to use it well was hardly possible. Sir
Hugh saw the new clothes and the fancy arms, the fine mount
and the company of men at his son's heels and was impressed.
He saw the same grin, the same mischievous twinkle in his eyes,
and he reserved his enthusiasm.

'Any man who befriends a Plantagenet is either a simple-ton or a blind man,' he declared. 'And since your eyes seem healthy enough, young Fergus, I can but deduce the former. All this is but a peacock's show and you remain the fool you always were.'

'Oh ye of little faith,' Fergus grinned, toasting Sir Hugh with a goblet of recently imported wine.

'Oh ye of little wisdom,' his father countered, with amusement.

'You'll sing a different tune, sir, when my plans come to fruition. I intend to build a fine house at Thorpe and ...'

'At *Thorpe*?' Sir Hugh interjected in disbelief. 'You seek to lay your foundations in *Thorpe*? My God, none but a fool would seek to establish his fortunes on that miserable and unprofitable patch of wasteland.'

'I intend to endow the church there for my fame, and I will give it a splendid altar dedicated to St Fergus himself.'

'St Fergus? You wouldn't dare!'

'I will do it,' Fergus grinned, marking the glint of respect in his father's eyes. 'Be sure I will.'

'The Church will not allow it, boy. They will see your arrogance for what it is and forbid that you attempt to exalt yourself by basking in the reflection of the saint whose name you bear. God's teeth! They will never allow it.'

'Oh yes they will, sir. My patron, Geoffrey Plantagenet, will insist upon it.'

'Why, you cunning, conniving whelp,' Sir Hugh exclaimed. 'What an ill wind was abroad the night I sired you. I swear you have the effrontery of the devil.'

'And the favour of the archbishop elect of York,' Fergus grinned.

'God's teeth, they'll soon be calling him St Fergus de Burton, patron of mischief-makers.' He rubbed his hands together and scowled deeply. 'If you can do this, Fergus, it will provide an enviable feather for our family's plumage. However, if you should cross swords with the Plantagenet, if your plans go awry and you fall from grace, I cannot afford to give you my support. You will not be allowed to put our

223

family at risk with your wild schemes.'

'You will disown me if I fail?'

'I will, and your uncles and cousins will disown you, too, in their own interests. The house of Burton will not be made to stand downwind of that archbishop's displeasure.'

'But if I succeed, I will have your full support?'

'Without question. My lad, if you succeed we will have just cause to be proud of you. Now, listen well to some fatherly advice. Have a care in all your dealings with the Plantagenet. He is as slippery as a tub of worms and no more to be trusted than a viper.'

'Oh, I have his measure,' Fergus smiled.

Sir Hugh smiled grimly. 'Just be sure he does not have yours. What will you do here?'

Fergus seated himself across a chair and spoke to his father over his folded arms. 'For years these canons of Beverley have been fighting amongst themselves without direction. Now Cyrus de Figham seeks to join them all against a common cause.'

'The lame scribe of St Peter's?'

'Who else? De Figham hates him with a passion.'

'And you?' Sir Hugh asked. 'Do you also despise this Simeon de Beverley?'

'Not at all. In fact, I hold him in the highest esteem. I have made it my business to learn everything there is to know about him, and what I know convinces me that he is worth more than all these squabbling canons weighed together. He's a fine man, father. I like him.'

'Have a care, Fergus. The role of Devil's advocate does not sit well on such young and frivolous shoulders as your own.'

'Nor will I try to suit myself to such a role,' Fergus assured him. 'My presence here is neither to condemn nor to protect him, but to stop de Figham in his plan to take control in Beverley. My lord archbishop is disinclined to see some canon gain at his expense.'

'*Some canon?*' his father repeated. He leaned forward in his seat to point an accusing finger at his son, and his face was suddenly grim. 'Have you no notion of what you will be dealing with in your plan to stop de Figham? That black-eyed priest is more cunning and more savage than a wolf once his blood is heated. His ally is Wulfric de Morthlund, who has neither conscience nor scruple to his credit, and together they could eat a man like you at one sitting.'

'Ah, but they'll have to catch me first.'

Sir Hugh's fist hit the table with such force that Fergus flinched. 'Damn it, boy, you'll fall at the first hurdle if you set yourself against them with the idea that either one is just "*some canon*".'

'You underestimate me, father. I have no intention of openly setting myself against them. I will simply make a place for myself in every camp and carry my information back to York.'

'And play all the ends against the middle, hoping that handsome smile of yours will ingratiate you far enough to stab every player neatly in the back? Fool's talk! See yourself for what you are, my boy, no more than a pawn in other men's clever games. Bishops and knights and kings are beyond your reach. They invented the game, Fergus, and believe me, you are barely qualified to play.'

'We'll see,' the young man said, smiling again. 'And now, with your leave, sir, I will ride for Beverley to begin my work.'

'I will not give my blessing in this,' Sir Hugh replied.

'I am disappointed, sir.'

'My good wishes you have, and my hopes that you succeed, but I will reserve my blessing until such time as you prove yourself worthy of it.'

'Be sure I will,' Fergus grinned.

'With you, my lad, I can be sure of nothing.'

When Fergus left his father's room, a man emerged from behind the hangings and poured himself a goblet of wine. This elder son resembled his brother closely, though he was more stocky of build and wore a fine red beard, and the backs of his hands were heavily marked with freckles.

'Well,' Sir Hugh demanded. 'What do you think of your brother's latest escapade?'

'Foolhardy,' Angus replied. 'If he believes he can manipulate such men as Geoffrey Plantagenet, Cyrus de Figham and

Wulfric de Morthlund, my brother is sadly mistaken.'

'One slip will see him out of this world and into the next with sickening swiftness,' Sir Hugh said acidly. 'The Plantagenet will have him hanged if he suspects any measure of treachery on his part.'

'Indeed he will. It seems to me that all Fergus will succeed in doing is bringing the wrath of powerful men to our door. I judge him to be dangerous and I believe he should be stopped.' He stroked his beard and paced the room before adding: 'We should let it be known that he is cut adrift from us to make or lose his fortunes as he will, and if his wild plan fails, no stain from it will come to us.'

'And if he succeeds?'

'If he succeeds, the name of Burton will prosper along with him. An altar to St Fergus, indeed! I believe the Devil himself would admire him for that piece of strategy.'

'He would indeed, but in the end the rightful saint of that place at Thorpe will surely win the day. Fergus plays York against Beverley, archbishop against canons, canons against each other. He will place himself between deadly enemies, de Figham and the lame priest, and expect to emerge unscathed. I fear he plays beyond his skills, Angus, and St Jude of the hopeless causes will love him for it.'

At Walkington that morning, the horse Fergus de Burton had loaned to the Jew came up for sale at a fraction of its value. The four men arrested for its theft claimed in their own defence that stealing from a Jew, who no doubt had robbed a gentleman of his mount, should not be counted against them as a crime. Fergus claimed back his horse and questioned the men closely before they were dragged off, still protesting their innocence. After that he rode directly to the lake at Beverley where the attack took place and, with his own men-at-arms and several helpers from the town, scoured the area in search of the missing Jew.

'He was stripped naked and beaten,' Chad observed in his dry tone. 'Four against one. Not pretty odds.'

'If reports of him are true, it would take that many to bring him to his knees. I'll wager he did not make their task an easy one.'

The soldier eased his body in the saddle, making the leathers creak beneath his shifting weight. 'And they would have paid him back four-fold for every blow he struck in his own defence. If he has survived, I will believe in miracles.'

'Unless he was aided.'

'Aided? A helpless Jew with skin the colour of mud?' Chad cleared his throat and spat upon the ground. 'I doubt it.'

Fergus de Burton would not concede that Aaron was lost. He liked the Jew. He admired him as he did the priest of St Peter's, for the breadth of his mind, his strength of character, and for the faith that made him what he was. Such men were rare and greatly to be valued. It angered him that someone of such quality could have his life snuffed out by common thieves.

He spoke to a monk at the nearby chapel of St Thomas and was told that no such person as he described had sought sanctuary there. Nor had those people living on the edges of the town seen anything worthy of report. The gateman on the bar angled for payment for his information, then told them nothing that might help their cause.

'He must be somewhere,' Fergus said.

'Aye, at the bottom of yonder lake,' Chad offered.

Fergus shook his head. 'My instincts tell me otherwise.'

Chad stared off into the distance beyond the town's Great Bar. He was beginning to recognise the twists and turns of his young master's mind. He saw in Fergus a leader in the making, and he blessed the day he was called from the tavern, and from his enforced idleness, to be this likeable upstart's man-at-arms.

'Two miles and more to St Peter's,' he said, then shook his head. 'He never made that journey. He's in the lake. They probably murdered him before they stole the horse.'

'Then damn them all to hell,' Fergus said angrily. 'No horse is worth such a price.'

'Tell that to them. Such men would slay a Jew for less than a horse, believe me. Give up the search and be glad that your

227

property is returned to you. We come too late to help him. Your friend is at the bottom of the lake.'

Fergus shook his head again and turned his horse for the bar that straddled the town ditch. 'I'll speak to Simeon before I end the search,' he said, and Chad, shrugging his leather-clad shoulders, rode after him into the town.

The conversation Fergus had with Simeon de Beverley within the compound of St Peter's was a cautious one, with neither sure how much to hide, how much to give away. Simeon listened closely to the story, watching and listening for the ring of truth in every word.

'I gave the horse to Aaron the Ethiopian for his personal use,' Fergus repeated. 'I gave it freely and it was stolen from him. Are you acquainted with the man?'

'You know I am,' Simeon replied.

Fergus nodded thoughtfully. 'When the recent troubles flared at the instigation of the canons, he rode from York in search of sanctuary. Where else would he come but here?'

'If he rode for Beverley, he was in gravest error. Despite the law, this town would not give sanctuary to his kind.'

'No, Father Simeon, but he knew that *you* would give it.'

Simeon shrugged, admitting nothing. 'All men are made in the image of God, even Jews.'

'I believe you two are of a kind. I saw in him yourself dressed up in different colours. You would have helped him, had he come to you.'

'Perhaps,' Simeon replied, hearing the question in the other's words. Then he met and held the steady stare of the younger man and said again, 'Perhaps.'

A small light danced in Fergus's eyes, but the smile it indicated did not reach his face. 'Do you believe he lives?'

'I believe it to be possible, since God is merciful to those in need. If Aaron has found a friend, then you can be sure he is safe from harm and on the mend.'

'If?'

'All things are possible,' Simeon answered carefully.

Now Fergus grinned. This conversation could have taken place amongst their enemies and still he would have read the deeper message in Simeon's words. The Jew was alive and safe. The cautious words and candid gaze of this priest told him as much.

'Then may I leave the horse with you and trust you will return it if you should encounter him again?'

'You may.'

'And will you assure the rabbi that his property in York is safely under guard? A few more days and it will be safe for him to return there. Tell him I will bring word and an escort for his journey. He knows he can trust me.'

'Does he?' Simeon looked closely at the veiled blue eyes. 'Very well, I will convey the message … *if* I should meet him again.'

Fergus paused with his hands on the saddle as he was about to remount. He glanced around him. Osric stood off at a distance and a group of men were working to clear a nearby stream of mud and garden debris. Chad stood by the gate, one foot placed on the water-trough from which the horses drank, his elbow resting across his knee and his chiselled profile betraying his Roman ancestry. Several nuns were walking in a nearby garden, and Fergus wondered briefly if the woman Simeon was said to harbour here was one of them. When he was sure his words could not be overheard he said: 'The archbishop has received ill word of you, Father Simeon.'

'Indeed?'

'Letters of complaint have already reached the palace from here in Beverley. I think he will not act upon them until he sees how things lie here, but act he must, since the petition is valid, and soon, if he is to keep his peace with Rome.'

'With Rome? Am I to be spoken of in Rome?'

Fergus nodded. He was no longer smiling and his eyes, without glint of laughter, were more readable. He knew the priest's reputation and did not fear his scrutiny. 'The journey is long and perilous, but be sure the petition will reach the pope in due course.'

'Then I hold the advantage until the papal legate gets here, if he is to come at all.'

'Don't count on it,' Fergus told him. 'Tactics, Father Simeon, simple tactics. The petition is on its way to Rome and the archbishop elect has been notified of the situation. The ground has been prepared and the proprieties observed. What, then, if certain men should force the issue?'

'Would they dare?'

'Why not? I certainly would if I were in their place,' Fergus admitted. 'I would make my strike while the iron was hot and plead that Rome's instructions, and the archbishop's decision, came too late to prevent the inevitable.' It was a warning Simeon could not fail to understand. 'For a man of peace and learning, you have many powerful enemies, Father Simeon.'

'My problems do not concern you, Fergus de Burton. Be advised that you play with fire when you seek to meddle in such matters. Should you be seen to make the acquaintance of Jews and disfavoured priests, you might find yourself tarnished by association.'

The smile returned to his face as Fergus offered his hand to the priest. 'I'll take my chances,' he said, then swung himself lightly into the saddle and added: 'And be sure to give my horse and my good wishes to Aaron of Ethiopia – *if* you should meet him again.'

At the gate the soldier, Chad, was already in the saddle and prepared to meet the others waiting outside. 'Well, do we call off the search for the Jew?'

'We do,' Fergus smiled. 'Are you a man of your word, Chad?'

Chad's chiselled face grew hard. 'Any man but yourself would know the edge of my sword for asking such a question.'

'Well then, my friend, since Aaron lives, you may believe in miracles.'

Watching them leave, Simeon pondered on the problem of Aaron's safety. For a week the Jew had lived in the cavern beneath St Thomas's chapel, regaining his strength and endearing himself to those who had saved his life. Neither

Osric nor Antony, nor even the ill-tempered Thorald, could find fault in him. His powers of debate were matched only by his extensive knowledge of philosophy and theology, and many long hours had slipped away unnoticed in his company. Father Cuthbert judged him a man above most men. Peter, ever hungry for instruction, hung upon his every word and dared to quarrel with him on any point that raised a question in his quick young mind. The men of St Peter's had taken him to their hearts, and in their easy, complex conversations, rarely recalled that he was a Jew and they were Christian men.

'All made in the image of God,' Simeon repeated, watching Fergus de Burton turn in the saddle and raise an arm in salute as the gates closed at his back. This week of friendship with the Jew had not been shadowless. Elvira sang his Hebrew songs, her light, soft voice uniting with his deeper tones to create a sound of undeniable charm. And in those underground caverns Simeon had seen the gift the Ethiopian gave in endless measure to his lovely nurse. It was the gift of laughter, and it caused her cheeks to flush and her eyes to dance with ebony lights. It chased the sadness from her heart and gave her the happy demeanour of a child. It was a gift that Simeon, in all his years of loving her, had but rarely had the privilege to offer.

When his prayers were finished Simeon slipped through a narrow opening behind the altar of his little church of St Peter. He had not known this place existed until young Peter had led them here to escape the great fire. The ancients who designed these churches lived with the threat of invasion and attack. They needed to pass with speed and safety from one building to another, often bearing away their altar plate, their treasures and their communion wine. They also knew the risks of venturing with their goods and jewelled robes into the streets, where vagabonds and thieves might lie in wait. These tunnels had been their lifeline, providing a swift, convenient passage between the Minster church and its many dependent churches. How Peter had known of them was still

231

a mystery, but without his knowledge and his courage they would surely have perished with all those other poor souls when the Minster took light.

Now Simeon crawled along a passage until he reached the ancient tunnels leading down. He had chosen the longest route in order to cross the lake beneath the Minster where St John of Beverley's original monastery lay half-submerged and partially preserved. Once there he paused to stare about him and feed his senses on the simple wonder of the place. Many hundreds of years had passed since the Saxons drained the beaver lake and Bishop John founded his monastery on the site. The town sprang up around the walls, the schools grew in their fame, the bishop was canonised and the pilgrims came. Now the great Minster dominated the town and the ancient stones had slipped quietly into antiquity, entombed beneath the greater edifice. Now the beavers were gone, but still the beloved abbey of Bishop John remained, an eerie, lost reminder of another time.

By little points and shafts of light from above, the lake was turned to polished jet with the cavern's vaults reflected on its surface. Simeon untied the old boat he kept at its edge. Here the painted heads of saints looked down on empty halls and squat stone pillars, on rounded arches and timeless scenes reproduced by the brushes of long-dead monks: the Fall of Eve, the Expulsion from the Garden, the Labours of the Months, the Agony of Christ. A stout stone staircase rose from the shimmering waters, supporting a carved arched door that led to nowhere. A pair of pillars, once the bearers of some massive arch, now stretched toward the roof with empty hands. A mound of fallen masonry, a curve of stone, the skeleton of a window: all resting here as if awaiting the day when time would be unlocked for them so that their splendour could be restored. Here, too, beneath the great Minster church, lay Beverley's treasures, its holy relics and its artifacts, made safe from the grasping hands of greedy men.

'God bless and keep you, John.' Simeon whispered as he steered his boat across the lake. 'We are the keepers at your shrine, the guardians at your gate. We will not fail you.'

Once beyond the lake, Simeon tied up the boat and walked the narrow pathway along the ancient stream whose waters, so vital to the monastery and its devotees, received the holy blessing of Bishop John.

'Be fresh and clear and pure for all time,' the saintly man had said, and so it would be, Simeon believed.

He followed its winding course until it looped away toward the Lairgate tunnels. Here he turned right and stooped into another opening that led to the straighter Keldgate passageways. Here and there the shaft of a well brought sounds from above; the cry of a child, the barking of a dog, the thuds and curses of some busy workman. He could hear the ditch as it made its sluggish way beyond the massive stone walls, and once he caught the unmistakable sound of a boatman's pole as it dipped and lifted, scraped and dragged, moving a craft along toward the landing-place at Hall Garth.

He heard their voices long before he came upon them, the deep rumble of the man's, the softer murmur of the woman's, the easy lilt of their shared laughter. He stopped to listen and his heart was troubled. For the first time in a decade he doubted Elvira and the unique, unconsummated love they shared. He had seen the way sweet words and laughter touched her heart, the way she came alive as she listened to stories of the outside world, the way the attentions of another man could warm her senses. She was a beautiful woman, young and worldly. The Jew was a handsome man with a life to offer. Without a faith to keep her locked behind the cloister walls, without a husband to love her in the flesh, how would she bear the temptations placed before her?

'Dear God, I must not lose her now,' he said aloud, then crossed himself and begged the Lord's forgiveness for his selfishness. Elvira deserved a life to call her own and the love of a man not bound by a vow that held her at a distance. He heard again the soft sound of their laughter and he knew that, if it came to it, he would steel his heart and set Elvira free.

He stooped beneath an arch into the cavern where they

233

sat, saw the table with its books and plates and cups, the bed with its wolf-skin cover and silken pillow. She rose to her feet, her long hair loose and glinting in the torchlight, her eyes bright as she flashed him a tender smile of welcome. His heart stirred as it always did at the sight of her, and yet his lips would not return her smile. Instead his eyes asked, 'Have I lost you?' and hers replied, 'My love, you have me still.'

CHAPTER TWENTY-FOUR

'G od's blessing, Rabbi Aaron.'
    '*Shalom*, Father Simeon.'

The two clasped hands, the rabbi and the priest. There was a bond of friendship between them which had been forged at their first meeting. In all their dealings since, and particularly in the matter of the Minster's restoration, each had found the other to be a man of high integrity. In this past week, while Aaron healed of his injuries and Simeon waited to learn the hooded figure's purpose, Simeon had found another friend and Aaron recognised in this enigmatic blue-eyed priest a kindred spirit.

Both men were dressed in grey and white. Simeon's cloak hung loosely from his shoulders. Aaron's borrowed shirt lay open to the waist, revealing the strips of white linen covering the wounds on his chest. His grip was firm, his eyes clear and alert. Osric was pleased with his progress and had declared him almost well enough to travel. Simeon had received this news with mixed feelings. He was reluctant to lose the stimulating company of this Jew, and yet he feared the consequences if he stayed too long among them.

'Your friend Fergus de Burton came in search of you,' he said.

'Ah, the handsome boy whose smile has the power to charm Plantagenets.'

Simeon smiled at that. 'He sends his greetings and returns your horse, with promises of safe escort home to York in a few days' time. Can he be trusted?'

'Aye, as any wayward child with a new toy can be trusted.'

'He says your house has been protected.'

'That is good,' Aaron nodded, 'though I have learned to keep little of any value there. You Christians are an unpredictable breed, my friend.'

'The fault lies not in our faith but in our temperament.'

'Your Christ was a Jew and stands amongst the most revered of our prophets. Because He loved all men and urged them to love one another, to live in peace, I fear there must be times when He despairs of us.'

'Especially when we squabble in His name,' Simeon observed. 'Your health seems much improved, my friend.'

Aaron's smile showed big white teeth near perfect in their shape. 'And how could it be otherwise when I have been sent an angel to nurse me back to health?' He glanced at Elvira and his gaze was soft. 'She has told me much about you, Simeon.'

'Then you have earned her trust. Do not betray it, Aaron.'

'Never. I am discreet in all I do and say. Neither you nor she will ever have cause to regret befriending me.' He drew the priest aside and lowered his voice to a husky whisper. 'This hooded man she speaks of, this black-robed apparition. How many of you have seen him recently?'

'We have all seen him,' Simeon answered gravely. 'Each man in his turn, though as yet we have no inkling of his purpose.'

'I too have seen him, Simeon.'

'You? Are you sure of that?'

'There can be no doubt. The black hood hiding his face from view, the height, the peculiar quality of the voice ... it was the same one.'

Simeon's concern was in his eyes and in the sudden tightness of his voice. 'When did this happen? And in what circumstances?'

'He came to me a week ago in York, on the day Fergus de Burton helped me flee the city. He appeared in my house although the doors were bolted and the shutters barred. He spoke one word and then he disappeared.'

'What word was it?'

'A word that brought me here and saved my life: "Simeon."'

The priest tapped his fingernail against his teeth in contemplation of the other's story. Daniel Hawk had admitted to glimpsing the figure on the eve of St Matthew's Feast. Edwin had seen it and now so too had Aaron, and what occurred to Simeon was that all were either living at St Peter's or had been driven there by circumstances shortly after their sighting.

'A gathering up,' he said at last. 'It is a gathering up, a bringing together of allies against some force that is yet to come.' He glanced at Elvira, who attended to her tasks with a small, contented smile on her lovely face, and his heart was anxious for her safety. Lowering his voice to a whisper, he asked the Jew: 'Has Elvira seen it?'

'Would she not have told you, Simeon, if she had?'

Simeon nodded. 'I do believe so.'

'Then perhaps his purpose does not include Elvira. If so, we should be grateful for the omission.'

The two were quiet for a while, each with his own thoughts, until Aaron broke the silence.

'You have not converted your lady to your faith.'

'Nor have you converted her to yours, I trust?' Simeon replied with a smile.

'Not I. Her soul remains her own. Elvira is a rare thing. This is a sorry life for her, my friend. Such flowers were never meant to blossom in the shade.' He saw the priest turn his head and hold his gaze with those wide eyes, as blue and as uncanny as the boy's, and he knew this Simeon had read his heart, and he was glad of it.

When Simeon left for the afternoon offices, Elvira went with him, leaving Aaron in conversation with Osric. The Jew's gaze followed them as they passed beneath the arch, Simeon

237

stooping to avoid the low curve of ancient stones, Elvira's fingers lightly entwined with his.

'God smiles on him,' he remarked in his low voice. 'He is blessed with a son in his own image and a wife most men would covet.'

Osric looked at him with some surprise. 'You do not know their story, then? You have not heard?'

Aaron shrugged and his smile was crooked, showing half his teeth. 'The story of a strange child given into Simeon's keeping? Of a woman he keeps and loves but does not bed? Ah, yes, I have heard, but I have not believed.'

'He did not sire the boy.' Osric confirmed.

'But Peter has his colouring and Elvira's dainty features,' Aaron protested. 'He is a perfect blending of the two.'

'Even so, his parentage remains a mystery. Elvira did not bear the boy and Simeon did not sire him.'

'I am astounded,' Aaron confessed.

'Nor does he bed the woman.'

'Now that I will not swallow, Osric. Any eye can see what lies between them. He beds her.'

'Not so. Simeon has never in his life enjoyed the pleasures of the flesh. He is sworn to celibacy, and he will keep that stubborn vow though Heaven itself should mourn the waste.'

The rabbi rose to his feet, his dark brow wrinkled into a frown. 'That cannot be,' he said, and again, more forcefully: 'That cannot be.'

'It is, much to his friends' regret.'

'They love and yet they do not *love*?'

'That is the way of it.'

'Then she is free to leave him?'

Osric shrugged his massive shoulders. 'As free as any who loves is free to abandon the other.'

The infirmarian watched the rabbi's face and saw his thoughts passing like shadows over the smooth, dark features. He knew the ways of men. This swarthy stranger had suffered an enchantment. His heart was lost and Elvira was the cause. He said as much to Simeon after vespers.

238

'I know,' Simeon replied.

'And she is much taken with him.'

'I know that, too.'

'Then if you must persist in your vow, send Aaron away before you lose her.'

Simeon shook his head. 'It is not safe for him to return to York. I will not endanger his life for my peace of mind.'

'St Theodore's rest is close enough, and with the lake and the marshes set between them . . .'

'Osric, we cannot send this man away simply because he loves without our full approval.'

'Then find another nurse to tend his injuries and to be his constant companion. This situation is unacceptable, Simeon.'

'Aye, we are sorely tested.'

'*Tested?* This Jew intends to take Elvira from you!'

'I know that,' Simeon sighed. 'I know that.'

During the afternoon offices, Cyrus de Figham chose a seat next to Wulfric de Morthlund and sang the psalms and responses in a lusty voice. The man beside him was sullen in his mood. He ate from a dish of honeyed figs, licking his fingers and sucking his lips more noisily than was necessary. He was resentful of the duties of his office and cared not who might notice his ill humour. From time to time he heaved a sigh of displeasure that warned those seated around him that his volcanic temper was simmering, and at such times Wulfric de Morthlund was not to be trifled with.

'Once again your priest is conspicuous by his absence, Father Wulfric,' Cyrus whispered maliciously.

The fat man grunted and his glance was sharp. 'Father Daniel is unwell after taking a bad fall from his horse. I have excused him.'

'Indeed? I hear the "fall" has lamed him.'

'He is temporarily indisposed, nothing more.'

'And temporarily out of favour, Father Wulfric?'

De Morthlund sucked the honey from his fingers, then tongued fig seeds from his teeth and spat them out. 'I keep my servants in their place,' he said.

'And leave them free to roam at will, it seems.'

This last remark was accompanied by a knowing grin. De Morthlund, as anticipated, rose instantly to the bait.

'What do you mean by that? Come, man, if you have something to say, speak out. I have no inclination to bandy words with you on the subject of my household. Speak out.'

Cyrus de Figham cleared his throat, then studied his elegant fingers and considered his words most carefully. He had no wish to bring about the fall of Daniel Hawk, though he knew enough about a certain Edwin to have de Morthlund raging like a bull. What he wanted was to use his information to the very best advantage, mainly to discredit Simeon but also to twist a favour from Daniel Hawk. He needed the key to Simeon's fortress, that den of secrets he called his scriptorium. He was convinced the woman and the boy were hidden there, and he wanted them: more than the Beverley treasure, more even than the relics of St John of Beverley and the Evangelist, he wanted Elvira and that son of Simeon's.

'Perhaps, this time, you went a little too far in your chastisement,' he said at last.

'Too far?' De Morthlund gave a derisive grunt and pushed another honeyed fruit between his glistening lips. 'I think not. A few cuts and bruises, a week or so of deprivation, and he will be more than ready to bend to my will.'

'Unless he finds some other means of comfort for his ills while he is exiled from your patronage.'

'What? What other comfort?'

De Figham looked sideways until his eyes were dark slits in his face, 'I hear he still frequents the enclosure of St Peter's.'

For a moment de Morthlund wrestled with his fury, then brought it under control and demanded: 'If what you say is true, then all it proves to me is that my priest still has the head to help himself. He must have his food and medicines from somewhere. The infirmarian there is the best this town can offer, and since my priest is penniless on his own account . . .'

'Ah, well, then, you have no cause to be concerned,' de Figham conceded with a sly grin. 'If your Little Hawk has injuries needing attention, and if St Peter's offers hospitality at little cost, then the time he spends there is probably innocent.'

De Morhtlund's head swivelled on his great shoulders, twisting the fat around his chin into a shapeless mass. His eyes shrank in his face and his mouth turned down at its outer edges, accentuating the bulbous hang of his lower lip and the juice dribbling from its corners. 'What more do you know of this, de Figham? What games does he play while my back is turned?'

'What games indeed?' de Figham asked. 'I simply wonder that he dares seek out the company of Simeon de Beverley on the heels of his chastisement for that self-same folly.'

'You know this for a fact? You have seen him there?'

'Not I,' de Figham said, 'but I have eyes and ears within those walls and I am kept informed. It would seem that Simeon has become his tutor, or else his confessor.'

De Morthlund's cheeks were reddening and the flesh of his chin began to quiver. 'His confessor? But *I* am his confessor. God's teeth, if Daniel Hawk has need of a priest he has no right, *no right* to go elsewhere.'

'Is he in the habit of making regular confession?'

'He certainly is not. Nor does he require tutoring by any sanctimonious priest with a shaven head. How *dare* he go his own way and make a public show of his defiance?'

'Perhaps it is God he seeks there,' Cyrus offered cunningly, knowing de Morthlund's feelings on the subject.

'I will give him God. I will give him confession. Hell's teeth, I will have him dragged from that place and ...'

'Rein in that temper of yours,' de Figham hissed, as the fruit bowl fell to the floor with a clatter and several choral priests turned in their seats to see what had happened.

De Morthlund's face was purple now with rage. 'He has gone too far,' he spluttered. 'This time he has gone too far.'

'Calm down, I have the situation in hand. My spies will tell me all that passes between Daniel Hawk and Simeon, and in the meantime, we are better served by doing nothing.' He leaned a little closer, waited for the next lull in the singing and whispered, 'By allowing him to run on a slackened leash, you will encourage him to catch the prey before you pull him sharply back to heel.'

'How so? What will it serve me to leave him there while Simeon fills his ears with religious bleatings?'

'Come to my house tonight and I will tell you how,' de Figham said. 'You will find my plan is faultless, and I wager you will be content to leave young Daniel to his own devices for a few more days. The lad can serve us well, but only if he believes you have no knowledge of his little indiscretions.'

'I will not stand off and play the dupe between those two.'

'You will, and gladly, when you have seen my plan for what it is,' de Figham said, and his smile ignited cruel glints in his quick-silver eyes. The fingers of one hand closed slowly over into a fist. His next words were spat in a venomous whisper. 'I will have that priest. I will squeeze him like a rotten fruit, and when I'm done Simeon de Beverley and his precious St Peter's will be no more.'

Three more days were to pass before Fergus de Burton returned to St Peter's enclosure with news that Rabbi Aaron had been recalled to York. The archbishop was eager to have him back so that his presence could underscore the peace which had been restored between the Christians and the Jews. Fergus had used his wits and his men-at-arms to turn the troubles to Geoffrey Plantagenet's own advantage. Now the archbishop was lauded as sage and peacemaker, since the clever use of rumour and counter-rumour had everyone convinced that a city-wide bloodbath had been narrowly avoided by the archbishop's diplomacy.

As Fergus waited now by the infirmary at St Peter's, he saw a man he recognised, a man with handsome, hawk-like features and dark hair growing well back from a fine, deep forehead. Daniel Hawk was limping and leaning heaving on a crooked stick, his gaze turned down as he listened intently to the words of his companion. Like tutor and pupil they walked together, the youngster animated, the man's expression grave. Fergus knew the youth to be Edwin, unmistakably the twin brother of the sickly-looking girl who helped Osric with his herbs in the infirmary. The scene was one of innocent interchange, just a man and a youth out walking in the open. No eye could conjure any trespass in it, unless the watcher wished to make it so.

'God's blessing, Fergus. Do you bring news from York?'

He turned to face the priest and once again was struck by the size and almost princely bearing of him. His shirt was loosely thonged so that a blaze of gold shone through the tapes, showing a flat disc set against a mass of thick blond hair and hard muscle.

Fergus nodded but did not return the greeting. 'The rabbi is to return to York without delay. Our archbishop requires a symbol of his own goodwill to parade before the people.'

'Or a convenient foil to set between himself and his enemies?' Simeon suggested.

'The Plantagenet cannot please all men at once.'

Simeon nodded. 'And what is one more Jew in the greater scheme of things? I think the archbishop's favour may prove as dangerous to Aaron as his animosity.'

But for the moment he is to be protected,' Fergus said. 'His good friend Hozah did not fare so well in all of this. Geoffrey considered it expedient to balance the scales by giving both sides their sacrificial lamb.'

'Hozah is dead?'

'He is. Word was put about that he was guilty of the murder of a priest, and that honour and justice would only be satisfied if he were given up and rightfully punished for the crime, and so . . .'

'But Hozah was innocent,' Simeon protested. 'And his cousin, who was brutally murdered for that same offence, was also innocent. Does Geoffrey Plantagenet keep his seat by tossing harmless old men to the masses like sweetmeats to a pack of savage dogs?'

Fergus raised his hands as if to ward off Simeon's anger.

'Believe me, Father Simeon, there was no other way to protect the rabbi and quieten the town's unrest. A repeat of the recent butchery had to be avoided at all costs. The people needed a scapegoat and the church had challenged Geoffrey to make a stand against the Jews in the name of justice. What else could he do but keep the peace by careful manipulation and the public sacrifice of a lesser man?'

'But in God's name, Fergus, you are his adviser. You could have helped him find a better way. He listens to you, he ...' As Simeon watched the young man's eyes he saw the truth and was dismayed by it. 'You? My God, he *was* acting on your advice. This murder of an innocent old man was manufactured by *you.*'

'I did what I could,' Fergus told him. 'When every other pathway was explored and found impassable, my advice came from a simple, clear-cut choice. It was Hozah's life or the rabbi's, and I chose to throw in my lot with the better man.'

'As simple as that?' Simeon demanded. 'You killed an innocent man because it was *expedient?*'

'Yes, and by so doing I saved the life of another. Can you be so sure you would have done otherwise? If you were faced with the same choice, to save a good man and avoid another spate of Jew-killing by making one timely sacrifice, would you have remained aloof and let them both be among the first to die?'

Simeon closed his eyes and groaned aloud. He could not answer the question put to him. Only God had the right to weigh the value of one soul against another. He could only pray that he was never called upon to make so cruel and calculating a judgement.

'I did the best I could,' Fergus reminded him.

Simeon nodded. 'And no man can ask more of you than that.'

The sound of a man's throaty laughter drew Fergus's attention back to Daniel Hawk and his companion. Something the youngster had said had amused the priest, who palmed his bruised face as if the very act of laughing caused him pain.

'I would have credited you with more common sense than to allow the jackal's whelp into your fold,' he said to Simeon.

'Daniel is his own man,' Simeon replied mildly.

'Not so. He is de Morthlund's creature. Get rid of him. De Morthlund will cut out his heart, and yours, if he discovers him here and sees that you have provided him with such a pretty companion.'

'Their friendship is innocent.'

Fergus snorted. 'Can you be so naive?'

'It is the truth. Daniel's heart is drawn to God. He does not share de Morthlund's appetites.'

Fergus met the priest's calm stare. 'Father Simeon,' he said, as if speaking to a child. 'He has shared de Morthlund's appetites since boyhood.'

'And now he turns in search of God. Should I deny him that?'

'In the name of God or of carnal lust, if you help divide that canon from his catamite, you will pay a heavy price for what you do.'

'I thank you for the warning.'

Frustrated by the priest's calm attitude, Fergus stepped back a pace, turned and pointed a finger at Simeon's chest. 'Get rid of the Hawk or you will put another weapon in the hands of your enemies.'

Simeon looked closely at the younger man. This matter seemed to have touched him deeply and Simeon, still uncertain of de Burton, was suspicious of his concern. When a man alters his colours as speedily and as regularly as de Burton, when he befriends all men in haste yet cleaves to none in truth, then his agitation is rooted in self-interest. If the presence of Daniel Hawk caused him concern, it was for his own schemes, not for Simeon's benefit.

'I will bring Rabbi Aaron to you at St Thomas's chapel in an hour,' he said.

'Two hours,' Fergus corrected. 'Cyrus de Figham has letters for me to carry to the archbishop.'

'More letters? Did ever a canon get better value from his priestly clerks?'

'He has charged me to discover if you keep a woman here.' He saw the blue eyes narrow on the instant and sensed the sudden tension in Simeon's body. 'A woman named Elvira.'

'And what will you tell him?'

'The truth, that if in fact you keep her here, you keep her hidden from all eyes.'

Simeon turned his face until he was watching the young man from the edges of his eyes. His voice held no emotion when he said: 'I think you play a double-handed game, Fergus de Burton.'

The young man spread his hands. 'Since the Lord thought fit to make me ambidextrous, I play all games according to my given skills. Perhaps you should be thankful that you know me for what I am.'

'I think you cannot be trusted.'

'And others can? De Figham has a man here, perhaps two.'

'And are you one of them?'

'I might well be. De Figham believes it to be so and pays me well on account of that belief. De Morthlund pays me too, as does our lord archbishop and a number of those Janus-faced canons who profess to serve him.'

'You sell your loyalties, then, to the highest bidder?'

Fergus shook his head. 'I sell only lies and half-truths, at whatever price they will fetch. My loyalty I give without a fee, and only where it is earned. I believe it to be a commodity grossly undervalued in the market-place. Deceit is the thing men want, the thing that sets their purses rattling.'

'Then you will surely be a rich man,' Simeon said, in the same dispassionate tone. 'Or else a dead one.'

The young man met his stare with confidence. 'Father Simeon, Cyrus de Figham has placed a clever noose around your neck and now he is ready to begin the slow process of choking you to death.'

'I see. And this he will achieve with your assistance?'

'So he believes.'

'But first he wants the woman?'

'If he can get her,' Fergus nodded.

Simeon's bland expression did not alter. 'And with what other devious tasks has de Figham charged you?'

'I am to ingratiate myself into your scriptorium.'

'To what end?'

'To steal the key so that he and his men have access.'

'Your answer means it is too late for that. Since I am forewarned I am also forearmed. I will double the guard at the door.'

'A very wise precaution, Father Simeon.'

The two men eyed each other as a hot, dry breeze blew between them, and neither was sure how thin the line was drawn betwixt enemy and ally. Then Simeon asked: 'What does de Figham want from me?'

And Fergus answered simply: 'Everything.'

CHAPTER TWENTY-FIVE

In the cavern beneath the chapel of St Thomas, Aaron was preparing for the journey home to York. Father Cuthbert had travelled by cart to the chapel and, with the assistance of his priests, had made the short but difficult journey to the caverns beneath the building. The frail old man had done this several times before, for his mind still hungered for higher knowledge and intellectual debate, and the Ethiopian Jew provided both in inexhaustible supply.

Simeon greeted his mentor with a blessing. Father Cuthbert was pale and his fingers trembled visibly, but his eyes were bright with interest and he carried with him an ancient book whose script no other man in Beverley could decipher. He tapped the cover of beaten brass with his knuckles and licked the constant dryness from his lips.

'Arabic,' he said, and his voice, though thin with age, betrayed his pleasure. 'Aaron reads it as flawlessly as he reads his Hebrew. He is a scholar of rare talent, a man of exceptional insight. I hate to lose him so soon, Simeon.'

'Our archbishop demands that he be returned to York without delay,' Simeon told him. 'Aaron, it seems, has a part to play in the Plantagenet's affairs.'

'Will he return to us?'

Simeon glanced at Aaron's brooding face. Elvira, too, was

glum. It was as if a light had dimmed inside her. She packed his few acquired possessions into a cloth with idle fingers, her eyes downcast, and Simeon sensed that this parting pained her heart.

'He will return to us,' he assured his canon, and he was unsettled by his own deep certainty when he repeated, 'Oh yes, Aaron will return to us.'

At a bench in the corner, Aaron stood with his back turned to the room. He was wearing a borrowed cloak and riding boots, and his new black robe had been stitched by Elvira during the long hours spent in his company. At no time had they been alone since those first few hours when he had been delirious, drifting periodically from unconsciousness to find her bending over him, her hands on his face, her dark eyes tender with concern. There were always other eyes to see, other ears to note the words that passed between them. They were never alone, and yet there had been many times when nothing existed for him beyond Elvira's presence. Unless this unexpected attachment blinded his eyes to truth, he had been aware of moments when, for her, his company was all in the world she needed.

Now Aaron was summoned back to York, to be the archbishop's trophy and to do what he could to help the exiled family of poor Hozah. The loss of his old friend pained him deeply, and the confiscation of Hozah's goods and property added insult to the hurt. There was much for him to do in York. He was needed there, where he must be seen to approve the so-called justice meted out by Geoffrey Plantagenet. The times were uneasy, the matter delicate, and yet he was loath to turn his back on all he had discovered here in Beverley.

'Aaron, are you prepared?'

He met Simeon's gaze and steeled his heart, knowing the truth, as yet unspoken, was lying openly between them.

'I have asked Elvira to come with me,' he said, and a heavy silence left the words to hang like the after-tone of a pealed bell in that cavernous place.

Simeon's voice was even. 'And has she given you her answer?'

'She has refused.'

'Then the matter is surely settled,' Simeon said, and thanked God in his heart for her constancy.

'Give her your leave, and your blessing, and she will come. You have no right to keep her here with but half a life to call her own. Give her your leave to travel with me to York. She deserves much more than you can offer her.'

Simeon caught the underlying meaning in his words and knew that Aaron was right. Her safety was his first concern, her happiness his second; this compelling, prosperous Jew confirmed that Simeon was falling short on both these counts.

Osric looked from one man to the other and felt regret, but no surprise, that their friendship had come to this, for this moment had been a decade in the making. In law Elvira was the wife of a man she had not seen for almost ten years; by choice the wife of a celibate priest; in truth no wife at all. She had no child to call her own, no settled home, no life but that of a fugitive, no future but that which love without true expression would allow. In that confrontation between the priest and the Jew he saw the situation as it truly was, and he knew that Simeon recognised it too. This priest loved Elvira more than he had any right to love her, and for that reason he would let her go.

'Give her your leave and your blessing,' the rabbi prompted softly.

Elvira stood with her head lowered so that her hair concealed her face. For a short time she had entertained a dream of being free. This Aaron had charmed her with his golden voice and watchful brown eyes. He had captivated her with his tender affections and his glimpses of a world beyond her reach. He was cast in Simeon's own mould, tall and strong, protective and scrupulously honest. In another time, another place, she might have loved him. Jew or Christian, rabbi or priest were interchangeable concepts to Elvira. The only true difference she saw between these two was that the rabbi was free to love her and the priest was not.

Now Aaron's words, 'you have no right,' jarred in her mind

to clarify her thoughts. She raised her head to look at Simeon, hoping to deny the accusation in those words, but found his gaze hard fixed on the darker face. Fear touched her heart. Peter no longer needed her to be his loving protector and Simeon would be unburdened if she were gone. These good men of St Peter's had risked their lives to keep her safe for ten long years, and doing so had earned them many powerful and dangerous enemies. Peter was safe now, quick and independent. Not for him were the men of St Peter's put at risk, but for Elvira, who could not hide in holes or live like an elusive rodent underground. If she were sent from here their fortunes all would be improved. Elvira saw her reasoning echoed in Simeon's handsome face and knew that her life, and her love, were hanging in the balance.

'Let me take her,' Aaron asked again, in a whisper.

Simeon swallowed the lump that was in his throat. 'Will you protect her?'

'With my life.'

'And . . . love her?'

'Yes, Simeon, I will love her.'

'Then you have my blessing.' He heard her sharp intake of breath and saw her hand come up to cover her mouth. 'And Elvira has my leave to go with you.'

The Jew nodded curtly. He knew what it had cost his friend to say those words, but he could only guess what price he would exact from himself for handing his woman over to another man.

Her face turned ashen, Elvira went to Simeon and placed her palms upon his chest, searching his eyes for what was in his heart. 'Do you no longer love me, Simeon?'

He looked beyond her. 'Elvira, if you are bound to me by any fault of mine then I release you.'

'Do you no longer love me?'

Simeon's sigh was almost a groan. 'Enough to set you free, Elvira.'

'Look at me, Simeon.' She reached up to cup his face in her hands, moving it until his eyes again met with hers, and all he felt for her was in his gaze. 'Tell me that you have changed, Simeon, that I have lost your love, that nothing binds us now but promises. Tell me and I will leave.'

'Elvira . . .'

'Tell me.'

He sighed again. 'Nothing has changed,' he answered hoarsely. 'God help me, nothing has altered but the growing depths of my love for you, Elvira.'

Smiling through her tears she whispered, 'And that is all I will ever ask of you. Never doubt it for a moment, Simeon. It is enough.'

For an endless moment they stood together, their gazes locked and their bodies barely touching, then she turned to Aaron, cleared her throat and said: 'You honour me, Rabbi, but I cannot accept your generous offer of a home with you in York. My life is here, with Simeon.'

'Half a life,' the Jew said softly.

'It is enough.'

'You could have so much more, Elvira.'

'Dear friend, I already have my fill. My heart is here.'

'So be it.'

With a flourish the rabbi snatched up his modest bundle, bowed once to all those present, muttered *'Shalom'* in his deep voice and strode toward the tunnel leading to the chapel. Elvira watched him go, then rested her head on Simeon's chest and smiled contentedly as his arms encircled her.

'I love you, Simeon,' she said, and he replied, his throat constricted with emotion, 'I know you do.'

While Aaron made his farewells and prepared to ride for York, Fergus de Burton was enjoying the sumptuous comforts of Figham House and the generous hospitality of its master. He had received a purse of gold for his services, and this he emptied on to a table in order to count its contents.

'You do not trust me?' de Figham asked. He was not surprised by this but was amazed that this young man should dare make such a conspicuous show of it.

Fergus smiled as he dropped the coins one by one into the purse. 'Would you trust me if this transaction went the other way?'

'Perhaps I would be less obvious in my doubt.'

'My friend, I am well aware that even Geoffrey Plantagenet weights his purse with stones or rings of base metal before adding coins in short measure. Should I trust a canon where I would doubt an archbishop?'

De Figham raised his glass and his smile was crooked. 'I suggest you temper your candour with a measure of tact,' he said. 'The more unscrupulous the man, the more sensitive he becomes to any suggestion that his honour might be in doubt.'

'I will remember that. The purse is two marks short.'

'What? That is not possible. You tease me, sir.'

'Not at all, my lord canon.' Fergus tossed the purse across the table, then sat back in his seat and raised his glass, grinning broadly. 'Count it for yourself.'

John Palmer had been sitting in a corner with a book spread over his knees, seemingly intent on reading every word on every page, though Fergus had suspected all along that he was there to note the subtle twists and turns of the conversation. His suspicions proved correct when John set down the book and gave them his full attention.

De Figham tipped out the coins and moved them around on the table-top with his fingers. 'God's teeth, you are correct. We agreed on twenty marks and there are only eighteen here.'

'Did you run short of metal rings, Father Cyrus?'

'Not I,' de Figham growled, 'but I can find the man who did. It seems I have a clerk who is also a magician. Between the coin chest and the hall, he has managed to transform my twenty marks into eighteen.'

'He has a clever hand,' Fergus replied, not sure that he believed de Figham's story.

The canon rose to his feet and beckoned John Palmer to one side of the great hearth, where they spoke in hushed tones with their heads bowed close together. The young priest left the room and returned a moment later with two silver marks which he placed on the polished table near the purse. Then he bowed to his master and said, 'It shall be done,' and left again, lowering the leather door-curtain behind him.

'You are lenient,' Fergus smiled.

'Not I,' de Figham said. 'That one is not the thief. John's loyalty does not come cheaply. Two marks would never be sufficient to slip him from his present pedestal.'

'I see.' Fergus tasted his wine again and decided to leave the matter where it rested. He believed de Figham had kept back the two marks on a point of principle, or perhaps to test the mettle of his guest. Whatever his reasons for lightening the purse, he now knew that de Burton had his measure and would not be taken in by such a ploy.

'Your wine is excellent, my lord canon,' he remarked. 'I have heard it said that your cellar would cause a king to weep with envy, and that your barn is so well fortified as to resist a whole garrison of soldiers.'

'I am a man of certain standards,' de Figham replied proudly. 'I also intend to keep what I have gained. As you have seen already for yourself, my barn is thief-proof and its vaults impregnable.'

'I am impressed. Perhaps I will beg your guidance when I build my house at Thorpe.'

'If guidance is all you need, then build your house elsewhere. What can you possibly want with a derelict church and a worthless village left crumbling in a wasteland?'

'I will prosper from it,' Fergus said. 'It will be known as Ravensthorpe and one day you will be honoured to sup from *my* fine cellar.'

Cyrus de Figham laughed out loud, reminding Fergus that he could be just as affable as any man when he was off his guard. Now was the time for Fergus to employ his latest strategy, that devised by himself and the Plantagenet over several hours of careful and detailed planning. Cyrus de Figham had made himself untouchable, and Geoffrey Plantagenet, cautious of allowing powerful men their freedom, needed a means of bringing him to heel. Fergus was charged with finding, or creating, the bridle that would rein this canon back whenever his ambitions threatened to carry him too far beyond his rightful place.

'I must return to York,' he said with a sigh. 'First my lord archbishop bids me ride as extra escort with his shipment, then he calls me back one day ahead of it. There are times when I dance exhausted on his indecision, but at least I will not be held responsible if the shipment should be lost.'

De Figham poured more wine into their cups and feigned but a passing interest. 'What shipment is this you speak of? Does his lordship transport goods over land when wells and springs are low and the roads are thick with thieves?'

'He does. A river-craft carrying furs and salt, sugar and French wine of the highest quality was recently lost to thieves. Our archbishop has therefore decided that its replacement should come by the Hull to Beverley, and from there to York by road.'

'A risky journey,' de Figham commented.

'Aye. It travels under the banner of York and with a suitable guard, but who knows how many soldiers might desert their posts or be enticed away in this crushing heat? My little company of men was meant to swell the guard, but now...'

'Now?'

'Since our indecisive archbishop has recalled me to his presence, his shipment will arrive or not, according to the fates.'

'Furs and salt, you say? And sugar?'

'And wine, the very best.' He closed his eyes and shook his head. 'God's teeth, how a man might dream. Just half that shipment of fourteen barrels would lay my cellar at Ravensthorpe in princely fashion.'

De Figham snapped his fingers and a servant approached with fresh wine in a jug. 'A man might dream and another man make it so,' he told his guest. 'I would hear more of this shipment and its inadequate complement of guards.'

'Not from my lips, Father Cyrus. After all, I am now the

255

Plantagenet's trusted servant and adviser, and with such standing my tongue must not run loose.'

'Come now,' de Figham coaxed, smiling again. 'Enjoy your fill of this excellent wine and consider the twenty marks already hanging from your belt. What is a little idle talk between two friends in a place as well secured as this? The archbishop is thirty miles away and shall never be the wiser.'

Fergus allowed himself a smile of satisfaction. The bait was taken. The bridle he had devised was slipping neatly over his head and soon the bit would be in place. The Plantagenet, once again, would have cause to bless the day he took his brash young friend into his confidence.

A man's cries from the courtyard drew de Figham to the window. He beckoned Fergus to join him there and together they watched a noisy scene unfold. A clerk in holy orders was dragged, screaming and babbling, into the open space close by the gate. Two men secured him to a fence while another bound his right arm to an upright stake, leaving the hand unbound to clutch and twitch at the air above his head. Shrieking, he called upon God and all His angels to intervene, but the men who held him were stronger and de Figham's justice swifter than Heaven's laborious turning.

'Lenient, am I?' de Figham asked. 'My dear Fergus, I have learned that theft will thrive where there is leniency. I punish according to the law and to my priestly rights within that law. Observe.'

In the courtyard the man who kept de Figham's dogs had raised a short sword in a two-handed grip above his head. He turned his face to the window and, at his master's signal, swung the sword in a downward arc that severed the upper inches of the stake. The hand flew through the air and landed close below the window, its fingers plucking in spasms at the cobbles. By now the clerk had fainted in pain and horror, only to be revived by a different agony when a blazing torch was rammed against his stump.

'Rough justice,' Fergus said.

'Fair justice,' Cyrus answered.

'The fairness escapes me, Father Cyrus. Would not a

clipping of the nose suffice, or the loss of an ear or a finger?'

'It was the hand that stole the marks.'

'The left hand, then? The clerk is of no further use to you now that his right hand has been lost. He can neither write nor use a broom nor tend the horses in your stable. His living is forfeit, his usefulness at an end, for the sake of no more than two silver marks.'

Once again de Figham laughed aloud. He drew Fergus from the window, his arm around the young man's shoulders and his dark eyes twinkling.

'You miss the crucial point in this, my friend,' he said. 'That foolish clerk did not lose his hand merely for stealing two marks. He lost it because he stole two marks from *me*. Now, Fergus, since you have whetted my curiosity, you must tell me all you know about the shipment that will pass through Beverley on its way to York.'

When Fergus met his men-at-arms outside the modest chapel of St Thomas, his head was swimming and his hands unsteady on the reins. The presence of crows and starlings, swooping low to see what pickings were to be had from this group of men, caused the horses to side-step and toss their heads in agitation. Fergus knew they would be tormented by these feathered scavengers along the route, just one more reason why he did not welcome this long journey. After supping so much wine at de Figham's table, he was better prepared for his bed than for a thirty-mile journey on horseback in stifling heat and swirling dust.

'We meet again, Rabbi Aaron,' he said, extending a hand in greeting to the glowering man before him. 'It is good to see you healed and well again.' He paused to study the scowling dark face and added: 'Does the prospect of returning home displease you?'

'It pleases me well enough,' the Jew replied. 'I am needed there.'

'But your brow is furrowed. Has something unpleasant happened here? God's teeth, don't tell me you have crossed swords with Simeon of Beverley?'

The look the rabbi flashed at him as he swung into the saddle was enough to silence Fergus on the instant. The black eyes glared a warning and the full lips tightened to an angry line, then Aaron spurred his horse to the front of the column and moved ahead to set the pace.

Bringing up the rear, Fergus called Chad to him and demanded to know what soured the Rabbi's mood. Chad told his young master all that had ensued beneath the chapel of St Thomas, about the woman Aaron loved and his daring confrontation with Simeon. When the story was told they rode a while in silence, then Fergus spat the dust from his throat and asked: 'Is she as beautiful as they say she is?'

'I have seen her,' Chad replied, 'and she is beautiful. Her hair is waist-length and as near to black as any, and it shimmers when light is on it, like the sheen on a raven's wing. Her eyes are as dark as the rabbi's, big and lustrous. Her skin is soft and white and ...'

'By the gods!' Fergus exclaimed. 'Is she a sorceress who enchants every eye that looks upon her? You speak like one besotted, Chad.'

'The woman is beautiful,' the soldier replied. 'Aaron asked for her. He challenged Simeon and demanded that she be allowed to travel with us to York.'

'And?'

'Simeon was persuaded. He wants her safe and under the protection of a man he knows is trustworthy, so he released her with his blessing.'

'So? Where is she? Why is she not here?'

'She stayed. For ten years she has cleaved to her celibate priest. When freedom was offered she turned her back on it and chose to stay with Simeon.'

'Perhaps it is as well,' Fergus suggested. 'A Christian and a Jew would make strange bedfellows.'

'This woman's faith is not strong enough to keep her from the rabbi's bed. She stays for love of Simeon, nothing more.'

'Then he is fortunate indeed. Cyrus de Figham is obsessed with her. He intends to have her, and to sell the boy, Peter, to certain men in Rome who have an interest in his origins and his purpose here in Beverley. It is said that Peter knows the whereabouts of the treasure and the relics of St John. Do you believe it to be so?'

Chad shrugged. 'He is a strange one. He neither smiles nor laughs nor plays like other children. Men speak to him as an equal and believe he has more knowledge in his head than was ever written down in books. He makes my flesh creep. I do not fear him but he unsettles me. I think I would believe anything of him. Yes, I would say he knows where the treasure is hidden.'

'I see. And how would I know this boy if I came across him?'

'By the scar on his throat, a puckered, crimson scar, just here.' Chad touched his own throat with his fingertips. 'And by the clear blue of his eyes and his yellow hair.'

Fergus de Burton nodded and added Chad's words to his store of information. He watched the rigid back of Aaron as he rode at the head of the company in advance of the clouds of dust their mounts created on the road. The prospect of a house at Thorpe was becoming more attractive by the hour. He liked the flavour of this town. He had a mind to press on with his plans in doubled haste, for he would make himself a part of the intrigues, the mysteries and the simmering plots that were afoot in Beverley.

CHAPTER TWENTY-SIX

Cyrus de Figham made himself conspicuous at the offices that evening. His huntsmen all were out with spears and longbows, swords and crossbows, their faces hooded and their horses stripped of their identifiable finery. On roads that were alive with wandering bands of robbers and vagabonds, such a force of men might move around unchallenged. The archbishop's carts had been advised to take the shorter route across the Figham pasture, thereby avoiding some trouble in the town. Long before they rejoined the road to York beside the Westwood, their progress would be halted by a fallen tree completely stopping up the dusty track. Here the bowmen would stand off at a measured distance with their weapons primed, and it was hoped the shipment would be given up without a fight. A longbow could kill a man in armour from two hundred yards, so none but a fool would set himself against a band of bowmen in defence of a few sacks of salt and wine intended for the table of an archbishop few men respected. The beasts drawing the carts would carry the goods to Figham House upon their backs. The empty carts would be left for a band of South Cave men to take away for the timber and the wheels. By the time the load was missed in York, none would suspect that the attack had taken place in Beverley.

Cyrus de Figham smiled grimly as he twisted the onyx ring on his index finger. 'Has the entrance to the barn been cleared and the cellar prepared for the wine?'

'As you instructed, my lord,' John Palmer said. He was laying out his master's robes, the embroidered alb, the jewelled mantle, the heavily decorated over-robe. 'The matter will be attended to while you are at the holy offices.'

'Be sure it is, and allow no lights on the pasture. I want no errors made that will cause suspicion to drift in my direction. I will have that shipment, John, and Fergus de Burton shall have his seven barrels of wine as payment for the timely loosening of his tongue. And the other matter? How many have been procured?'

'Twenty, my lord. Seven men and thirteen women.'

'Good, good. If rumour can spread like a flash-fire from one tongue, we may expect a decent blaze from twenty. What will they say, these witnesses of yours?'

John Palmer did not miss the emphasis cunningly placed on that last word. Should fault be found in any witness, should it be proved that falsehoods had been purchased, no blame would be attached to this sly canon. 'They will say that Simeon raised thieves and robbers from the dead, that he preached against the Holy Catholic Church and all its servants.'

'What more?'

'Some women will say he mocked his vows of chastity by lying with them in fornication. A herbalist will swear he purchased holy water from Simeon for magical purposes. This one has much to say of sacrilege and crimes against the Church, and there is more, much more.'

Cyrus nodded his dark head. 'And so his end draws ever closer. That priest of St Peter's will not survive a third examination, not while he taints the church by such a weight of personal ill-fame. You have served me well in this, John Palmer, though not, I hope, in your canon's name.'

'No, my lord. In this, as in all things, I have served only my personal ambitions.' He handed a sheet of paper to his master. 'Here is the list of books you asked me to acquire.'

Cyrus grinned. 'You amaze me, John. Did it cost you dearly?'

'Yes, my lord, it did.'

'Then you shall be amply reimbursed. What of the key?'

John shrugged. 'My man in St Peter's is hard pressed to keep suspicion from himself. He saw the books by stealth after feigning a sudden sickness while passing the guard who keeps the door. He needs more time, but the list will interest you while you wait, my lord.'

'God's teeth!' De Figham's face lit with a grin as he slapped the backs of his fingers across the sheet. 'These books are priceless rarities. Aristotle, Adelardus, the Evangelists – who gave him leave to claim such treasures and lock them away from all eyes in his scriptorium?'

'He is a scribe of some repute, my lord. I believe our last archbishop, Roger du Pont L'Eveque, requested copies to be made.'

'Hearsay! Any thief could steal our treasures and claim as much.'

'Indeed they could, my lord.'

'And written here are the titles of several books that vanished from our provost's library at the time of the great fire. Is this Simeon guilty of looting, then? Or do these two, the priest and the provost, conspire together to rob the church of its literary treasures?'

John smiled his admiration. 'A convincing argument, my lord. If Jacob gave him leave to keep the books, by what right did he do so and why were the other canons kept in ignorance of the fact?'

'And if Jacob de Wold did *not* consent to these precious volumes being spirited away to Simeon's scriptorium ...' He spread his elegant hands and his smile was wide. 'Why, then, the charge is theft by any reckoning.'

'And sacrilege, my lord.'

'Indeed, and if he steals our books what more has this profane priest stolen from us? Our relics, perhaps?'

'Sound reasoning, my lord.'

De Figham laughed heartily. 'We have him, John. By God, this time we have him.'

*

'Simeon.'

The night was still and oppressive in its heat. From the deep shaft of the scriptorium well soft scuttling sounds could just be heard as rodents searched for food amongst the shadows. The fluttering of bats' wings in the dark mimicked the whisper of breezes in the eaves. Simeon was sleeping half-propped on a couch, his only garment the linen breeches covering his legs from waist to thigh. His feet were bare, his muscular chest exposed, the flat disc glowing dully against his skin. In the crook of his arm Elvira lay curled in sleep, and in the space allowed by his bent knee, Peter's small body lay face down, one arm hanging from the couch.

There were others in the scriptorium on that night of October 4th, 1190. Thorald was sprawled on a cloak spread on the rushes, snoring softly through his open mouth. Close by him lay the little monk, Antony, sleeping on his own bent arm, his pilgrim's staff just inches from his fingers. Osric lay on his back with one leg bent up and his arms thrown out. A few clerks and copyists were curled inside their cloaks, old Cuthbert nodded in his high-backed library chair, an open book on the revolving table before him. Here too was Edwin, sleeping beside his sister, their fingers lightly entwined, their faces close together, each the mirror image of the other.

'Simeon.'

Two candles burned in the centre of the room. Other, much smaller candles flickered around the corner shrine. Bright moonlight flung a shaft of silver light from each high window to lie in softened pools upon the floor.

'Simeon.'

The whispered calling of his name pierced through his dreams. His eyes snapped open and he knew their troubles had begun.

The figure was standing just inside the door. Simeon felt no fear, only a deep regret that their short peace was at an end. 'God bless and keep you, friend,' he whispered.

'God grant you courage, Simeon.'

Elvira stirred and pressed herself against him. Peter, his sleep rarely more than cat-like, came to his senses, instantly

263

alert. Simeon tightened his grip on Elvira and placed his free hand lightly on his godson's head.

'The time is come?' he asked, and the figure nodded.

One by one the others came awake. Edwin scrambled from his bed and approached the figure without hesitation. Knuckling sleep from his eyes he peered into the shadowed hood, then smiled his sleepy smile and bowed politely in greeting.

'I know this man,' he said. 'This is the guardian at the gate, the priest who bade me bring my sister here. I greet you, sir, and thank you for your care. My sister Edwina is much improved. In a few more weeks she …'

Coming silently up behind him, Thorald slid his arm around the boy's shoulders and drew him gently back. 'Come away boy. Come away.'

Now Peter left the couch to approach the figure. His lower body was covered by a wound cloth of white linen. The rest of him was naked and pale in the soft light of the scriptorium. Elvira's breath caught in her throat as the figure reached out a hand and placed it on the boy's bowed head. He seemed so small and vulnerable to her then, a skinny ten-year-old, as much a helpless orphan now as he had been ten years ago. She felt Simeon's heartbeat quicken beneath her cheek and she was glad of it. He knew, and shared, her deepest fear that Peter would be taken. Then she heard the whispered words, *Keeper at the Shrine*, and was reminded that the boy belonged to Beverley, to Simeon and herself.

When the figure beckoned, Simeon left the couch and placed himself beside Peter. He was tall and broad and yet the figure dwarfed him with its height. It seemed as if the two looked closely into each other's faces, as if their eyes were locked in a searching stare, each probing for the strength within the other. Then Simeon slowly lowered himself to one knee and bowed his head to receive the figure's blessing.

'God grant you courage, Simeon de Beverley.'

Just then they heard a sudden, heavy pattering at the high scriptorium windows. Startled, every face turned up to find the cause, and every eye saw the first rain falling down upon the glass.

'God be praised,' Osric exclaimed, and the others echoed, 'God be praised.'

'It's raining!' Edwin shouted. 'The drought is at an end. It's raining. Look, *it's raining*!'

'Dear God, we thank thee from our hearts for this.' Simeon crossed himself from lips to breast and shoulder to shoulder. The rain had come. The streams would all run fresh again and the exhausted wells fill up. The stinking ditch would rise again to carry its waste away, and the dust that had shrouded Beverley for many weeks would either fall to earth with the rain or else disperse itself. Even as he watched the windows, the downpour began to drive itself in a deluge against the glass. This was no isolated shower of half-fulfilled promise. This was the answer to their prayers. The drought was over. Pestilence and fire had been avoided: it was raining.

He turned to the figure and, as he had half-expected, it was gone. They went outside to welcome the rain and found that those others who lived within the walls were already gathered there. Some stood in prayer, some sheltered where the cool rain could splash their skin, others danced and gave their thanks with a joyful heart. It was a happy celebration. Daniel Hawk had been given a bed in the infirmary when his master once again denied him access to his house. Now he laughed and danced with the others despite the pains in his leg. A priest rushed in to toll St Peter's bell and soon the other churches in the town took up a similar joyous pealing.

Simeon stood close by the open door of the scriptorium with the light behind him. He was drenched from head to foot. His breeches clung to his hips and thighs like a second skin and he was laughing as he watched Elvira and Peter, their hands joined, spinning and turning together in the rain.

There was no warning when the blow was struck. His arms were in the air and laughter was bubbling from him when the arrow struck his chest and he went down. Elvira's scream rose shrilly above the sounds of merriment and the pounding rain. In seconds Osric, Antony and Thorald were bending over him.

He lay as still as death, his face impervious to the downpour, a short, stout arrow protruding from his chest. A stupefied hush descended on the watchers. Nobody spoke. Nobody dared even to pray, until young Edwin uttered a torturous cry:

'They've killed him,' he wailed, holding his horrified sister close against him, and the disbelief in his voice was in his eyes. 'They've killed Father Simeon!'

A dozen men ran off into the woods, rushing like wild beasts into the trees from where the deadly arrow had been fired. The rest stood in a press around the fallen priest.

'Get him inside ... gently, now, gently. Support his head. You there, fetch cloths to stem the bleeding.' Osric's voice was calm as he gave orders with a soldier's authority. 'Thorald, we have to get this arrow out.'

'But if the head is hooked behind his ribs ...'

'I'll have to cut it free. I need water to swab the blood away. This arrow must be drawn, and quickly.'

Elvira watched them lay Simeon down with loving hands on the very couch where she had slept in his arms such a short time ago. She saw the short, thick arrow sticking from his chest, the deathly pallor on his face, the blood seeping into the mass of hair where she had recently rested her own head.

'Dear God, don't take him from us,' she said aloud, and in her distress was not aware that she was praying for the first time in her life.

Peter's hand slid into hers and gripped it tightly. 'He cannot die,' he said, and his words were neither prophecy nor prayer but the heartfelt cry of a child who saw his father facing death. *'He cannot die.'*

Now Osric's voice boomed out to astonish them all. 'The arrow has pierced the brow-piece. Its force was halted by the thickness of the gold. He's stunned but he's alive – Simeon's *alive*!'

They removed the brow-piece with the utmost care, easing the arrow head, with its cruel, double-edged barbs, from the flesh in which it was deeply, but not mortally, embedded. The point had struck the ribs below but, once the flow of blood

266

was stopped, a wound no deeper than an inch was found in Simeon's chest.

Thorald freed the brow-piece from the arrow and handed it to Elvira. Her hands were trembling as she took it from him. She pushed her thumb through the hole made in the gold and a wave of sick relief washed over her. That arrow would have killed him but for this. She saw herself ten years ago, stealing the brow-piece from a dead horse, hiding it in her clothes so that her greedy husband could not claim it from her and later, in the infirmary, handing it to Simeon.

'Cephas.' She read the word still visible on the disc, where its capital letter scrolled around the arrow's hole. Her gift had saved him. Some wicked man with murder in his heart had sought to take his life but this, her gift, had saved him.

'Elvira?'

She dropped to her knees beside the couch and pressed his cold, wet fingers to her lips. His eyes were clouded, barely focused. He tried to raise his head but could not lift it from the pillow.

'Elvira? What ... what happened to me? Was I struck by a thunderbolt?'

'You were struck by a crossbow bolt,' Thorald informed him, holding up the arrow. 'It came from the trees across the way. Our men are scouring the woods for your attacker, but if he is de Figham's creature, he will simply hide the weapon and join the search. I doubt we will ever punish him for this.'

'A crossbow bolt?' Simeon, still dazed, seemed confused by Thorald's words.

'In the light from the open door of the scriptorium you made an easy target for a bowman of any skill. The light was good, the distance short, so even in all that rain he could not miss you.'

'Shot at close range? But how?' Simeon glanced down at the pad of blood-stained linen on his chest, at the stains on the couch and the blood on Osric's hands. He frowned, perplexed. 'Do I still live?'

'You live,' Osric informed him, 'though you'll be devilish sore for a day or two. When that bruising shows itself you'll carry this night's work in a rainbow on your chest.'

Simeon tried to laugh but only a ragged sound came out. He winced against the pain and spoke again. 'Did God produce a miracle? Was the arrow deflected?' He winced again and avoided filling his lungs with too much air. 'How could a man take such a shot and be merely bruised by it?'

'The brow-piece saved you,' Elvira said through her tears. 'It took the full force of the blow and stopped the arrow head piercing your body through.'

Simeon groaned and his head rolled on the pillow. 'Thor's hammer could not have felled me with more force.'

'Heathen priest,' Osric grinned.

'I did not heed the warning,' Simeon said. 'Two minutes after he was gone I lowered my guard and made myself a target. Are my ribs broken?'

Osric shook his head. 'I do not believe so. You are a fortunate man, my friend. Had you possessed a lesser physique, your ribs would have snapped like twigs when the arrow drove that disc against your chest. All that running and chopping of wood has served you well.'

'God and that golden brow-piece served me well,' Simeon corrected. He lifted a hand to Elvira's cheek to wipe the tears away. 'Your gift to me, Elvira.'

'My gift,' she answered simply.

He looked beyond her to where his godson stood beside the couch in his wet body-cloth. The two looked hard and long at each other before the injured priest began to falter in his gaze as pain and weariness threatened to overcome him.

'Be extra vigilant, boy.'

'Yes, father, I will.'

Peter did not use the formal 'Father' but the personal one, and in that simple word the special bond they shared was vividly conveyed. The last thing Simeon saw before he fell into a deep sleep was the face of Peter lit with a smile; not the wispy thing he sometimes showed but a grin so wide it showed his teeth and revealed him as an ordinary, and very happy, little boy.

CHAPTER TWENTY-SEVEN

They came for him in the early morning while he was
praying at the altar of St Peter. They were kept outside
the gates until Canon Cuthbert could be found to ascertain
by what authority they intruded upon his ecclesiastical
privileges. After that they were allowed to gather in the open
area just inside the gates, where stone seats were arranged
against the walls and a tiny spring offered water for their
needs. Cyrus de Figham led the group of canons, priests and
clerks that was to escort Simeon the short distance to the
provost's court in Hall Garth. He paced impatiently inside
the gates, obliged to allow the canon elect to complete his
morning prayers before he took him from this place. Despite
his air of authority and taste for leadership, he was keenly
aware of the strict church protocol by which his conduct was
hampered. Stephen Goldsmith, canon and legal owner of
the land on which St Peter's compound stood, had wider
jurisdiction here than any other man. He also held high
status as the provost's designated representative, and only on
his direction would this matter be conducted.

'This Church does not drag canons from their prayers to
answer charges that may yet prove false,' he told de Figham.
'Or would you rather make a Becket of him by having him
cut down at his own altar?'

269

'You misjudge my motives,' de Figham smiled benignly. 'I seek only to protect our Church from knavish canons. The evidence was gathered and verified by my priests and I am bound by canon law, as our lord provost is so bound, to act upon it. I do so in good faith and in the interests of the Church. I have no personal grudge against Simeon de Beverley.'

Stephen Goldsmith bit back the words he might have said in response to this. Instead he stood off a pace and muttered bitterly to his clerk, 'If that were true, we would all be in our beds, not gathered here to persecute an innocent man.'

Wulfric de Morthlund, garbed in great splendour and here at St Peter's for reasons of his own, seated himself upon a low stone bench and gathered several men around him. 'Slip away when any opportunity arises,' he told them. 'If my priest is here, I want a full report of his activities.'

At his altar Simeon received the whispered message, gave a brief signal and watched two priests slip behind the altar curtain before returning his attention to the morning offices. Another psalm and two short hymns would end it, and then the blessings as the worshippers filed from the church. That was all the time he had to impede de Figham's progress, and he prayed that Father Cuthbert's stubborn influence would do the rest.

Outside, the quick-witted Edwin had already darted through trees and bushes and scrambled through muddy gardens to reach the scriptorium without being seen. This building stood well beyond the others, its back close against the boundary wall in Eastgate, its north walls shadowed by woodland. Instead of going inside he gave a hasty message to the priest on guard, then raced to the little garden where Daniel Hawk was observing the morning offices in solitude.

'What is it, Edwin? Why do you run so hard?'

'Come quickly. You must not be found here. Hurry, Father Daniel, hurry.' Edwin grasped the priest by the arm and pulled him roughly from his seat. 'You must hide yourself, Father Daniel.'

Grabbing his stick and his prayer-book Daniel hurried

after him, ducking to avoid low-hanging branches that threw down a shower of rainwater when disturbed. He covered the ground with difficulty, struggling to keep pace with Edwin's agile sprint. The way was rough underfoot and treacherously laid with tree roots and slender young saplings. Daniel's injuries had not yet fully healed and the herbal remedy Osric had prescribed in regular doses slowed his body down to assist the healing process. He limped along behind the boy, slithering and sliding where the heavy rain had turned that summer's dust to mud. They did not speak again until they reached the spot where Father Bernard and Alice had been buried. Exhausted, Daniel gripped his stick in both hands and leaned his weight upon it, breathing deeply. Edwin retrieved the fallen prayer-book and wiped its muddy covers with the sleeve of his shirt.

'What has happened, Edwin?'

'Father Cyrus is here and he has your master with him. They have come for Simeon.'

'For Simeon?' Daniel looked aghast. His damaged left eye was halfway open now, the sight unimpaired but the skin around it still discoloured with bruising. His mouth, too, was healing well, though the wound on his head suffered a mild infection which had required yet another opening with the infirmarian's knife. 'On what grounds? By what right have they come for him?'

'They have papers signed by the provost,' Edwin said. 'That is all I know of it, except that they will take him to the courts when the morning prayers are ended.'

'And my master is here with them?'

Edwin nodded. 'I saw him for myself and I swear I have never seen such a man as he. I would have taken him for a king.' He looked about him quickly. 'Father Daniel, I must go where I am needed. Stay here until I come for you. If someone approaches this place and you do not hear my whistle, conceal yourself beneath this undergrowth. It can be lifted like a mat and a man may slide beneath it without hurt. Do not be discovered here, Father Daniel. Your master will raise the Devil for it if you are.'

As he turned away Daniel caught him by the arm. The handsome young face turned back to him, the eyes a soft, deep brown beneath heavy lashes, the expression open in its innocence. 'You are a good lad, Edwin. Now listen to me and heed this warning well. Cover your head and keep your face from Wulfric de Morthlund's notice. Never allow your hood to be lowered in his presence. Avoid him at all costs. Do you understand?'

'No, sir, I do not . . .' he paused, recalling rumours he had heard concerning the obese canon and his ungodly appetites. Comprehension dawned to flush his cheeks and cause his gaze to waver momentarily. 'Yes, sir, I understand.'

'And you must not fall asleep in his presence.'

Edwin smiled sheepishly. 'I will endeavour not to do so, sir.'

'Go then, and do what you must do, but have a care, Edwin. That man is dangerous.'

He watched the boy lope off, swift and sure-footed on the slippery ground. Then he lowered himself into a sitting position, lifted the carpet of ivy and let it rest against his back, the better to conceal himself if others should approach that quiet spot. His master had beaten him without mercy and turned him from his house, but if he found him here at St Peter's, and with a book of prayer in his possession, Wulfric de Morthlund might well be moved to kill him.

By now the enclosure was a hive of activity. The priests were unable to keep the impatient visitors together, so that the pathways teemed with curious strangers seeking to learn the secrets of Simeon's domain. When Edwin reached the corner of the scriptorium that was farthest from their view, the guard allowed him to slip inside unhindered. He dropped the bar behind him and let the heavy chain hang free so that no hand could unlatch the door from the outside. Those others who were already inside were rushing to clear the precious books and manuscripts away. The grid of the well stood open. Osric and Thorald were passing the heavy volumes through the opening while others, Antony and Richard among them, carried the treasures by ladder down below. Edwin saw what was yet to be done and went to work without instruction, wrapping manuscripts, sheets of paper and bundles of gold leaf into linens and knotting them safely at the corners. When this was done he helped Elvira roll her small possessions into a bundle, assisted her into the well and passed the cloth down after her. His eye was keen as he glanced around the room, marking this item and that as either safe or incriminating. The clerks and copyists, having helped in the hasty clearing, now took their seats at their allotted tables, dipped their pens and prepared to begin their day's work in earnest.

'Go now,' he said to Peter. 'Conceal yourself.'

'Tell Father Simeon I will come to him.'

Edwin shook his head. 'Do not come here again. The Father is to be taken to the courts . . .'

'I will come,' Peter repeated, then swung himself lightly into the well and lowered the grid behind him.

Edwin watched the small hand reappear between the bars, saw the small, deft fingers shift the lock along its ancient fittings, then scattered the rushes around the wall of the well to hide the signs that many feet had trampled there. Only then did he pull his hood well down over his face and seat himself in the farthest, gloomiest corner of the scriptorium.

When the office was ended and the church cleared of its worshippers, Simeon de Beverley stepped out to face his accusers. The sky was overhung with blackened clouds and distant thunder rumbled over the wolds. The air was fresh and clean with the sweet smell of rain on grass and thirsty soil. It was a morning for the giving of thanks and the singing of grateful praises, not a day for bitter enemies to lock their horns.

Stephen Goldsmith stepped forward, the Celtic colouring of his hair and beard thrown into contrast against a hood and mantle of brilliant green silk. 'Simeon de Beverley, you are charged to appear before the lord provost at his Hall Garth court, where certain charges will be brought against you. These men are sent to escort you there. Do you accept the summons?'

273

'I do accept,' Simeon replied.

The goldsmith's gaze flickered to the wrappings on Simeon's chest. A circle of blood had seeped through the cloth to stain his habit. 'You are injured, Father Simeon?'

'Last night an attempt was made on my life. As you see, it was not successful.'

'Even so, it will be reported to the court. Was the culprit apprehended?'

Regrettably, no. We lost him in the woods. It was dark and raining heavily at the time.'

Here Cyrus de Figham cleared his throat. 'May we proceed with the business in hand? But first . . .' He turned to Simeon, his eyes bright with malice. 'First there is the matter of certain books and manuscripts which we believe are in your possession contrary to the law of our mother Church.'

'I am a scribe and copyist,' Simeon answered. 'What books are here come from my private library, or else were borrowed with the full consent of our lord provost.'

'Then you will have no objection to opening the doors of your scriptorium for our inspection,' de Figham said.

Simeon looked back at Stephen Goldsmith and prayed that Elvira and Peter were by now far from this place. 'If such is the provost's desire, sir, I will take you there.'

The door of the scriptorium was open wide upon its hinges. The huge oak bar had been taken away and a long, ornate key pushed into the keyhole so that a stranger's eye might judge it worthy of its assumed purpose. They found the clerks and copyists, the translators and the colourists hard at work, and when the place was searched only a handful of books belonging to the church could be identified. De Figham was furious. The door of the scriptorium had been watched since their arrival. Neither books nor chests nor bundles had been carried out, and yet the place held little or nothing that might serve his case against Simeon. He insisted that the roof-space, the alcoves and the recesses be searched. With a flaming torch held high above his head, he inspected the guard-robe for himself, expecting to find some priceless items hidden in that rank place where men and women left their excrement. Much to his chagrin he found nothing there but holes in the ground with a stream running below them, and not a single window-slit wide enough to pass a book or manuscript to anyone on the outside.

'Perhaps our fellow canon uses the black arts, aided by stolen holy water, to spirit the evidence away,' he suggested pointedly, then thrust the torch into the hands of a clerk and strode for the door, his eyes glinting on the key as he approached it. He paused there to allow his provost's representative and his party to pass ahead of him, noting that Wulfric de Morthlund was holding back, his stare fixed on a corner beyond the candlelit shrine.

'You there!' the fat man called. 'You in the corner! Show yourself!'

Edwin rose obediently to his feet and shuffled forward, his head bowed low so that his face was hidden.

'He is just a servant, my lord,' a clerk hurriedly explained. 'A poor boy with a …'

'I need a boy for my household,' de Morthlund said, still watching Edwin. 'This one looks healthy enough. How old is he?'

'Not yet sixteen, my lord.'

'He is tall and graceful,' de Morthlund observed. 'He has good shoulders and fine hands and lacks but a little meat upon his bones to bring him to manhood. I could use such a boy as this in my employ.'

'But my lord …'

Ignoring the clerk, Wulfric stepped forward a pace and beckoned to Edwin. 'Come closer, lad and lower your hood. If you are comely, you shall have a place in my house. I doubt that Simeon will have use of you when he is brought to trial.' He licked his lips and waddled forward with one arm outstretched. 'Come, lad, be obedient to your canon. I would see your face. Remove your hood and raise your head to the light.'

Edwin's heart was pounding in his throat as he drew near the fat man. He could see the embroidered boots and the beaded robes, the full red cloak and the massive silver girdle holding a mound of flesh in place. For want of courage and a place to run, he turned his body limp and did exactly as Daniel Hawk had warned him not to do; he pitched to the ground, face down, at Wulfric de Morthlund's feet.

'God's teeth!'

'He has a sickness, my lord,' the clerk explained.

'A sickness?' de Morthlund echoed, stepping backwards and lifting his sleeve to cover his nose and mouth. 'Is he infected?'

'A falling sickness, my lord.'

Wulfric de Morthlund glared at the crumpled figure at his feet, then turned and strode for the door, his great cloak billowing in his wake. 'God's teeth, what madness is this? These misguided priests of St Peter's would harbour lepers in their midst if such came begging at their gates. Let me out of here before this vermin touches me with his pestilence.'

The clerk stood at the door until the party had travelled halfway to the gates. He noted that the ornate key was missing from the lock. As Simeon had predicted, his enemies had seen the key and looked no further for the source of the scriptorium's security. The clerk wished he had been more diligent, for there was a spy abroad in their enclosure, and it would have pleased him well to catch that traitor at his work.

When he judged it safe to end his watch, he closed the door and rushed to assist young Edwin to his feet. The lad had bloodied his nose in the fall but he was laughing nervously as he cleaned the mess away.

'Who would have thought this illness of mine could be put to such advantage?' he remarked to the clerk.

'What, are you saying that you were not overcome, that you cast yourself down deliberately at de Morthlund's feet?'

'How else was I to save myself?' Edwin asked, sniffing blood into a scrap of cloth. 'Fear of sickness can be more useful than a weapon, in its place.'

'Quick thinking, lad,' the clerk said. 'You did wisely.'

'I acted out of terror,' Edwin admitted.

'Then you may thank the Lord for the heart of a coward and the wit to use it wisely.'

Jacob de Wold was sickened in his heart. The charges against Simeon de Beverley were very serious, and a string of witnesses were to be brought to say their piece against him. He did not doubt that money had changed hands to make it so. The rumours in the town had sprung up too fast and with too much detail to be dismissed as mere coincidence. Already the word was out that Simeon had taken a crossbow bolt full in the chest and received but a small wound and a patch of livid bruising. No ordinary man could have survived that shot. Jacob could not explain it to his own satisfaction, since he did not believe in miracles, but he would not, could not entertain the alternative, that magic of the blackest kind had saved him. Someone was bent on laying Simeon de Beverley in a lead-lined coffin, and the nails were cast that would hammer the lid in place.

At this preliminary inquiry, at which the presence of the archbishop was not required, it was to be decided if formal charges should be made and Simeon should be brought to trial. If this proved to be the case, Geoffrey Plantagenet would decide if the trial of this Beverley priest should take place in the Minster's own court or at the palace at York. Either way, the Plantagenet would judge the case in person, and Jacob feared that Simeon would be his scapegoat. The eyes of Rome would be on them, eager to see this unpopular archbishop prove himself equal to his holy office or else hold up his failure to them all. He had subdued the troubles in York between the Christians and the Jews and he had done so admirably. Now he would seek the same success in Beverley, and if ever a man was wont to use a hammer to crush a flea, that man was Geoffrey Plantagenet, Beverley's overlord.

'Where is the middle way?' Jacob muttered as he thumbed through the pile of papers that recorded so many complaints, both petty and severe, against Simeon. 'This evidence is enough to damn him simply by its volume. Where is the middle way?'

Stephen Goldsmith stood with his arms folded across his

chest, glowering at the papers. 'Someone has been more than a little clever here,' he said. 'One charge or two can be dismissed as scurrilous. Even three or four can be handled with diplomacy, but this . . .' He heaved a heavy sigh and his thick red brows knitted more fiercely across the bridge of his nose. 'This quantity of grievances beggars all hope of justice.'

Jacob de Wold looked up with a tired expression in his eyes. 'How will we help him, Stephen? De Figham is a clever manipulator of words. He is well practised in the art of twisting questions and answers to his own advantage. He will bedevil the minds and loyalties of everyone here, and how will he be stopped, since he speaks without the lawful fetters of formal charges? By the time we have sifted the wheat from the chaff in this, Simeon will be floundering through a maze of doubt and suspicion. What can we do? How will we help him?'

'I do not know,' Stephen admitted. 'God help us, Jacob, I think this Cyrus de Figham has tied our hands.'

The most serious charges laid against Simeon were those of procuring and selling holy water for magical purposes and of stealing precious books from the church for his personal profit. These accusations might be argued by a clever advocate and found unproven, but the stain of them would leave his reputation sorely damaged. The sheer quantity of lesser charges might yet prove to be more injurious, for men will always presuppose a fire where there is smoke, and few would be left convinced of his innocence. Those who hated him would have their satisfaction, while those who loved him now would soon come to despise him for their own uncertainties.

'All this is hearsay,' Jacob de Wold complained when the charges were read. 'The words of the rabble against the reputation of a canon. Cyrus de Figham, if all were to be tried on the strength of tittle-tattle from the streets, this court would never rest and you yourself might yet be standing in Simeon's place.'

'His claims to sainthood are more than common prattle,' Cyrus replied. 'His raising of the dead is more than mere gossip. He professes to be lame, yet is as healthy in both legs as you or I. He professes to be celibate yet lies regularly with the women of the town and keeps a whore and a bastard son at the expense and embarrassment of the church.'

'Hearsay,' Jacob growled. 'Where is your proof?'

'A score of witnesses will be my proof.'

'Hearsay and prattle.'

'At his instigation a dead man was staked through the heart lest he rise up to point a finger at his murderer.'

'Lies! This priest has never held with such foolish superstition.'

'My witness will say otherwise.'

'Then your witness will lie, Father Cyrus.'

De Figham pulled a small sheet from the stack of papers in his hand. 'Lord Provost, here is a list of books recently seen in his scriptorium.' He placed the list on the desk before the provost. 'Many have now been confiscated, but those volumes underscored have not yet been recovered.'

'Nor will they be, since they were lost in either the floods or the great fire. These others were being copied with my full consent.'

'But there is no record of such consent,' Cyrus protested.

'A small omission on my part,' Jacob told him bitterly. 'I believe my lord archbishop will forgive the oversight.'

Cyrus narrowed his eyes maliciously. 'He meets with Jews in secret.'

'What man does not?' Jacob demanded pointedly. 'Since our church has forbidden usury, a man must raise needed cash where he can.'

'Needed cash? How much can one man need? Does he claim to support the entire populace of Beverley with his alms?'

'No, but he does support the entire Minster Restoration Fund without the assistance of his fellow canons,' Jacob answered curtly.

'Ah yes, the rebuilding of our holy Minster church. Less gullible men might say he has been hiding behind that pretext for too long, while he lines his bottomless pockets with our treasures.'

'Father Cyrus, be warned,' Jacob growled in anger. 'Such talk is slanderous.'

'Perhaps, but I will ask, in due time and for the benefit of his peers, with what collateral he tempted these Jews.'

'Simeon de Beverley has never professed to be without certain means.'

'Ah, yes, his *means*. By your leave I will question him briefly on the matter.'

'You have that right, if he consents to it.'

The discourse was moving and turning according to de Figham's thrust and parry. He turned to Simeon and demanded: 'Is your father Sir Rufus de Malham, a man much favoured by our late King Henry?'

Simeon stood erect, angered to hear his father's name spoken by such a man and in such circumstances. 'He is.'

'And has he not disowned you as his son?'

The question was like a slap in Simeon's face. 'That is a slanderous lie, sir, and well you know it.'

'And did he not set your younger brother, Thaddeus, in your place, making him the rightful heir instead of you, the elder son?'

'You twist the facts, de Figham.'

'Well, Simeon? Is it not true that Sir Rufus has disowned you?'

'I was crippled,' Simeon said. 'Sir Rufus had two sons, a noble house and extensive holdings. To preserve his line he chose the healthier child to be his heir. The practice is not uncommon and it had the king's approval.'

'So, you were stripped of your birthright and handed over like some chattel to the Church? Little wonder, then, that you have scant love for your present master, that you strip the Church of its treasures to redeem your losses.'

'That is a wicked lie,' Simeon declared.

'Then perhaps Sir Rufus de Malham could be summoned here to speak on your behalf?'

Simeon's eyes grew narrow at this suggestion. 'Cyrus de Figham, you know I would never sanction such an outrage.'

'Because your father has no love for you?'

'No sir, because he loves me well and a father's love is not to be hung up for inspection by those who scheme to besmirch his family.'

De Figham, satisfied that this exchange had coloured the minds of all those who witnessed it, turned back to the provost elect and made another skilful lunge in this verbal contest. 'A clerk from York was disposed of at St Peter's.'

Jacob de Wold allowed the sudden murmur of amazement in the room, then fixed de Figham with a steely stare. 'Disposed of?'

'Witnesses saw him enter but not come out. He was carrying gold and silver in his purses and made it known that he had business with Simeon de Beverley. That clerk has not been seen since he entered the gates of St Peter's two weeks ago.'

'This town was plagued with mud flows and sudden swamps at that time,' Stephen Goldsmith interceded. 'Hundreds of souls were lost without trace. Perhaps this clerk was one of them.'

'There were no floods within St Peter's walls,' Cyrus said coldly.

Jacob looked at Simeon. 'Do you know the whereabouts of this clerk from York?'

'I do not, my Lord Provost,' Simeon replied. 'He did not come to St Peter's.'

'I tell you there are witnesses to the fact,' de Figham suddenly shouted, banging his fist on the arm of a chair. This was the signal for the clerks at the door to allow a man in ragged furs to enter the room unannounced. Before he could be stopped he rushed to Simeon and pulled him roughly around to stare him in the face.

'This is the man,' he shouted. 'He sold the holy water. I saw him at his magic and I was present when he gave a portion of the holy relics of St John to a travelling Jew.'

'What? Silence! Silence!'

A cry of protest went up from all those present. Men stamped their feet and shook their fists while others merely smiled at this performance.

'He sold the relics,' the man, a herbalist, shouted. 'I have the proof. He sold the relics to a Jew for gold and silver.'

'Subdue that man! Silence him!' Jacob de Wold was rapping with his ring upon the desk. The room was in tumult as clerks rushed forward to drag away the herbalist and Cyrus de Figham, feigning surprise, gestured as if to protest his innocence. When silence was at last restored the provost's face was reddened by his rage.

'Cyrus de Figham, what is the meaning of this outrageous outburst? How dare you bring a witness here to speak against a man who is not on trial? How dare you seek to influence this inquiry by such wicked means?'

'My Lord Provost, this is none of my doing,' de Figham cried. 'Someone has acted unwisely. It was not my intention to show this man the face of his accuser while he is still free to do the witness harm or offer bribes to still his tongue. I beg the court's indulgence, my Lord Provost. Give me two days to gather certain necessary papers and to have that over-zealous herbalist better schooled before he gives his evidence. Two days, then let these goodly men decide if Simeon de Beverley should be tried for wicked crimes against the church.'

'Cyrus de Figham, do you intend to formally accuse this canon of taking away, of *selling*, the holy relics of our blessed St John of Beverley?'

'I do, my lord, when the time is appropriate.'

'God's teeth!'

Stephen Goldsmith stepped forward and pointed a threatening finger at Cyrus de Figham. 'Be very cautious, sir. It will go ill with you if such a loathsome charge is made in the absence of irrefutable proof to support your claims.'

'The herbalist is my proof,' de Figham countered. 'What he has to say will convince the court of Simeon de Beverley's guilt. When he has spoken and shown his evidence, both Geoffrey Plantagenet and His Holiness the pope will know beyond doubt that we have evil in our midst. I beg you for two more days to present my case.'

'Denied! I will not lock this man away while you prepare a suitable case against him. This matter should never have been brought before the provost's court while still deficient in its preparation. I have a mind to dismiss him without charge.'

'Then I will be forced to take these serious charges to York, and then to Rome.'

'God's teeth, de Figham ...'

'Two days are all I ask. My charge is not vindictive, therefore I am content to see him freed until this court recalls him.'

Stephen Goldsmith growled: 'Your generosity astounds me, sir.'

'My lord, I insist on it.'

'Why? How will it serve you if he is freed?'

Cyrus de Figham spread his hands. 'Not I but justice, and the reputation of this honoured court, will be served by it.' He turned to the gathered canons, smiling. 'A show of hands, then. Free Simeon de Beverley to the goodwill of his canon, Father Cuthbert. Recall him in two days' time to hear the formal evidence against him, and then decide if he should go to trial.' He paused, then added slyly: 'Despite the nature of many of these charges, I doubt he will dare use the black arts to escape our Christian justice.'

Now the objective of this cold-hearted priest was clear to Simeon and many others in the room. De Figham aimed to have him excommunicated, denied the Church, the fellowship of other human beings, the right to shelter and food, water and fire. It was the ultimate punishment, worse even than death, for a man might die in grace and hope for Heaven, but to be excommunicated robbed him of his place on earth and deprived him of his seat in Paradise.

The show of hands decided that Simeon would be brought before the court again in two days' time. When the rapping of Jacob's ring declared the hearing at an end, John Palmer leaned toward his master and said, in urgent tones, 'My lord Cyrus, two days from now this plan will turn against you. How can you hope to succeed in this? You have no proof.'

'Oh ye of little faith,' de Figham smiled. 'I need no proof, John. I have the herbalist.'

Close by the provost's desk, Simeon blinked his eyes. 'I am astounded.'

'De Figham was too keen to have you freed,' Stephen told him. 'Had he but made these charges formal, and demanded your incarceration, he would have got his way, and well he knew that. He angled for your freedom, but why?'

'To demonstrate his generosity?' Simeon suggested. 'To show the court that he is not vindictive in his accusations?'

Jacob de Wold shook his head. 'Stephen is wise to suspect de Figham of yet more underhand work against you. There is more to his generosity than meets the eye. Do not forget that by canon law a man may be condemned by common report. Be on your guard, my friend.'

'You can be sure I will.' Simeon rubbed his face vigorously with his palms, then shook his head as if to toss his perplexity away. 'The holy relics sold to a travelling Jew,' he said. 'What a sacrilege with which to brand a man. He seeks my excommunication. I am sure of it.'

'And Geoffrey Plantagenet might well oblige him with it,' Jacob said.

'But he has no proof,' Simeon protested. 'Even with a score of witnesses to speak against me, how will he possibly convince the court, and our archbishop, without just and reasonable proof?'

'He will have his way without it.'

'Never.'

Jacob de Wold leaned over his desk and peered at Simeon sternly. 'Simeon de Beverley, you underestimate your enemy and place too much honest faith in your archbishop. To put an end to this embarrassing squabbling among his canons, all Geoffrey has to do is remove the bone of contention that excites them. He is a huntsman with a hunter's reasoning. He will waste neither time nor energy, nor risk the intervention of the pope, by struggling to make peace here. To end the conflict, quietly and cleanly, he will simply shoot the fox. He will excommunicate you.'

CHAPTER TWENTY-EIGHT

I n York Geoffrey Plantagenet turned a gold seal-ring in his hands and whistled through his teeth in admiration of the craftsmanship. It bore a seal contrived from the arms of England and of York, entwined about with the *Planta Geneta*, Geoffrey's family motif. He probed its edge until the ring sprang open to reveal a yellowed object under glass.

'Do you believe this relic to be genuine?'

Fergus de Burton turned up his palms and shrugged his silk-clad shoulders. 'Would he dare present it to you, my lord archbishop, as the fingernail of St Timothy, if he even suspected that it might be otherwise?'

'I think not.' Geoffrey placed the ring on his finger and moved his hand this way and that to view it from all angles. He scrutinised the fine and intricate engraving around the band. 'This goldsmith is a craftsman of extraordinary skills. My brother Richard will be envious of this. I doubt he owns any item that will match it.'

'Stephen is also a wealthy man with power enough to rule the roost in Beverley, if his ambitions ran to it. He owns the ground on which St Peter's enclosure stands. Provosts and archbishops in their long succession have tried without success to coerce that land from his family. They would not be swayed and nor will he. A stubborn man from a stubborn line, this goldsmith.'

'He begs my intervention on behalf of Father Simeon. He says these Beverley canons plot against him, that the authority of the Church is being used to advance Cyrus de Figham's personal obsession. It is a complex, tightly knotted net they weave in which to snare a solitary priest.'

'De Figham has also petitioned Rome,' de Burton reminded him.

'Aye, and I would rap his elegant knuckles for it, if I could find a discreet way to do as much.'

Fergus grinned at that. 'By now your carts of wine and salt sit snugly in his barn. You could disarm him at a stroke, or else persuade him that these charges against Simeon should be dropped.'

'Do you not think I have sufficient plots and intrigues of my own to unravel without rushing to embroil myself in this?'

'They will involve you, whether or not you will it,' Fergus said. 'When formal charges are made and a trial set, you will be called upon to decide the issue. It promises to be a dirty business, sire, and Rome will be eager to see how your hands are soiled with it.'

Geoffrey Plantagenet scowled and pursed his lips. 'If this Cyrus de Figham believes he can shift archbishops and popes around like petty pieces on a board he is mistaken. I will play no part in his unsavoury intrigues. Damn it, Fergus, I will not be manipulated by this canon.'

'I doubt you will avoid it, sire, when the time comes.'

'What?' His eyes closed into slits and his face grew dark with indignation. 'I am York's archbishop elect, the son of one king and the half-brother of another. Geoffrey Plantagenet paces his steps to *no man's* tune.' He glowered at the seal-ring on his finger. 'If this sly fox of Figham could be removed, the sharp thorn that is Beverley might give my side some ease.'

This was the moment Fergus had anticipated. He leaned forward in his seat and placed his forearms on his knees, his gaze intense. 'Sire, the balance of power in Beverley is delicately hung. I merely offer that it would serve you better to contend with the Devil you know than to remove him and risk a younger, stronger demon springing in to take his place. De Figham's heart is set on reclaiming the artifacts and treasures that were lost in the great fire. By bringing Simeon to his knees he hopes to strike a double blow, to destroy his enemy and take hold of Beverley's wealth.'

'But that treasure rightfully belongs to York.'

'Indeed it does.'

'God's teeth, St John was York's archbishop for thirty-six years! Any treasure of his belongs to me by right. His relics should be lying here, where we can claim the revenue from his pilgrims, not in that godforsaken hole where canons war with each other like fretful children.'

'Indeed, sire,' Fergus repeated. 'And what a wealth you would possess if all those assets were in your hands, enough to buy your immediate consecration as archbishop, enough to buy the devotion of your brother the king. There is no ambition you could not realise at a stroke if you were master of Beverley's treasure.'

The Plantagenet's eyes were bright as he turned his imagination loose upon the words. The magnitude of power to be harnessed by such wealth was more than even his covetous mind could calculate with ease. 'Does Simeon have it?'

Fergus nodded. 'It is almost a certainty that he knows its whereabouts and has set himself up as its protector.'

'But will he give it up?'

'He might, once Cyrus de Figham has him trapped. Such charges as will be brought against him could result in a sentence of outlawry or perpetual pilgrimage, and either one would break a man like Simeon. He would be sent from Beverley naked and in chains, with none to befriend him and no hope of ever returning home, and every man in England would have the lawful right to kill him on sight. A dreadful sentence for any man, sire, and I doubt if Simeon would pass the town gates before his enemies struck him down. His only hope would be to purchase pardon from the Church.'

'And I would set the price on his redemption?'

'You would indeed, sire. And what a price you would be free to levy in those circumstances.'

'This priest is honest and stubborn to a fault. He might prefer a martyr's death.'

'I doubt that very much. Whatever else he is, he is no fool.'

'Then I need do nothing in this but set the appropriate sentence when the time comes, and then haggle the cost of his redemption?'

'No more than that,' Fergus assured him. 'And when the Beverley treasure comes to you, pope and king alike will be eating from your hands.'

'God's teeth, your mind is devious, Fergus de Burton.'

'Fertile,' Fergus corrected with a smile.

'Then it is settled. Instruct my clerk to inform Stephen Goldsmith of my decision. I do not choose to intervene in these intrigues until I must. He has my sympathy, of course, but I cannot be seen to use my position within the Church to further the prospects of an obscure canon already judged delinquent by his peers. Let him keep me well informed of events at Beverley. Other than that, this Simeon stands alone.' He held his hand up to the light. 'And you may tell the goldsmith I will keep the ring.'

In Beverley a group of priests and clerks were on their way from the Minster to St Mary's, passing alongside the ditch in Eastgate which ran a parallel course with the eastern wall of St Peter's enclosure. Their presence there at twilight was unusual, for those of the church preferred to pass by those of the streets in less uncertain circumstances, lest one group should seek to profit from the other. John Palmer led the churchmen and all were armed: twelve men to bring one witness from the chapel of St Mary to the Minster church. Their business was conspicuous, for when the words of a witness might defame a canon, others became desirous of his tongue. Rumour had been spread that Simeon knew the face of his accuser, and so this herbalist must be protected.

So was the scene prepared and the wheels of de Figham's clever scheme set in motion. Even as his escort came for him, the herbalist was being induced by wine and coin to leave St Mary's for the streets.

All along the Eastgate ditch small fires burned with huddled figures gathered around the flames. Those lacking shelter for the night would spend the hours of darkness by the wall, with one amongst them wakeful to protect the pot and the ale jug. The group of priests and clerks made tardy progress, hampered as they were at every camp fire by those seeking a blessing in exchange for coin or some item of little value. A rabbit-skin or a cockerel, a brace of crows or a strip of well-tanned leather could buy ease for a poor man's spiritual needs. A coin could purchase forgiveness for omitted sacraments, a candle might be offered for atonement of a minor sin. Business, as ever, was brisk among the poor, the more so since the drought was over, and who but these priests and clerks, with their constant prayers and their special kinship with Almighty God, could be responsible for that?

From the other end of Eastgate a man came tottering, weaving an erratic course along the edge of the waterway. A priest he did not recognise had brought him as far as the fish market, then urged him make the remainder of the journey alone. He knew only that he must follow the ditch until he could be met, and after that his poor life would be altered for the better.

Between the oncoming herbalist and the party of priests advancing in the opposite direction, the high wall of St Peter's loomed, its ancient brickwork shadowed in the fading light. If any eye had looked beyond to mark the shadowed contours of the wall, the figure of a lurking man might have been seen and Cyrus de Figham's plan undone before it was enacted. Lying flat and still atop the bricks, this lurker, in a dark cloak and a hood, fingered a long-bladed knife as he watched the staggering figure of the herbalist drawing closer. Only a few yards remained between them when the ever-watchful John Palmer,

289

travelling with the priests, yelled an alarm.

'Look there! An armed robber has scaled St Peter's wall from the inside! Stop him! Someone grab that man before he gets away!'

In the confusion that followed the shout, several men bore witness to a foul and cowardly attack on the herbalist. The cloaked man dropped from the wall and leaped the ditch, his long blade flashing in the firelight for an instant. Then the herbalist uttered a guttural cry and fell to his knees clutching his bleeding chest. Something was snatched from his clothing before the heavily cloaked attacker ran off at speed. Those who watched the attack were agreed on but one fact, that the killer was a cripple who made his escape at a rapid lurch, dragging one useless foot behind the other.

'Simeon!' John Palmer yelled as though aghast. 'My God, see how he limps! It's Simeon!'

A clerk shook his fist after the departing figure. 'No other man in Beverley has such a limp. It was he. There can be no doubt. It was Father Simeon.'

'That is impossible,' someone else insisted. 'Simeon is no common lawbreaker to lie in wait for an unarmed man and …'

'This man is dead,' John Palmer informed them all. 'And see, he is the chief witness, the herbalist, the one who would denounce that same Simeon with his testimony. He's dead, stabbed through the heart before he could give his damning evidence. We all saw what happened here tonight. Simeon has murdered the witness to save himself. We saw it. We all can testify to the fact.'

'Not I. I cannot be sure.'

'Nor I. Dear God, I pray it was not he.'

John Palmer crouched down to sign the cross over the dead man's chest. 'I know this knife,' he said. 'It has the crossed keys of St Peter on its hilt. The truth lies right here before our very eyes. This knife belongs to Simeon de Beverley and he has murdered the only man who could speak out against him.'

*

Simeon was sitting with Elvira in a secluded garden near the woods when the gates of St Peter's enclosure were breached by a large force of armed men. The gateman and a priest were struck down when they tried to stand against the sudden intrusion. A dozen men came running from the kitchens and infirmary, but they were no match for such a force and many were injured in the bloody scuffle that ensued. When Osric saw that they had come under attack by men of the church, he called at once for peace and all stood off.

'By what right do you breach the gates of St Peter's?' he demanded of Cyrus de Figham, who had the bright glinting eyes of a hunter now that his blood was heated and his quarry in his sights. 'By what right do you bring violence to this peaceful and godly place?'

'By the right of our holy mother Church,' de Digham snarled into the other's face. 'I have the papers here, and this time the rabbit will not bolt to avoid the snare. Where is the evil-doer?'

'There is no evil-doer here,' Osric replied, matching de Figham's excitement with his own hostility. 'Of whom do you speak, my lord canon?'

'I speak of the liar, the fornicator,' de Figham shouted so loudly that all about could hear. 'The sorcerer who dares to make magic without first calling on the name of God, then claims the black art miraculous. I have come for the thief who strips our mother Church of its artifacts, who sells our holy water for a profit ...'

'Have a care, Cyrus de Figham. Rein in that viper's tongue before I take my surgeon's knife to it.'

'Don't threaten me, infirmarian. These men are witness to all that is said and done within these walls.'

Osric's fury was cold and tightly checked. 'If you have come for Simeon then you act above and beyond your powers as a canon. The charges against him have yet to be confirmed, and until they are ...'

'Until they are, he will languish in a cell below the courts. He will take privation for his daily bread and be forced to make atonement for his sins.'

'A cell? He is to be interned?'

'Below ground with the rats, where he belongs.'

'On what charge?'

Now de Figham had the ear of every man, the outsiders and those who followed Simeon. 'The charge is murder, and for that I hope he hangs.'

In the garden some distance away Simeon had risen to his feet at the sound of the furore at the gates. He set Elvira at his back as Edwin came running, his long, thin body skirting the trees and bushes for cover.

'They have come again for you, Father Simeon,' he told the priest in a breathless whisper. 'New charges must have been brought against you because they come in force. They are armed and one man is carrying a neck-brace and manacles.'

'What? Am I to be trussed up like a dog on some trumped-up charge of Cyrus de Figham's imagining?'

'You could escape them,' Edwin urged. 'Go by the far wall and the marshes. They will never dare to follow you now that so much rain has fallen and the land is turned to swamp. You know the way. Go now and thwart their efforts. Take the lady and go, and when the matter is settled ...'

Simeon shook his head emphatically. 'Were I to abscond, de Figham would claim others in my place. Father Cuthbert ...' He saw the white-clad figure in the distance, a frail old man on whom the full responsibility for an erring priest would hang, and he knew he could not save himself while Cuthbert might be taken. He turned to Elvira and took her by the shoulders. 'My love, you must not risk crossing the open space between here and the scriptorium. Go with Edwin. He will conceal you in the woods until he knows it is safe for you to return.'

Her eyes were wide. 'What will you do?'

'I will face them.'

'Be careful, Simeon.'

She spoke so calmly that she appeared unconcerned by these events, but he felt the trembling of her body as he held her close in a swift and fierce embrace. He watched the two shapes vanish into the shadows, saw the pale oval of Elvira's face reappear briefly, heard her say again, 'Be careful, Simeon,' and then the two were gone.

They were upon him before he had walked a dozen strides, eight men in all, each wielding a stick or a cudgel for the purpose of restraining him. Before he could make a move to defend himself, he went down beneath a rain of savage blows. He took a hefty kick to the ribs before the brawling men were pulled away and he was hoisted to his feet, gasping and dazed.

Cyrus de Figham pushed himself forward, dragging others aside to reach the priest. 'Simeon de Beverley, eleven independent witnesses saw you kill the herbalist who was to speak against you at the provost's inquiry. Your knife was found embedded in his heart and all the evidence he carried was taken from him at the killing. Do you have anything to say in your defence?'

'I am innocent of this charge,' Simeon gasped, knowing now why de Figham had angled for his release. 'I am innocent, and well you know that, Cyrus de Figham.'

'You will be taken to the provost's court and held there in a cell until the charges can be formalised and while the due process of canon law is scrupulously observed. You have overreached yourself this time, Simeon de Beverley. The Church will not suffer a murderer to go unpunished.'

At a signal from de Figham a man with a metal restraint stepped forward and another, bearing lengths of chain, took hold of Simeon's arm.

Simeon shrank from them. 'In God's holy name, there is no need for this. Call off your blacksmiths. Take these shackles away.'

'You cannot do this!' Osric shouted. 'The man is already under restraint.'

Another, bigger voice cut through these protests. 'You proceed with this outrage at your peril, Cyrus de Figham.' Father Thorald's great bulk had ploughed a rough way through the knot of armed men and curious bystanders. He towered above de Figham with his fists clenched and his face a mask of fury. De Figham yelled his orders without taking his brazen stare from Thorald's face.

'Should any man here seek to oppose the rightful duties of the Church, let him be subdued, shackled by the neck and limbs and taken forcefully to the cells as a co-conspirator in this villainous matter.'

'Damn you, de Figham,' Thorald growled.

'It is not I who shall be damned, my friend.'

'The charge is false.'

'I have eleven witnesses, all priests and clerks in holy orders, who will swear on oath that it is otherwise.'

'The charge is false,' the huge priest said again. 'And any who dares to bear false witness against another will burn in Hell.'

'Hell's fires do not concern me,' de Figham smiled.

'Then be sure the fires of this world will, for I will personally set the sticks under you and put a lighted torch to them, if you persist in this.'

De Figham turned away contemptuously. 'Shackle the prisoner and take him away.'

In the woods Elvira had broken free of Edwin's guiding hand and turned back at a run. She had heard nothing of the heated exchange between de Figham and the good men of St Peter's. All she knew was what was in her heart, that Simeon was in trouble while she crept away to hide herself from danger in the woods. She ran back through the trees, her long hair flying and her linen slippers sliding in the mud. As she approached the clearing she caught sight of Simeon bent beneath a cruel iron yoke, his ankles shackled and his arms held fast behind his back, a score of jeering, angry men surrounding him. A cry rose in her throat as she rushed forward at a sprint, but before she could break through the thickness of the trees a man's hands were on her, gripping her by the waist and gagging her mouth with a large, rough palm. She felt herself lifted up so that her feet could no longer gain purchase on the ground, and a man's face pressed itself against her own.

'Be silent, lady. Be silent and be still.'

She recognised the voice of Daniel hawk and, though she was struggling hard and he barely recovered from his injuries, she could not manage to break his grip on her. All she could do was stare in horror as Simeon was led away, a proud man hobbled by iron bars and chains, a good man treated no better than a common criminal.

It was Father Richard who instructed Daniel to release Elvira when the gates were safely closed behind the stumbling Simeon and his escort.

'Have courage, lady,' Daniel told her. 'Simeon will come through this.'

'Do not mislead her,' Richard countered. 'Elvira is brave enough to hear the truth and bear with it.' He took her hand. 'The herbalist is dead and a charge of murder has been brought against Simeon. Let Edwin take you back to the scriptorium, where I will come to you when something is decided. As his canon, Father Cuthbert has the right to see and hear all evidence before it is presented to the court and, as his priest, I too have many rights. There is much to be done and it must be dealt with quickly.'

'There are eleven witnesses to this murder,' Daniel Hawk reminded him. 'You know the law as I do, Richard. A man may be condemned by common report and given eight days to leave the country or else be outlawed. And if they elect to have him tried by secular, rather than canon law . . .' his voice faltered, unwilling to express the consequences of such a circumstance.

Richard voiced it for him. 'If he is excommunicated on the other charges, then tried by secular law for the herbalist's murder, his freedom is ended now and his life in jeopardy.'

'Protect him, Richard,' Elvira pleaded. 'Find a way. Protect him.'

'We will, Elvira. Edwin, see the lady safely within the scriptorium, them come at once to the infirmary. You, too, will have a part to play in this. Daniel, are you with us?'

The dark young priest shook his head. 'No, Richard, I will ask Osric's leave to return to my master's house and beg forgiveness for my transgressions against his humour. If I am to repay the debt I owe St Peter's, I can do it better from that other camp.'

'No man can serve two masters,' Richard reminded him. He was only half-satisfied with Daniel's motives and he doubted his strength to be his own man while standing in Wulfric de Morthlund's awesome shadow.

'I know that, Richard,' Daniel said.

They had left Elvira in Edwin's care and were striding toward the scriptorium when Richard said: 'They beat him and kicked him, Daniel. Simeon has served this town, its people and its Church since he was ten years old. They know him well, and yet they tried to break his bones and then they locked him in that iron contraption and dragged him off like an animal.'

'Most men are as fickle as quicksilver in their souls, my friend, and they fear the terrible power of the Church.'

'No, Daniel, they fear the power of men like Cyrus de Figham and Wulfric de Morthlund. There is no evil in the Church, only in some of the men who profess to serve it.'

Daniel nodded, at pains to match his limping pace to that of the fitter man. 'Our immediate concern must be in gaining his freedom from the cell. He will not survive it, Daniel. All Cyrus need do is contrive to keep him there, while time and enforced "atonement" do the rest. They seem to have him every way. However he jumps he will meet another trap. He will die in there, Richard. Cyrus will make sure of it. We have to get him out.'

'We?'

Daniel looked sideways at his bearded companion. 'You have no reason to trust me, Richard, since I have had neither time nor opportunity to prove myself, but my words are sound enough. You may doubt my loyalty but do not doubt my reasoning. Simeon will die unless a way is found to free him from that dungeon.'

They reached the infirmary to find the others waiting, all crowded into the little chapel where their words would not be overheard. Daniel Hawk made no attempt to cross the threshold. Instead he waited outside for Osric's leave to offer the olive branch of peace to his own master.

'We should have known,' Thorald was saying to the others. He sat on a low stool with his shoulders hunched, and it seemed the whole of his strength had drained from him. 'When de Figham engineered for Simeon to come face to face with his accuser, then angled for his freedom until the court could be recalled. We should have known.'

Antony handed him a jug of ale. 'Simeon needs neither our regrets nor our recriminations. He needs our help. We must find a way to free him or he will die.'

CHAPTER TWENTY-NINE

The cell beneath the provost's courts was cold and very dark. One window-slit, set at an angle in the slope of the stone roof, let in a haze of light and a steady fall of rain. The walls were running with damp, which gathered in rank pools at every corner. The ground was laid with ancient stones covered over with layers of rushes, and every previous occupant had added to the stench that rose each time the rushes were disturbed. There was a slab of stone against one wall where a man might stretch his body out, though the chill that seeped through the walls drove many to seek the dubious comfort of the rushes. A metal sconce hung on the wall close by the squat oak door. Here visitors and inquisitors could rest their flaming torches while the black smoke fed the sticky, dripping sludge lining the roof. Simeon did not fear the cold, the darkness or the damp that chilled him to the bone. He only feared to die like this, alone among the rats. He heard the bell Great John, begin its mournful tolling of the hour and knew that, through this darkness, only his prayers and his faith remained to him. He spoke the psalms out loud, and by this simple act of trust he was sustained.

'Father?'

At first he was not sure he heard a voice. He looked toward

the window-slit and felt a spray of rain upon his face. Great John still tolled the long midnight offices and rats were scuttling noisily in the rushes.

'Father?'

Now he was sure. He hauled himself to his feet, his limbs stiffened by cold and bruising. 'Peter? Where are you, boy?'

'Here I am, father. Here.'

Simeon raised his arm above his head, stretching his fingers to the window-slit. He found the small, thin hand, felt the fingers entwine around his own and knew, in that one moment, that somewhere a candle still burned in the night for him.

'God bless you, son. Where is your mother?'

'She is safe. I saw her weeping, and when the arrow felled you I heard her pray that you would live.'

'Tears and prayers,' Simeon said grimly. 'My Elvira must be torn of heart to lend herself to either.'

'Have they hurt you, father?'

'No more than God gave me the strength to bear.'

A stab of lightning forked across the sky and flung itself to earth, and in the brief flash of light he saw his godson's face. The boy was clinging to the sloping roof, one arm thrust to its shoulder through the window. His hair was plastered in wet strands to his head and cheeks. His eyes were wide and very blue, and the raindrops looked like tears on his thick lashes. Elvira called him beautiful, and in that flash of silver light no other word sufficed.

'God grant you ease and courage, father,' he said. In the eerie light he had seen the cuts and bruises on Simeon's face, the ragged wetness of his clothes and the pain in his blue eyes.

'This meeting has strengthened me, Peter.'

'The canons are divided over the date of your trial. Jacob would have you dealt with right away, but others vote to await the news from Rome and the sanction of the archbishop.'

'If they wait on Rome's approval, I might be here for weeks or even months!'

'That is why de Figham is so set on it. The atonements

will begin at dawn. You are charged with many crimes and, because one of those charges is murder, your jailers may do as they wish to ensure your penitence. It is their solemn duty. The church allows it and de Figham demands it.'

Simeon sighed and gripped the boy's fingers more tightly. 'Guilty or innocent, I must be cleansed in order to face my accusers, and my God, with a humble heart. All men by turn might be the loved sheep or the scapegoats of the Church they serve.'

'We fear the carting, Father.'

'Would they stoop to that?'

'For murder, yes. They say you killed a townsman, and by the law his equals have the right to admonish his killer.'

'And if I am then judged innocent of the crime will these law-abiding equals take back their blows?'

'You will not be judged innocent,' Peter told him bluntly. 'Too many charges are levelled against you for that. What we fear most is the executioner hiding in the crowds, the one de Figham bribes to cut you down so that you die unshriven, untried and guilty by default.'

'Then I am doomed,' Simeon declared. 'You must look now to your own and Elvira's safety. Protect the holy relics of St John and ...'

'No, father, we will not abandon you to save ourselves. I have found a well-shaft underneath the cells. Osric and Thorald, Antony and Richard are working right now to clear the debris from it and release the opening. There must be a cover lying beneath the rushes. Find it and raise it up. Take this, it will help you in the task.' He passed a metal bar through the window-slit. One end of it had been flattened and sharpened, the other angled and forked to provide good leverage. 'The cover has lain for centuries untouched. If it is made of wood, time might have weakened it, but if of metal its raising will not be easy. Have you the strength to do it?'

'I have the strength,' Simeon said without conviction.

'Is there a place to hook a rope? I can scale the shaft to reach you but I doubt you will get down without a rope.'

'The ring in the door will support my weight.'

'When the bells of St Peter's ring ahead of all the others, or when they ring between the hours, you must be ready to lift up the cover.'

Another flash of lightning lit the boy's pale face against a rain-filled sky. Simeon could not see how this plan could work. Four men to move the rubble of centuries, one injured man to lift a time-sealed cover, and all before de Figham could make his move. It was too desperate, too uncertain a plan.

Simeon gripped his godson's fingers, wishing he could embrace the boy just once before he faced what lay ahead.

'Peter, you must find a way to get word to Fergus de Burton at the bishop's palace in York. Tell him all that has happened here. He knows the colour and shape of de Figham's schemes, and he has the ears and the confidence of Geoffrey Plantagenet. Tell him he was right, that John Palmer is the key. He'll understand what might be done to help me. Do this in haste. If Fergus de Burton is not to be found, the same message must be taken to Aaron the Jew, in Coppergate. I believe he can be persuaded to approach the archbishop to plead the urgency of my predicament. Will you see to it that this is done?'

'I will,' Peter replied. 'There is danger. I must leave you.'

'Go safely and with God, Peter.' He felt the small fingers tighten and then release their grip, and by another flash of lightning he saw that the window-slit was empty.

It was well before dawn when Richard set out across the Westwood on a sturdy horse, taking the shortest, most direct route to York. The vital message was carried in his head, no word of it committed to paper. The men of St Peter's were aware that Cyrus de Figham would anticipate their efforts on Simeon's behalf. Even now the vast, timber-rich acres of the Westwood might harbour a dozen men bent on preventing any rider passing through. Written words might fall into the wrong hands and so be turned against Simeon at his trial. Nor was it safe to let it be known that Fergus de Burton, that grinning, amiable guest at every man's table, had made himself approachable to such a petition. They needed every ally they could muster, however questionable. If that young man with the too-ready smile could use these circumstances to his own advantage, then they would gladly use him in return. The Devil called the tune and they must dance to it, no matter if their partner wore the Devil's own colours.

Over the Westwood clouds were gathering, with grey light filtering feebly at their edges. The sun would not be up for another hour. Father Richard rode hard, cutting a crooked course across the pasture, keen to be clear of the area and on the old Roman way before the town began to stir. His purpose was now extreme, for the well beneath the cells defied all efforts to clear it, and there were demands for Simeon to be carted.

'God bless and keep you, friend,' Richard muttered now. 'And the Devil take your enemies.'

It soon became apparent to him that he was being followed. Behind him the figure of a horseman, still in shadow, kept irregular pace across the uneven ground. This one rode a course as straight as an arrow, ignoring the many detours necessary for the safety of his mount. Richard urged his own mount to a faster pace. He was riding with woodland on his right and pasture on his left, and up ahead the trees that would give him cover were still some distance off.

The whinny of a horse alerted him. He turned in the saddle to see that his pursuer had been unhorsed, perhaps when his mount was tripped by a hidden hollow. A moment later the rider was on his feet and struggling to regain his seat in the saddle. Richard used the other's mishap to gain some extra ground, only to slow his pace when he heard another whinny from behind him. This time the rider had gone down on his back, a heavy fall that left him prostrate while his mount pranced and pawed at the earth. If Cyrus de Figham, expecting a hasty ride to York, had sent a man to apprehend any rider leaving St Peter's, then he had erred uncharacteristically in his choice.

Richard steered his horse for the trees on his left and,

sheltered by heavy foliage, observed the one who sought to dog his heels. He drew his sword and freed his sword arm from his cloak. No man had ever died by Richard's hand, but if this rider chose to be the first, so be it. He saw the man stagger to his feet, regain his horse and make several clumsy attempts to mount before he managed to haul himself into the saddle. Then he whipped his mount into a gallop, only to be flung to the ground again by the sudden momentum of the animal under him.

'What the . . .' with a curse Father Richard resheathed his sword and turned back at a canter, squinting into the darkness to confirm his suspicions. He caught the wayward animal by the reins and walked it to where its rider still lay winded on the ground.

'What in God's name are you doing here, Edwin?'

The youngster propped himself on his elbows, wincing. 'I intend riding to York with you, Father Richard. You might need my help.'

'Is this what you call riding, this pathetic show of ups and downs with never a thought for where your mount might be setting its feet?'

Edwin looked amazed. 'Does the horse not watch its own feet, Father Richard?'

Richard looked to the Heavens and signed the cross. 'Edwin, the route to York is likely to be littered with de Figham's men, watching for any rider leaving Beverley. He cannot think for a moment that Simeon's friends will stand by in silence while this outrage runs its wicked course.'

'All the more reason why you should not go alone.'

'I go alone for speed, and because no other can be spared.'

'I can be spared,' Edwin insisted. 'I will ride with you.'

Richard's smile was hidden in his beard. 'Go home, lad. Two hours of instruction and one brief spell in the saddle never made a rider of any man. Go home.'

'But I want to help you, Father.'

'You can help me best by going home and learning how to ride a horse. Your mishaps can only be a hindrance to me now. Already you have lost me precious time, Edwin. Go back and help the others.'

'Yes, Father.' Edwin got to his feet and touched himself all over, expecting half his bones to be broken. Then he accepted the reins of his horse with a sigh. 'They will not let me underground to help them with the digging. They say my illness makes me a danger to myself and them.'

'Then you must be content with guarding Elvira,' Richard told him. 'And walk beside the horse. He's a fine animal, too strong and energetic to be mastered by a novice like yourself. Walk him back to his rightful owner and take more expert tuition before you attempt such a ride, and in such poor light, again.'

'Yes, Father.'

As the boy began to lead his horse away, Richard remounted and, mindful of Edwin's eagerness to please, called after the shadowy figure: 'You're a good lad, Edwin. I will not forget this brave attempt of yours to lend a hand.'

'Thank you, Father.'

In the east a brighter light was already shafting through a layer of cloud. Soon the sun would be climbing into the daytime sky. The colours and textures, the shapes and hollows of the Westwood would be fully visible, and a single rider made conspicuous. He turned his horse, nudged at its flanks with his heels and set his sights on distant York.

Edwin muttered and grumbled as he made his way back to the town and the enclosure of St Peter's. He turned but once to mark the speedy progress of the priest, and what he saw caused him a havoc of indecision. A group of dim shapes peeled themselves from the distant trees to surround the single rider, and, in an instant, they had struck him down.

'Father Richard!'

Edwin clamped a hand across his own mouth. He could not help the priest by crying out, nor could he reach him where he lay unmoving on the ground. A quarter of a mile of treacherous land lay between them, and he could see the riders heading back in his direction, cutting him off from the spot where Richard had fallen. If help were to come at all then Edwin must be the one to fetch it, and he could only do that by staying free of these attackers. With a courage he had not known he possessed, he hauled himself into the saddle, wound the bridle straps tightly around his wrists, lay flat against the horse's neck and kicked the animal into a gallop. Clinging thus, he closed his eyes and fled for home.

The handbell-ringers were out with the first dawn pealing of the church bells, raising the slackers from their beds and drawing the early risers from their labours. People streamed from houses and hovels, huts and sheltered corners to gather in the streets, and rumours flew like buzzing insects from one group to another. Some said the archbishop had come from York to eject every canon in Beverley from his seat. Some said the papal legate had arrived with a sackful of excommunications to enforce. Others whispered of war or plague, of marauding Scots or an invading army from some seaward country. And others said that a once-loved priest, one Simeon of Beverley, was to be chained and carted through the streets as a damned man and a murderer.

Still bound to his horse, Edwin passed through the North Bar as the gates were opened and reached the wall surrounding the modest grounds of St Mary's chapel. Here a priest helped him down and a groom took the nervous horse away to drink at the trough by the gate. Other priests gathered close as Edwin's words came out in a hasty tumble. He told his story rapidly and priests were immediately sent in search of the stricken man.

'Come inside and rest yourself,' the good priest said, but the lad drew back.

'No, Father, I must hurry to St Peter's and … what noise is that? What is happening?'

A loud cry had gone up amongst the swiftly increasing crowds out in the streets. A seller of vegetables had his cart stripped and his produce passed piece-meal from hand to hand. Stones and rocks were being collected, lengths of wood ripped from window openings and door-frames, slates pulled from roofs and loose bricks prised from any available wall. The people of the town were arming themselves and every group in every street was whipping itself into a frenzy. Edwin saw the shutters close across the painted windows of the chapel. The animals were being herded into the nave, the women of the chapel into the crypt and keeps below.

'What's happening?' Edwin asked again.

'Do you not know? Have you not heard?'

Edwin shrugged. 'I know there is talk of war, of excommunications and foreign invaders.'

'Foolish talk,' the priest said bitterly. 'There is to be a carting. A man accused of murder and serious crimes against the church is to be paraded for the town's amusement. They will pelt him with rotten fruits and vegetables, food they can ill afford to spare, and with anything heavier that comes to hand.'

'He is guilty then?' Edwin asked.

'He is innocent,' said the priest. 'Falsely accused and not yet brought to trial.'

'Then why the carting? Surely he will not survive it?'

The priest crossed himself and clasped his hands in prayer, his head lowered and his eyes closed. At last he said: 'It is the townspeople's right to have him so displayed so that they might help his conscience to atone.'

'But they will kill him,' Edwin said, and cold fingers of apprehension scraped his spine.

The priest nodded. 'His enemies seek to avoid the trial this way. They want the man defamed because too many already see him as a saint. And when the rabble has done the foul deed it will turn upon the churches and the clergy, because the evil-doer is one of us.'

Now Edwin's eyes were round with alarm in his narrow face. His voice was a whisper when he spoke the name: 'Simeon.' Then he turned, vaulted the chapel wall and raced toward the corn market.

'Come back!' the priest yelled after him, but when he saw Edwin already plunging into the throng, he shook his head and finished, in a smaller voice: 'You foolish, loyal boy, they'll kill you, too.'

Quick and slight enough to wriggle through the crush of

bodies, Edwin came out of the market at Walker Gate, where he found the tiny pavements choked with townsfolk. Unable to pass by them, he waded through the stinking stream that ran down the centre of the street, thigh deep in the filth of felters' waste, household excrement and animal dung. At Toll Gavel the crowds were jostling shoulder to shoulder as he fought his way to the fish market, where Eastgate and Fishmonger's Row came side by side from the Minster, divided by a wide strip of timber hovels. There was something in the atmosphere, a taste or a smell that made his skin crawl. He had experienced the same sensation at another carting years ago, and now he knew the thing for what it was. These people generated it by their hysteria, their blind, unreasoning hunger for what they believed to be moral justice. It was blood-lust, and it affected every screaming man and woman gathered there.

By climbing the market cross he saw the cart, a sturdy open conveyance guarded by four armed men and drawn by a single, slow-moving ox. At the rear of the cart a man was standing, bound like a crucified Christ to a makeshift frame of wood. He wore a metal restraining yoke about his neck and shoulders, and every jolt of the cart sent rivulets of fresh blood running down his battered chest. No part of him was left unbruised, no portion of skin unblooded. His face was raised, a mask of agony beneath his yellow tonsure, and even from that distance Edwin saw that he was praying.

'Simeon! Oh, Simeon!'

The sound of another's voice, anguished and feminine, brought Edwin scuttling down from the lesser market cross. He caught Elvira by the shoulders and drew up her hood to conceal her raven hair, anxious that she might be seen and instantly recognised. 'Come away, lady. You must not stay here. Come away at once.'

'Simeon . . . Simeon . . .'

'Please, lady.' Edwin was a twin who loved his sister more dearly than he loved himself, and in Elvira's eyes he saw a similar bond reflected. She was in torment. Whatever tortures they had inflicted on him, whatever tribulations befell

307

him now, this woman bore Simeon's suffering as if it were her own.

The crowd surged like a wave across the market-place and Edwin, moving against it, struggled to draw Elvira back towards the safety of Eastgate and St Peter's enclosure. Armed riders had come along Fishmonger's Row from the Minster, led by the impressive figure of Cyrus de Figham, cloaked in red. He wielded a broad sword and a golden shield, and on his head he wore a metal helmet polished to a shine that glinted even in that dismal light. On his instructions, Simeon was cut down from the stake and the heavy yoke removed. The crowd roared out its protest at this theft of their rightful entertainment, but de Figham's men drove them back with swords and lances. The cart was pelted with a fresh hail of stones, bricks and rotten fruit, so that even de Figham's fine attire was stained. A large rock struck his thigh and, infuriated by the sudden pain, the black-eyed priest lashed out with his sword and struck down an innocent man who stood too close.

'This is a sacrilege. No carting will take place while the morning offices are in progress,' de Figham bellowed above the mayhem. 'Get this prisoner on to a horse and take him back to the Hall Garth cells, then send for the infirmarian without delay. If this man dies I'll have your eyes. Ye gods, this carting business is *barbaric*.'

Even as he spoke, the cart was overturned and the crowd became a swarm of grasping scavengers. Huge chunks of flesh were cut from the ox while the bellowing beast was still on its feet. By the time it breathed its last its entrails were being divided by many hands.

'He frees him? Cyrus de Figham frees him?' Elvira's voice was thin with disbelief.

'He has his reasons, lady.'

'But why?'

'God knows, Elvira,' Edwin said. They had reached the small gate set into the wall below and behind Simeon's scriptorium. Here Thorald, filthy with earth and masonry dust, came running to meet them. 'De Figham has played a master-stroke,' he growled. 'He halts the carting, supposedly in respect of the dawn offices, and openly condemns it as a barbaric act, offensive in the sight of God. Knowing as he does that the Church must eventually allow the tradition of carting in these circumstances, he sends a whisper through the town that it will take place tomorrow, immediately after the dawn.'

'So allowing the mob more time to prepare,' Elvira said flatly.

Edwin was shocked. 'A *second* carting, when this one, only half its measured length, has all but killed him?'

'A master-stroke,' Thorald repeated fiercely. 'The crowd will be armed to the hilt. They will not allow their prize to escape them so easily a second time. If Simeon survives this night in de Figham's clutches it will be a miracle, and the good men of this town will tear that miracle to shreds at dawn tomorrow.'

'Perhaps the well ...?'

'I doubt it can be undone,' Thorald said, rubbing his dusty face with the palms of his hands. 'Not even if we work without rest throughout another day and a second night. Those stones have stood for centuries. They refuse to yield. We can only pray that Richard's message ...'

'Oh, no.' Edwin gasped.

'What is it, lad? Are you taken ill again?'

Edwin shook his head. His face was ashen. 'There were men lying in wait for Father Richard. They struck him down on the Westwood near the oak forest. Help will not come from York, Father Thorald. It will not come. I fear Father Richard may already be dead.'

CHAPTER THIRTY

The Minster bells were still pealing in the dawn when Simeon stirred. His senses returned to him in sickly waves. He was slumped on the floor of his cell, the stink of the rushes in his nostrils and pain in every limb. The morning sun was slanting on him through the window-slit, its pale ray both a hope of light in darkness and a mockery of the ease beyond his reach.

'Father?'

He turned his head and felt the ground shift under him with the effort. The shaft of light was broken now by a small face at the window.

'Peter.' He mouthed the name through swollen lips, unable to speak out loud. 'God bless you, boy.'

'Here is water, Father. Drink and be strengthened.'

The water came in a small gourd, lowered on a length of rope from the window. It was cold and fresh, as sweet as nectar on his tongue. A second gourd contained a fatty mutton soup with herbs and spices added. The third was no larger than his own palm. It contained a sticky liquid with a rich, familiar smell.

'For the pain,' Peter whispered. 'Unfasten the pouch from the rope and conceal it beneath the rushes. Take sips, just a little at a time. Have courage, Father.'

'The well?' Simeon asked hoarsely. 'Have they undone the stones?'

'No, father, but our friends will soon begin again with the blacksmith's help. I will go there myself to see what aid I can offer them.'

'The power of binding and loosing, of barring and admitting.'

'St Peter's gifts,' the boy said.

'I cannot undo the lid of the well,' Simeon said, falling back on the rushes, exhausted. 'The iron is too deeply embedded in the stone. It will not yield. I cannot shift it.'

'Hush, father. Do not distress yourself. If God is with us, we will clear the shaft and lift the cover from below.'

Simeon groaned. 'I saw faces in the crowd I recognised, men and women I have blessed, who have loved and trusted me.'

'It was ever thus,' Peter reminded him. 'We stone or crucify the best among us, then regret the heat of the moment and call them saints.'

'I think our God intends me to die in infamy.'

'I think He does not intend you to die at all.'

'But will He stay de Figham's hand?'

'He will,' Peter promised and, from where he lay, Simeon could see the small hand stretched down through the window-slit. He could not hope to raise his body up to reach that hand, but by its presence he was comforted. 'Have courage, Father, and when the …'

He saw the bigger hand that clamped across Peter's lower face to stop his words, heard the scuffle on the slanting roof as boy and man rolled and tumbled downward to the ground outside.

'Peter? Dear God in Heaven; *Peter*!' No answer came from the window-slit and in the stillness Simeon knew such fear as could stop a man's heart inside his breast.

Simeon struggled to his knees, hung his head as a wave of nausea threatened to empty out his stomach, then used the stone slab of the bed and the angle of the wall to claw himself to his feet. Still calling out his godson's name, he reached in futile desperation for the window-slit, saw the face of a bearded man and felt his senses rushing away from him. As he hit the ground and slipped into unconsciousness, he distinctly heard a guffaw of laughter and the chilling words: 'We have him, priest. We have your whelp at last.'

The toe of a boot aroused him. A sharp pain seared his ribs to pierce his oblivion and drag him back to bleak reality. He was still in his cell beneath the provost's court, cold and in much pain. A flaming torch was resting in the wall-sconce, burning as fiercely, it seemed to him, as the very fires of Hell. Great John was tolling still, that deep and sorrowing sound marking alike the continuation of the morning offices and the death knell. It tolled for Simeon, facing death in a stinking cell, and for Beverley in her blind surrender to corruption. It tolled for the Minster church, soon to be abandoned to those who would milk it dry and callously discard it and, saddest of all, that bell tolled for its namesake, the blessed St John of Beverley.

'Wake up, priest. Open your eyes and your ears. I have a mind to share my victory with you.'

Cyrus de Figham stood in the torchlight by the door, tall and handsome, his dark hair and aristocratic features shown to best advantage against the gold folds of his cowl. His eyes were flashing gems in the flickering light, brilliant beneath their fringes of jet-black lashes. Even the great black stone on his finger glinted with flares of amber in its depths.

'Wake up, priest, and greet your canon with due respect.'

The boot jabbed at his ribs a second time. Simeon rolled on to his side and curled his knees up close to his chest, expecting further violence.

'I have your whelp, Simeon.' The voice was soft and deep, the voice of a man speaking in friendship rather than in hatred. 'That puckered scar on his throat is as clear an identification mark as any hot-iron brand.' The emphasis on that hateful last word was intended as a reminder that this man was a law unto himself; untouchable, unmoved by anything but his own base passions.

312

'Peter?'

'I have him,' de Figham repeated, 'and he will lead me to a wealth most kings would envy.'

'Never. Never!' A fit of coughing choked off Simeon's words. De Figham's laugh was cruel.

'If he talks, the carting will be stopped and the charges against you dropped. You will be given eight days to quit these shores, and after that your life, and his, will be your own. If the boy remains stubborn, you will die. The choice is a simple one, even for a ten-year-old to reason. I think the laws of atonement will persuade him.'

'My God, would you have a small boy tortured?'

'Be sure I will,' de Figham grinned.

'I'll kill you. I'll …'

He was silenced by another kick to the ribs.

'You'll do what, priest? Look at yourself, cringing like a whipped cur at the feet of its master. All you can do is wait upon my favour, and my mercy. I will have you outlawed, Simeon de Beverley, outlawed and disgraced, and while you suffer your excommunication, I will enjoy the pleasures of Elvira.'

Simeon raised his head, his blue eyes narrowed against the torch flames set around de Figham's head. 'Elvira?'

De Figham laughed aloud. 'Did you think I would not find her? Did you think your conspicuous little ruse with the key of your scriptorium, carelessly left in the lock, would fool me for a moment? Within the hour my man will send word that the chain is through the hole and I will have her. Do you hear me, priest? *I will have her!*'

'Dear God in Heaven.'

'Perhaps she too will benefit from the atonement? She will eventually be released into my care, of course, and I will undertake to teach her the error of her ways.'

'I'll kill you, de Figham. As God is my judge I'll kill you if you lay one hand on her.'

'Well, now,' de Figham scoffed. 'Is this the saintly Simeon who speaks of murdering a canon? And how will you kill me, priest? You cannot even stand on your feet, let alone protect

313

your whore from my intentions. I will have her. She will bear my brand and warm my bed and breed me a hoard of handsome brats to carry my name. I will have her and whether you live in exile or fry in Hell, your soul will writhe each time I touch her flesh.'

'No, no!'

As Simeon tried to rise de Figham kicked him down again and, snatching up the blazing torch, guffawed with laughter as he left the cell. The heavy door slammed at his back and willing hands secured it with bolts and chains. In the darkness behind the door the injured priest was on his knees. His face was pressed to the rushes and he was weeping.

Elvira rose from her bed, her thoughts now running clear after the shock of seeing Simeon so broken.

'Will that bell never cease its tolling?' she asked with a sigh. 'It is too much like the passing bell. It cuts the heart with every stroke.'

'The morning office was delayed by the carting,' Edwin reminded her. 'It has not yet been an hour...'

'An hour? No more than that? Eternity itself must move at a swifter pace.'

She was standing by the hearth where Edwinia, Edwin's twin sister, was struggling to kindle a fire in the grate. The girl's arms were as thin as sticks and the bones sharp in her face, but already her brown hair had lost its lankness and her eyes their haunted look.

Elvira was pale but very calm. Her hands no longer shook and the sense of panic which had overtaken her in the market-place had ebbed away, leaving her strength intact. Distress had fogged her mind but now she saw the situation for what it was, and she knew the cold, hard anger in her heart would now sustain her. She saw de Figham's plan with clarity. Like the donkey shown the carrot it could not eat, this town had anticipated a bloody spectacle, only to have it snatched away almost before the first bite could be taken. At dawn tomorrow they would be better prepared. A Beverley man had been murdered and the church had an obligation to the town. Knowing this, they would demand their rightful share of the justice to be meted out.

'Lady, your gown is hanging too close to the flames.'

'Thank you, Edwinia.' Elvira smiled and the girl scuttled away to her place on the far side of the well's low wall. She joined her brother and together they knelt against the wall, their elbows on the bricks and their faces propped between their hands. They resembled each other so closely that, with nothing but their hair and faces visible, their own dear mother might have been hard pressed to know which was the boy and which the girl she had borne.

Elvira turned to stare at the glowing coals. If Simeon died from his injuries during another long night in the cells, de Figham's ends were neatly served, and who could guess what further hurts might be inflicted on him behind locked doors? If he survived, the mob would oblige de Figham now that it had been so cleverly primed to do so. And out of it all that demonic canon would rise as a man of deep, if misguided compassion for the doomed man. By halting the carting of Simeon he had served himself two-fold: he had painted himself in godly colours and edged Simeon closer to his death.

Elvira picked up a knife with a long and narrow blade, a knife she had seen Simeon use many times to trim his leathers or to shape his quills. One edge of its blade was curved with use and the handle, made of bone, was smoothly worn where it fit into his palm. She held the knife against her chest, seeking the essence of him in the cool, smooth metal. Then she opened her robe and slipped the knife inside where it could nestle safely amongst the folds.

'I will go to him,' she said without emotion. When this is over and Simeon is dead, I will go to Cyrus de Figham and seek his bed. He will die in the night with Simeon's blade between his ribs.'

'No, lady,' Edwin begged. 'You must not even think of such a thing.'

'No other hand can touch him. He covers his tracks at every step and always sets his minion, John Palmer, between

315

himself and those who would challenge him. No man may call him to account while every scrap of evidence points to John Palmer as the villain who plots behind his master's back.'

'He is too cunning for any man to snare,' Edwin agreed.

'For any man, yes, but not for any woman. I will kill him, Edwin, when my Simeon is dead. This is my solemn oath. I will stop de Figham's evil heart when Simeon's heart is stopped.'

They fell to silence then, and Edwin placed his arm around his sister's trembling shoulders. Such a quiet passion from so serene a lady shocked them both, and neither was in any doubt that Elvira would keep her vow. They shared a special bond, these two, and love was something both could understand.

'Tell me the truth, Edwin. Was Father Richard taken?'

'Yes, Elvira. I saw him attacked and felled near the forest that divides the Westwood from the Old Roman Way.'

'Is he dead?' Elvira asked.

'I do not know. The priests of St Mary's were sent in search of him. I think . . . I think he is dead.'

'Then who will ride to York in his stead?'

Edwin jumped to his feet. 'I will.'

She shook her head. 'Not you, dear boy. If your illness does not defeat you in such an attempt your lack of riding skills surely will.' She paced this way and that before the hearth, her brows puckered in a frown. 'We must not lose hope so long as Simeon lives.'

'Does he still live? Does he, Elvira?'

She closed her eyes and placed her palms against her breast as if she might find some trace of Simeon there. At last she raised her head, smiling a little. 'Yes, Edwin, he still lives.'

'Like the bond between twins,' the boy whispered, intending the words only for his sister's ears.

'He is my life, Edwin,' Elvira said. 'When he is dead my heart will know of it. Now, you must find a man to ride for York. Promise him anything. Let him carry the message as it was given to Father Richard, then seek out Aaron the Jew and tell him this.' She took up a pair of clippers and snipped a thick strand from her hair. 'I send this token of my good faith, and I swear that I will come to the Jew if Simeon can be saved.'

Edwin was clearly shocked. 'Will you abandon Simeon for the rabbi?'

'Gladly, if it will save his life.'

'And will you then remain with him while Simeon lives?'

'I will honour my pledge to Aaron, if he will help save Simeon,' Elvira said calmly.

'But lady, he is a *Jew*.'

She shrugged her shoulders. 'Your own Messiah was also a Jew. I will take the rabbi's faith if I must and live by it if I am able. More than that I will not pledge. All else belongs to Simeon.'

'You are very brave,' Edwinia whispered.

Elvira took a package from a cupboard in the chimney recess, unwrapped the cloth that bound it and held the shimmering brow-piece in her upturned palms. Ten years ago she had stolen this from the bridle of a warhorse and, hoping to buy her dead babe's place in heaven, had handed it to a handsome priest. Now the golden brow-piece bore a neat round hole at its centre where the crossbow bolt had struck, but its value to the Jew would be unimpaired. There were tears in her eyes when she turned again to Edwin.

'This, too, must be given over to Rabbi Aaron. Take it, Edwin. If Simeon is to lose this precious keepsake, let it help to buy his safety and his freedom. Now, who can we trust to carry these pledges to York?'

'Elvira, I do not know. Perhaps the herbalist who helps Osric in the infirmary, or the clerk who does Simeon's special copying, or the gardener who helped him chop the old trees down, or . . .'

'Find someone,' Elvira told him.

'I will.'

She placed her palm on his cheek. He was taller than her by several inches and yet she saw him as little more than a

317

child. It seemed ironic that, in the end, the last of their hopes should be placed in the hands of a willing but untried boy. 'Edwin, the priest in the black hood sent you here and bade you pledge your life for Simeon. If you err in your judgement now, he is surely lost. You too must honour your pledge.'

He took her hand and placed its palm against his lips. 'I will not fail you, Elvira.'

'No, Edwin, you will not fail Simeon.'

Great John had ceased its tolling and the office of lauds was at an end when a clerk came from the infirmary with a platter of food for Elvira to break her fast. While she took the tray and called the twins to eat, the clerk replaced the bar across the door. He busied himself at the hearth, tending the fire. The twins divided portions of bread and cheese for themselves and returned to the far side of the well to eat. Elvira watched the clerk. His head was tonsured and his face familiar, but his presence in the room left her vaguely unsettled.

'What is your name?'

'I am John, Osric's helper.'

'Another John. Our saint has many who bear his name. How long have you lived and worked here at St Peter's?'

'A little time,' the man replied.

Elvira ignored the food. The Minster bell had suddenly resumed its tolling. That sound, untimely as it was, had a strangely ominous ring.

'You may go now, John,' she said.

'Let me fetch more logs from the basket.'

'No!' Her voice was high and urgent. She swallowed a sense of foreboding and added, in a softer tone: 'That will not be necessary. Please leave at once.'

Edwin rose to his feet, concerned by the note of alarm that had crept into Elvira's voice. He made as if to speak but then his jaw fell slack and his eyes began to close. His legs buckled beneath him and, as his sister dropped her cup and reached up to support him, the youngster muttered a sigh and fell prostrate beside her in the straw.

The clerk did not rise from his crouched position before

the hearth. 'I will need to return the platter and the jugs.'

'Just go,' Elvira told him. 'I have private matters to attend to and ...'

She heard the sound of feet outside and glanced toward the door. The heavy chain had been lifted and its end passed through the hole. Any hand, be it the hand of friend or foe, might raise the bar and enter at its owner's pleasure. This clerk, this John, this helper of Osric's, had put them all at risk.

With a cry Elvira rushed towards the door, but before her hand could reach the chain to pull it back inside, a heavier hand took hold of it and yanked it through the hole. She threw herself at the bar as it came up, but neither her speed nor her weight were enough to bring it down again. Too late she saw it spring free of its iron casing slots. With another cry she jumped back as the great bar clattered to the floor and bounced towards her, heavy enough to break a bone on contact. Then her breath caught and she knew the very worst had come to pass. The scriptorium door was flung open with tremendous force and Cyrus de Figham stepped across the threshold.

'So, Elvira, priest's whore and ditcher's wife, we meet again.'

Cyrus de Figham slammed the door behind him, shutting out the men who had come with him. His cloak was black, trimmed with a lining and a hood of gold, and his boots were heavily hung with decorations worked in silver and in gold. As Elvira backed away he advanced towards her. His smile was crooked, his eyes aglow as he appraised her from head to toe and, by his expression, found her not wanting in beauty.

De Figham licked his lips, savouring the moment. Here was the woman he had coveted for years, the woman he had searched for, dreamed of, desired and despised with equal passion. She was more beautiful than he remembered. Her face was as pale as alabaster and perfectly proportioned, with a full mouth, sculptured cheekbones and a high, intelligent forehead. Her hair was black without a trace of grey, though colours shone there like the oily hues from a jackdaw's wing.

319

She was perfection from head to toe, full-breasted and with slender, delicate hands, but it was her eyes that held him. Those eyes had haunted him since first he saw them; eyes so large and warm, so darkly toned, so inviting, that a man might drown himself in their inky depths and never want for more.

'Get out,' he snapped to the clerk without taking his gaze from Elvira.

'But my lord canon, there is ...'

'I said, get out, damn you!'

The clerk scuttled out and de Figham, still staring at Elvira, kicked the door to close it at his back. Elvira's hands were on the knife hidden in her gown. In her own defence she might have drawn it out, but for Simeon she dare not take the risk. While he still lived, while there was still hope for him, however tenuous, she must not, by any hasty act of hers, deprive him of it.

De Figham moistened his lips again. This woman excited him beyond measure. She was looking back at him with neither fear nor defiance in her lovely eyes. She was proud and calm. This was Simeon de Beverley's whore and now de Figham had her safely in his possession. For him it was a heady, long-awaited triumph. Desire for her stirred in his loins but he would not take her now. He would have her come to him, begging on her knees. He would have her denounce her priest and call *him* master. He would have her humbled and subservient, and with Simeon and the boy as his leverage, her decline was sweetly, tantalisingly within his reach.

'So, Elvira,' he said again, 'It seems I have you.'

'Never,' she answered calmly.

'Ah, but I will, as I do your lover ... and your son.'

He watched her eyes grow wide. 'Oh, no.'

'The whelp with the puckered scar across his throat, a scar that might be reopened with the sharp edge of a hunting knife.'

She whispered hoarsely: 'It cannot be.'

'Aye, lady. Your man lies dying in the provost's dungeon

and your bastard is bound and gagged in a miller's sack. And now the bar is across the door and the chain left hanging loose. It seems to me, Elvira, priest's whore and ditcher's wife, that I am to have you for myself at last.'

CHAPTER THIRTY-ONE

Lying flat beside her brother in the rushes, hidden from view by the low wall of the well, Edwinia clasped her hands in silent prayer, terrified that de Figham would find her there. This canon's reputation struck fear into her heart and she was sure that her safety, and Edwin's, depended on their silence. Her brother would regain his senses quietly, as one emerging from normal sleep, and Edwinia prayed that she could warn him as his eyes came open, before he stirred or màde a sound to attract the intruder's attention. She pushed the golden brow-piece beneath the rushes, then placed her hand on Edwin's cheek and waited.

De Figham strode to the fireside, close to the well, and pulled a sheaf of papers from his tunic. They bore the provost's seal and a scarlet ribbon, and when he threw them down they made a loud slap on the surface of the table.

'These are the formal charges against Simeon de Beverley,' he declared. 'And this is the written evidence of every witness, as collected by my priest, John Palmer.'

'The man behind whom you hide,' Elvira said.

De Figham spread his hands and smiled. 'When a man has power, as I do, he takes the trouble to protect it. I have no stain against my character that can be proved, since I act only upon John Palmer's evidence and advice. A man in my

322

position requires a scapegoat upon which his enemies may focus their petty jealousies. If Simeon was a wiser man his loyal priest, Richard of Weel, would even now be suffering in his place.'

'Have you no conscience, sir?'

He laughed at that. 'What need have I of conscience? The servant serves the master and, in return for his loyalty, the master buys that servant's freedom if the need arises. Mine is the better way. No circumstance will ever reduce Cyrus de Figham to the indignity of a stinking prison cell.'

'Why have you brought these papers here?'

'You have a pleasant voice, Elvira. Perhaps I will have you read to me. Do you read well?'

'Why have you brought them here?' she asked again.

He sighed, still smiling. 'No copy of these documents exists. They are my gift to you, Elvira. Burn them, if their destruction is your pleasure.'

'Burn them?'

'Aye, and he'll go free.'

Elvira glanced from the papers to the fire, then met de Figham's gaze and spoke her mind. 'What trickery is this, sir?'

'No trickery. Burn the papers and he goes free.'

Behind the well, Edwin had opened his eyes to find Edwinia's hand pressed tightly over his mouth. He felt her fear as if it were his own, raised himself without a sound and took in the situation at a glance. That Cyrus de Figham was here, in Simeon's impregnable scriptorium, was unthinkable. The viper had invaded the safest nest in Beverley and Elvira, left alone, would be its victim. Edwinia signalled that others were standing right outside the door, reminding her brother that any move on his part would be futile. The two could only watch and listen and pray that they might find a way to help her.

Elvira was standing with her hands clasped at her waist, calm and brave as she faced the man whose power knew no bounds. Her voice was steady when she asked: 'What must I do in return for Simeon's freedom?'

'Denounce him. Speak out against him at his trial.'

'Never. I will die first.'

'As well you might,' he smiled, 'when I am done with you.'

'So be it, but I will not speak against him.'

'Your loyalty is touching,' de Figham said acidly. 'And foolish. Be sensible, Elvira. Denounce him as a fornicator and a sorcerer. Confess that he stole and sold the holy water, knowing it was to be used for unholy purposes. Admit that he procured our Minster's precious books for his own use.'

'Never. For all that he will be excommunicated. He will be *outlawed*.'

'Indeed he will. That much I cannot prevent.'

'I will not do it.'

De Figham sighed again. 'Outlaw or dead man, the choice is yours, my dear. Without this written evidence, your testimony will ensure that he is convicted only of the lesser charges. I will prevent tomorrow's carting, have him removed from his cell at once and given the services of his infirmarian. I will return your son to you unharmed. So, speak out and he is saved, keep silent and he dies. A simple choice.'

Elvira stared into the man's dark, metallic-toned eyes. She neither trusted him nor believed that Peter would be freed. There were men in York, in Canterbury and in Rome who would pay highly to have that mysterious boy in their clutches. Nor did she hope that Simeon would be saved, or that she would escape the lust she saw in those quicksilver eyes.

'I will not speak against him,' she said softly.

'Then he will die tomorrow, and you . . .' He paused, his head cocked in a birdlike manner, listening. The bell had stopped again, another signal. With a speed which took Elvira by surprise, de Figham snatched up the papers and flung them into the fire, kicked over the stools around the hearth and made a grab for her. In an instant her gown was ripped from shoulder to waist, revealing the linen shift beneath and the small knife held by her belt. She fought like a tigress, clawing and kicking at her attacker. The back of his hand came down across her cheek and she went sprawling, and then the two were grappling on the floor, the knife between them. With a cry Edwin attempted to leap to her defence, only to trip and fall as his sister clutched at him in panic. She had heard the steps and voices beyond the door, and she feared more for her brother's life than for Elvira's safety.

When de Figham's men burst into the scriptorium, they found the canon wrestling with the woman on the ground, his cloak ripped and his clothes in disarray. Two priests, aided by the canon of St Catherine's, dragged Elvira to her feet and then restrained her.

'My lord canon, are you hurt?'

'Hurt?' De Figham almost screamed the word. 'This witch attacked me. See, here is the knife with which she tried to take my life. It was hidden in her clothing. She offered me her favours and then attacked me.'

'Then she will surely be punished, my lord. But you are injured.'

De Figham was sucking his hand where Elvira's teeth had penetrated almost to the bone. 'She bit me. The whore dared to bite me when I tried to arrest her. My God ... the papers ...'

While the others looked on and the twins cowered behind the well, de Figham fell to his knees and made a vain attempt to pull the blazing papers from the fire. When this was unsuccessful he got to his feet and shook his head, staring at the grate as if he saw a tragedy unfolding there. 'The papers are lost,' he told them all. 'Simeon's whore has burned the only written evidence against him. The formal charges, the statements of witnesses.'

'There is a copy, my lord canon.'

'There is?' He feigned surprise and crossed himself. 'Thank God for the efficiency of my clerks.' He pointed a finger at Elvira. 'I want this woman arrested and thrown into the cells.'

'It will be done, Father Cyrus.'

'She must be encouraged to make full atonement for

this – this outrage. Have formal charges prepared without delay. She is a witch, a sorceress. She called upon the forces of darkness to help her cause against me. She tried to murder me. You saw for yourselves how she fought like a demon against the authority of the Church. Three men ... three strong and healthy Christian men ... were needed to restrain her in her madness. She has received the Devil's aid in this.'

Every man present signed the cross at this, and those restraining Elvira stood well back, holding her by the wrists with her arms outstretched, her hair so tightly gripped from behind that her head strained backwards at a painful angle. De Figham's gaze went from her face, where his blow had left a mark upon her cheek, to the pale skin of her exposed throat, the firm swell of her breasts and the taut nipples clearly visible through her shift. The urge to take her there and then burned like a branding iron in his belly. He drew his cloak across his body to conceal the evidence of his arousal, then dragged his gaze from her with some reluctance.

'Cover her sinful flesh,' he snapped. 'Bind her, lest she turn herself into a crow and fly to her master, and get me a surgeon for this hand. My God, I fear the witch has bitten poison into me.'

They took Elvira from the scriptorium with her hands bound behind her back, a small, dark figure flanked by many guards. She held her head high, her face impassive and her steps assured, and none would guess the anguish in her heart. Men wept as she walked by them, and women stood with aprons to their faces. All of St Peter's enclosure were there to see Elvira taken, the still shapes lining the pathways from the scriptorium to the gates, a distance of many hundreds of yards. The silence within the walls was almost uncanny. No bird sang in the trees, no person spoke to his neighbour, no child cried out. When an isolated spear of lightning forked across the sombre, brooding sky, some took it as a portent and fell to their knees, afraid. This was the sorriest of days when Elvira, having survived amongst her enemies for a decade, was taken like a criminal from their innermost sanctuary.

326

Within the empty church an old man in a long white robe lifted his sleeve to wipe away a tear. He moved with hesitant steps towards the little open tower, took up the hanging rope and leaned upon it. For the doomed Elvira Father Cuthbert, frail and ageing canon of St Peter's, wept bitter tears as he rang the passing bell.

'You must not do it, Edwin,' Edwinia cried. 'You must not. It is foolhardy.'

'Who else will help us?' her brother demanded. He found the brow-piece amongst the rushes, wrapped it in a linen cloth and pushed it inside his tunic. 'This saved his life when the arrow struck. Perhaps it will again. And this' – he lifted the thick lock of hair and watched the firelight dancing on it – 'if the rabbi is true to his word, will save Elvira.'

'Edwin, in God's name, let some other go in your place.'

'No, sister.' He took Edwinia by the shoulders and shook her gently. Her eyes were wide with fright and wet with tears. 'Osric and the others are back beneath the ground. Half our friends are out searching for Peter. What other can be trusted, Edwinia?'

'It is too late for them. You will throw your life away to no avail.'

'It is never too late, Edwinia, not while any one of us still lives.' He kissed her then, full on the lips, then pushed her from him and ran from the scriptorium, not daring to glance back lest her tears dissuade him from his purpose.

There was still some unrest in the streets, which Edwin avoided by hugging the shadowed passageways and animal tracks as he hurried to St Mary's. He felt conspicuous with the golden brow-piece in his tunic. Where men will kill for bread or a decent pair of boots, a slender, unarmed youth risked life and limb to carry such a thing on his person. In Hengate he was forced to hide himself in a timberyard while a gang of young men wielding sticks and chanting obscenities went by. From there he could see that the church had suffered some damage in the fracas which had broken out at this end of the town. One shutter had been ripped off and the glass behind it shattered. The door was marked and scarred where rocks had struck it. Even the stone walls were chipped in places where the mob had vented its frustration. For many moments he crouched in the woodman's yard before racing across the open street, scaling the low brick wall and crossing the burial patch at a run. When he reached the church he pounded on the door with his fists until a priest came to admit him.

The big horse was tethered in the nave with many other animals, its saddle and bridle still in place. The animal rolled its eyes and side-stepped as the boy came near, already made wary and nervous by his incompetence.

'Whoa, horse, be calm. We have a job of work to do, you and I, and who's to say which one of us most dreads the task? We ride for York, full thirty miles, all at your fastest pace, and I intend for us to arrive intact.'

A priest came running with a broad smile on his face, scattering hens and goats as he approached. 'Edwin, I have good news for you. Father Richard is alive.'

'Thank God! Is he able to ride?'

The priest shook his head. 'Not for a long time will he sit on a horse again. He is injured but awake. Would you like to speak to him?'

'Thank you, Father.'

He found Father Richard lying on a bed of straw behind the altar. His hair and beard, face and hands were wet with perspiration. His brow was hot and yet he shivered so violently in his bed that his teeth were chattering.

'He has a fever. Some ribs are broken and one of his arms is badly wrenched at the shoulder. The rest is as you see. The herbalist from Lady Gate is doing all he can.'

'Send word to Osric. He will come when he is able. Meanwhile, the herbalist at St Peter's will make up the best of brews for this fever. And bring another cover. Keep him warm.'

'I will do as you say,' the priest nodded. 'He can speak a little, but he is still very much confused.'

Edwin nodded, then dropped to his knees beside the bed

of straw and took the sick man's hand. 'Father Richard? It is Edwin. I did not abandon you. I saw what happened but there were too many of them, so I rode for help.'

Richard's eyes flickered open and he squeezed Edwin's fingers. With an effort he managed a single word: '*Rode?*'

'I cannot stay,' the boy said urgently. 'I must ride for York at once.'

'No.' Richard turned his head on the pillow and struggled to focus his eyes and his senses on the boy kneeling beside him. '*No!*'

'I must. Simeon is to be carted again at dawn tomorrow. Peter is missing and ...'

'Peter? Missing?'

'We think de Figham has him.'

'Oh, God forbid.'

'And worse: we were betrayed. He has Elvira.'

Richard closed his eyes and groaned aloud. 'Sweet Jesus, has it really come to this?'

'I fear it has,' Edwin replied. 'No rider can be spared, no stranger trusted, and time is scarce. It must be me, Father Richard. There is no other.'

'Go, then, lad, with my blessing. God speed and keep you.' He signed the cross in the air between them. 'And bring you safely home.'

He was not aware that Edwin had left his bedside. A fit of coughing left him exhausted, his ribs so painful they might have been trapped in a vice. He welcomed the thick fur cover that was slid over him and the warm bricks that were placed on either side of his shivering body. He slept fitfully for a while, then awoke to find another man bending over him, a man with a fine, thin face and one half-closed eye.

'Wake up, Father Richard,' the man was saying, shaking him by the shoulder. 'Open your eyes. Good, good. Now look at my face. Do you know me?'

The injured man nodded. 'I know you, Daniel Hawk.'

'And do you know me as Edwin's friend?'

'I do.'

'Then tell me where he is, Richard. I know he was here,

329

that he spoke with you less than an hour ago. His sister says he has ridden to York for help, but surely that cannot be so? Where is he, Richard?'

'York. He rides for York.'

'Damn! Damn his courage! He is sick and he is no rider. He can neither master a horse nor defend himself if he is waylaid by thieves along the way.' He clenched his teeth and hissed: 'Even if he makes the journey safely, which he will not do without a miracle to aid him, how will he persuade the archbishop to hear his plea?'

'Through Fergus de Burton. He will go first to him.'

'Aye, if he can find him.' Daniel moved from the bed to pace distractedly, his steps made awkward by his injured leg. At last he grabbed an elderly priest by the shoulder and barked rapid orders into his startled face. 'Get me a horse, the best you have, and prepare an extra mount to travel with me. That animal he borrowed is too lively for Edwin to control.'

'Daniel?' Father Richard caught the young priest by the lower edge of his cloak. 'You? You will go after him?'

'I must.'

'But the message? Who will plead on Simeon's behalf, for Elvira and for Peter?'

'By God, *I* will,' Daniel said. 'I will find the boy and speak to Fergus de Burton, and I will persuade him that Simeon must be helped, even if I must draw my sword to do it.'

'Are you forgetting Wulfric de Morthlund? He will never allow it. As your lord and master he will ...'

Daniel bent his knee and took Father Richard by the wrist, releasing the grasping fingers from his cloak. His eyes were steely when he said: 'The time has come for me to make a choice. Today I am my own master.'

'Tomorrow you might be called upon to pay a heavy price.'

Daniel smiled and nodded his handsome head. 'Aye, I might at that, but I will have had my day, Richard.'

'God bless you, Daniel Hawk. I do confess I never took you for your own man.'

'And you were wise, my friend. I have never been my own man until this moment.' He turned and limped away, calling out loudly as he pushed a pathway through the animals gathered in the nave. 'Bring me horses! Two horses, if you please, both fresh and ready for a swift, hard ride to York!'

Near York four men rose from the long grass in the hedgerow at the sound of hooves approaching. They had been resting beside a little spring of clear, cool water, breaking their long night's fast on stolen produce from a local farm. They were still some distance out of York, carrying cloth and silver to their master there. All were soldiers, armed and battle-scarred, and all were alert to the risk of surprise attack in this isolated spot.

The oncoming horse kept to the Old Roman Way, ignoring the succulent grasses in the hedgerow, a weary beast with lathered snout and flanks. A man was slumped over its neck and it seemed that only his mount's controlled and steady pace was keeping him in the saddle. The soldiers drew their swords and formed a barrier across the road, their senses alert for robbers skulking at the rider's back. Their voices, though low, carried far in the open countryside.

'Is he dead?'

'Dead men do not ride so well as this man rides.'

'Injured, then?'

'He's no more than a boy, by the looks of him.'

'That's a fine animal if ever I saw one.'

The horse came to a halt and pawed the ground, watching the men draw near. The whites of its eyes were showing and its flanks twitched nervously. It side-stepped and whinnied as if preparing to bolt. The soldiers stopped, cautious lest their presence cause the beast to take fright and throw its rider down. Instead, it danced awhile and then grew calm, as if strong hands and considerable skills controlled it.

'Easy, boy, easy,' the tallest of the soldiers coaxed, extending his hand as he came near the uneasy animal.

He took the reins and led the horse forward while his companions helped to keep its senseless rider in the saddle. At the spring where they had rested the animal drank its fill. Its rider was supported while one soldier drew his knife and slashed the reins right through, for the straps were so tightly bound around the youngster's wrists that the flesh was broken and the hands discoloured. They eased him from the saddle and laid him in the hedgerow, dripped water into his mouth and bathed the dust from his face and head.

'He looks half-dead,' one soldier remarked, then smiled grimly as the boy's eyes flickered open. 'Well lad, and who might you be?'

'Sir? My name is Edwin. I have ridden hard from Beverley . . .' he looked around him anxiously. 'Where am I? Where is this place?'

'You have fallen among friends, since you seem to own the luck of the Devil.'

'And York?'

'A few miles off.'

'I must get there. I must speak with Fergus de Burton without delay.'

The boy was struggling to raise himself but the soldier held him back. 'What business might you have with Master Fergus, lad?'

Edwin stared into the soldier's chiselled, weather-hardened face. 'My business with him is private, sir, but vital. Many honest lives are hung on his goodwill.'

'Give me a name, lad. Prove to me that your urgency is honest.'

Edwin put his hands to his chest and sighed with relief to feel the brow-piece hard against his ribs. 'Simeon,' he said, and saw the chiselled features of the soldier change, the creased eyes grow narrow and the mouth compress.

'So be it,' the soldier said, and helped the youngster to his feet.

It took but a little time to peel the leather from Edwin's wrists, smooth an ointment into the raw flesh there and rub the circulation of blood back into his numbed fingers. His bridle straps were bound with twine, but when he went to mount the horse shied off, tossing its head. Only by a combined effort did they manage to get young Edwin back in the saddle.

'If you rode this beast all the way from Beverley you have my admiration,' one man said.

'I fear it has little liking for me,' Edwin admitted with a sheepish grin.

'I fear you are no rider,' the soldier remarked dourly.

'Nay, where's the truth in that? We all saw how the horse came in, well checked by a masterly hand and ...'

'Look there! Two riders at the gallop! Mount up! Be on your guard!'

The alarm was immediately acted upon, swords drawn and mounts prepared. Not two men but a single rider was bearing down on them with a riderless horse in tow. Meeting a barrier of five mounted men across his path, he drew his beast to a halt and came on at a slower pace.

'Edwin! Are you harmed?'

'Father Daniel!' In his excitement, Edwin heeled his horse and it reared under him, throwing him back across the saddle with his arms flailing and his legs askew. A soldier broke his fall, the horse ran off a little way, calmed itself and returned to the spring to drink.

Amid much laughter and disparaging remarks, the lad regained his feet and limped to greet the priest. 'Father, are you fit to ride?'

'Are *you*, Edwin, you foolhardy whelp?'

Edwin grinned. 'Father, you came to help me.'

'I did, though it seems I might have spared the horses. Who are these men?'

'They are friends. They will take me to Master Fergus in York.'

Daniel looked up suspiciously as one of the soldiers walked his mount towards him. 'I am Father Daniel of Beverley,' he said in a loud, clear voice. 'I am known as Daniel Hawk and I am here to assist the boy.'

'I am Chad,' the soldier said in his deep growl. 'I am

333

Fergus de Burton's man-at-arms. Who sent this boy to do a grown man's job?'

'His own stout heart is all that brings him here,' Daniel replied. 'He saw the task and rose to it.'

'Then he is to be commended. Come, lad, mount up. We should make York within the hour.'

Edwin was helped into the saddle of the spare horse and rode alongside Daniel at a steady pace, two riders ahead and two behind, with the big horse led by a loose rein at the rear. They rode in silence, each with his own thoughts, until the youngster said: 'I saw a shadow, Father. My senses were swimming. My mount was on the verge of bolting and I could not hope to keep myself in the saddle. I was exhausted, my illness was upon me, and then . . .'

Daniel Hawk looked sideways at Edwin's troubled face.

'. . . and then I looked down at the road where the sun had cast my shadow, and that of the horse, in the dust. I saw that a man, a tall man in a hood, was mounted behind me, holding me fast so that I would not fall. The horse grew calm and settled into a steady trot. I saw his shadow, and yet I was alone and senseless when Chad and his fellows found me.'

'You had an arduous ride and you were ill,' Daniel replied. 'And you sell your courage short by seeking to lay your achievement on some other's shoulders.'

In the distance they could see the pale stones of York's Minster church, St Peter's, standing tall on the horizon. Here they turned off from the Roman Way and rode across open land, taking the shortest, speediest route to the city.

'Father Daniel, I know what I know,' Edwin persisted. 'I saw that shadow clearly on the roadway. I felt a presence at my back and a strong grip on the reins. I did not make that ride unaided.'

Those words gave Daniel hope as he heeled his horse to keep pace with the others. Such talk of supernatural forces still had the power to cause his flesh to crawl, yet he was content with Edwin's easy acceptance of it. If there was some other hand in this, if higher forces were at work on Simeon's behalf, they might yet save that good priest from his fate.

CHAPTER THIRTY-TWO

Wulfric de Morthlund stuffed another sugared fig into his mouth and raised a silver goblet to his lips. He was resting on a fur-covered bench, soft cushions at his back and a padded stool beneath his feet. He wore a green and yellow robe, a jewelled alb and a belt of threaded silver. He had broken his fast on crow pie and mutton pasties, on butter cakes and red wine from the cask, and his mood was one of drowsy joviality. The constant bickering of these priests amused him. He watched de Figham's performance with a measure of admiration. The man took a malicious delight in aggravating others, in setting one man against another, playing the devil's advocate, the paddle that stirred the pot.

De Figham was seated in an upright chair, one forefinger against his lips and his brows folded in a scowl. For the better part of an hour these priests had harangued him with their arguments, entreaties, criticisms and open threats. They made demands, they quoted canon law, they paced and fumed. Through it all de Figham held his peace – and the only key to the cells in the provost's keep.

A placid spectator at de Figham's games, Wulfric de Morthlund smiled as he studied the exasperated performers.

'You must not deny him his last rites and confession,' Canon Cuthbert said again. 'To be properly shriven is his right, whatever the charges against him.'

Cuthbert was growing swiftly into his dotage. He barely knew what he was about and the long hour spent standing on his feet to plead for Simeon had left him weary.

'Nor have you any right to deny him the benefit of ease for his many wounds,' Thorald insisted. This man was huge, as big as his reputation and no doubt as fierce as rumour had him painted, but Cyrus de Figham now had that ferocity hampered. Whatever else this Thorald of the Holme church claimed to be, this day he had been rendered impotent.

Now Stephen Goldsmith cleared his throat and spoke his piece again. 'As the provost's representative and acting upon his full instructions, I demand to question the prisoner privately.' His face was almost the colour of his hair and bushy whiskers, reddened under the pressure of suppressed rage. Father Wulfric knew these men would eventually have what they demanded, but they would not have it until Cyrus de Figham had grown tired of his game.

The moment came abruptly. De Figham jumped to his feet, snatched up his coat and strode to the door. 'See to it,' he told his priest, then he was gone.

'Hell's teeth!' Thorald spat. 'That devil was toying with us all along.'

Wulfric de Morthlund released his laughter in a bellow that set his mounds of flesh quivering and propelled a spray of half-chewed fruit from his mouth. 'To win de Figham's game,' he choked, wagging a short fat finger at the priest, 'first you must be made to *play* it.'

The expression on Thorald's face was murderous. As a clerk began to usher them from the room, de Morthlund drew John Palmer to him and made an observation. 'That priest will kill your master, given half a chance.'

John Palmer smiled and glanced at Thorald's back. 'My lord canon, I fear he'll have to stand in line with many others and wait his turn to strike the fatal blow.'

As Thorald and Stephen Goldsmith helped the frail old canon negotiate the stairs beyond the room, Wulfric de Morthlund's bellowing laughter was ringing in their ears.

They found Elvira in the smaller cell. Her face was badly bruised and on her robe were stripes where blood from the lashing had seeped through. The atonement, intended to encourage sinners to repent and make their peace with God, was severe enough to break a man in spirit and in body. That Elvira bore it so bravely was mute testimony to her quiet strength.

'Will you take confession, lady?' Stephen Goldsmith asked.

She smiled and reached to take his hand with fingers that were bloody and torn at their ends. Her voice was broken and hoarse, for her throat was injured. 'No, friend, but I will pray with you for Simeon.'

In a cell not far away, Thorald had spread his cloak on the stone slab and was lifting Simeon on to it, packing the folds of the hood beneath his head and pulling its ends around his shivering body.

'They have used him ill,' he told the old canon. 'My God, they have used him ill.'

The priest's eyes came open slowly, pained by the bright light of a burning torch. 'Is there water?'

They gave him sufficient to quench his thirst.

'God bless you both. Is Peter taken?'

'We have not yet given up hope,' Thorald assured him.

Simeon groaned. 'They know of him in Rome. There has long been a price on his head. Watch the port, Thorald.'

'Aye, I will. We have watchers at every road and waterway and loyal men out searching everywhere. Simeon,' Thorald cupped his friend's bruised face in his big hands, 'the work on the well-shaft has had to be abandoned. We can do no more to help you, my friend. We must give our all to saving the boy.'

'That is as it should be,' Simeon replied. In the torchlight his eyes had never looked so blue or so untroubled. He gripped his old friend weakly by the arms. 'Look first to Peter.'

In the smaller cell, the goldsmith had ordered water to be

brought so that Elvira could wash the smears of grime and blood away. Her hair was smoothed and bound into the nape of her neck with a strip of cloth torn from his canon's robe. Other strips were used to cover the tears in her clothing and to bind up her injured fingers.

When Thorald came at last he spoke no word to them. He had left Simeon alone with his canon and confessor, to be shriven of his sins and faults in private. He was being prepared for his passage to the other world by the man who had loved him as a father in this. Still well short of his thirtieth year, Simeon de Beverley was facing death while many less worthy men were left behind, and Father Thorald was crushed to his soul by the injustice, the awful waste of it.

The huge priest stooped low to clear the doorway into Elvira's cell, stared at the pale, hurt figure sitting there, then turned and pressed his forehead to the damp stones of the wall. That giant of a man, priest of the Holme church and self-styled master of the teeming port, was weeping.

Stephen sat beside Elvira on the stone slab on which she was expected to sleep. His arm was around her shoulders, his cheek lowered so that it rested against her hair. His heart was aching but his thoughts were savage.

'St Peter's will not be lost to us,' he vowed. 'Nor will it fall into the hands of those who bleed the Church for their personal advancement. I own that land and, while I live, every tree, every blade of grass on it will prosper. When I die it will be gifted to those who seek no worldly profit from the Church. Neither canon nor archbishop will ever own St Peter's enclosure.'

'Antony of Flanders has persuaded you, then?'

'He has. The monks shall have it.'

She nodded. 'Simeon will approve of that. Stephen?'

'What is it?'

'De Figham said that Peter is bound and gagged and tied up in a miller's sack.'

'The power of binding and loosening,' Stephen answered, as if he spoke his thoughts out loud.

338

'Such superstition will not strengthen a mother's heart,' Elvira told him. 'Peter is no saint with saintly gifts at his disposal. He is a child, a little boy in danger and all alone. They have him, Stephen. We failed to keep him safe and now his enemies have prevailed.'

'Have faith, Elvira.'

'In what?' she asked.

'God and St Peter will protect the boy as they have done so many times before. He will survive. He *must*.'

Much later Elvira was taken to Simeon's cell to find him standing with an arm outstretched toward the empty window-slit. She heard his whispered, 'Peter,' and she knew that, while he suffered this hateful 'atonement' and faced the ordeal of a second carting, his thoughts and fears were only for the boy. He turned his head and met her gaze as the door closed at her back, and it seemed to her the past had come again. She saw the torch flames dancing in his eyes, the golden tones of his hair, the handsome contours of his face. She saw his height and his aristocratic bearing and felt the subtle yet compelling magnetism in his presence. As Elvira had loved him then she loved him still, with the core, the very essence of herself. His eyes grew soft and bright with tears as he lowered his arm and opened both to her. She went to him at once, pressed her face against his neck and felt those arms, still strong and muscular, close around her with an aching tenderness.

'My love,' he whispered, and she echoed the greeting, and in the first moments of their sad reunion they had no further need of common words.

At last Elvira led him to the sleeping-slab and drew him down beside her. He lowered himself with pain in every movement, wincing as he stretched out his legs, groaning a little as he leaned his battered back against the wall. His hands, like hers, had suffered the cruel tortures of the atonement. Such disciplines were devised by the holy Church to remind the sinner of his human frailty. By showing him the agony of his mortality, it hoped to cleanse and elevate his soul in preparation for God's holier chastisement. Elvira would never understand such reasoning, but she had learned that the priests who kept the cells performed these sacred duties with devotion.

When Simeon slid his arm around her she leaned against him, turning her head to kiss the injured fingers on her shoulder. He felt her hot tears on his hand, sharp and salty where the skin was broken, searing the exposed flesh. They reminded him that worldly love was never painless. It came with its own inbuilt and unique pains, its fear of loss, its torments of the flesh, the heart, the soul. All love was precious, this he did believe, but for himself and Elvira he would cast this love aside and free them of it, if he could.

They remained thus for a long and silent time, too full in heart to speak, too empty of hope for words. Simeon watched the torch's flaming reflections on the walls, where rain and slime created a mirror-bright surface for them to play upon. Small sparks spat from the torch to die with a sizzle of sound in the rushes. Two years ago such sparks had caused the horrific conflagration in Beverley, but here, in this damp and filthy cell, they leaped and fell to earth and were extinguished.

Elvira's tears had stopped when Simeon spoke at last. 'This love of ours was doomed from that first day you came to me after the tempest,' he said. 'We knew, then, there could be no future for us.'

'We have had our future, Simeon,' she reminded him. 'Ten precious years of it. Give thanks to your God for that.'

He tried to smile, touched by her simple view of their short lives. He thought of Alice, degraded by Cyrus de Figham's brand, hanging alone and unshriven in the hunchback's squalid burrow. He thought of the poor child Maud, the fishmonger's daughter, dying in filth as she gave that black-eyed priest a son he would never acknowledge as his own. He did not voice his fears but asked instead: 'How will you face the future now, Elvira?'

'With strength,' she answered readily. 'Your love will help me bear it, Simeon.'

'If you could only accept God's love as you have accepted mine, be confessed and . . .'

She touched a bleeding finger to his lips to silence him. 'Simeon, your God will know me for what I am. Neither priest's words nor recitations will alter that.'

He held her as closely as their hurts would allow, and in their silence both remembered all that had brought them here. He looked to the empty window-slit where spots of rain, blown on a fitful wind without clear direction, came sharp and cold through the opening. He saw again that unholy tempest savaging Beverley like a beast from Hell let loose to prevent the baptism of a child. And he recalled the words of that hooded figure as it held the naked infant up and railed against the storm as if the simple deed of baptism was more than equal to it: *Behold the Rock, the Guardian of the Shrine. Behold, ye Forces, Peter of Beverley!*

'Peter will be returned to us,' he said at last. 'It was ordained at his baptism. He is the Keeper at the Shrine.'

'Do you still believe that?'

He nodded. 'We must believe it, Elvira. Why else has all this come to pass? God has His own purpose and Peter his. For Beverley and St John, he will survive.'

The torch in the metal wall-sconce spluttered and dimmed, then flared and burned again with a steadier flame. A shadow passed the window-slit, perhaps a cloud scudding across the sky, and in the silence Great John, the ancient Minster bell, began its slow, sad tolling.

While Simeon and Elvira drew some comfort from each other, a man was shown into the Minster Moorgate house of Wulfric de Morthlund. He wore a leather hood and mantle and carried a bulky miller's sack thrown casually over his shoulder. As he stamped upstairs he left muddy traces from his boots on every tread. His movements released a blend of odours from his clothes which caused the servant who led him to grimace in distaste. On the upper floor she drew back a leather hanging and jerked her head as a signal for him to enter. He winked and leered at her as he stooped into the room and, as she lowered the curtain at his back, she cleared her throat and spat into her apron.

Several clerks and priests were gathered in the room, all with their girdles loosened and their bellies filled, all nursing goblets of wine and replete expressions. The carrier's glance flickered to the table and lingered there on the debris of their meal. What remained was fare for servants and for dogs, though it might feed a poor man's family for many days. He licked his lips and his mouth watered at the scent of roasted meat, poultry and rich sauces. These priests had gorged themselves and left a half-feast on the table, and he could not recall a single day in his own life when he had turned away, fully stuffed, while there was a morsel of food left in the pot.

Cyrus de Figham set down his goblet and rose from his chair to greet the carrier. He took a fat purse from his palmer and held it out, only to withdraw it as the carrier's sack hit the floor with a resounding thud.

'I do not pay good money for damaged goods,' he growled.

'Damaged?' The man showed twin rows of rotten teeth in a grin. 'A knock or two might help to cool its temper,' he said. 'This thing bites and scratches like a wolf-cub.'

De Figham rubbed his hand where Elvira's teeth had pierced the skin, then touched his neck where the marks of her fingernails were clearly visible. 'It had a she-wolf for its mother,' he remarked. 'Untie the sack.'

'I'll take the purse and go, sir, if I may.'

'You'll untie the sack,' de Figham told him.

With a shrug the man stooped, set the sack on its end, withdrew the binding straps and stepped back in haste.

'By the gods! What manner of animal is this?' Wulfric de Morthlund heaved himself up from his cushions and waved aside the priest whose broad back now partly obstructed his view. His gaze moved up and down, the eyes growing narrow, as Cyrus de Figham strutted around the sack with a superior, almost triumphant air.

'Wait outside,' he told the carrier. 'Your stench offends me. You will have your purse when the goods are safely delivered to my house.'

The boy was standing naked save for a linen cloth wrapped

tightly around his skinny body from navel to thigh. His skin was pale and scrupulously clean, his hair a silky mop, saffron in colour. He stood with his hands at his sides, neither defiant nor afraid, and de Figham's emotions seethed as he observed him. The fishmonger's daughter had produced a whelp singularly lacking in beauty, a swarthy thing that could not look so princely and so noble even if it were dressed in a king's attire. That whelp had wary eyes and the quick, instinctive cunning of his class. This one had all the hallmarks of excellent breeding. That other whelp was coarse and vulgar; this one was stamped with an aristocratic bearing. The obvious differences raked through his heart with blade-like sharpness. That the priest and the ditcher's wife should produce so fine and handsome a son was pain enough; that a swarthy rodent should spring from his own loins was salt in the wound.

He reached out to grasp the boy by the hair and, as Peter's head came up, the puckered scar on his neck was clearly visible. Two years ago de Figham had held this boy by the throat, high on the inner walkways of the Minster church. He had held his life in the balance, then found the situation reversed and his own life hung upon the strength of Simeon's arm. That hated priest had spared his life and left him in his debt, but now de Figham's chance had come again. He had them all at last, first the priest, then the ditcher's wife, and now their son.

'Your father will die at the carting at dawn tomorrow.' He spat the words into the upturned face.

'Only if God so wills it,' the boy replied.

'Your mother will then become my property, to use in any way I choose to use her.'

'Only if God so wills it,' Peter repeated evenly.

'Cyrus de Figham wills it, boy. *I* will it.'

De Morthlund clapped his hands. 'Hold up, have ease, Father Cyrus, if you please. There are some here who would study this intriguing creature for themselves before you decide to tear him limb from limb.' He beckoned to the boy with one bloated finger. 'Come, lad, step closer so that we might see you more clearly.'

Peter stood his ground until Cyrus de Figham struck him between the shoulder-blades, a full, closed-fisted blow that sent him sprawling. Without a sound he raised himself where he had fallen and stood before the fat man and those priests who scrutinised him with suspicion in their eyes. Though a livid mark grew on his back, no trace of pain or distress showed on his face.

'Is it true there is no language you have not mastered, no book you have not read and memorised?' de Morthlund asked.

'Is it true that you possess the power of binding and loosing?' a priest demanded.

'Is Simeon de Beverley your natural father?' another inquired.

'And the ditcher's wife your mother?'

The boy maintained his silence, his demeanour respectful and his gaze untroubled.

De Morthlund asked de Figham: 'What will you do with him?'

'I intend to sell him to the highest bidder.'

'Indeed? Well, now, I just might be persuaded to join the bidding. He's a pretty enough lad, though as skinny as a starving rabbit. He rubbed his chin and smiled. 'Name your price, de Figham, and the matter might be settled here and now.'

'Three thousand marks.'

'What? Are you insane? My friend, I fear you will bring him home unsold. Your price is extortionate.'

De Figham's grin was lopsided as he seated himself in his chair, one leg draped elegantly across its arm, his head tipped on one side as he viewed his prize.

'The bidding *begins* at three thousand marks. I expect to raise three times that figure, once the eyes of York, Canterbury and Rome have rested on him. The papal legate will assess his knowledge and his special skills, and after that the price on his head will soar. This is no ordinary boy, de Morthlund, no common lap-child to be had for half a penny. The bidding begins at three thousand marks.'

'You price your own people out of the market, Father

Cyrus,' a priest complained. 'This child belongs to the Church, the *Beverley* Church, and we should be allowed first say in his appraisal. He should be tested here, by us, before the papal legate can thwart us all by serving papers upon you for his immediate transportation to Rome.'

'Father James is right,' another said. 'We should have first claim on him. We are entitled to it.'

'Father Wulfric?' de Figham asked, lifting one dark brow into the creases on his forehead, inviting the other's opinion.

The fat man spread his hands and licked his lips, then sipped his wine and studied Peter's impassive face over the rim of his goblet. 'I can but agree with my fellows here. We all have a special interest in this boy. I would welcome an opportunity to question him.'

'I do not doubt you would,' de Figham laughed. He rose from his seat and snapped his fingers for the servant. 'There is a man outside in a leather mantle. Bring him to me at once.' He placed his palm on Peter's head and addressed the others in a quiet tone. 'In view of your interest, gentlemen, let me start the bidding at a more realistic sum.'

De Morthlund's face brightened. 'Name your price.'

'Four thousand.'

'What? This is an outrage. You have no right ...'

'Come, come, Father Wulfric, do not speak to me of rights. Possession is the law and four thousand marks begins the bidding. This creature belongs to me and by all the gods of Heaven and Hell I intend to profit from the ownership.'

As Peter was bundled back into the sack, one small sneeze, brought about by the finely ground flour trapped in the cloth, was all the sound he made. The neck of the sack was secured and by its straps the boy was hoisted roughly across the carrier's shoulders. John Palmer and a lesser clerk accompanied the man from the house and set their feet for the Figham pasture, determined to keep the prize in their sights until he was safely in the keep and the catching-fee handed over. By dawn tomorrow Beverley would be changed, its balance of power shifted and its fortunes drastically

345

altered. By the time the boy was auctioned off to the highest bidder, Cyrus de Figham would have his secrets from him. At Figham House that priest was god and law combined, with none to stay his hand. He would have the treasure, the artifacts and the relics, and the court of Rome was welcome to the rest.

A drizzle was falling and the sky was dark, with shards of lightning flashing here and there in the brooding distance. The men trudged over mud and softened grass, cursing each time their feet sank or slipped where the going was made treacherous by the rain. The house of Figham was in their sights when several hooded riders appeared as if from nowhere. So intent had they been on reaching their destination without mishap that none had seen the band approach, and so it was upon them without warning. The carrier threw down the sack and drew his short, wide-bladed dagger. John Palmer tossed back his cloak and pulled out his sword, exposing the bulging purse clipped to his belt. The clerk behind him crossed himself and began to pray with a frantic intensity, too frightened for his life even to consider defending it.

'We are on Cyrus de Figham's business,' John Palmer announced, counting seven men in all. 'You hamper us at your peril.'

'And you resist at yours,' one voice replied. 'What's in the sack?'

'Flour for Cyrus de Figham's table,' John replied. 'I fear the rain has been the ruin of it. Take it and risk the canon's wrath, if you have a taste, or a use, for spoiled flour.'

The other expelled a derisive snort as he dismounted and moved to face John Palmer at close quarters, his face well hidden by his dripping hood. 'Put up your sword, priest, or I'll cut your arm in two.'

John stood his ground. 'We are on de Figham's business. He will not be ...' A back-handed blow from the man sent the palmer sprawling in the mud. Several others moved their mounts around the carrier, rendering his dagger arm useless

346

by their numbers. The praying clerk threw up his hands and fled in fright, slipping and sliding across the wet ground until his own momentum brought him down.

John Palmer was hoisted to his feet, relieved of his purse, cloak and sword, then shoved aside. The carrier was searched, relieved of his dagger and leather mantle and similarly discarded. Then the robber remounted and, with a signal to his men, rode off and was soon lost amongst the rain-misted shadows of the pasture.

It was a sorry, bedraggled trio which reached the Figham house and ordered riders to be dispatched in pursuit of de Figham's purse.

'You should have let them take the sack,' the carrier complained. 'This spitting creature would soon have repaid their impudence in kind.'

'You can thank God for my swift thinking,' John said acidly. 'If the sack were lost, I doubt de Figham's wrath would be contained.'

'Spoiled flour, indeed! And will your swift thinking replace my leather? Will it pay my catching-fee?'

'Hold your babbling tongue,' John Palmer snapped, 'and help me get this sack into the keep.'

The little vaulted room was at the bottom of a flight of steps lit by a single torch. They set the sack on the rushes and stood between it and the door as the straps were unfastened.

'What? Ye gods!' John Palmer leaped back in alarm and disbelief. 'Bring the torch, man. Quickly.'

In the flickering light they opened the neck of the sack and tipped it out, spilling its contents of ruined flour across the dirty rushes.

CHAPTER THIRTY-THREE

At the bishop's palace in York, Daniel Hawk was deeply impressed by all he saw and heard. Such pomp and circumstance as he encountered here was stunning to his senses. Richness he had seen before, and splendour in fine measure in his master's house, but here in York the everyday brilliance of it dazzled him. These men of York paraded like pampered peacocks, dined like princes at every meal and lived such lives as even a canon might envy. The palace itself was decorated in gold leaf, hung with priceless tapestries and silks, bedecked with works of art and precious objects. Gold and silver, ivory and jade were in profusion, with every room more splendidly embellished than the last.

In Geoffrey Plantagenet's private chamber, Daniel watched a master craftsman at his specialist work. The artist was none other than Fergus de Burton, his task the manipulation of his archbishop. His arguments were not merely persuasive, his tactics not only clever. This young man's skills were remarkable to observe. Here was Geoffrey Plantagenet, slippery and volatile, sliding from this end to that in every argument, with never a hint of where his mood might next alight. And here was the young de Burton, skilfully following after him, judging every shade and subtlety, every shift and side-step of the other's mood. This was no self-serving youth hot with ambition. This one was clever to a fault, and dangerous in the extreme. He could become another Simeon or a second de Figham, depending upon which way, for him, the winds of fortune blew. Soon he would own a church, roof, stone and altar, not two miles outside Beverley, and with it much land and property. A dangerous man indeed to be left to blow upon the fickle breath of Fortune.

Daniel followed the conversation where he could, already familiar with the essence of it. He was intrigued by Fergus de Burton's verbal skills and amazed by his subtle influence over the Plantagenet.

'... and restore the balance of power before it is fully lost to you,' Fergus was coaxing now, 'by saving Simeon, your only link to the treasure and the relics. Chastise de Figham, but do it indirectly. Leave the serpent to his nest but pull his fangs and neutralise his venom.'

'So,' the Plantagenet suddenly boomed, so loudly that Daniel started. 'I arrest his priest, this palmer, and have him charged with conspiracies against the Church, and against the authority of his lord archbishop.'

'Indeed, and when the charges are proven, those against Simeon de Beverley will be negated. Hang the scapegoat if you must, that much you can do without fear of rebuke from Rome. De Figham will be obliged to thank you publicly for the service you have rendered him. Every man among them will be firmly in your debt, including Simeon. And how will the pope and his council fault you then, when you have uncovered such vile and sacrilegious plots against the mother Church?'

Daniel watched the resolution light in the archbishop's eyes as Fergus, in his low, persuasive tones, convinced him that the idea, with all its subtle twists and turns, was Geoffrey Plantagenet's own. Such cunning would put de Figham himself to shame. His grasp of the situation was astute, his solving of it little short of brilliant.

'Your enemies will think long and hard before daring to plot against you after this, my lord archbishop.'

'And you will lead my army to the gates?'

Fergus nodded. 'Your presence might be misconstrued. I will undertake the task and suffer the consequences, should the need arise.'

The Plantagenet rubbed his hands together gleefully. 'This upstart canon, thinking to rule the roost in Beverley, will find his fine tail-feathers clipped away when his puppet-priest is arrested and held to account for every ecclesiastic misdemeanour in the town.'

'You might even slip your own man in his place,' Fergus suggested. 'If the viper needs new fangs, why not provide them ready-shaped to your own requirements?'

'Yourself?'

'If it serves you, sire,' de Burton answered with a bow.

Outside the chamber Daniel asked: 'Would you really be prepared to serve a man like Cyrus de Figham?'

'Make no mistake,' the young man chuckled. 'I serve no man but myself.'

'None but this Plantagenet archbishop,' Daniel countered.

The eyes were bright, the grin as cheerful as ever when Fergus de Burton touched Daniel's chest with a forefinger and said, with heavy emphasis, 'I serve no man, *especially* this Plantagenet archbishop.'

The night was black, dry but crackling with distant storms, when the army began to gather in the courtyard of the archbishop's palace. Daniel had waited impatiently while the necessary documents were being prepared by clerks kept from their beds to complete the task. He slept a little, unwilling to do so, but quickly seduced by the sumptuous padding of the couch on which he rested. The invocation of the choral priests disturbed him. Their voices seemed to hang on the air, so deep and melodic that the sound almost had him mesmerised. His smile was wry as he rubbed the sleep from his eyes. Here in York, even the voices of St Peter's choral priests were lined with gold.

His horse was a fresh mount from the archbishop's stables, a gelding with a white blaze in its forehead. He was to ride between Fergus de Burton and the soldier, Chad, until they passed through the gates of Beverley. Only then, being of no further use to the archbishop's envoy, would he slip quietly away and hope to keep his involvement in this affair from his master's notice.

'Will we cover the distance in time?' he asked, concerned that not a moment should be wasted. 'We must reach the town by dawn, before the carting can begin.'

'We will cover the distance,' Chad assured him, too busy counting, checking and rechecking his men to pay much attention to Daniel Hawk.

'Where is Edwin? Has anyone seen young Edwin?' Daniel took hold of a clerk and was immediately rebuked for doing so, and thereby sharply reminded that this was not Beverley but York, where clerks enjoyed a higher status. 'Forgive my ignorance, sir,' he responded graciously. 'My business is urgent. I seek a certain boy, close to my height but skinny, brown eyes and long brown hair. His name is Edwin. Have you seen him?'

'I cannot help you,' the clerk said curtly, then jerked his head in a perfunctory bow and turned away.

Daniel asked his question of many men until Fergus de Burton called him to the gates. A soldier was lighting torches one from another, and passing them around the mounted men, and the gates of the bishop's palace were swinging open.

'We must leave the boy behind,' Fergus said. 'We cannot wait for him if we are to reach Beverley before sunrise. He spoke of some errand.'

'An errand? Did he mention the Jew, Aaron?'

Fergus shrugged. 'I doubt he will find any money-lender willing to ply his trade at night. You should have kept him in your sights, my friend. The streets of York are no place for an untried lad with more enthusiasm than wisdom to his credit.'

'I am loath to leave without him,' Daniel confessed. 'I fear he will try to follow us in the dark.'

'You risk too much if you stay behind, Daniel. Wulfric de Morthlund will have the gates of Beverley closed against you for all time if you are implicated in this affair, and do not think you will ever be safe in York. Your master has a long reach, and a long memory.'

Daniel looked at the grave blue eyes above the friendly smile and once again was surprised by this young man's keen observance of other men's intrigues. 'Must I abandon him, then, after all he has done on our behalf?'

The big man-at-arms, Chad, who had been standing off a little way, now nudged his horse forward, his features grim. 'The lad is foolhardy enough to attempt the ride alone, and Heaven knows he rides like a novice. Let me send a man to search for him and bring him after us. Will that suffice?'

Fergus nodded and Daniel said: 'It will, Chad. I am grateful to you.'

'Oh, you priests,' Fergus de Burton laughed without disparagement. 'You would save every soul in sight, whether it profit you or not.'

The small army, made up of two score and ten mounted men, began its clattering journey through the streets of York before the lengthy midnight offices were at an end. They went by Bishop Hill, crossing the river at the Ousegate bridge and following a winding course toward the Monk's Bar. The streets were narrow and unlit, with shops and dwellings crammed together on either side, all chimneys stopped by fire-plates, all windows tightly shuttered against the night. At the bar Fergus produced his written authority marked with the archbishop's seal, and the troop was allowed to pass through the city gates with a thunder of hooves on timber. They travelled with lighted torches, an eerie, menacing sight in the darkness beyond the city.

They had covered four miles when three riders were spotted running a diagonal course across open country to meet the road, all guided by a single torch. One rider was a clerk from the bishop's palace. He wore a pale grey cloak over a crimson robe, a heavy crucifix swinging across his chest and a glowering expression on his face. Splashes of mud thrown up by his galloping horse had stained the lower section of his cloak and this, more than the arduous ride or the lateness of the hour, had made him peevish. His companion was Edwin, dressed in a fur cloak many sizes larger than himself and sporting a helmet and sword borrowed from one of the palace guards. He came on smartly, heeling his horse so that the startled animal met its flanks sharply with those of Daniel's mount. In the brief scuffle which followed, the gelding side-stepped into Fergus's mount, which reared up in alarm.

'God's teeth!' Chad growled. He grabbed the reins of Edwin's horse to calm it as Daniel helped right the lad in the saddle. Then he leaned toward the priest and growled again, this time directly into his face. 'In the name of heaven, Daniel Hawk, do us all a service and teach this lad to ride!'

In the commotion the third rider had been forgotten. Now they saw that the man behind the flaming torch was Rabbi Aaron, garbed as a soldier beneath a wide brown cloak, his near-black face divided by the nose-piece of a splendid helmet.

Fergus came forward to greet him, grinning sideways at the incongruous sight of a Jew prepared to ride with the archbishop's private army.

'Has the lad converted you to our cause, Rabbi Aaron?'

'I ride to help free Simeon de Beverley,' the Jew said softly, 'and to claim the fee I have been promised. The woman, Elvira, will return with me to York.'

'Elvira? She will return with you?'

'That is the bargain.'

'But she belongs to Simeon.'

'No more. She is pledged to me if Simeon can be spared. It is arranged. She will come willingly.'

'You strike a hard bargain, Jew,' Fergus said bitterly.

'The bargain was her own. She thinks fondly of me and I will give her a better life than Simeon ever could. Are you aware that Cyrus de Figham has taken her?'

'I am, and you can be sure he will put her to the sword before he gives her up. I suggest you make her safety your sole concern. Ride with us as far as the town, then do what you must to reach her before de Figham knows what you are

353

about. Save her if you can and let all else remain between yourself and Simeon. I will allow six of my men for your protection. Beyond that, I will have no part in this bargain of yours.'

The Jew nodded his head. Torchlight danced across his polished helmet and shone in his black eyes. Then he nudged his horse into line and the troop moved forward, making a steady pace along the Old Roman Way to Beverley.

They heard the bells before they reached the town, pealing across the open Westwood while the sky remained as black as pitch. Every bell in the town was ringing, and through the streets men and women ran this way and that with flaming torches held above their heads.

'The carting!' Edwin cried in a strangled voice. 'We come too late. The carting has begun.'

'No, lad, take heart,' Daniel said. 'The town is merely preparing itself for the spectacle. The bells will be stopped when the cart is released.'

'Aye, and the priests will sing their morning offices in empty churches,' Chad remarked.

They covered the last mile at a steady gallop and reached the North Bar gates to find them barred and unattended. It was the custom to keep the town secured during these dawn events when men could not be trusted to guard the gates. Were it not so, too many traders, merchants and vagabonds would flood the town, paying no tolls or tithes for the privilege.

It seemed the friends of Simeon were to be thwarted after all. The gates were made of solid oak with metal inlays, their enormous weight hung on massive iron hinges, their load-bearing beams sunk several feet into the ground. It would be no easy task to break them down, and while they were at their labours the element of surprise would have to be abandoned, an army might be raised against them and their quarry lost.

'Look! I see a man! How did he come here? The place was deserted a instant ago!'

A tall and slender figure, hooded and all in black, stepped from the shadows close to the gates and moved toward the men who led the troop. Unsettled, Fergus raised his sword in challenge, only to find his hand stayed by the rabbi.

'It is the hooded priest,' Edwin whispered. 'The Guardian!'

'I care not how men style him,' Fergus growled. 'One man alone will not guard these gates against my army.'

The rabbi held fast to his sword arm. 'Hold up your sword, young Fergus. And if ever you meet this one again, stand off and let him pass without impediment.'

'Who is he?' Fergus marked the figure's stillness, its silence and its extraordinary height. '*What* is he?'

'I have heard him called the Guardian at the Gate.'

'Will he admit us?'

'If he does not we will never enter here, not even with an army a hundred times our present number.' Aaron urged his mount forward a few short paces and raised the nose-piece of his helmet to reveal his face. The figure neither moved nor made a sound. When Aaron turned away his face was grim. 'The Guardian will allow us to pass,' he told de Burton.

'But how? The gates are barred from within and ...' Fergus gaped. The gates of Beverley, so firmly closed against them, were swinging open on their great iron hinges. 'How in the name of God ...?'

'He is the Guardian,' Edwin grinned. 'The gates of Beverley will always open or close at his bidding.'

'Fairies' tales, lad. There is some trickery here.'

'Perhaps, but it works for us.' Aaron heeled his horse and the troop surged forward and, as the last man passed through, the gates swung closed, as if unaided, at his back.

The town was in uproar, with such a clamouring in the streets that even these mounted men made but slow progress to the Minster. Shops, dwellings and churches along the way were shuttered. Men, women and children, all armed with sticks or bags of stones, jostled and fought with each other along the route the cart would take. The noise of bells and excited voices had reached a deafening pitch. At St Mary's Daniel slipped away, pulling the protesting Edwin's mount by the reins, to take a safer and less conspicuous route to St Peter's enclosure.

When Cyrus de Figham arrived at the provost's hall with his priest, John Palmer, he found a band of soldiers in the courtyard and Fergus de Burton waiting in an ante-room.

'Explain yourself, de Burton,' he demanded.

The young man made an apologetic gesture. 'My hands are tied in this matter, my friend. Our archbishop sees plots in every corner and has his spies in every household. He came this close', he measured a small distance between his finger and his thumb, 'to arresting you and making an example of you before his enemies.'

'My signature does not appear on any charge or accusation,' de Figham protested. 'I cannot be touched. I am innocent in this matter.'

'As I was at pains to show, on your behalf, my friend. However, the Church may hold you responsible for the actions of your priest, convinced that you turned a convenient blind eye to his conspiracies.'

'I will not suffer this,' de Figham hissed. 'I am above such things.'

De Burton shrugged his shoulders. 'No man is invulnerable when the full power of York is focused upon him. I did all I could, Father Cyrus, and now you must act to keep the Plantagenet from your door. Surrender John Palmer. Speak out against him as the sole conspirator in this unsavoury business. Do so and you will emerge unscathed, an innocent canon duped by an ambitious priest. Defend him and Geoffrey Plantagenet will destroy you.'

De Figham's face had blanched to grey. 'I will not surrender my prisoners.'

'You must. If the palmer is guilty then the charges against them are false. And if he is innocent, who but yourself could have orchestrated such plots as have been uncovered by our archbishop?'

'My God, he has me cornered.'

'Aye, and he would have had you hanged, but for my intervention,' Fergus reminded him.

De Figham sat down heavily on a chest, all his emotions etched upon his face. 'Give me an hour,' he said at last.

'I can give you nothing. The die is cast.'

'But if you had arrived too late . . . if you were delayed . . .?'

'My borrowed men-at-arms owe their allegiance to Geoffrey. They cannot be bought. They will report the truth of it, that we came in time to prevent Simeon's carting.'

'Damn it! One hour is all I ask.'

'Impossible. Even now the provost is on his way here to hear the formal charges and verify the archbishop's seal. When that is done, John Palmer will be taken.'

De Figham slapped a fist into his palm and said again, his face now ashen: 'By the gods, am I to be undone for want of one miserable hour?'

'You or him, my friend,' Fergus pressed. 'The choice is simple. Geoffrey Plantagenet will have his scapegoat, whether that one be John Palmer or Cyrus de Figham.'

While Cyrus seethed and spat and Fergus performed his verbal manoeuvres, the dungeons below the provost's house teemed with activity. The keepers of the cells were herded out and all the prisoners freed, the doors of their cells caved in by picks and axes. At Simeon's cell they found the door standing open.

'The yard!' A soldier shouted. 'They have him in the yard. They are preparing him for the carting!'

Thorald and Osric, who had kept the long night's vigil outside the prison, were at work with axes on the door of Elvira's cell. Aaron took up an axe and bade them follow the soldiers up to the covered rear yard.

'Look to Simeon. I will free Elvira. This lock is halfway broken. Go! Look to Simeon!'

She was standing with her back against the wall when the door burst open, her hands bound up with rags and clasped to her breasts as if in prayer. Her face was pale and bruised, her eyes dark-rimmed and, though she stood quite still, her fear was obvious.

The Jew stooped through the doorway and approached her slowly, with his hand outstretched. 'I have come to free you, lady.'

A moment later Elvira was in his arms, clinging to him and

357

weeping with relief. 'You came . . . you came. But Simeon . . .'

'He will be freed at once,' Aaron assured her, and felt her body sag against him. He slipped the lock of hair and the golden brow-piece from his clothes, then raised her head up so that she might see them. 'I must hold you to your word, Elvira.'

'When Simeon is safe,' she whispered, 'I will keep my word.'

'Bless you, lady.'

'And you, for your timely arrival, Aaron.'

As he helped her from the cell they met Osric and Thorald coming down. 'Simeon is under heavy guard, bound to a two-ox cart with chains and leathers. They hold us off with spears and bows and threaten to release the cart if we try to cross the yard. We must bring de Figham here to order this rabble aside and Simeon freed.'

'We will go at once,' Aaron agreed. 'Fergus has him in the provost's hall where charges are being heard against his priest. Leave the soldiers here and come with me.'

They went up, bearing Elvira between them, and when they reached the provost's chamber they were held back from the room where the formal charges were being heard. Word met them here that Cyrus de Figham had already left the building.

He had seen his opportunity and pounced upon it. He left a senior clerk behind to deny his part in John Palmer's conspiracies, then raced down a narrow stairway to the keep. Once there he concealed himself in an alcove while Elvira was brought up from the cells. Enraged by her release, he slipped into the street and joined the crowds gathered like teeming rats along the carting route. He was bruised and dishevelled when he reached the Minster. The place was filled with those allowed to shelter there, with many who carried boards to block the windows or sacks to gather up candles, all striving in their small way to protect the great church and its contents from the tumult outside its walls. One more priest could pass unnoticed in the confusion. The choral priests were singing in the choir stalls, their voices seeming to mock de Figham's fury. Great John was ringing in his ears, tolling like the passing bell for all his grand ambitions. When that cursed bell stopped ringing the carting would begin, and neither man's law nor God's would hold back the rabble from its intent.

In the little bell tower a priest was at the rope, pulling a steady rhythm for the huge, black metal bell. Cyrus de Figham drew his sword and struck down the priest where he stood, opening a wound in his neck that all but severed the unfortunate's head. Then he swung his sword arm again and, with a scream of rage, severed the bellrope.

'My God! What have you done?'

The monk from Flanders was at the door of the tower. He had seen de Figham arrive and guessed his purpose. He glanced at the dead priest, saw the severed rope and took in the situation at a glance. With a cry he threw his wiry body into the air, hoping to catch the rope to keep the great bell ringing out. His hands fell short and he dropped back to meet the full force of de Figham's swinging arm. The hilt of a sword caught him a savage blow to the temple. As he slumped to his knees the sword's point sank deep into his upper thigh.

Prepared to strike the helpless monk again, de Figham stopped with his face turned up and his eyes alight. Great John was slowing. The massive bell was losing its momentum. He turned and ran from the tower, laughing out loud, while Antony, feeling his senses ebbing, still strained to reach the idling rope so far beyond his grasp. Another strike and the clapper itself was idle. Great John fell silent and one by one the other bells of Beverley were also stopped. Then a roar went up from the mob. The bells were stilled. The carting could begin.

CHAPTER THIRTY-FOUR

They knew the worst had happened. In one part of the provost's court the friends of Simeon pleaded for his immediate release while, in another part, his fate was decided. The bells had stopped. The gates of the yard were thrown open and, as the crowd roared out its frenzied satisfaction, the oxen were goaded and the wheels were turned.

'It has begun!' Osric's voice was tight, his soldier's face contorted.

'God help him,' Jacob de Wold muttered.

And then the cry went up inside the hall. '*Stop the carting! Stop the carting!*' Two score of men, uncaring that their fancy robes put them at risk from thieves, took up their swords and rushed toward the doors. Outside, Fergus de Burton mustered his men, their numbers swelled by those who knew that Simeon was innocent. The gates were opened and the force surged out, cleaving a pathway through the screaming mob. At their backs came gatemen, servants, kitchen staff and gardeners, all wielding makeshift weapons. In other parts of the town similar scenes were taking place. Word had spread that the charges against Simeon de Beverley had been cleverly fabricated to serve one man's ambition. The populace had been duped. The good people of Beverley would be damned by Church and God alike if Simeon were killed. Small armies of honest men, led by the priests of every church, braved the pandemonium of the streets to put an end to Beverley's shame.

'Simeon is innocent,' these men chanted, and soon others were taking up the cry. 'Simeon is innocent.'

'John Palmer is the guilty one,' many cried, and quickly this cry, too, was echoed by many others. 'John Palmer is the guilty one. Give us John Palmer! Give us John Palmer!'

The cart, raised up on massive solid wheels and drawn by two oxen whose flanks were protected with leathers, ploughed through the crowds around the provost's courts. A man in a shelter made of sticks and hung with leathers crouched in the front of the cart, prodding the oxen with a sharpened stick to keep them moving. Behind him, Simeon stood aloft, bound to a sturdy frame, wearing only a pair of linen breeches tied at the waist and knee. The large round bruise on his upper chest, pierced through with a bloody wound the size of an arrow head, gave him the look of a martyred St Sebastian. So marked was this effect that some who stood close to the passing cart fell back with lowered weapons and startled gazes. The high cart bore its helpless burden across the drawbridge at the Keldgate crossing, its shadow thrown upon the glittering surface of the water, and began its steady trundle into the chaos around the Minster. As it came the cry was heard more loudly: 'Simeon is innocent. Simeon is innocent.'

The morning sky crackled with distant lightning and grumbled with thunder, its rolling clouds shot through in places by shafts of vivid sunlight. The storm which had been threatening for several days still simmered, and there were many who feared the skulking presence of those restless elements.

Daniel Hawk led a band of men from St Peter's enclosure. Some were priests, many gardeners or ditchers. Some had abandoned their kitchen duties, others had left their beds in the infirmary. Young Edwin was by his side, too brave, too stubborn to be left behind. They chanted as they battled

361

their way to the Minster to meet the cart. 'Free Simeon! Free Simeon!' Some distance westward, Thorald and Osric were making similar progress, and from the north-west came Fergus and his soldiers. Coming northward were several other loyal bands, dividing the mob and proclaiming Simeon's innocence. These groups converged on the area around the Minster with but one thought: to take the prisoner from the cart by force, and damn the consequences.

In the Minster yard a flash of brilliant crimson caught Daniel's attention and he saw a familiar figure being manhandled by the mob. Wulfric de Morthlund had sought to reach the safety of his house in Minster Moorgate, only to have his priestly guards struck down. His cloak was ripped away, his girdle and cross stolen, his rings prised from his fingers. He was in terror when Daniel saw him, floundering and screaming. For an instant Daniel merely stared. To his left the cart was just coming into view. To his right the terror-filled gaze of Wulfric de Morthlund met his own across a sea of lawless, rampaging people. A moment later Daniel was moving again, driven by instinct, yelling and thrusting for leeway through the masses. When he reached the spot he soon realised that he was fighting for his life as he shielded his master's fat and vulnerable body with his own.

They managed to halt the cart at the corner of St John's Passage and the packed Minster yard. Here the tumult had grown to riot proportions as soldiers and townsmen, priests and rabble fought a bloody battle for the spoils. The cart was pelted with sticks and stones and clods of muddy turf. A man struggling to cut the priest's bonds was struck in the back by a spear. Another was felled by an axe, yet another by a hail of rocks that split his skull wide open.

Fighting her own way toward the cart, Elvira screamed Simeon's name as Stephen Goldsmith struggled to hold her back. Osric and Thorald were ahead of them and even the Jew, still helmeted and cloaked, was striking men and women aside in his haste to reach the innocent priest. From the rear a group of men came yelling, bearing a screaming priest upon their shoulders. 'Here is your guilty man! Here is the rogue, John Palmer! Simeon is innocent! Simeon is innocent!'

A rain of rocks came down upon the cart and Simeon, one wrist cut free by his rescuers, slumped sideways so that his body hung grotesquely on the stake. Another rock struck his hanging arm, drawing much blood but no response from him. Now a different cry went up, beginning softly and passing like a wave through the clamouring masses, gathering strength and volume as it went: 'The priest is dead! Simeon is dead!'

Another wave, this time of silence, swept the immediate throng. Then a voice from near the cart cried out: 'God help us! The priest is dead!'

The rumbling and crackling in the sky could now be heard distinctly. A fork of lightning hissed to earth and caught the highest timbers of the Minster roof, causing a snap of sound and a flashing show of sparks. Seeing this, many had their faces turned in that direction when the Minster doors swung open and a figure swathed all in black appeared in silhouette against the torchlight at its back.

'The priest is dead! Father Simeon is dead!'

The black-robed figure moved from the Minster doors in the direction of the cart, parting and silencing the crowds in its path the way a farmer parts the corn with his scythe. A heavy chunk of masonry struck the hood, which neither turned nor flinched against the impact. Those nearest to it fell back in awe. Some crossed themselves, amazed to see a man survive, let alone ignore, such a wicked blow.

At the cart two men had cut the bleeding Simeon down and Thorald, weeping openly, received the body as tenderly as if it were that of a child. With Osric's help he set it down on a cloak spread on the ground. This was how Elvira came upon him, near-naked and bloody, his face turned on one side, his chest unmoving. She dropped to her knees beside him and touched his bruised face with her fingertips.

'We came so close to saving him,' Osric choked. 'Dear God, we came so close to saving him.'

Elvira placed her palm on Simeon's chest and uttered a small and tragic cry. She had felt the cold, sharp emptiness in her heart that told her she had lost him.

Cyrus de Figham drew too close in his haste to see the priest's death for himself. He met the stare of Thorald across a dozen other heads and, seeing the other's rage unleashed, turned on his heels and fled. With a roar the huge priest of St Nicholas went after him, drawing his dagger as he rampaged like a bull in pursuit of the fleeing figure. The two men moved against the flow of the masses, one fleeing for his life, the other bent on ending it. At the lowered drawbridge de Figham glanced back and saw his pursuer clearly, saw the murderous intent in his face and the long, thin dagger in his hand. He leaped on to the timbers and raced across them, seeking the cover of the trees beyond. One foot had met with safer ground when the blade sank in his back. He halted, arching his body against the blow, then slowly turned to his enemy, his features showing utter disbelief.

'By the Devil, you have killed me, priest.'

His eyes grew wide and glistening black, then he toppled sideways and hit the water with a noisy splash. The sluggish current bore his unprotesting form downstream.

In the Minster yard the cart was moving again. Many willing hands had lashed the shrieking palmer to the stake in Simeon's place, and two score of mounted soldiers made a path to guide it through to the chaos filling the Fishmonger's Row. The screaming, struggling palmer, held aloft by the cruel stake, was an easy target for the hail of rocks which met him there.

The chant continued: 'Simeon is dead!'

Those gathered around the prostrate priest were quieter now, their voices lowered to whispers, each swearing he had taken no part in stoning an innocent man to death. A circle of loyal men and women had set themselves to guard the body, braced shoulder to shoulder to keep the press at bay. No howling mob would take him while they lived, to break and mutilate him and divide his mortal flesh amongst themselves.

'Simeon is dead,' the voices said. 'Simeon de Beverley is dead.'

The hooded figure was standing by the body, his hands concealed in his sleeves, his head bent down as if in prayer. From Fishmonger's Row came another wave of chanting, and the bellowing of the dying oxen rose over a wave of fresh hysteria.

'I have lost him,' Elvira whispered, as if her beloved's corpse and the icy coldness in her heart were not enough to tell her it was so.

Now the black-robed figure crouched over the stricken body of the priest and muttered words that many thought they heard but none would ever repeat with any certainty. The dark hood obscured the still features of Simeon's face and the cloak concealed the hands that worked in rapid movements across his battered chest. When the figure rose up again the deed was done.

'He moved! Dear God in Heaven! *He's alive!*'

'It cannot be! The priest is dead!'

'I say he moved! Look there! His eyes are open!'

'A miracle! It is a miracle!'

A score of voices spread the word about, soon becoming a hundred that were joined by a hundred more, until it seemed the entire town had taken up the cry. 'Simeon is saved by a miracle! Simeon lives!'

Elvira's face spoke more than any words, until she saw the rabbi, Aaron, watching her above his prayer-clasped fingers. She kissed her hurt fingers, pressed them to Simeon's lips, then rose and walked beside the rabbi while Simeon was hastily carried to the Minster.

'We leave for York at noon,' the rabbi said.

'He lives,' was all she said, and turned away.

They did not meet again until the morning was almost spent. There was much merriment in the town. The riots had petered out soon after the carting, eased by the death of John Palmer and the cunning orchestrations of Fergus de Burton. Not a man to miss a golden opportunity, he had requisitioned every scrap of food from the provost's cellars, then opened up the alms-boxes and the pilgrim's chest with his sword. All this was widely distributed throughout the town by his own hand. Flanked by his full complement of soldiers, he rode like royalty through the streets, tossing his gifts about with all the charity of the saint whose name he bore. In return the mob roared its thanks to Fergus de Burton, to the holy mother Church and to Simeon, in that order. Their shouts and cheers could be heard from St Peter's enclosure, and their merriment left a sour taste on the tongue.

'They turn their minds and hearts by how the wind blows.'

An exhausted Simeon was seated on a bench outdoors, his body strapped with linen cloths, one wrist held close to his chest in a narrow sling. His fox-fur cloak was draped loosely about his shoulders, and even now he could taste the sweet, thick syrup which had been hidden in his cell, the thick liquid he had consumed in one long gulp before the carting. Word had reached him that Daniel Hawk was at the bedside of his injured master, lauded for his bravery and once again de Morthlund's favoured catamite. Father Richard and Brother Antony would survive their injuries, brave Edwin was reunited with his sister, but many who had fought had died that day in Simeon de Beverley's cause. The town was being scoured from end to end for the boy who had vanished from a miller's sack. Amid the excitement and the merrymaking, amid the prayers and heartfelt thanks, not one among them could forget that Peter had not yet been found.

'You leave him with nothing,' Osric told the Jew.

'I take only what is mine by right. We struck an honourable bargain,' Aaron replied.

'And many will despise you for holding her to it.'

The big Jew shook his glossy head. 'They will learn to thank me when they see how well she lives, and when that patched-up ruin they call a Minster is restored. Your Simeon will have all the money he needs for its rebuilding, with my goodwill and Geoffrey Plantagenet's blessing.'

Osric narrowed his eyes. 'I say again, you leave him with nothing.'

Simeon rose to his feet as Elvira approached. They had already said their farewells and shed their parting tears. Now she was cloaked for her journey, more beautiful to him now than she had ever been, and it pained him to the soul to look at her. She rested the palm of her hand to his chest and looked into his eyes. He stooped to brush her lips with his, a fleeting, tender kiss that was the last he would know of her.

Aaron turned away, stricken to the heart by what he had observed. He had thought himself enamoured of the woman for her beauty. He had duped himself into believing that her simple honesty and purity of heart had captured him, but now he saw all that as only part of the hold she had upon him. What he wanted from her was the impossible. He coveted that which she could never give to any man but Simeon: her love.

They were still standing close together, their gazes locked, when he approached. He cleared his throat and handed to Simeon the brow-piece that was part-payment for his life. To Elvira he handed the lock of hair, reluctantly closing her bruised, torn fingers around it.

'Lady, you are released from your pledge.'

'But sir ...?' He silenced her protests with a long dark finger.

'Let our friendship be enough,' he told her. Then he turned and said, with a formal bow, 'God bless and keep you, Simeon of Beverley. *Shalom.*'

He strode away, pausing only to bow and mutter his respects to Father Cuthbert, replacing his helmet as he hastened to the gatehouse.

'I must ride with him,' Fergus de Burton said. 'He is a man of honour and much valued, for the moment, by our archbishop.'

'You have served God and man in many ways this day,' Simeon told him. 'We thank you. With all our hearts we thank you, friend.'

Fergus shrugged and flashed his impish grin. 'You have your heart's desire and I have mine,' he said. 'My church will be restored at the Plantagenet's bequest, with a splendid

367

altar dedicated to my own saint, the blessed Fergus. I will gain a handsome profit from this. What I did was for none other than myself.'

Simeon shook his hand as firmly as his injuries would allow. 'Well, Fergus, I will be sure to remember that.'

'Be sure you do, and never call me friend. I might yet prove otherwise.'

'That, too, I will remember,' Simeon said.

As Fergus walked away Simeon drew Elvira into his arms and let her unwanted travelling cloak fall to the ground.

'I felt you go, Simeon,' she whispered. 'Out there in street as I knelt beside you.'

'A simple error, my love. I drank from a healing syrup that dulled my senses. I did not leave you.'

'No, Simeon, I felt it here, in my heart, as I have always known I would, if I lost you. For a moment I knew that you were gone. I felt it, Simeon.'

'Elvira, perhaps . . .'

'Simeon.'

In the sudden hush that followed the calling of his name, Simeon heard the ominous growling of thunder and the snap of lightning overhead. The hairs at the nape of his neck began to prickle, and as he drew Elvira more closely to him he heard the voice again.

'Simeon.'

The figure came on with steady strides, passing the storehouse and the scriptorium, its great cloak billowing around its feet and its hood concealing its face.

'God bless and keep you, brother,' Simeon said. 'We owe you much.'

'The Keeper at the Shrine.'

'Not I, but Peter.'

'The Keeper at the Shrine.'

The voice seemed to reverberate through Simeon's chest. The figure stopped some distance off and once again it seemed that their gazes locked. Then the great black cloak came open and all who watched beheld another miracle as the missing boy stepped out.

'Peter!'

A cheer went up around St Peter's. Elvira gasped and covered her mouth with her hands. Simeon, too full to speak, merely bent and opened his big embrace to receive him. The boy came at a sprint and threw himself into Simeon's arms, laughing, safe again.

The figure raised a hand and inclined its head, giving the reunion its holy blessing.

'God bless you,' were all the words Simeon could offer.

They watched the black-robed stranger turn away and stride toward the gates. When it reached the wall that marked the lower boundary of the enclosure, it joined the deeper shadows there and vanished where there was no opening.

Now sunlight edged the storm clouds overhead, confirming Father Cuthbert's prophecy that there would come a storm that carried no rain with it. A deep, full-throated boom was heard, to be followed by another and another. The bellrope had been renewed. Great John was tolling, despite the evil which had sought to still the saint's own voice and place the future of his beloved Beaver Lake in jeopardy. The shrine was still intact, the saint preserved, and Great John was booming out the midday offices.

POSTSCRIPT

The relics of St John of Beverley remained hidden for a further seven years. His casket, including four iron nails, three brass pins, six beads, several scraps of bone and hair, 'and a dagger, much corroded', vanished again in the disaster of 1213 and was not located for another hundred years.

St Martin's church was never rebuilt. Its scant remains lie beneath the south-west corner of the present nave.

As recently as 1960 the water in the well to the right of the high altar of Beverley Minster was found to be still pure and sweet, almost a thousand years after it was blessed by St John of Beverley.

The ever-mysterious tomb of the unknown priest, to whom this book is dedicated, rests on the east side of the north transept of the Minster.

In 1221 Stephen Goldsmith, master craftsman and a canon serving Beverley Minster, gifted those lands in Eastgate described as St Peter's enclosure to the Dominicans, or Friars Preachers.

Only traces remain of the mediaeval village of Ravensthorpe, close to Bygot Wood, near Beverley.

Geoffrey Plantagenet, illegitimate son of Henry II, was consecrated as archbishop of York in August, 1191.

Aaron of York, teacher and money-lender, went on to become one of the twelve leading Jews in the land. His father Aaron, the wealthiest of all York's Jews, was slain in the 1190 riots, his assets confiscated and his debts collected by the crown.

Excavations undertaken between 1960 and 1983 at the site of the Old Friary enclosure (St Peter's) in Eastgate revealed the foundations of a mediaeval church, much of which lies in the trench of the present railway station. Also found was evidence of twenty-six burials, some grave slabs, tiles, masonry, cooking-pots, jugs, spouted pitchers, fragments of painted window-glass and pieces of leather shoe-soles, all dating from the eleventh and twelfth centuries. Many skeletal remains were also uncovered. Details of these excavations can be found in *Excavations at the Dominican Priory, Beverley* by P. Armstrong and D.G. Tomlinson (Humberside Heritage Publication No. 13).

Keeper at the Shrine

Domini Highsmith

A freezing winter's night, a mysterious hooded rider; a sudden storm of sinister and devastating power: strange forces are unleashed on the Minster town of Beverley in the see of York ... and worse is yet to come.

It is December 1180. At the height of the tempest the hooded figure brings a new-born child for baptism ... a child whose divine task it is to defend the sacred shrine of St John of Beverley. In the great Minster Church a crippled priest is healed of his affliction and made the boy Peter's guardian when the figure vanishes.

United with Elvira, the beautiful young woman engaged as wet-nurse, Father Simeon is driven to unforeseeable lengths to protect the child from the evil elements within the church. Together they become both catalysts and scapegoats in a game with ever-changing rules, a game in which the priestly players are capable of anything, even murder.

The church is divided, the shrine of St John besieged, the town itself in danger of destruction ... and then the hooded figure reappears.

☐ Keeper at the Shrine	Domini Highsmith	£5.99
☐ Leonora	Domini Highsmith	£4.99
☐ Lukan	Domini Highsmith	£5.99
☐ The Heaven Tree	Edith Pargeter	£4.99
☐ The Green Branch	Edith Pargeter	£4.99
☐ The Scarlet Seed	Edith Pargeter	£4.99
☐ The Marriage of Meggotta	Edith Pargeter	£4.99

Warner Books now offers an exciting range of quality titles by both established and new authors which can be ordered from the following address:

> Little, Brown & Company (UK),
> P.O. Box 11,
> Falmouth,
> Cornwall TR10 9EN.

Alternatively you may fax your order to the above address.
Fax No. 01326 317444.

Payments can be made as follows: cheque, postal order (payable to Little, Brown and Company) or by credit cards, Visa/Access. Do not send cash or currency. UK customers and B.F.P.O. please allow £1.00 for postage and packing for the first book, plus 50p for the second book, plus 30p for each additional book up to a maximum charge of £3.00 (7 books plus). Overseas customers including Ireland, please allow £2.00 for the first book plus £1.00 for the second book, plus 50p for each additional book.

NAME (Block Letters) _____

ADDRESS _____

_____

☐ I enclose my remittance for £ _____
☐ I wish to pay by Access/Visa Card

Number ☐☐☐☐☐☐☐☐☐☐☐☐☐☐☐☐

Card Expiry Date _____